Words
of the
Witches

Edited by

YVONNE JOCKS

BERKLEY BOOKS, NEW YORK

B

A Berkley Book
Published by The Berkley Publishing Group
A division of Penguin Putnam Inc.
375 Hudson Street
New York, New York 10014

Collection copyright © 2002 by Yvonne Jocks, Denise Little, and Tekno Books
Book design by Tiffany Kukec
Cover design by George Long
Cover art: *The Golden Stairs* (1880) by Edward Burne-Jones, oil on canvas, © Tate Gallery, London/Art Resource, NY, and *Summer* (1869) by Edward Burne-Jones

PRINTING HISTORY
Berkley trade paperback edition / August 2002

Visit our website at
www.penguinputnam.com

Library of Congress Cataloging-in-Publication Data

Words of the witches / edited by Yvonne Jocks.
p. cm.
ISBN 0-425-18497-8
1. Witches—Fiction. 2. Occult fiction, American. I. Jocks, Yvonne.

PS648.W5 W67 2002
813'.608037—dc21
2001052921

PRINTED IN THE UNITED STATES OF AMERICA

10 9 8 7 6 5 4 3 2 1

Words
of the
Witches

Hear now the words of the witches
The secrets we hid in the night,
When dark was our destiny's pathway,
That now we bring forth into light . . .

—DOREEN VALIENTE,
from "The Witches' Creed"

Contents

Introduction

Good Witches. Magical powers. Bubbling cauldrons and moonlight rituals. Most people believe these are the stuff of fairy tales and fantasies.

Most people are wrong.

Welcome to a collection of stories and wisdom by modern-day witches and their friends which may just set the record straight. Unlike some pure fantasy stories, these will not only entertain you, but do so while showing what Witchcraft and Modern Magick are *really* about.

Do real Witches ride through the night on broomsticks? Wiggle their noses to make things appear? Worship the devil? Put curses on their enemies?

No.

Do they work real magick, foretell the future, heal the sick?

Yes.

Do they have hopes, dreams, and heartaches like the rest of us? Absolutely! But sometimes, it takes a little magic to set things back on course.

This collection of stories, by a mix of both established and new authors, shows the variety of the modern Craft of the Wise. Some of them, like Maggie Shayne's "Anytown, USA," could have been lifted from the headlines. Others, like Rosemary Edghill's "The Iron Bride," reveal what headlines might not always tell. Many of the Witches you'll meet are still seekers, like the one in Val Taylor's "The Reluctant Psychic," just finding their path. Others, as in Zelena Winters's poignant "Tambourine Moon," introduce Witches from old traditions indeed. Most importantly, all of the women within these stories, from a despairing wife in Lorna Tedder's "A Reverence for Trees" to a wife who may regret her magical victory in Celia Moon's "The Letter," are not simply Witches. They are real women and men.

Enjoy the words these Witch and Witch-friendly authors have to tell. If they bring you entertainment, that is enough. If they haunt you with a sense of unexpected familiarity, even better. Either way, enjoy the magic.

And believe.

—*Yvonne Jocks*

Anytown, USA

MAGGIE SHAYNE

Mary pushed her shopping cart along the aisle of her local Wal-Mart store. The place was crammed with every Halloween item imaginable, from costumes to candy to scary decorations. The new favorite was the flattened witch on her broomstick, which people hung on trees or front doors, to give the illusion the poor thing had crashed there. Mary thought it was in poor taste, but what could you do?

The place had a nice selection of candles in varying sizes and colors, most of them heavily scented. Of course there were other places she could buy candles. That brand-new shop on the corner, Pandora's Box, had them in regular and beeswax, scented and unscented, in the standard pillar, taper, and votive shapes, but also in other forms. They had candles shaped like animals or even people, and those tiny little altar candles as well, in every color of the rainbow. She had seen them through the wide glass windows in front. Wal-Mart didn't carry anything like those. But she would far rather use what she found here than be seen in that shop. It was a small town, after all.

She found a nice white pillar candle with tiny silver diamond shapes decorating its surface. It looked perfect. Picking it up, she pulled it close to her face and sniffed, silently willing it not to emit an overwhelming floral scent. There was a subtle hint of vanilla to it—just enough. Smiling, she set the candle carefully in the cart with her other purchases—a jumbo-sized bottle of liquid Tide, a new head for the sponge mop, and a supply of candy for the trick-or-treaters who would show up tomorrow night—and headed for the checkout counter.

As the girl at the cash register carelessly dragged each item across the scanner and tossed them into a bag, Mary kept her eyes on the candle, bit her lip, willed herself quiet. But when the girl reached for it, Mary grabbed it first. The girl shot her a look of surprise.

"Sorry. I, um . . ." Shrugging, she slid the candle over the scanner. "I'll just, uh, carry this."

The girl lifted her eyebrows. "Whatever you say, Mrs. Sunquist."

Mary blinked and looked up sharply, though she supposed she shouldn't have been surprised that the girl knew her name. It was a small town. She was the minister's wife and the only pianist in town. Therefore she was seen onstage with the kids at every school concert and play. She was the unofficial assistant to the vocal music teacher at Arlen High School. She'd been serving in that capacity for ten years, and three music teachers.

She paid for her purchases, taking an extra bag and wrapping her candle safely inside it before tucking it into the top of one of her shopping bags. Then she carried the bags to the minivan. On the way out she passed a pair of teenage girls, walking arm in arm, dressed in black clothes and army boots, and wearing too much eyeliner. One wore a pentacle on a chain around her neck. Another had earrings in the shape of crescent moons. They were laughing as they passed on the sidewalk, and had apparently just come from that strange little shop on the corner. They had bags in their hands with the shop's familiar logo, an open treasure chest with wafts of purple sparkles spiraling from it.

For a moment, she just stared, amazed that they were so . . . obvious.

The shop had only opened a couple of weeks ago. Mary walked past it as often as possible, surreptitiously peering in the windows as she did, eyeing the items on display. Big glittering crystals, miniature reproductions of ancient images, small black cauldrons, crystal balls. She'd glimpsed the woman inside most of those times, and once she'd seen her outside, sweeping the sidewalk outside her door. She only knew the woman by reputation, even though she'd been in the same small town for as long as Mary could remember. Maybe all her life. Her name was Rose MacArthur. Her hair was mostly stunning silver, with a few streaks of black still remaining. Her face was deeply lined, and yet her eyes were sharp and clear, and potent when they locked with Mary's each time she passed.

Most of the people in town shunned Rose MacArthur. Everyone knew she was a Witch. Mary couldn't understand why the woman felt the need to be so open about her private beliefs. Maybe she *liked* being the object of ridicule and disapproval. God, opening that shop in Arlen, of all places, was like waving a red flag in front of a born-again bull.

Mary wondered vaguely what sorts of treasures those teenage girls had found in that shop. Then she put that out of her mind, sighed, put her groceries into the back of her van, got behind the wheel, and drove the mile and a half back home.

The house was large, old, and right next door to the church. It was provided free of charge as a part of the minister's pay.

Mike had an office in the back of the church, and a den in the house so he could work in either place. He was in the den now. She could see him pacing back and forth by the window as she pulled into the driveway. A little knot formed in her stomach. He seemed agitated. She wondered why, and then felt the familiar fear that it had something to do with her secrets. But that was foolish. He couldn't know what was in her mind, in her heart. Those thoughts were hers alone.

But what about her books?

Her heart sank. That had to be it. The books. Those pieces of radical female subversive literature that he would consider heresy. Oh, God. She thought she kept them hidden so well!

She closed her eyes and braced herself for the worst, then got out, gathered up her bags, and headed in to face her husband's rage.

HE turned when she walked into his study. She'd taken her time, put the groceries away, tucked her special candle into the cabinet all the way in the back part of the pantry. Mike never so much as glanced into the pantry. And from the looks of things, he still hadn't. The cabinet was closed, the books undisturbed. She allowed herself a small sigh of relief and, with no more excuses, went through the house to face her husband.

The study door was closed. She knocked, then waited patiently until he called, "Come in."

Stepping inside, she offered him a smile and felt guilty that it wasn't genuine. She didn't feel like smiling anymore when she saw him.

"Can you believe this garbage?" he asked.

She blinked at the tone in his voice. "What's wrong, Mike?"

"That damn shop. I brought it up with the council at the meeting this morning. No one wants to do anything about it."

"Do anything?"

"Witches. They call themselves Witches, and they're selling their blasphemous books and graven images to our friends and neighbors right out in the open as if there's nothing wrong with it."

She tipped her head to one side. "I see. But, Mike, what is it you think you can do about it? I mean, it's a free country. Don't they have a right to—"

"A right? You're worried about their rights? What about our right to live in a town free of heathens? Satanists, for God's sake."

She swallowed hard, lowering her head. "Actually, they're not."

"Not what?" he asked.

"Satanists."

He blinked, lifting his head slowly. "And just how do you know that, Mary?"

"Well . . . there was an article in last month's *Woman's Journal*. It was really interesting. I saved it, if you want to read it—"

"You saved it?"

His voice was dangerous now. She met his eyes, suddenly worried. "Isn't it something you can use? Before trying to fight these people, wouldn't you like to know more about them?"

"I know all I need to know." He reached to his desk, picked up a Bible, flipped through the pages. " 'Thou shalt not suffer a Witch to live,' " he read. "Exodus 22:18."

He snapped the book closed again.

She lowered her head and muttered, "Poisoner."

"What?"

Licking her lips, she shook her head. "Nothing, never mind."

"What did you say, Mary?" He asked the question in that quiet voice that frightened her.

She wished to God she hadn't said anything. What was getting into her?

"Something else you found in that article?" he asked. "Come on, tell me. I want to know."

Mary cleared her throat. "Well, there was a note about that verse. According to a Hebrew scholar, there were lots of people practicing various types of magic in biblical times. There were different words for most of them. The word they translated to 'Witch' in that verse was *M'khashepah*. It referred to a specific type of magical person, one who cast harmful spells in absolute secret, cursed the cattle, blighted the crops, and used herbs to poison their enemies. That's hardly the way I'd describe these modern-day Wiccans."

He was staring at her through narrowed eyes, now. "Get that article for me."

She almost sagged she was so relieved, and she ran from the room, thinking she might have reached him, convinced him to learn more about his subject before launching any attacks. She brought the magazine back with her, handed it to him.

He took it from her, glanced at the cover. She only noticed the lighter in his other hand when it flared to life. He held the flame to the corner of the magazine.

She reached toward it, but he dodged her and sent her a look that told her not to dare do that again. He let it burn until it singed his fingers, then tossed it into the empty wastebasket beside his desk where it flared higher for a moment, then belched dark smoke as the fire died.

"If I catch you with any more articles like that, Mary, you'll be sorrier than you know. And in case the insane notion gets into your head to visit that shop, you'd better think again. Don't let me catch you there. Ever. We have an image to uphold. I'm a minister, for God's sake."

She blinked in disappointment. She should have known better. "But what if you're wrong about this?"

"You tell me one place in the Bible where casting unnatural spells is a *good* thing, how about that?"

She blinked. "The loaves and the fishes."

His hand came hard and fast across her face.

Mary covered her stinging cheek with her hand, lowered her head, and blinked back the stinging tears.

"How dare you compare the miracles of Christ to the hocus-pocus bullshit of those bitches?"

She felt herself cringe smaller, her shoulders hunching in around her. She thought that he wasn't acting Christlike at all by treating her this way. She thought that miracles and magic were the same thing. But all she said was "I'm sorry."

"You're sorry. All right. You want to do some biblical study, Mary, I'd suggest you begin in the book of Ephesians, chapter five, verse twenty-two. Do you know the verse? Do you?"

Lifting her head, her face still stinging, tears blurring her vision, she recited the verse. " 'Wives, submit yourself unto your own husbands as unto the Lord.' "

"Maybe you'd better spend some time thinking about that, then," he told her. "Now go on, I have work to do."

She nodded, backing away quickly, pulling his study door closed behind her. Then she pressed a hand to her stinging face and wept.

FOURTEEN-year-old Iris MacArthur skipped down the steep stairs of the old Victorian house with Tansy right behind her. She looked great, she thought. They both did. Grams had talked them into ditching their goth look and going for something a little more mundane. As warm as it was they didn't mind. It was their first day in a new school, and while Iris still ached with missing her old friends, she was excited too. Besides, it was only for one semester until their mom got back from Europe.

Grams looked up from the plates she was heaping full of gooey omelets and smiled. "There are my girls! Did you find everything you needed in town yesterday?"

Iris held up a bulging book bag. "We hit every store in town."

"Yeah," Tansy said, grinning. "All three of them." They both laughed. "But I still say yours is the best, Grams."

"Oh, yeah. By far," Iris agreed. "The bookstore on the corner is a joke. They don't even carry the *Harry Potter* books!"

Grams licked her lips. "Well, they did. At first. But um . . . well, the locals didn't like them."

Blinking twice, Iris tilted her head. "Come again?"

Grams sighed, plopping two heaping plates on the table and waving the twins into chairs in front of them. They eyed the eggs, eyed each other, made an unspoken joke about how fat they would be by summer vacation, and then dug in. They did that a lot, communicated without speaking. Iris was never sure if it was because they were twins or because they were Witches. Maybe a bit of both.

"We've hardly had time to talk since you arrived," Grams said, sitting down with her own plateful. She wore a caftan in African print, and a shawl with fringe. She was effortlessly beautiful. Iris wanted to be just like her when she was old—except that she would keep her hair cut short and colored, not let it go all long and silvery. Still, on Grams, it was perfect.

"It was pretty sudden, us showing up on your doorstep," Tansy said. "I hope we don't cramp your style too much, Grams."

Grams waved a dismissive hand and rolled her eyes. "It must have been very upsetting, having to pull out of your own school."

Iris shrugged. "It was horrible, but don't tell Mom."

"Yeah," Tansy agreed. "She's been waiting her whole life for an opportunity like this. I mean, it's a real honor."

"She didn't want to leave us," Iris said. "It took a lot of talking to convince her to go to Scotland without us. One sign that we're having trouble, and she'll be back here like *that*." She snapped her fingers. "Besides, it's only for three months."

"Three months of bliss for me," Grams said. "I'm thrilled to have you two all to myself for a while." Her warm smile waned slowly, and she licked her lips. "But I am a little worried that you aren't quite aware of how . . . different things are here."

"Yeah," Iris said with a big grin. "It's warmer! I love it. I don't miss the snow at all!"

"I don't think that's what she meant, Iris."

"No," Grams said. "No, that's not what I meant." She drew a breath, sighed softly. "I don't want you thinking badly of this town, or its people. But, um . . . maybe it would be better if you toned it down just a little on your first day."

"We did!" Iris looked down at her outfit. She wore an ordinary pair of jeans, and a tiny T-shirt with the name of her favorite rock band spelled out on the front in glitter. Her sister's outfit was basically the same.

"I mean, the jewelry," Grams said. "The pentacles, specifically."

Blinking in shock, the girls looked at each other. Iris wore three pairs of earrings, onyx pentacles, silver crescent moons, and gold suns. Tansy had a black velvet choker with a silver pent front and center. She lifted a hand and fingered the five-pointed star in its perfect circle. "Why?"

Grams shrugged. "Just get the lay of the land first. I have no idea what the students here are like, but honey, this is the middle of the Bible Belt. It's different here."

"But Grams, you just opened an occult shop in town."

Grams smiled slowly. "I'm old and tough as shoe leather.

And I have insurance. I knew what I was doing going in, girls. I knew the risks. But what I didn't know was that my precious granddaughters would be spending the next three months with me. And the last thing I want is for either of you to suffer any kind of . . . prejudice, because of my little act of rebellion." She bit her lower lip. "Maybe it would be better if you didn't advertise that fact that you're my grandchildren. Or that you're Wiccan."

Two Weeks Later

"Ms. Sunquist?"

Mary looked up from her piano to see Rebecca Longworth and Sarah Lee Cooke arm in arm. Rebecca held a wad of blood-soaked tissue to her nose. Mary had been going over the sheet music for the spring concert next week, using the small music room at the Arlen High School.

"Oh, my gosh, look at you," she said, getting up from the piano and hurrying around it. "Put pressure right here, hon. Tip your head forward. That's it." She led the injured girl to a desk, and sat her down. Then she shot a stern glance at Sarah Lee. "You want to tell me how this happened?"

"Those new girls did it, Ms. Sunquist! The smaller one, Iris. She hit Rebecca right in the face!"

Mary frowned as she hurried to Adam Abrams's desk and rummaged for the first-aid kit. Finding it, she extracted some gauze pads and helped Rebecca exchange them for the blood-soaked tissues. "The MacArthur twins?" Mary asked. "Why, Sarah, what happened?"

"Nothing. Iris MacArthur did it for no reason at all."

Mary looked at Sarah Lee, narrowing her eyes. "No reason at all?"

The girl averted her eyes. "Well, we were singing and she

told us to stop, and we didn't. It is a free country after all. We can sing whatever we want to."

It made no sense whatsoever. Mary had been tense, expecting something to erupt from the moment she learned the two new girls were the granddaughters of Rose MacArthur, the woman who owned the odd little shop in town. But over *singing*?

She looked at Rebecca now. "Where did this happen?"

"Girls' roob," Rebecca replied, still clutching her nose.

Which explained why they had come to her instead of heading straight to the nurse's office. She was much closer. "And do you two always spend your time singing in the girls' room?"

They looked at each other. It was a speaking glance, and Mary knew there was more to this story than she was hearing just now. "Just what song was it you were singing that set the new girls off like that?"

"It was just one of the songs from chorus!" Sara Lee said, her tone defensive. "They're singing it, too, for the concert next week. We were just getting some extra practice time in."

"I see." She glanced at the sheet music, wondering what song she would find in the stack that could elicit violence among freshmen. Lifting the gauze, she checked Rebecca's nose. The bleeding had stopped. "And when I call the MacArthur girls down here and ask them their side of the story, they'll tell me the same thing?"

Rebecca made a disgusted sound as she snapped up more tissues to wipe the blood from her face. "Who knows what that kind might say? I wouldn't believe them if they said it was warm in July."

"Besides, they're already down at the principal's office."

"Yeah. Mrs. Haines will probably call their lunatic grandmother, if she's not too scared of being turned into a toad." Both girls laughed at the joke.

"That was uncalled-for, Sarah Lee," Mary scolded.

"Oh, come on, Ms. Sunquist. You of all people can't defend them. You're married to a minister!"

"My mamma says they're Witches," Rebecca said softly, conspiratorially. "I don't like Witches in my school."

"Yup, it's true," Sarah Lee rushed on. "That's why they're throwing fits about the songs we're doing for the spring concert. Probably reminds 'em that they'll burn in hellfire someday."

"I'm surprised they don't burst into flames every time they sing along at rehearsals," Rebecca said. "Can we go back to class now, Ms. Sunquist? My mamma's just gonna have kittens if I don't get an A this semester."

Mary scribbled her name at the bottom of a pair of late passes, thinking she finally understood what was going on. When she sifted through the sheet music Mr. Abrams had left on the piano for her to go over, she knew for sure. Mr. Abrams himself walked in while she was perusing the sheets. She looked up, caught his eye, and he smiled. He was a young man, in his first teaching position since college. And he was handsome, tall and dark in a way that had attracted the notice of most of the older female students already. She sensed he was having a hard time dealing with all the adolescent crushes, and maybe with teaching in this particular school district. He came from a much more liberal community.

"Hi, Adam," she said as he crossed the room and sat at his desk. "I'm glad you're here. I, um, I wanted to talk to you about these songs you've chosen for the spring concert."

He licked his lips, looking uncomfortable. "I'm thinking about canceling it, actually."

"Why?" Mary asked, surprised.

He shrugged, not answering. "Not your problem. What did you want to ask about?"

"Well, it seems a fight broke out today between some of the

girls over one of the songs. I just finished mopping up Rebecca's bloody nose. She says Iris MacArthur did it." She tipped her head to one side, lifting the sheaf of papers. "I think I'm starting to see why."

Closing his eyes, he sighed long and slowly. "My first mistake," he said, "was telling the kids they could pick their own songs. I expected pop or even rap, figured obscene lyrics would be my biggest challenge. I thought I'd just rewrite them a bit, and . . ." Shaking his head, he nodded at the music she held. "Instead, they came back with these. 'Jesus Loves Me,' *'Pie Jesu,'* 'Old Rugged Cross,' 'Savior King' . . ."

"All Christian songs," she said softly.

"I know. There's no way the kids picked these songs. No way. I've heard what they listen to, and this isn't it."

Sighing, she returned the music to the piano. "It's not your fault, Adam. You haven't been here long enough to have picked up on the tension in this town." She sighed. "It's been building up for over a year. First there was the big prayer-in-public-school controversy, then the arguments about the Ten Commandments being posted in the hallways. Then the *Harry Potter* protests. And then, Rose MacArthur opened that shop in town."

"MacArthur? As in, Iris and Tansy MacArthur?" he asked.

"Rose is their grandmother. And she did everything right, got all the right permits and licenses. The town never saw it coming, and they can't find a way to shut her down. It was like a slap in the face to the ultraconservative fundamentalist majority around here."

He was listening intently, nodding slowly. "So you think it was the parents? They gave the kids the ideas for the songs?"

"Of course it was the parents. Left to their own devices, kids don't launch holy wars."

"I guess the locals saw this as their chance to shout back. To be honest, I was gonna just let it slide, until the two new girls joined the chorus."

"And then . . . ?"

"They're not Christians. They're offended that all the songs are. They've asked that we cut a few, and add a few songs from other cultures and religions around the world. It's one of the most reasonable requests I've had since I started teaching here. They suggested a Native American song, a Buddhist chant, an African tribal song, and something called 'From the Goddess.' "

"And you said?"

"I thought it was a great idea. The rest of the class didn't love it, but they didn't get fired up or anything. Hell, I was even thinking of suggesting a traditional Hebrew prayer." He smiled bitterly at her. "Guess I forgot where I was for a second there."

"You're Jewish," she said softly. "I didn't realize."

"I don't advertise it. Not in this town. I'm only here until I can find something else."

"I understand."

"Anyway," Adam went on, "the kids went home and told their parents, and apparently, that was all it took to start— whatever the hell has started here. I got irate phone calls all night long, until I finally took the receiver off the hook. Then they started showing up at my door. My mailbox was stuffed full of furious letters this morning. The parents are insisting that it's unfair of me to change the program just for the sake of two students. Especially these two students."

"Because of their grandmother," Mary inferred.

Adam nodded. "I guess if she owns that shop, she's openly Wiccan?"

"Yeah."

He shook his head slowly. "Brave woman."

The door opened, and Principal Haines stepped inside. "I think we have a situation on our hands, Mr. Abrams."

He nodded at the woman. "Speak freely, Mrs. Haines. Mary knows all of it."

Mrs. Haines came in, closing the door behind her. She wore a navy skirt and blazer over a white blouse, and pearls around her neck. Her blond hair was twisted into a tight knot at the back of her head. "I'm very much afraid that we're going to have a riot on our hands if we alter the concert program to include pagan songs."

Adam nodded. "I was just telling Mary I was considering canceling it."

"No," Haines said. "Absolutely not. This school has held a spring concert every year for over fifty years. We aren't going to break that tradition. We'll go with the songs the children selected, in keeping with the Easter holiday, and that's final."

Adam opened his mouth, closed it again, seemed to be searching for words.

"Mrs. Haines, I have to tell you, I think that is highly inappropriate," Mary said, getting to her feet. "This is a public school. We can't give the appearance of endorsing one religion over another."

"This is a democracy, Mrs. Sunquist. And in a democracy, majority rules. The majority in this town are Christians. The two new girls have simply been outvoted. Surely no one can find fault with that rationale."

"I think a good civil-rights lawyer could," Adam said softly.

Mrs. Haines blinked at him. "Come on, you two, surely you can see the folly of stirring up the entire town over this. These two girls are only here for one semester. I mean, even I can see why people who've done things the same way for as long as they can remember would resent outsiders coming in and trying to force them to change." She shook her head. "It's not as if we have any *real* members of the community who want these other religions represented at the concert."

"Other than Rose MacArthur, you mean," Mary said.

"Members of the *school* community," Mrs. Haines corrected herself.

Adam was nodding now as he rose from his chair. "Would you consider me a real member of the school community, Mrs. Haines?" he asked.

"Of course I would, Mr. Abrams."

"That's great. I'm Jewish. I want a Jewish song at the concert. And I think that Mrs. Ashworth has some Native American blood in her background. In fact, if I look hard enough, I'll bet I can find enough ethnic and cultural diversity hidden in the halls of Arlen High to make your lily-white skin turn even whiter."

Mrs. Haines blinked at him. "I'm sorry if I offended you, Adam. I didn't know you were Jewish."

"Was I supposed to have my Star of David tattoo visible at all times? No, wait. Wait, that was under Hitler, not Bush. Right? I get so confused sometimes."

"I am not a bigot, Mr. Abrams. . . ."

"No." He eased his tone. "I know you're not, Mrs. Haines. But you are stomping all over the Constitution here. We can sing songs from many religions, or we can sing songs from no religions. But we will not, under any circumstances, sing songs from only one religion. Not while I'm leading this chorus."

Licking her lips, she nodded her head. "The board won't like this. They can vote to have you fired."

"Not without giving me notice, and by then the concert will be over."

"And if they fire him, the next chorus teacher had better also be a pianist, because I won't ever help out again," Mary put in.

Nodding slowly, Mrs. Haines turned and walked stiffly from the music room.

Adam's face went a shade paler. He clasped Mary's hand, closed his eyes, and sank into his chair. "God, what have I done? I need this job."

Mary silently wondered what *she* had done as well. In a town this size, she estimated Mike would hear about this episode in a matter of hours.

"TELL me what happened," Rose MacArthur said to her granddaughters. Because she knew there had been something. The first few days of school, the girls had come home amazed and slightly pissed off. They'd gone on about the Ten Commandments that were still posted in the hall, and how that would be fine if they would also post beloved rules from other belief systems, the Wiccan Rede among them. And they were surprised by the prayer meetings after school and the bumper stickers on the cars and the WWJD—What Would Jesus Do—bracelets on most of the kids. Rose advised them to just ignore it. It was the way things had always been here in Arlen.

On the second day of school, the girls joined the high school vocal chorus, and had come home even angrier once they had seen the list of songs slated for the next performance. Rose's advice had been to suggest to the teacher that they might want to aim for a bit more diversity, and maybe even give him a list of possible additions to the program.

Encouraged, they did that the next day, and came home angrier still. Apparently, the teacher's reaction had been open-minded, but a few of the other students had been petty and mean about it. Nothing they couldn't handle, they assured their grandmother. Name calling, crosses drawn on their lockers, people yelling, "I'll get you, my pretty" and cackling at them in the halls.

Today, though, their anger had changed to something else. They looked tired. Beaten down. Maybe even a little bit afraid.

They had gone straight from the school bus to the bedroom they were sharing, with barely a word.

Sighing, Rose had gone upstairs, tapped on the door, then stepped into the room and asked her question.

The girls looked at her. Strawberry blond hair, and green eyes that matched almost perfectly. Iris was just a bit smaller. Tansy had the narrower face.

"We had kids following us around in the halls all day," Tansy said. "Singing 'Jesus Loves Me.' "

"Not just singing it, screaming it," Iris put in. "Mobs of them, screaming it at the tops of their lungs, right in our faces everywhere we went. Even into the restroom."

"It was awful, Grams. We couldn't get away from them in there. I mean, it was like they backed us into a corner. It really wasn't Iris's fault."

Rose tipped her head to one side. "What wasn't your fault, Iris?"

Licking her lips, Iris said, "Well, they wouldn't knock it off. I didn't hit her all that hard."

"You hit one of them?"

She nodded. "Rebecca Longworth." She lowered her head.

Tansy didn't. "Knocked her right on her butt, bloodied her nose, too."

"Oh, dear."

Iris peered at her grandmother's face. "I shouldn't have done it, should I?"

Rose drew a breath, grounded and centered herself. "You have every right to defend yourselves. Both of you. Especially against that kind of attack. But—well, the girl you hit is the daughter of the president of the school board."

"Oops." They said it in unison.

Iris sighed. "Figures. She's also the most popular girl in school. She was leading them, though, so she had it coming."

"Are they going to change the songs?" Rose asked.

"Mr. Abrams really loved the idea the first day. Today, though, I don't know. Some of the kids' parents are fuming, and a lot of the teachers are on their side," Tansy explained.

"Maybe we should just let it go."

Rose licked her lips. "Girls, did you ever wonder why I opened a shop like Pandora's Box in a town like this one?"

Staring at her, they shook their heads.

"Have you noticed, since you've been down here, how few customers I have?"

"Hardly any," Tansy said. "I don't know how you stay in business."

"Oh, business is booming. But most of it is done by mail order. Over the phone, privately. I have to ship the stuff out in brown paper wrappers, unmarked." She shook her head slowly. "I opened the shop because it was desperately needed. There are pagans down here. A lot of them. They're just—"

"In the broom closet?" Iris asked.

Smiling, Rose nodded. "Yes. They see all this religious hatred and bigotry, and they decide that it's better to just . . . let it go."

"But that's so wrong," Tansy said. "No one should have to hide their religion out of fear. Gosh, this is America."

"That's right, it is. But this little town—like a hundred others just like it—has been doing things the same way for a long time. People who live here are used to it. They get complacent. They don't believe change is possible."

"Well, I'm not from here, and I'm *not* used to it," Iris said with a small stomp of her foot.

"And we're not going to just let it go!" Tansy added. Then she looked up at her grandmother, as if seeking approval.

"It's not legal, what they're doing. It's not constitutional. You girls are in the right here."

They both nodded, but still seemed doubtful. Their eyes round, waiting.

"What?" she asked, searching their faces.

The girls exchanged a glance. Iris said, "Gram, we're outta here in June. But you have to live here. Your house, your shop . . . if we let it go, it might be better for you. You know, in the long run."

Rose felt a pool of warmth in her chest and she had to blink her eyes dry. She cupped the girls' faces, one cheek in each hand. "You are so like your mother. By the Goddess, I am so proud of you. Now you listen. Your Grams has always been a scrapper, just like your mom. It's high time we locals stopped 'letting it go.' If you want to fight for what's right, then I'm right behind you. Understood?"

They smiled broadly. "Okay, then." Iris glanced at Tansy. "We fight?"

"We fight," Tansy said.

Rose nodded. "Now come with me. No self-respecting Witch goes to battle without a little prep work."

Taking the two by the hand, she led them down the stairs and into the large room in the back, her special room. There, they sat on silk cushions on the floor. Rose lit the candles, consciously relaxing her tense muscles, slowing down her breathing, knowing her granddaughters were doing the same. Rose lit a bundle of purifying sage, and when it was wafting its fragrant smoke around the room, she used a turkey feather fan to wave it toward each of the girls in turn, then waved the smoke over herself.

She cast the magic circle in the palm of her hand, poured power into it until it expanded, growing larger, encompassing the entire room and all in it. Then she turned and faced north.

"I call on the Earth, her energies and her power. The force and might of the north, of nature, of mountains and stone and winter. Come now, and join us. Lend your spirit to us. Be our shield as we enter into battle."

"Welcome, Earth," the girls said together.

Iris turned to face the east. "I call on the Air, with its wisdom and knowledge. The rebirth and renewal of springtime, of flowers and incense, and youth. Come to us now. Bring us wisdom and clarity as we fight for justice."

"Welcome, Air," the three said together.

Moving to the south, Rose raised her hands and said, "I call on Fire, the power of will, the passion and courage of the summer sun. Come to us now. Bring us your force to make positive changes."

Together the three chanted, "Welcome, Fire."

Tansey moved around the circle to the west. "I call on Water, compassion and healing. Bring the transformative power of Autumn to the hearts of Arlen."

"Welcome, Water," they said as one.

Lowering their hands, they all faced center. "The Goddess is alive and magick is afoot," Rose said. "Let the ritual begin."

"OH, my God." Mike Sunquist's fist tightened around the newspaper the next morning as he read the headline. His cereal and coffee sat unnoticed in front of him. Mary had been feeling as if she were walking on eggshells for days, ever since their confrontation over the occult shop. "Have you seen this garbage?"

He dropped the paper, got to his feet, snatched his coat off the back of his chair, and stormed out of the house.

Hands trembling, Mary reached for the newspaper and drew it to her, smoothing the wrinkles her husband's fists had put in its sides. She scanned the page he'd been reading. It wasn't difficult to find the piece that had upset him.

An Open Letter to the Witches of Dunwood County,
*   I know you are out there. And I know you are afraid. But right now, two young girls are showing us all the meaning of courage.*

Their high school had scheduled an all-Christian chorus program for next week's spring concert. These two girls, my granddaughters, have asked that the program be altered to include songs from other religions and cultures. Because of that request, they are being bullied and harassed. I don't know what the school will choose to do. But I do know that I will be there to witness it on the night of the concert. And I also know that I am no longer content to be forced to keep quiet about my beliefs, or to watch others struggle to keep their spirituality a secret. Bigotry and prejudice are not what Jesus taught. True Christians, like true Wiccans, show respect for the sacred beliefs of all people, even those they don't agree with.

I am publicly declaring that I am a Wiccan. I am a Witch, and I am proud of my beliefs and my heritage. I encourage every one of you out there to come out of hiding, and take a stand.

Rose MacArthur, Pandora's Box, 21 East Main St., Arlen

Mary swallowed hard as she folded the newspaper, cleared the table, carried the dishes to the sink. Through the window, she could see Mike in the church next door. His shadow was pacing back and forth in the office, and its window lined up with this one. He was speaking into his recorder. That was how he wrote most of his sermons. Orally, on tape, so he could listen and work on getting the right tone and inflection into his voice in the right places. She reached up, cranked open the window, and heard him, his voice raised in anger.

"Therefore shall a wife be in all ways submissive to her husband!" he railed. "But Rose MacArthur wouldn't know about that, would she? No. She's never even *had* a husband. Bore her daughter out of wedlock and raised her without a father. Now, while the daughter is off gallivanting around the world, shirking her responsibilities doing God knows what, her two daughters are in the hands of their grandmother. And they are stirring up revolt against God Almighty Himself! I say we won't stand for it! I say we must band together. I say we drive the devil out of Arlen!"

The telephone shrilled, and Mary went so rigid she thought her spine would snap as she picked it up.

"Hi, Mary. It's Reverend Phelps. Is Mike there?"

Will Phelps was a minister from the next town, and a good friend to Mike, although Mike often disagreed with his more open-minded approach to certain things. "He's . . . a little occupied at the moment. Can I take a message?"

Will Phelps sighed, then said, "No, I think I'd better talk to him in person. He's . . . he's not gonna like what I have to say."

"Is it about that letter to the editor?"

"Yeah. Frankly, Mary, I think the woman is right. We teach tolerance, love, and kindness in our churches. If these girls are being harassed in school because of their beliefs, then it's our duty as clergy to speak out against it."

She nodded slowly. "You're right. He's not going to like it."

"I know."

"For what it's worth, Will, I agree with you. I'll . . . I'll leave Mike a note, have him call you."

"Okay. Thanks, Mary."

"You're welcome." She hung up the phone, jotted the note to Mike, and set it on his desk. Then she hiked her bag up to her shoulder and went to school.

SHE saw Iris and Tansy MacArthur in the hall two days later, smiling, so she stepped into her doorway, leaning on one side. "You two know something I don't?"

Tansy smiled even wider. "Mr. Abrams changed the music program. We're still singing most of the original songs, but he added three new ones. A Jewish prayer, an African chant, and a Wiccan song. He said he'd have the sheet music for you by tonight."

Mary felt a ton of tension lift right off her shoulders. "That is wonderful. You girls should be so proud of yourselves. You've really—"

A large red *something* splattered against the back of Tansy's head. At first Mary thought she'd been shot, and her head had exploded. But no, it was a tomato. Tansy cried out, fell to her knees. Iris and Mary crouched beside her, helping her up and into the music room as Mary scanned the hall behind her in search of the culprit. Crowds of students stood around, many of them laughing and pointing. From somewhere in the halls she heard someone singing a melodic version of the Lord's Prayer.

She slammed the office door behind her.

THERE was standing room only the night of the concert. People were fired up, and Adam Abrams looked scared to death as the curtains rose and he faced the packed room, with his vocal chorus lining the risers behind him. He cleared his throat, tapped the mike, and began. "Welcome to the Arlen High School Vocal Chorus's spring performance. As you can see from your programs, we have something for everyone tonight, and we hope that you will enjoy hearing some of your old favorites as well as some songs you may have never heard before."

The applause was lukewarm. Just a smattering.

He turned to face the students, lifted his baton, and signaled Mary at the piano at the far right side of the stage. Mary hit the first few chords of "Jesus Loves the Little Children," and the kids began to sing. All of them, she noted with a sigh of relief. Including Iris and Tansy MacArthur. The harmonies Adam had worked into the arrangement flowed beautifully, and she felt a great deal of the tension ease from the room.

As the song wound to its close, the crowd applauded wildly, whistling and shouting, stomping their feet.

Smiling, Adam Abrams faced them again. When the applause died down, he said, "Now we're going to do something a little different. I hope you enjoy it." As he turned, he sent a nervous look down at Mary. She began tinkling the piano keys softly as the children hummed the opening, haunting strains of a beloved Wiccan song called "From the Goddess." The crowd was quiet for a moment, but Mary heard their programs rustling as they hurried to check the song's title.

The kids began to sing. "We all come from the Goddess, and to her we shall return, like a drop of rain, flowing to the ocean. . . ."

Someone in the audience rose to his feet and started singing as loudly as he could. And Mary cringed, because the voice was a familiar one. It was Mike's, and he was singing "Onward, Christian Soldiers," a song that hadn't even been a part of the original program.

The children on the stage faltered. One by one other adults rose and joined Mike in singing the hymn. And one by one, the kids on the stage joined in as well. Iris and Tansy MacArthur tried to keep singing the pagan standard, and Mary tried to keep playing it, but the voices in the room combined and rose to such intense power the place was virtually vibrating with it. And the kids, the kids were leaning toward the two new girls, shouting the lyrics into their faces.

Mary got to her feet, staring at the crowd around her, suddenly ugly and angry, all of them. Adam spoke rapidly into the microphone, begging for calm, for quiet. And suddenly Tansy and Iris stumbled from the risers and ran off the stage in tears.

Mary looked from them, toward where her husband stood in the crowd, leading them all in their battle song. He met her eyes, and she knew right then. She knew that it was over. She thought maybe he knew it too, because he stumbled over the words, and then fell silent, his brows drawing together as if he were only just now realizing the finality he saw in her eyes. He shook his head as if in denial and started toward her, and she saw his lips form her name.

She shook her head from side to side, just once, and, turning, went backstage.

She found Iris and Tansy wrapped in their grandmother's arms, crying.

"I'm so sorry," Mary said. "I honestly don't know what these people are thinking, but this is wrong. It's wrong, and it never should have happened."

Rose nodded. "I think I'll just take them home. Maybe look into home-schooling them for the rest of the semester, until their mother can get back and help me figure out what to do."

"Where is their mother, anyway?" Mary asked, suddenly curious.

Rose MacArthur smiled. "She's the priestess who was chosen to represent American Wicca at the World Council of Religions meetings being held in Scotland. After that she'll be staying at least two months, working on an interfaith committee to foster cooperation and understanding between religions."

Mary closed her eyes slowly at the irony. "You must be very proud of her." Then, licking her lips, she said, "Do me a favor, and don't leave just yet."

Then turning, she walked back out onto the stage, right up to where Adam Abrams stood, holding the useless microphone in his hands, looking close to panic as the roaring audience finished their song.

Smiling, she took the microphone from him and sang the last few notes along with them. They clapped and roared, and she held her hands up until they finally quieted down.

When she had their attention at last, she spoke. "You all know me," she said. "I'm Mary Sunquist, the minister's wife." Wild applause. "It was so nice of you to let my husband lead you all in a song. Now I would ask you to give the same courtesy to me. Or, you can interrupt and try to outshout me. Which means your taxes will go through the roof when this school district has to pay several million dollars in damages after the civil-rights suit I plan to file against you for discriminating against me based on my religion. I'm a Wiccan, you see."

A few people gasped, some muttered.

"Or, you can let me get through one simple song. It's your decision. Here's a thought to help you make it, though. What would Jesus do?"

She took the microphone to the piano, propped it on top, and began to play. And softly, she began to sing. "We all come from the Goddess . . ."

At first, she sang the words alone. But within a few beats, Rose MacArthur and her two granddaughters walked out onto the stage and joined her. And then, though it surprised her, someone in the crowd stood up and joined in. And then someone else. And another, and another. There seemed to be a Witch in every section, two or three in some of them. They rose from the crowd of hatred, and they joined, bravely, in the song, to the shock and outrage of their friends, neighbors, and, in some cases, families.

Adam Abrams's eyes were warm with approval as he came up beside Mary and joined in the song. And then Principal Haines stepped onto the stage and joined them as well, picking up the words and tune as she went along. She slid her hand into Mary's, met her eyes with a slight nod, and sang.

When the students saw this, they began to sing too, until the harmony filled the room to the rafters.

When the song ended, the room was dead silent. No one seemed to know what to think, what to say or do.

Adam took the microphone. "If it's okay with everyone, I'd

like to share a song from my tradition. It's a Jewish prayer."
There was a tug on his shirt, and he looked down. A student
whispered something to him, and he smiled. "Tommy says his
grandfather taught him a Native American song honoring the
earth, that he'd like to sing. And maybe after that, we can take
requests. What do you all say?"

There was a long, drawn-out silence. Then someone began to
clap. Someone else joined in, and gradually, almost grudgingly,
the applause spread throughout the room.

Adam looked at the two girls, at Mary. "Thank you," he said.

Mary smiled and said to Iris and Tansy, "Looks like your
mother isn't the only one doing her bit to change the world."

Iris shook her head. "This is just one tiny little part of the
world."

"Yeah," her sister said. "But Mom always says that's how
you change the world. One tiny little part at a time."

Author's Note

While this story is set in a fictional town, in a nameless state, I feel compelled to tell the reader that stories like this one are happening all over our country, with one important difference. The ending you see here is entirely of my own creation. It's a dream I'd like to see come true one day. But in real life, stories like this one end differently. In May 2001, it ended with Shana McNelly from North Carolina being driven from the concert stage at her middle school in tears, and being taunted and teased as she and her mother tried to leave the parking lot.

A few months earlier, on February 20, the story ended even more tragically when beautiful fourteen-year-old Tempest Smith of Lincoln Park, Michigan, hanged herself. Her suicide note said she couldn't bear the teasing of the kids at school any longer.

Teachers are fired from their jobs when it is learned they are Wiccan. Mothers lose custody of their children in certain courtrooms. This is happening, here. In the twenty-first century, in America.

Let us all take a moment to remember that our country was founded by people seeking freedom from religious persecution. Let's strive to remember that freedom of religion means freedom of *all* religions.

—Maggie Shayne

A Spell to Promote Healing and Tolerance in Your Community

MAGGIE SHAYNE

Items needed (and where to place them on your workspace):

- ◖ A stone, found locally (center)
- ◖ Some local soil (north)
- ◖ The dried petals of a locally grown flower (your town or state flower would be ideal!) (east)
- ◖ Water from a local spring, river, lake, or well (west)
- ◖ A yellow candle (center-east) and a blue candle (center-west)
- ◖ A disk of charcoal designed for burning loose incense (east)
- ◖ A small red candle to represent fire (south)

Magickal timing: Do this rite on a Friday (day of Venus, for harmony) when the moon is in Aquarius (friendship, hopes and dreams, groups). The moon should be waxing—that is any time from new to full (building something new).

Purify your work area and create sacred space in any way you like. Light the charcoal. (It takes time to get going.) Ask Deity to join you and help you in your rite.

Light the blue candle. Focus on water, love, healing. Light the yellow candle. Focus on wisdom, understanding, communication. Light the red candle, focus on the might of fire.

Take the stone in your hands, hold it, and visualize it clean and pure, an empty vessel waiting to hold the energies with which you will fill it.

Taking a bit of the soil, rub it over the stone, saying:

By the power of Mother Earth, by the earth spirits of this place in which we live, I fill you with love of all who dwell on the earth and the awareness that you and they are one.

Take the dried flower petals and drop them onto the glowing charcoal. As their smoky scent wafts, hold the stone in the smoke, saying:

By the power of Air, by all the air spirits of this place in which we live, I fill you with wisdom and clarity, that you will see things as they are, without the blinders of hate.

Run the stone through the flames of the red candle, saying:

By the power of Fire, and by all the fiery spirits of this place in which we live, I fill you with the will to do justice, to defend the wronged, to speak and act to right injustice!

Next, dip the stone into the water, saying:

By the power of the Waters of this place in which we live, I fill you with healing love and understanding, tolerance and kindness.

Now, hold the rock toward the heavens, in your open hands. If you are outside aim for the sun or the moon. Picture the energies of earth and sky beaming up and down into it. And say:

By all the positive forces of the universe, I empower this stone. All who pass by it shall be touched by the energies of Earth, Air, Fire, Water, and now, Spirit, with which I have filled it. It will open the minds and hearts of all who draw near it, and it will speed healing to my community. Because I will it, with good to all and harm to none, so mote it be!

Take the stone to a public place, a centrally located place in your town, such as a town square or a park, or to your school if that is where your energy is aimed, and hide it or bury it. Let its energy beam out and create a forcefield of love and understanding, felt by all who pass within its reach.

Angel Web

Carol Lynn Stewart

Titan College of Engineering and Physics, Berkeley,
California, Spring 2001

The paper had merit.

Professor of Physics Peter Angelakos tapped the crisp edge of Maíre O'Donnell's doctoral thesis proposal on his thigh. The calculations were a bit crude and her conclusions were shaky, but it had some merit. Her description of the electro-magnetic properties of her proposed "ISIS" factor, the quantum missing link between a particle and a wave, was bold, to say the least.

Yet the paper was unacceptable.

He placed the proposal back on his desk and turned the pages again until he found it—the "deal breaker," the flawed formula. A formula so poorly crafted that even a first-year student would sneer at it. Yes, there it was on page eleven. How could she have been so clumsy? His fingers itched to scribble a note, point out the unfinished equation, and give the paper back to her for more work, have her finish the damn formula. He couldn't do that. She'd turned it in. Once students turned in their proposals, it was all over. There was no giving them back. Not only was this a Physics Department rule, it was his own as well, and he'd *never* broken his rules. Not one. His Greek father would have had Peter whipped if he broke his own code. Worse than that, his dad would have quoted Aristotle. Just thinking about that was like biting on tinfoil. Peter *had* to fail her.

Still, it was a damn shame. Maíre had shown promise. Intense promise. And, well ... *Admit it, Angelakos!* She was easy on the eyes. Small woman, triangular face, pale skin, black hair that had a sheen of cobalt in the sunlight. Turquoise eyes. Low, husky laugh. Made it real hard to give her the boot.

Be honest. It wasn't just her beauty that pulled at him. She had a way of smiling that made his pants feel too tight, and what she said in class and at the graduate student parties revealed an offbeat intellect. Damn, he'd like to keep her around. He couldn't date her but at least he'd be able to see her each day. Wait—maybe his own calculations were wrong. He'd done a quick-and-dirty check on her theoretical formula; maybe his computer would arrive at a different conclusion.

He pulled up Smartchip's AdaByron math program and punched some number values for the variables in Maíre's formula, then pushed his chair back and put his hands behind his head. Maíre was his student. Nothing could happen between them. He'd never broken that rule either, though plenty of the other faculty made it their life purpose to do so. Not that it was easy for him. In Maíre's case, it was incredibly hard.

Still, there were things that had given him pause, things that had pulled him up short when he found himself glancing Maíre's way a little too often. She was multiply pierced: a filigreed silver hoop graced her nose and star-pattern earrings both dangled from and studded all the way up both her ears. A silver ring lanced her belly button, exposed by the skimpy T-shirts and low-slung jeans she wore. When she laughed once he caught a flash of silver on her tongue that made his own mouth ache in sympathy. A Celtic interlace tattoo circled her right thumb, and whenever she was near, the faint odor of some exotic herb from the local Lhasa Karnak shop had tickled Peter's nose.

The powerful G4 Macintosh whirred as the yin-yang processing ball tumbled, taking the numbers he had entered into Maíre's formula and running them through AdaByron's elegant math programs. The processing symbol stopped. A sign popped up in the results field: FORMULA ERROR. Peter placed his hand against the computer screen, his thumb blocking the answer. It was gratifying to know his own slide-rule brain had come to the same conclusion, but damn, he hated what he had to do about it.

Peter rolled Maíre's paper into a tube and rested his forehead on it. She was one of the brightest kids he'd had the pleasure of teaching. He'd miss her, piercings and all. If only she hadn't botched the final formula. Damn, damn shame. There still weren't many women in physics. He'd have the Committee on Science and Gender down his throat for this, but so be it. If one of his male students had turned this in to him Peter would have called the student into his office and made the kid watch while Peter tossed the proposal into the infamous "breath of God" shredder Peter kept parked next to his desk.

He wouldn't do that to Maíre. She might *cry*.

No, no, no. That was wrong. Maíre wouldn't cry. From the way she behaved in class and at the Roaring Rock Brewery graduate student sessions, he suspected she'd be more likely to throw something at him. Either way he might be tempted to place his feelings ahead of his responsibility to his students, to the department, and to science. Couldn't have that. He just would not accept her proposal.

Ms. O'Donnell would have to leave with dual masters in physics and computer science, two good degrees. Yes, there it was. Ms. O'Donnell. Not Maíre of the turquoise eyes and lusty chuckle, but Ms. O'Donnell. His student. He didn't need to feel guilty. She'd have no problem finding a cushy job.

Peter straightened Ms. O'Donnell's paper and fed it, page by page, into his shredder. The pages caught the sunlight that struggled through his narrow office window and the text shimmered. God, but he hated this. When his shredder ate the last page, with a sound halfway between the powerful breathing of Tibetan Qigong Master Khenpo and the expensive purr of a Jaguar XJ6, Peter leaned back, ran his hands up through his hair, and rumpled it until his scalp burned. Very well. Done. He shook his head, reached over to his computer without looking, and fumbled for the Apple-Q keys that would close AdaByron, both deleting Maíre's formula and ending the program.

All right now. Time to write the letter that would give Ms. O'Donnell the bad news.

Peter took a pen in his left hand and scribbled the words that would pitch Maíre O'Donnell right out of the doctoral program.

He stood, gathered up his lecture notes, and marched to the door to Edwards Hall 126, on his way to teach Physics 210, his "Hole in the Universe" course.

Behind him, the computer whirred. AdaByron blinked. A dialog box popped on screen.

APPLE-S. FILE SAVED.

*   *   *

Rose Street, Berkeley, California
April 30, 2002

"By the balls of Eros!" The fifth wooden kitchen match broke
in two right in her hand. Maíre O'Donnell stood at the north
quarter of the Beltane circle, trying not to hurl the matches, the
candle, and herself across the room. She glanced behind her
where Delphine sat looking goddamn amused, Nur was hyper-
ventilating again, Joanna was zoning out, and Cedar . . . Damn,
the high priestess was giving Maíre that *look,* the fixed stare
that told Maíre Cedar knew exactly what was going on in
Maíre's life, including all the things Maíre didn't want to tell
her.

Maíre turned back to the north quarter candle. Just because
everything in her life was going down the goddamn toilet
wasn't a reason to let her responsibility to her circle slide along
with it. Beltane was one of the major ceremonies; drawing the
sacred space where the sleeping Goddess would be coaxed from
Her long slumber was a big deal to Hearthfire coven. Maíre was
not going to let them down!

Maíre's hands shook as she drew out the sixth match to call
forth the guardians of the north, the powers of Earth. "Damn
cheap matches." Where was the rest of Hearthfire coven? There
should be thirteen of them here, not five. The rest couldn't all
be sick. Could they?

Delphine snorted, "Way to go, Maíre. Why don't you light it
with your *laptop?*"

"Don't start that." Nur's tiny hands fluttered. "You know it's
bad to say negative things in the circle. Maíre, it's also rude to
say things about the God's . . . you know." She looked down and
played with the cascade of moonstone beads that spilled in an
opalescent tumble over her chest.

Delphine bent her head, raised one eyebrow, and looked over
her glasses at Nur. "Who died and made you high priestess?"

Maíre spun around. "Will you give it a rest! It's just a frickin' match, okay? And Eros has balls if you care to look." She pointed toward the center of the circle where a statue of Aphrodite showed the naked Goddess rising from her shell, abundant Botticelli hair held discreetly, while a rust-brown statue of the god Eros stood adjacent. A very anatomically correct statue of Eros. A very *happy* Eros.

"It's disrespectful."

Maíre counted to fifteen. "Oh, for the love of Diana, Nur! Wicca is a fertility religion!"

"Chill, Maíre." Cedar strode over to Maíre and placed a strong, square hand on Maíre's shoulder. Cedar's waist-length, ash blond hair jangled as she moved. Fifty tiny bells were woven into the ends of her hair and brought the silver-laced chime of summer into the circle haven. "And Delphie, put a sock in it." She turned back to Maíre. "I think Eros wouldn't mind your expletive, Maíre. But others here do."

Maíre looked at Hearthfire's high priestess. Damn but she wished she was more like Cedar. The high priestess never got her feathers ruffled. "Yeah, sure." She swept her arm around the circle. "Sorry, guys. My bad."

"Continue."

"Okay, Cedar. We're styling. It's cool; it's tight." Maíre rasped another match against the sandpaper block. The match flared, sputtered, then steadied. "See? Six is a Goddess number. Had to work." She lit the indigo candle of the north, stepped back, drew in a breath, and intoned the plea,

> *"Powers of Earth, land under our feet*
> *Bones of Gaia*
> *Wrap yourself around this sacred place*
> *Open the space between the worlds*
> *Guard this circle."*

Cedar gave a brisk nod and stepped into the center of the circle, spreading her hands. "Gods above and Gods below! Hasten to this place. Guide us. Be with us now!" She took up the sapphire urn of May wine. "We offer our gift of wine with strawberries, blueberries, and sweet woodruff leaves." She dipped her finger in the white wine-soaked berries and placed it against the god's terra-cotta lips. "Lord of the Greenwood, accept our offering of love and laughter." She touched the rose-stone lips of Aphrodite. "Lady of ocean-tide and deep forest, accept our adoration. Bless us with your bounty." She turned and lifted the urn above her head. "So mote it be!"

"So mote it be." Maíre whispered the words with the others but she barely listened as Cedar walked the circle and spoke the invocation and charge of the Goddess. What the hell was wrong? Why was it so damn hard to focus?

Maíre sleep-walked through the remainder of the ritual and when it was over, she collapsed on a pale rose velvet-covered feather pillow. Nur clasped and unclasped her hands. Delphine plopped herself down and lay spread-eagled on the faded kilim. Only Cedar and Joanna were left standing.

"Let's share news." Cedar climbed onto her Isis throne, an Egyptian chair of wood, leather, and sisal.

What the hell was this? Maíre leaned forward and stared up at her high priestess. Hearthfire always shared any news *before* ritual, not after. Must be something important for Cedar to break pattern.

"Nur, you start."

Nur pulled at her beads; their clicking punctuated the wind-chime quiver of Cedar's bells as the high priestess nodded at every sentence. "So many things are going wrong, all around me. Three of my friends are getting divorced—one of them only just got married and all of them don't know why they are splitting up. And a whale washed up on shore yesterday." She bent her head and smoothed the gold paisley fabric of her skirt. "There's more but that's all I want to say right now." A hiccough bubbled out and had her beads shaking again. "S-sorry. Hic. Hic. Hic."

Delphine groaned. "Pollution's been around a long time, Nur. And in case you haven't noticed, over fifty percent of all marriages fail."

"But there is usually a reason. People have a reason when they get divorced."

"Oh, really? Men need a reason?" Delphine gave her signature braying laugh.

Nur crumpled in her seat.

No reason. Ice skittered down Maíre's back and settled around the base of her spine. First vertebrae meant security issues. Yeah, right. All that safety first–chakra stuff Nur would go on and on about if she even suspected Maíre had felt this. Still, it was weird. Why did what Nur was saying spook Maíre? She stared at the urn. She hadn't had much of the wine, so it wasn't alcohol that was making her stomach quiver.

Delphine yawned. "Next you'll be telling us about your little green space friends, Nur."

Damn, why wasn't Cedar reining in Delphie? Nur would start crying before too long.

Maíre shook her arms, snapped the tension out of her wrists, and lurched from the depths of the pillow to her feet. "Back off, Delphine."

Delphine rolled over and jumped up. "Try and make me, cyberqueen."

"Fricking Luddite."

"What about you, Maíre?" Cedar placed her hand on Maíre's bunched fists. "What have you been experiencing?"

Maíre looked down and relaxed her hands. Had she really been ready to pop Delphie? Not that she couldn't take her on, but damn, Maíre was losing it if she even considered getting into a tussle with Ms. I'm-an-artist-and-so-much-better-than-all-of-you. "I've got my own troubles, Cedar."

"Such as?"

"I lost four clients. Four! I mean the economy sucks right now after most of the dot-coms tanked but businesses still need network support, right?"

"Our little cyberslut."

"Can it, Delphine." Cedar took Maíre's wrist and pressed gently on her pulse. "Share with us, Maíre."

"I hate losing clients. I don't live like a yuppie and I watch my money so it hasn't burned me yet, but the reasons the clients gave were ludicrous. One didn't like my logo. After three years of his contract he decided all of a sudden that he didn't like it."

"It's phallic." Delphine smirked.

"It's *Greek*." Maíre rubbed her left hand on her soot-black jeans and wondered for the millionth time why she hadn't changed the Hermes pillar on her business cards. It wasn't like Peter had ever cared. He'd never answered any of her calls about her proposal. The rat-bastard. Maybe she should have gone to the department chair after all, even though that would have harmed Peter.

"See what I mean?" Nur jumped up and jiggled. "Even Maíre is feeling it, and I bet Delphine is too." She flinched at Delphine's glare but continued, "It's got you two fighting. Not that you never fight, but . . ."

Delphine backed away from Cedar and Maíre. Cedar touched Delphine's arm and gently pulled her back, all without releasing her hold on Maíre. "Delphine?"

Delphine sighed. "I need a cigarette."

Cedar stroked the inside of Delphine's elbow.

"Dammit! Quit that. I'll talk already. I'll talk." Delphine

bowed her head; her tawny hair shimmered forward to hide her face. "I haven't been able to paint for the past month." The words drifted from the curtain of her hair.

Nur moved forward and opened her arms. "Oh, Delphie!"

"Don't you start! I just can't and I don't know why."

The slimy trickle down her back oozed forward to Maíre's belly. "Delphie, has this ever happened before?" She suppressed a shudder. What the hell was *this*? Was she coming down with something?

Delphine looked up, startled. "No."

Joanna frowned. "I haven't noticed anything, Cedar."

Cedar released Maíre's wrist. "The members of our circle who are not here all mentioned differing levels of this problem." She shrugged. "Perhaps it is affecting some more than others. Animals have been affected as well."

Nur nodded. "And plants, too. All the seedlings I planted this month have soured."

Cedar took her place on the Isis throne again. "I believe the balance has shifted."

"Bull." Delphine rubbed at her arm.

"Hear me out. None of these things taken separately means much at all. But all of them?"

"It's just coincidence." Delphine had control of her voice again.

Maíre glanced at Nur. "We just need a little research, that's all. Maybe you can cast a chart?"

Nur shook her head. "I have already. There is a Neptune-Pluto aspect, but not enough to explain this."

"Maybe something in the atmosphere? Charged particles like the electro-plasma people called swamp gas? I could look it up." Maíre pulled out her Palm Pilot.

"Right, use your computers to solve this."

"Maybe I will."

"Yeah, sure, Maíre. Crash the Department of Defense."

"I can hack *anything*." By the gods, Maíre would like to wipe that smirk off Delphine's face.

Delphine leaned forward so they stood nose to nose. "You are a rubberband. Stretched way too tight."

"Hack. *Anything*." Maíre's clenched fist rose.

Delphine drew in a long breath and poked Maíre gently in the solar plexus.

"Damn!" Maíre fell back, arms windmilling. She caught the edge of Nur's chair and steadied.

"Twang! I rest my case."

"Stop it, both of you. Delphine, take that chair over there, please." Cedar stared at Delphine until she sat. "I appreciate your ideas, Maíre, but we need magick as well as science and technology to research this." Cedar peered around the circle. "Any volunteers?"

Maíre looked down and picked at the black polish on her thumb.

No one spoke.

"Very well. The pendulum will choose."

"CHEERS!" Peter smashed his glass of ouzo into the Jack Daniels tumbler of his partner so hard it cracked.

"Christ!" William Reston of Smartchip jumped back from the splash of ouzo. "Watch the Armani, *compadre!*" He grabbed a napkin and dabbed it at his muted teal and scarlet tie.

"Aw, s-sorry." Peter made a swipe at William's shirt. "Whatever. Doesn't matter. We're going to be rich." He stared at William's smooth face. "Hey. Why'd you shave off your beard?"

"So we could get the money, dude. The bucks. Gotta look corporate to get venture capital with a cha-ching!"

"We're rolling!"

"Mega-mega-gigabytes of data, any kind of data, the bloody Library of Congress, transmitted wireless anywhere on earth."

"Why restrict it to this planet?"

"Anywhere. And instantaneous download. No waiting."

"No muss, no fuss."

"Did I tell you about the Department of Defense contract?" William now moved to single malt, pouring a splash of Highland Park into his tumbler and gulping it down. He didn't look up.

"No DoD, Will."

"Why not? Their money is as green as anyone else's."

"Two words: black ops."

"You've been watching *X-Files* reruns again."

"What's wrong with that?" Peter pushed his ouzo away and leaned back in his chair. "I like Gillian Anderson, so what?" Though the face that popped into his mind was triangular, pale with dark hair surrounding it, amazing turquoise eyes. But the mouth, yes. The mouth was the same—that natural, lush, near-pouting curve of the lower lip. The mouth.

William gave a wink and a nod. "I haven't committed us."

"Good."

"But I wish you'd—"

"No." Peter glanced around the bar and then looked through the windows at the San Francisco skyline just across the bay. Did Maíre ever come here to His Lordship's restaurant?

William sighed. "Eventually someone will copy it, Peter, and they will sell it to the DoD." He shrugged. "I just think if we do it we'd at least have some control. For a while, anyway."

"You have to be kidding."

William looked away. Peter reached over and jabbed his arm.

"It's all in here, Will." Peter tapped his forehead. "Nothing is written down." Except on his hard drive, and he'd coded that.

"We had to provide enough of it for due diligence, my man."

"Just enough, Will. There is no one who could complete this formula."

"All right." William fingered his tie again. "Hey. To us!" He extended his tumbler and clicked it against Peter's glass.

"Angel Web is on its way."

"Get this man another drink!"

"DAMMIT, Cedar!" Maíre gripped the edge of Cedar's kitchen chair. "I'm with Delphine on this one. The pendulum is complete bull."

Cedar approached the table with a steaming kettle. "Ginger tea, I should think." She poured the hot water into the honey and ginger in Maíre's cup.

"It's just the ambient electromagnetic flow in the room that makes that fricking thing sway." Maíre raised the cup to her lips and took a deep breath. Sweet, hot, and spicy. She swallowed. Bliss!

"So you say. However it works, it chose you." Cedar poured her own tea and returned the kettle to the stove. "As I hoped it would." Cedar took Maíre's hands. "What is troubling you, girl?"

Oh, man. Here it goes. "You're my family, Cedar. My *only* family. Years ago when I was kicked out of my house and lived on the streets it was you who took me in."

"Not so many years ago." Cedar's eyes did a crinkled coyote twinkle. "I've never regretted that. Have you?"

"You may regret it now." Maíre took another gulp of her tea. "I broke the Rede."

"Ah. *Harming none, do what you will.* Deep personal responsibility for individual action. Each one of us struggles with that."

"I didn't think any harm would come of it."

"Come of what?"

"You remember my initiation when the gods gave me my Wiccan name and my gift from Isis?"

"I know it was a powerful gift. The atmosphere crackled when your initiation was over. I had to use de-static on my rug for a week."

"My gift was a formula, Cedar. In the initiation trance I was given a formula. And I'm a physicist. Yes, yes, I know I don't have the advanced degree. But I'm still a physicist so the formula I was given, well, I knew what it was."

"And it was?"

"I was given the formula for the frequency of the gods. The paths of Hermes. And damn it all, I gave it away!"

"What makes you think you gave this formula away?"

"Cedar, all that you have taught me has told me something is going on. You are right. Something has shifted." Maíre pulled her hair back and twisted it into a loop. "You must have seen the things happening around the world, violence breaking out in places that have been quiet for decades, like the riots in Zurich, the assassination in Australia, the whole-scale abandonment of children in Nepal, the poisonings in the Vatican."

"Yes. I have been following these things, but what does that have to do with you?"

Maíre touched Cedar's arm. "Bear with me on this. You know that Peter Angelakos was my doctoral advisor?"

"I know that name very well."

"I haven't . . . well, I've tried not to think of him for the past several months, tried to wipe even the image of him out of my life."

"Not so easy to do."

"As I found out, Cedar. But I thought I had succeeded." Peter had never even touched her, let alone kissed her. It was just a crush she had on him, that's all. "Then some things started happening, in the way they do when the gods are trying to get your attention. His name just kept coming up. First I was at the library standing in line behind a woman who wanted to tell me all about this book she was reading, like she had found God or something."

"What was the book?"

"The fricking *Peter Principle*! And the man standing behind me was named Peter. Damn, and that man's little boy was Peter Junior!"

Cedar quirked a brow and nodded. "What else?"

"At home I went online to Beliefnet. You know of it? It's a web site for spirituality. They had a lead story on pagans in film." Maíre mashed her face in her hands. "But the rest of the site had stories all on Saint Peter this and Saint Peter that."

Cedar took her hands. "Maíre, listen to me. You never had any closure with this man. There was no cutting of the loop that bound you. It's time to do that. It doesn't necessarily mean that this has anything at all to do with the shift in balance. It doesn't mean that what is happening is your fault."

"But I gave him the formula. Not the whole formula, but a part of it was in my thesis. I wanted so much for him to be, well, dazzled."

"And he wasn't. Look. You did not give him the complete formula."

"Right."

"Could he complete it with what you gave him?"

"Get real. He's a man! And I'm pretty sure he's not a techie. He even had a wooden case built around his computer at school so it would look more *organic*." Maíre snorted. "He couldn't hack his way out of a paper bag, let alone finish that formula! It wasn't just a physics problem; it was a material science and engineering equation. He couldn't complete it." Unless he knew magick, completion of the formula was impossible. This was

Maíre's biggest secret, one she had never shared with anyone, especially Cedar. The only way Maíre could solve an equation was to take it to the still place inside her where magick dwelled. "He'd never be able to solve it."

"Then there is no problem."

"There shouldn't be. What I'm afraid of is that even with the little bit I gave him he may have been able to shift the balance."

"You must have noticed I'm not asking what this formula would do."

"I noticed." Maíre pushed her tea aside and set her head on the table.

"Is it that bad?"

"It would be bad, Cedar. A catastrophe. The first magickal people of Ireland had this formula, too. When they could have used it as a weapon against an invading army, they all walked into the Otherworld rather than unleashing it." Maíre shuddered. "I've broken faith with the gods. I have to set this right."

"You don't know that he kept the formula. I mean, he failed you."

"Exactly. He failed me, the rat-bastard."

Cedar shook her head. "I swear, Maíre, I swear." She squeezed Maíre's hands. "Someday you will stumble over your arrogance. But for today—yes, today, it is one in the morning now—I want you to go home and do something that has nothing at all to do with physics." She smiled. "Plant something, or bake something, or weave something. It doesn't matter. Put all of this aside."

"And then?"

"And then go see this Peter. Close off the loop that binds you. In love and forgiveness, not in hate. That is the only way you will be able to move on. Have your say. And let it go."

A fluttering clutched Maíre's throat. "S-see Peter?"

"I'm your high priestess, Maíre, and your adoptive mother. I ask you to do this."

Maíre nodded. "So mote it be."

JASMINE tea made a kick-ass dye. Of course, she had to boil it and boil it and boil it until it was pretty much goo. Then it needed salt water to set the dye and she had to soak the fabric in it for practically a year and a day. Maíre caught the edge of the buttery muslin with her wooden yardstick and lifted the saffron-tinted Victorian blouse out of the dye bath on her tiny gas range. Well, not a year and a day, just a few hours, but it sure as hell felt like a year and a day! She grinned and whispered the words of completion as she danced from her postage-stamp kitchen to her even more miniscule bathroom, "Gentle Lady Aphrodite, my thanks."

She spread the dripping blouse over the edge of her claw-foot tub and stood back to admire it. Cedar was correct. This kind of work was therapeutic, and the blouse would look *tight* with Maíre's black leather jeans. A little bit of time in the dryer on gentle cycle and she'd be all set. With jeans, jacket, ritual jewels, and antique blouse, she'd venture out to Roaring Rock Brewery where the physics graduate student crowd would be having their weekly meeting.

Maíre raised her arms and rubbed the back of her neck. She'd been up since five making the dye bath. It was worth it, though. The blouse had just the right amount of lace and was antiqued to the nth degree by the jasmine tea.

The very thing to face the lion in his den.

THE crowd on Shattuck Avenue was pretty thick for a sunny Friday afternoon. Why weren't all these people over at Pac-Bell Park watching the Giants game? Ah, well. Maíre swung her arms as she strode past Carlton Street, grinning as she caught several sidelong glances at her blood-red lips, black polish, studs, leather, and lace. Roaring Rock Brewery was a fair piece up the street. Plenty of time to figure out how to toss rock salt in Peter's path without him knowing, so when he stepped in it she could do a quick truth-telling spell and discover if he had done anything with her formula. Maybe Cedar was right and Maíre's formula had nothing whatever to do with the inexplicable events of the past month. By the gods, she hoped so.

First of all, she needed a plan to approach Peter. The best opener would be something wry, a Gallic shrug, perhaps. Something from an old movie. Maybe a young Lauren Bacall smirk from *To Have and Have Not.*

She faltered. Now why the hell had she thought of that? Damn. Something about whistling, wasn't it? Putting your lips together. She stopped in front of Delta Software's storefront, where a group of people stood staring in the window at the big-screen television displayed there. Maíre glanced at it and prepared to move on. Dave generally had computer games patched into it. It was great for his business—people on the street would be transfixed by the characters of Knights of Vengeance six feet tall on the huge screen, then would come in to buy the game. Maíre did Dave's network support and thanked the heavens *he* hadn't bolted from her Hermes Pillar company. She turned her head away and prepared to walk on when a sound grabbed her.

It was a voice, a silken, deep near-growl issuing from within Dave's store. Maíre swiveled and pushed through the crowd to stand, face nearly against the window, hand splayed against its cool slick surface.

"One major barrier to taking the next step to becoming a phase one planetary civilization is the ability to transmit huge amounts of data instantaneously. . . ."

It was Peter's face, his almond-shaped, firelight-through-sherry eyes. God, she loved those eyes. His mother was Tibetan; his father was some kind of Onassis clone. At least, that was what he'd told Sandy, his graduate secretary, and Sandy had told Maíre this when Maíre had plied Sandy with Godiva chocolates. Damn all crushes! It hurt just to see him, even on television. Maíre pressed harder against the window. Yes, it was Peter, the same shock of black hair, same shake of the head, same grin, same barking laugh. How could she face him, see him in person? She frowned. What was he doing on television, anyway?

"To what do you attribute the success of your procurement of venture capital?" The reporter was a milk-fed Midwest blond who leaned into Peter with her microphone. Maíre curled the hand she held against the window; her nails streaked the surface with bits of her polish.

"We have a viable product and the tests we just ran show it works. Sorry, but I have to run." He glanced at his watch. "I'm off to a meeting." He grinned, gave a triple wave of his hand, and walked off.

The hayseed bimbo reporter lost her cool and fumbled through her next lines. "Well. Yes. Well, there you are, Titan College's own Professor Peter Angelakos. Founder of Angel Web, and the Angelakos factor that allows billions of gigabytes to be transferred anywhere, wireless, in the wink of an eye." A stock picture of Peter's face filled the screen.

Mist covered his face. Damn! It came from her open mouth. Maíre stepped back, shaking. Goddamn that man! It *was* him! He'd stolen her formula! Worse than that, he'd finished it! Oh, my gods, blessed mother of the universe. He was using it to trespass in the Otherworld!

They were all in deep, deep crap.

*   *   *

MAÍRE stood poised at the entrance to the microbrewery. It was pretty much the same crowd at the physics table at Roaring Rock. Dan Jessup was practically genuflecting at the Saint Peter altar, stumbling over himself in his effort to shout out the news of Angel Web. Both Dan and a girl Maíre didn't recognize were checking out Peter's butt as he strode to the back toward the bar.

"Goddess help me." How in Hades would she get through this? Ah. Brazen it out. Always worked for her. She tripped through the green-frame glass doors before she could think about it. "Hey, Dan."

"Hey, beautiful! How is your network business doing?"

She smiled. "Still kickin', Dan."

"Well. Maí . . . Ms. O'Donnell."

The voice came from behind her. A sober, reflective voice. A deep voice that grabbed her between her heart and a blossoming ache between her legs. A beloved voice. Damn, she was not ready for this. It was the voice of a thief, a traitor, soon to be a killer if Angel Web continued. Maíre pulled air deep into her lungs, then turned. "Professor Angelakos." She stood and waved her hand at the door. "Can we speak privately?" Maíre ignored Dan's whoop and the steely dagger-glance the new girl was sending her way.

Peter merely nodded and gestured for her to precede him outside, then walked silently beside her and around the corner until they reached the street behind the Body Time Soap and Lotions store.

Maíre stopped and looked up at him. But did she say, "Hello Peter?" Did she say, "Please reconsider running the Angel Web harmonic resonance program?" Hell, no.

She stared him in the eye and said, "You fricking bastard. Why did you steal my formula!"

*   *   *

JESUS, Joseph, and Mary. Lord Buddha and all the monks, saints, and holy relics. He'd forgotten how stunning Maíre was. Wait. What was she saying? "Your formula?"

"The formula you worked out for Angel Web. The one in my proposal. The proposal you turned down."

"What are you talking about? I had the Angel Web formula in AdaByron." He'd come upon it in an unnamed file when he was doing some purging of his system. He couldn't remember having saved it but he was sure it wasn't Maíre's work. He'd erased that. "What is this? You want a piece of my business?" God, was she truly like that? He'd been warned that once the venture capital and the lucrative nature of his business was out there in the media something like this might happen. But to have this from Maíre . . . "You want money?"

"No."

Well. "Then what? You want me to get you back into the doctoral program?"

"I want you to kill it. Kill Angel Web."

He gave a sharp laugh. "Lady, you are nuts." She didn't turn away; she just stared at him. "Do you know how much I have riding on this?" He fingered the worry beads he kept in his pocket. "If you really think this is the case, why don't you go to the department chair?"

"That would bring harm to you. I won't do that. I just want you to kill it." She stepped in closer. "Peter, please. This thing you are doing, it's dangerous."

"How so?"

Her face went still. "You think this is a joke, don't you?"

"No, I don't." If it were anyone else but Maíre he might have thought that. He was hard-pressed to determine exactly what Maíre was doing, but he was sure it wasn't a joke.

She looked down. "Thousands of years ago, a people in Ireland, some say it was the first people there, were given a gift, a device so terrible that they destroyed all traces of it and destroyed themselves as well so no one would ever know this thing existed."

"I'm not into myths, Maíre."

She shook her head. "It's not a myth."

"Look, I have a lot I have to do so why don't you cut to the chase?"

"I already did."

"You want me to kill a project I've worked hard on, for months and months." Eight months, in fact. Damn, why did he feel like a flurry of ice shavings just blossomed in his stomach? It had to be coincidence that the idea for Angel Web had come after he'd turned down Maíre's proposal. "A project that will help bring this world together. Information can be transmitted all over the globe, wireless, just like that." He snapped his fingers and stepped closer, so close that he could see each individual lash framing her turquoise eyes. "I'm not going to do that." He was so close the Lhasa Karnak herbs she wore enveloped him. "I'm not going to kill it."

"You are going to do that."

Goddamn her! His hands came up of their own accord, circled her neck. She stood her ground. The pulse in her throat beat wildly against his fingers. God, he just wanted to *shake* her! Damn, he couldn't do that, he couldn't. . . .

He dipped his head and took her mouth with his, burrowed between her lips, and found her teeth. She opened for him with a moan, met his tongue with hers. The rasp of metal underneath his tongue and along his lower lip took him by surprise and shook him to his core. He broke contact, leaped back, and looked at her, aghast.

She touched her lips with her fingers. "Well!"

"I'm sorry." What was he *thinking?*

"I'm not."

"It won't happen again."

"I know." She seemed okay now; she folded her arms and gave him that "Don't mess with me" look he remembered from class. "I can see you need convincing."

"I can see your time is up." He backed farther away.

"This is not over."

"When the bell rings, class is over, Maíre." He swiveled around and said over his shoulder, "Good-bye, Ms. O'Donnell."

MAÍRE pushed through her front door and flung her keys on the couch, then followed them, rolling into the couch's soft depths in a wet, sloppy mass, sobbing and raging. Damn that man. She'd have to face him again, she knew this. She had to convince him. But how? She wasn't all that good at math. She was an intuitive scientist, not a mathematician. Might as well admit it. She got through her college math classes using magick. So how could she convince him? Now that he'd kissed her she had no credibility at all. "Face it, Maíre, you never were credible in his eyes. He flunked you." She held a pillow against her belly, tried to still the sobs that kept welling up from her gut, took up the remote, and punched the "on" button. CNN was running Peter's spot again. Maíre kept it on but closed her eyes until it was over.

"In other news, a five-point-eight earthquake rolled through Wyoming and Montana today. Another earthquake shook Tierra del Fuego and yet another rocked Belgrade. Professor Musgreaves at the U.S. Geological Survey stated that this kind of seismic activity is highly unusual."

Maíre leaped up from the couch. By the Gods! Was it already too late? She reached out to turn off the television. Her glance fell on her collection of objects sitting on top of it: a slide rule, a gyroscope, a small fulcrum. All silly little gifts from Cedar when Maíre had found her true vocation. She picked up the fulcrum and stared at it. Of course. Physics. She looked up at the clock. Peter should be home by now. She strode to her bookcase and pulled out the volumes she would need.

PETER sat in front of his computer in his basement lab, staring at the screen and cursing. She was right. Dammit, but she was right. Somehow her formula had gotten saved to his computer instead of erased. He'd looked up the date the AdaByron file had been saved and it was the very day he'd turned down her proposal.

"Sloppy." It was damn sloppy of him to not check to see that he'd erased her formula from AdaByron. What could he do now? He'd have to give her at least a quarter of his profits. It was only fair. He'd created three-fourths of the formula but her part was what had started it. He poured a juice glass full of Manderine Zest and sipped it. He needed the ginseng. It made him go all zen. Only way he could do what he had to do. He picked up his phone then stared at that, too. Had she changed her number in the last year? Well, he had to start somewhere. He punched in the numbers on his student list beside Maíre O'Donnell's name.

A sharp rap on his door had him dropping the phone and grabbing for his Mandarin Zest before it could crash to the floor. He only just caught it when his door opened. The air in his throat went thick. "William? Did you need something?"

"Professor?"

"Ah. Come in, Maíre." He offered her a chair. She remained standing. "You were right. It was your formula."

"I know."

"I don't understand why you want me to kill Angel Web."

She pulled a photograph out of a file folder she held close to her side. "You can't do any more tests, Peter. The formula is a killer. It sets up a resonance, a harmonic, pulsed, electromagnetic resonance."

"That's how it works. It's a quantum bidirectional data transceiver, essentially quantum teleportation." He glanced at the picture she held. "What is this?"

"It's the Tacoma Narrows Bridge. Remember what happened to it?"

"Bad civil engineering. It shook apart . . ."

"Exactly. Peter." She reached over and placed the file in his hands. "Read these."

He held the file but didn't open it. Several minutes passed while he struggled to open the file and see what he suspected he would see.

The death of Angel Web.

MAÍRE stood and watched Peter, watched his face as he read through the packet she'd put together. Dismay, sorrow, rage, despair, acceptance, resignation; one by one these expressions washed over his face. All the steps to bonding with death. The death of his dreams. Or the death of the planet. She held her breath when he closed the file.

"It's a planet buster." He looked her straight in the eye. "Angel Web is a planet buster. Isn't it?"

Maíre sagged against the table. He leaped up and helped her to a chair. "You see why I want you to kill it."

"I've only run two tests." He tapped the file. "And the effects have been horrendous."

"Plants were affected first, then small animals."

"And people." He waved his hand at her printout of the seismological report. "Not to mention the earth." He took her left hand in his and squeezed it. "I'll kill it right now." His hand paused over the keyboard. "Is it already too late?"

"I don't know. But there are some people I know who may be able to counteract it as long as the tests stop." At least she hoped Hearthfire and the other covens around the world could do this.

He nodded and brought up file after file. Maíre's gut clutched. All that work. Each time he hit the delete key, she trembled. Finally he leaned back. "That's it."

She took his hand. "May I do something?"

He vacated his seat. "What did you want to do?"

"Your files could still be retrieved. I have to do something to ensure that no one can steal them." She went to Control Panels and pulled up his internet connections.

"What are you doing?"

"Your regular files will be fine. Wait." She closed her eyes and leaned against the screen. The configuration of his system spread out behind her closed eyelids. Dozens of red, blinking capillaries flowed away from his hard drive to the internet portal. She lifted her head, opened her eyes, and turned to him. "Someone has hacked into your computer."

"How do you know?"

"It would take too long to explain. Do you trust me?"

He looked down at his hands. "Yes."

"Very well." She cracked the knuckle of each of her fingers then grinned up at him. "I can trace it back and set up a program on their system that will only change the formula so they won't be able to detect it right away. You can watch but don't say anything." She swiped her hand across the screen and closed her eyes again. "Welcome to *my* world." The machine hummed under her fingers. She spoke to the computer, drilled down deeper, danced with the particles and electrons that made up the electrical and mechanical parts of the machine, and finally saw it. The rogue signature of the hacker. "Found it. Huge system." She typed in the code that would change the formula, twisting it so it was harmless. Once the next person logged on to the hacker's network the change would be complete. At each computer in their system the formula would change. "They shouldn't discover this for a while." She stood.

"How did you do that? How did you find it? Your eyes were closed the whole time."

"It's a long story." He'd probably cringe if she told him it was magick, that she wasn't a true physicist.

He touched her cheek. "I think I know who hacked my computer." He kept stoking her cheek. "These people are dangerous. What are we going to do to make sure they didn't move it to another system? Or that they would just work out the right formula with what they have?"

We? "The way I twisted it they won't be able to complete it. And I thought I told you I know people . . ." It was difficult to breathe. His touch ignited a sweet fire trail from her cheek to her neck.

"No. I want you to tell me how you did this. Tell me."

She sighed. "I'm a Witch, Peter. A Wiccan."

He moved back but held on to her chin. "So?"

"What?"

"Did I ever tell you about my mother? She used to talk to demons." His hand now stroked down her arms. "She was a big-deal Tibetan Buddhist nun before my dad married her." He smiled into her face. "I think she'd like you. Just be who you are, Maíre."

She entwined his fingers with hers. "We'll use Magick to fight them, Peter. Real Magick. It will be a lot of work but in the end they won't know what hit them."

A deep chuckle rumbled up from his throat. "I guess you'll be the teacher now."

She rubbed her cheek against his. "Class is in session."

Clearing and Grounding

CAROL LYNN STEWART

I have a really simple "house clearing and grounding" spell I adapted from a feng shui remedy told to me by an old Chinese man I sat next to on the bus from the Now and Zen festival at Golden Gate Park in San Francisco to the Powell Street BART station. If you find yourself feeling unaccountably anxious and depressed in your living space, or in your office space, you may be experiencing "stale or stagnant Qi"; that is, the living and breathing energy from the unseen world that interpenetrates this realm may have gotten caught or snagged, and has stagnated. To remedy this, and to allow the Qi to flow as it should flow, you can do a few simple things. You will need these items:

- Four small quartz crystals
- Sage "smudging stick"
- Small bell
- Lavender oil

First, if it is possible, open all the windows to your space. If you want to clear and ground your office space, and you work in a high-rise where the windows will not open, you will want to take several minutes to visualize open windows and a breeze fluttering the curtains. Once the air is flowing freely, or you can "see" it flowing freely, make a schematic of your space, to identify the four corners. If your house is oddly shaped, just get as close to the four corners of your house as you can. Charging the ground floor or the basement, if you have one, is best for this spell, but if you live in an apartment on a higher floor, don't worry! The spell is intended to ground and clear your space, so it will work just fine on upper floors, as long as that is where you live.

Second, light the sage smudging stick and use it to "cleanse" all the windows and door, starting at the back of your space and working your way to the front of your space, traveling counterclockwise, the "banishing" direction. As you do this, chant, "All evil out! All evil out!" Of course, if you are doing this in your office you will want to choose a time when you are not likely to disturb your coworkers. In clearing an office space, you can forgo the sage and use four drops of lavender oil in a cup of water, sprinkling the space as you travel "widdershins," or counterclockwise, around your space. Once you reach the front door, open it, allowing all that is negative to slide around you and out the door.

Third, you need to "anchor" your space. Take the lavender oil and anoint all the crystals, pouring into them at least three good things you would like to see happen in your life in the coming six months. You can actually breathe these hopes right onto the crystals! What you are doing here is talking to the unseen world, the place where all things begin. The things you would like to see happen may or may not occur within the next six months, but at least you have let the unseen world know what you want.

Now take the anointed crystals and the bell and march clockwise from the front door to the first corner of your space. Place the crystal in that corner, ring the bell three times, and go to the next corner, repeating this process until you have placed all four crystals. At this time, there is nothing else for you to do. It is good to "tend" the crystals from time to time, making sure they are not disturbed. If one is accidentally knocked out of place, simply take some lavender oil, breathe your hopes into it, and replace it.

The best thing about this spell is that it combines feng shui with magick. In feng shui you don't have to believe in it to get good results! Just follow the instructions, even if you feel a little silly doing them, and then see what happens. You may be pleasantly surprised. In any case, your space should feel lighter and more calm.

A Reverence for Trees

Lorna Tedder

Beltane

We sat very still in the grass, and naked. We had made love for the last time, and both of us knew it.

I kissed Sam's broad shoulder, then laid my head against it as I stared out at the pastel hues of sunset. I tried to memorize everything about the moment: the smell of the spring grass, the darkening shadows under the double oak on the hill, the distant chirp of crickets. And Sam. Most of all, I wanted to remember Sam the way he was this night. The way he would never be again.

He slid his arm around me, pulled me close, and then kissed my forehead. His hair was a little too long on top, and the fringe tickled my nose.

I should cut it, I thought. *I should wait until he's asleep tonight and snip a few of those beautiful blond locks. Something to remember him by.*

My hand fell to my belly. Automatically. Protectively. Goddess willing, I would have something else to remember him by. Goddess willing, because after tonight, there would be no chances of children. Not for Sam. Not for us.

"What are you thinking?" I asked, snuggling against him.

Ah, damn it! The question was a matter of habit. Just a sweet nothing I whispered whenever we cuddled. I hadn't even considered the question or the possible answers I didn't want to hear. He was most likely thinking about the ten years we'd lost, about what a fool I'd been, about the dismal survival rate for newly diagnosed leukemia patients—even with aggressive treatment. I didn't want to hear his answer, not when I had to be the strong one. How could I be strong if I burst into tears every five minutes?

"I was thinking about that old oak tree," he said.

Probably a lie to spare my feelings. Sam was always like that.

He pointed at the oak on the hill. It had grown from two acorns and entwined into one tree. "It must be a hundred years old. Not many trees last that long."

Or people, I thought.

"Too many trees are cut down for parking lots and so-called progress," he continued. "No one plants oaks anymore."

"We did," I reminded him.

He nodded and glanced up at the grassy ridge where we'd planted acorns as part of our Imbolc ritual. Just the two of us, barefoot and wrapped in our ritual robes of black velvet, laughing and freezing our butts off as we celebrated the first signs of spring. Little had we known . . .

I pressed my cheek against his shoulder and hugged him. Not a fierce embrace as it would have been a few months ago. No. Gentle, as if he would break.

We had made love in much the same way this evening as the light had faded from the sky. Soft. Somber. *Sacred.* No more wild tumbling or rough kisses. Instead, our bodies had taken on the subdued yearnings of two weary people who would not have this again and needed to feel the subtlest tenderness in every touch. Tomorrow would begin the hell of tests, the chemotherapy, the radiation, possibly a bone marrow transplant. The memories of tonight would have to last the rest of our lives.

I shifted my cheek from his shoulder and blinked back stinging tears. I wouldn't have him feel their wetness on his skin and know I'd been weak.

He was trembling! I drew back, then quickly covered my surprise with a polite cough. It wasn't desire that shook my Sam, but rather exhaustion. That's how it had all begun. Fatigue. A lingering flu. A cut that wouldn't heal. More fatigue. Sam was a big man in his prime, and for all the times I had quivered in his strong arms, now he shook in mine.

"Sam . . ." The lump in my throat swelled, and I couldn't form words around it. I swallowed but still could not talk.

"Don't," he whispered.

I tilted my head enough to gaze up at his pale face, but he stared off determinedly at some imaginary spot in the distance. To some place where I could not follow.

"We should go inside," I finally managed. "You're tired."

He ignored me and nodded toward that damned tree again. "Beth, I never told you. That oak is why I bought this land. A semi had jackknifed on the interstate, and I took a detour on this little country road. There he was out there. Majestic and alone." A frown plowed across Sam's forehead. "I wondered how many other oaks had once shaded that hill. The rest were gone. Lightning, winds, people. That oak called to me. He was the last of his kind. I knew that if I owned this land, then one day you and I would plant more oaks. We'd fill these fields with trees. We'd return this land to the groves that once stood here."

I raked in a sob. "But you bought this land seven years ago."

"I know."

"Sam, we weren't even together then." I backhanded the tears. We weren't together because I had left Sam over a stupid argument and married someone else. A giant mistake, all right, but one I'd realized too late. I'd spent the next eight years trying to make a miserable marriage work and then another two years of aimless wandering before getting drunk enough on margaritas to call Sam and see if he remembered me. All that time . . . lost. Time I could have been with Sam.

"You're right," Sam said. "We weren't together then, but I knew one day we would be."

"How?"

"I prayed that the God and Goddess would give me one more chance with you in this lifetime. When the time was right. And that we wouldn't waste it this time. All I had to do was wait." His eyes met mine for an instant, then looked away to spare me. "I was willing to wait the rest of my life if that's what it took."

I flung one hand over my face and looked away to keep my tears from betraying me. I couldn't breathe. Couldn't talk.

"Beth, please. Don't cry. Please. Promise you won't cry over me."

"Don't ask me that," I sputtered. "Don't ask me to make a promise we both know I can't keep!"

He held me then, rocked me back and forth as I sucked in the tears. I was supposed to be strong. I had to be strong. I sniffled and then straightened beside him.

"I've been so selfish," I said quietly when a long while had passed. The first stars of night glittered above us as they had for lovers who had lived thousands of years before us. The lovers were long since cold but the stars still burned. "Sam, when we worked magick tonight, my intentions were selfish. I wanted to make a baby with you. To make up for all the time lost. To be here with me when you're"—I choked—"gone. Tonight's magick was so strong. Our ritual should have been for your healing. I made you misspend your energies!"

He shook his head. "I've told you before, Beth. Healing is not meant for me. But I'm sure our magick worked." He smiled in that secret way of his. Sam's spells always worked.

"Won't you even try?" I wailed. "You're the most powerful Witch I know, but you won't do anything to heal yourself. The two of us together are so powerful. Sam, I just don't understand!" Was he punishing me? Did he know how much I deserved not to have him after I'd thrown him away all those years ago? And then I hated myself for yelling at him and hated myself for feeling resentful.

"Beth, it's not that I don't love you. It's not that I want to die and leave you. But in my heart, in my *soul*, I know what has to be."

"Don't—"

"I've asked for healing, and I've received my answer. But Beth, if you'd like, you have my permission to perform a healing ritual on my behalf."

I stared up at him, gratitude welling inside me, and nodded furiously. Magick can change the course of a life and working magick on other people would be unethical without their permission. At last, Sam had given me a chance to save him.

"Thank you. Thank you, Sam." I kissed his cheek and nose and chin. "Thank you." Tears still streamed down my face, but I was nearly giddy now.

Sam rose wearily and stumbled, still naked, down the hill toward the house we'd finished building last autumn just before we married. I watched him fade away into the night.

"I will always love you, Beth," he said softly. The spring breezes caught his words and carried them back to me.

I rose and ran all the way up the hill. In my head, I composed my ritual, the most important spell I would ever cast. My unsure feet fell on clumps of tall grass and in night shadows, but I didn't stop running until I stood before the mighty tree. This oak had been Sam's covenant with the God and Goddess that he and I would be together again. I wanted this tree to bear witness to my magick because if intent and intensity had anything to do with spell-working, then Sam would be in remission and maybe even cured by Lammas and his nonpagan doctors would be congratulating themselves on saving him.

This would be a spell unlike any other spell. I didn't consult my astrological tables or select my mail-ordered athames or exquisitely carved wands from our altar. I had my chance at last to save my husband. It was just me, the power inside me to connect with the Goddess, and my heartfelt wish to cure Sam.

With no tools but my own hand, I cast my circle there in the grass with the oak, crickets, and stars as witnesses. Electric blue light shimmered around me as I raised my arms to the sky. Even before I called the quarters, I felt the life force of Mother Earth surge up through the roots of my feet. The energy of all the heavens entered my fingertips and tingled down into my arms and torso. I became a conduit between the earth and sky, an exchange of energy and magick and power. I sensed the presence of Deity as I hailed the watchtowers of the four corners and asked the guardians to bear witness to the rite.

I welcomed the Goddess into my circle. Warmth jolted through me, an otherworldly current, and humbled me. The words of my chant tumbled off my tongue, my voice rising with each syllable.

> *"And in this place and in this hour,*
> *I call upon the Ancient Power*
> *To give to one who has a reverence for trees*
> *A gift of—"*

Stop. I heard it clearly. A woman's voice, but in my head. I knew better than to dismiss it as wind. *Do not ask for healing.*

What? Panic rose in my chest. I was in the presence of the Goddess. I knew it without a doubt. Asking for healing was what I was here for. Asking for healing was *everything* I was here for. Nothing else. My pulse thrashed in my ears. What was I supposed to do now?

Do not ask for his healing. Ask instead for strength.

Strength? For what? For Sam? Strength to take him through the torture of chemo and radiation? Strength to fight and win? Or strength for me? To deal with his dying?

You must be strong. You must be his strength to see him through.

I understood then, or thought I did. Magick is seldom an overnight miracle. It can take days or weeks or even months. If Sam was to survive this ordeal, then I would have to be there for him in every way. To make up for lost time. And for Sam, I would send him all my strength, straight from my soul.

I swallowed hard, then altered my words to do as the Goddess had bid.

> "And in this place and in this hour,
> I call upon the Ancient Power
> To give me strength to lend
> And give him strength to mend.
> I give it willingly from my body and heart
> To atone for that which has kept us apart.
> As I will it, so mote it be!"

No sooner had I thanked the Goddess and dismissed the quarters than a heaviness overcame me, and I collapsed in the dew-laden grass.

*   *   *

Lammas

"You look like death warmed over."

I jerked my head up and peered between my fingers at the entrance to the intensive care waiting room I now called home. Oh, Goddess, it was terrific to hear a friendly voice!

"Anna!" I leaped to my feet and threw my arms around my high priestess. She was a couple of dress sizes bigger than I was, maybe a fourteen, and solidly into her forties. She'd been my surrogate mother since before Sam and I had been accepted into her coven. She gave me a quick hug, then held on when she realized I wasn't ready to let go. I sobbed into her shoulder. Goddess knew, I couldn't cry in front of Sam.

"I'm so sorry I didn't come sooner," she murmured into my ear, "but I just found out this morning when I couldn't get you on the phone. I called Sam's sister. Beth, why didn't you tell me things had turned sour with Sam?"

"I . . . I . . . ." I hung on to her for dear life. My knees gave way under me. I needed Anna's strength to stand. I was alone in the waiting room for now and so glad to have her company. "I guess I lost track of time. I'm sorry I won't be able to attend tonight's ritual."

"Shhh. Don't be silly. You have your priorities straight." She guided me back to the torturous chair where I'd slept the past three nights amid the nervous chatter of other patients' relatives and the fumes of chemicals the night janitors used to wash the floors. Anna frowned and sniffed the air. "When did all this happen?" she asked.

"Oh, no." I twisted away from her, suddenly embarrassed and afraid I'd offended her. "I'm sorry, Anna. I haven't had a change of clothes since Tuesday morning."

"Oh, hon. You're worn out. I'll stay with Sam while you go home and get a shower, if that's what you want. Why don't you get a nap, too, while you're at it?"

"No. No!" Even before I answered, I was shaking my head furiously. "I don't dare leave. Not even to go to the cafeteria. What if the doctors have news?"

"Caf— Beth!" Anna took my hands and steadied me. "Are you telling me you haven't been eating?"

I ran one hand across my forehead. My hair felt greasy, dirty, under my touch. "I'm not very hungry."

"Beth, look at me." Anna forced my chin up. Still, I refused to meet her gaze. "Beth, you're three months pregnant. You've got to eat. Come down to the cafeteria with me now and tell me all about Sam."

"I . . . can't." I dared not leave. I'd waited for four days for news. "They had to give him a second bone marrow transplant. He didn't want it." I inhaled and blew it out raggedly before I spoke again. "He did it for me. He wants to know that this pregnancy's safe and I'm not going to miscarry before he dies." I blew my nose on the tissue Anna handed me. "I don't know what he thinks he can do about it if I miscarry. The doctors say even if he goes back into remission, there's virtually no chance he'll ever father another child."

Anna scooted onto the seat beside me and drew my head against her shoulder. "I wish I'd known. Last we talked, he was doing so well."

And I'd thought for certain my spell had helped. Maybe it had. Until four days ago, we'd thought he had at least a twenty percent chance of surviving.

"He started feeling weak again," I explained. "I knew it before he ever said anything."

"Your intuition."

"No." A long silence passed between us. "I made some kind of connection with him. I could feel it. I was so tired."

"Hon, that's the baby. On the inside, your body's climbing mountains. You may not feel pregnant yet, but you're exhausted because of all that unseen work going on inside you."

I kept my head on her shoulder. She smelled of sandalwood. "I understand all that. This is different, Anna. I took him to the doctors. He was dying. I could feel it."

"What do you mean, you could feel it?" Anna asked carefully. The tone of her voice frightened me.

"I could feel the life draining out of my arms and legs. I was so incredibly tired. After the transplant, it got better, stronger. But the doctors still haven't told me anything. I just keep waiting and waiting for them to tell me something, anything."

"Beth, I don't mean to pry, but something's not right here. You're not an empath. You shouldn't be feeling everything Sam is, but you've made some kind of connection with him."

I nodded against her shoulder. "I know. I meant to. The Goddess told me to be his strength, so I've been sending my strength to him and taking his pain where I could."

"You *what?*" Anna framed my face with her hands and studied my eyes. I saw her wince. "You connected directly to a dying man? Oh, hon! You've got to stop this. You should never connect directly with a terminally ill man. Ever."

"But it's helped," I protested. "The doctors have been so surprised at how strong he's come through chemo and radiation."

"I don't doubt it, but what you're doing is a risk to you, Beth. And to your baby."

I pulled away from her. She knew how much Sam meant to me. How could she question me? "I have to do this, Anna. If it means he'll beat this thing, I'll give him the last ounce of my strength."

"And you will, if you don't choose a smarter way. Hon, why didn't you call me? You don't have to be alone. Why do you keep cutting off everyone? Why are you punishing yourself like this? There's a safer way."

"Then tell me!" My head pounded. I just wanted to sleep.

"A battery."

"A what?" My arms hurt. My eyes hurt. I ached all over. I thought I was going to throw up or fall down. I was so tired. So ready to give up.

"A battery. Instead of sending your energy directly to Sam, send it into an object. Then he draws energy from the object. You need something natural and solid. Say, a crystal or a meteorite."

"Or a chunk of petrified wood?" My eyes widened and for the first time in days, I felt a flutter of hope. "For his birthday, I gave Sam a petrified stump. I found it on our honeymoon while we were wading through a creek in the mountains. It weighs about thirty pounds and it's—"

"Too heavy. You need something lighter you can haul into the hospital with you. Something you can leave at his bedside."

My hopes fell again. The intensive care unit had little use for personal objects. Sam was in there, without me, without anything he owned or held dear. Dressed in hospital gowns, his Celtic wedding band removed, he was as naked to the life we had as he'd been on the day he was born. A thirty-pound rock would end up in a Dumpster, I was sure.

"I'll find something," I told Anna. "Then I'll break the connection."

"Good. Break it before it breaks you."

I stared past her and let out a long sigh at the flourish of white in the hospital corridor. "There goes Sam's doctor. Again." I sat up straight and dabbed my eyes with the soggy, wadded tissue. "I know it's bad news. Dr. Minter keeps avoiding me. He hasn't come to see me in days, and every time I try to chase him down the halls, he disappears into a restricted area."

Anna was up and out the waiting room door before I could drop the tissue in my lap and stand. A few seconds later, she stalked back into the room, triumphant, leading a stammering Dr. Minter by the sleeve. The white lab coat he wore had his name embroidered in blue script above the heart. "Dr. Minter, this is Beth Fisher. She'd like an update on her husband, Sam Fisher. I believe he is still a patient of yours?"

The doctor extended a jittery hand, then seemed to recognize me. "Uh, yes. Hello, again, Mrs. Fisher." He glanced at Anna and recognized true authority when he saw it. "Uh, I don't really have anything concrete to report."

"How about something in Jell-O?" Anna snapped. "This poor woman is pregnant, sleeping in straight chairs, and won't leave to shower, let alone grab a bite to eat because she's scared she might miss the five minutes that you finally bother to tell her how Sam is doing. She wants to hear something from you. Anything. Firm or not. Or would you rather she suffer a miscarriage right here in the waiting room?"

"Oh." His jaw worked as embarrassment spread over his cheeks. "I didn't want to report anything until it was firm. I don't like to get the family's hopes up."

"Doctor, her husband has leukemia. The only thing she has is hope."

"Something's happened?" I caught my breath and waited. The doc just didn't want to have to deliver bad news. He wasn't comfortable talking to worried wives. That's why he'd been avoiding me. He thought no news was good news. "He's better, isn't he?" I could feel it.

"Yes."

"Oh, thank you." I wiped away fresh tears. "Can I see him?"

"Not yet. If he's holding steady on my morning rounds, you can see him for a few minutes then."

He turned to leave but Anna pulled him back by the sleeve. "But there's nothing she can do tonight, right? She should go home and rest, right, Doctor?"

"I can't leave Sam. If something should happen . . ."

I'm not sure if Anna squeezed the doctor's wrist or what, but he flinched, then regained his composure. "Your husband is better, Mrs. Fisher. But there's no way you will see him before tomorrow morning. I'll expect to see you back here at seven A.M., and you'd better be well rested or Sam's going to worry about you and that's not good for him right now. Understand?"

I nodded. I knew I wouldn't sleep well, even in the bed I'd shared with Sam for the past year, but thanks to my won't-take-no-for-an-answer high priestess, I'd been given a reprieve for a bath and a hot meal. And to find a battery for Sam.

I made it home from the medical center in just under an hour. The house seemed unusually quiet, expectant, when I walked inside. I could feel Sam all around me, an electric tension in the rooms. I took a hot shower and changed into my ritual robe, hair still wet at my shoulders.

Barefoot, I walked into the backyard and stared up the hill to our favorite meadow and the giant oak tree. The sun was low in the sky, just as it had been that Beltane evening when Sam and I had made love in the grass. Crickets hummed in the distance, but everything felt one step removed from reality. As if I were walking there in an astral projection dream. My arms and legs ached. It was so still here and peaceful and so far removed from that sterile waiting room.

I trudged up the hill, toward Sam's favorite oak. Baby oaks dotted the hillside, some eight to ten inches tall already, and marked in circles that kept out the grass. My hand fell to my stomach, to the other seed Sam and I had planted.

Reaching the crest of the hill, I panted for breath. A jagged stripe marred the tree. I could see it from a distance. *No!* I ran the rest of the way. *No, Goddess, no!*

I reached the tree and nearly fell to my knees. By willpower alone, I tottered a few more steps and slumped against the trunk. I stretched my arms as far around the tree as they would go and leaned my cheek against its rough and torn bark where a bolt of lightning had cut a deep swath to the ground. I didn't even remember a storm.

Then I spotted a limb no larger than my wrist and tall enough to pass as a staff. The lightning had splintered it from the tree and stripped the bark down to the beautiful, gnarled sheen of oak. For someone with a reverence for trees, I knew I had found a battery.

Samhain

Through the waiting room window, I stared out at the flutter of fallen leaves in the hospital courtyard. The light autumn breeze plastered the leaves against a stone fence with an engraving I couldn't read from this angle. This time last year, Sam and I had moved into our new house and decorated the front lawn with pumpkins in hopes of our first trick-or-treaters. This year, our best-loved Sabbat was to be spent inside hospital walls with perky employees dressed as green-faced hags and red-horned devils. Even Dr. Minter, who knelt before me, wore silly clown hair.

"How much?" I asked, careful to keep the tone of my voice even. I'd come to know the doc quite well since that day Anna had commandeered him, but I couldn't help frowning at that damned wig.

"I . . ." Dr. Minter sighed and jerked off the rainbow hair. "Um, five percent."

"That's all? The tests showed only five percent cancer cells in his marrow this time? That's good, isn't it?"

The doc cursed, twisted the wig in his hands, and then slammed it into a nearby trash can. "Mrs. Fisher . . . *Beth*. It's such a small percentage but . . . but it means . . ."

I finished the sentence for him. "It means he's not going to make it. Okay, so what's next? Another bone marrow transplant? We'll do it. More chemo? Whatever it takes."

The doc shook his head. "No, Beth. Not again. He's just not strong enough. He's tired of hurting."

I knew what Dr. Minter was thinking. Sam had already left his body once. I'd been warned he was dying and I'd thought I'd be okay with it. I'd stood watching at the bedside with a team of hospital personnel. Instead, the instant the doc said Sam was gone, I started screaming, begging, for him to bring Sam back. I hadn't cared how much pain life held for Sam. I had just wanted him back. I couldn't bear the thought of being without him. Dr. Minter had resuscitated my Sam, and after that, we'd gone for transplant number three, followed by more chemo. Sam had been in constant pain since then, most moments clinging to the oak staff I'd imbued with my own strength and love.

"Can't we do something?" I pleaded.

Dr. Minter shifted on his knees in front of me and let me get a good look at the defeat in his eyes. "He's *ready*."

I slumped in the chair and wrapped my arms around my belly. At six months, my pregnancy had become obvious to everyone. "How long?" I whispered. "Is Sam going to see his baby?"

The doc shrugged. "I don't know. He could. It's possible he could hang on for another three or four months. Or, more likely, he could go tonight."

"Tonight." I sucked in my breath. I might have only one more night with Sam. And because I'd been so immature and made a stupid mistake all those years ago, I'd missed ten years with him. Over three thousand nights I could have held Sam in my arms. Lost.

"Beth? Are you still with me?" The doc touched my shoulder and waited for me to nod. "I've instructed the ICU staff that they're to let you sit with him whenever you like. We're going to give him something for pain. He'll be out of it after that, but I thought you might want to talk with him first."

Dr. Minter walked me down the corridor. Someone, probably a well-meaning volunteer, had taped cutouts of ghosts and scarecrows to the painted block walls. A cutout "Happy Halloween!" hung from the ceiling with little green witches dangling on cardboard brooms. I fought down the nausea and smashed my hand against the two wedding bands that hung from a chain around my neck. My heart pounded in my throat.

We stopped at a pair of huge steel doors. Dr. Minter punched a five-digit code into a panel on the wall, and the doors swung slowly open.

"Third curtain on the right," he said, and I walked forward, leaving the doctor behind.

I counted the curtained rooms, one by one. I was vaguely aware that my feet moved onward while I seemed to float somewhere behind. Numb, I stopped outside a half-open curtain and just stood there, staring at the hospital bed and all the machinery on either side.

A nurse in blue scrubs nodded at me and motioned me inside. "Stay as long as you'd like," he said and then headed for a set of monitors at the main desk.

I stood at the foot of Sam's bed and refused to recognize the man on the sheets. My outer eyes saw the bony weight loss, the stubble of hair, the pale skin. My inner eyes saw the curve of muscles on his arm, the sexy flash of a smile, the wild mane of hair. I looked down at the frailty of a tired soldier and remembered the first night we'd made love after we'd found each other again, how his passion had erased all those years. I saw his battle scars and thought instead of the nights under the stars and the ethereal radiance in his eyes when he was deep inside me.

"Sit with me," he whispered. His soft words startled me.

Suddenly I was moving, finding a tall metal stool, pulling it close to his bedside. He lifted his right hand, wrapped in tape and tubing, and let it drop. I knew what he wanted. I gathered his hand carefully in mine and brought it to my pregnant belly. He splayed his fingers to feel the roundness. Then . . . he smiled.

"Remember the acorns we planted?" I desperately had to say something, anything, to fill the silence. "They're getting big now."

"So are you," he whispered.

"I . . . I brought you something from your oak." I fished in my pocket for three acorns and slipped them into his other palm. His hand closed around them. I wouldn't tell him that lightning had struck the oak or that half of it had dropped its leaves. The other half thrived, its branches loaded with acorns, and our coven would help me plant every seed we could pick with the exception of the three acorns Sam now held.

"Beth, I've seen it. The Summerlands. They look just like our hill. Wildflowers. Green grass. Lots of oaks. And it doesn't hurt anymore."

"We lost you not long ago," I reminded him, "but you came back."

"I saw them then. I wasn't afraid. I'm not afraid now. I see them again."

I gasped. "Oh, Sam." He'd never make it to see the baby born. I bit my lip and looked skyward. One of his nurses had taped a Polaroid of my last ultrasound to the ceiling above him. "You were just dreaming. Looking out the window."

He shook his head slightly. "I can't see out the windows from here. Can't see the trees in the courtyard. I don't even know what time of day it is."

"It's early afternoon. The last day of October."

"Samhain."

"Yes."

"Maybe that's why the veil is so thin now."

I raked in a sob. I wouldn't let him see me cry. This time last year, we'd spent the day cooking a Samhain stew representing every animal and plant we'd eaten in the previous year. A little chicken, a little fish, a little potato, a little corn, a little of everything to honor the end of one cycle and the beginning of a new one.

"Beth, you have to let me go."

I gritted my teeth, shook my head. "Can't."

"Beth, it's time. I want you to take my staff." He inclined his head to the safety rail at his left side. The oak staff—his battery—pressed against the silver bars. It still seemed to buzz with energy.

"I'll recharge it for you. Right now."

"No. There's only so many times you can recharge it. I . . . I want you to destroy it."

I stared at him. Sam had never allowed a tree on his property to be cut down, no matter what. He even recycled limbs and sticks into trellises for the garden or saved them for Sabbat and Esbat bonfires. Even the ashes from the fireplace went back into the flower beds. But destroy the staff I'd made for him?

"I want you to take it outside. I want you to close your eyes and break it in half. Be sure you close your eyes, Beth. When the power leaves the staff, it could blind you."

I nodded, but with no intention of carrying out his ridiculous request. As long as he had his battery, he could hang on. As long as he could hang on, there was hope. Leaning forward, I placed my cheek near his shoulder, but I was careful not to let my weight rest there.

"Aren't you going to ask me what I'm thinking?" he whispered.

Abruptly I sat up. Since Beltane, I had not once asked what he was thinking. I was too nervous to ask. I guess he'd noticed.

"I was thinking about how lucky I am. Not many people get

the chance to say a long good-bye. People who die suddenly never get to say those last *I-love-you*s."

Just like Sam. Finding the good in this hell he'd endured.

"I was thinking, too," he said, "about a ritual I did alone. It was a few nights after we first heard the diagnosis."

"You did one alone? I didn't know." Since our marriage, our rituals had always been either with the coven or together. The only exceptions were the ones I'd done since he'd given me permission to perform magick on his behalf. "What was your ritual for?"

"Healing."

I sighed. Then it was still possible. Sam was so powerful, so powerful. With an illness as dangerous as leukemia, healing might take a long time.

Then Sam smiled weakly. "Healing for *you*."

"What?" I pressed his hand hard against my belly, against the "little oak" growing inside me. "Sam, what are you talking about? I don't need healing."

"In the past six months, I've been in and out of hospitals and I've seen more sick people than I ever thought possible. But you, Beth—you need healing more than any of them."

"I—I'm fine." What was he talking about? Here he lay at death's door and he was worried about me?

"No, you're not fine. You see, that night when I asked for healing, I already knew that my purpose in this life had been served, except for this." He wet his cracked lips. "I got a strong message not to ask for my own healing but to ask for yours."

"But you're the one with leukemia! *I'm* fine!" My voice echoed in the small chamber, and I purposely lowered my pitch. "I'm fine, Sam. Really. I just want you to be well again. I want things to be like they were."

"Like they were last year? Or like they were the first time? You have to forgive yourself, Beth."

I looked away and focused on a nearby IV pole, but my vision blurred. "I don't understand."

"Yes, you do. You keep blaming yourself for all the time we lost. Don't."

His words ripped at me. He'd meant them to be gentle, comforting, but instead they tore through me. "I was so stupid," I mumbled. "God, I can't believe I was so stupid!"

"You're not the same person now." He lifted his hand to wipe a tear from my cheek. "Without the past, you wouldn't be the woman I love now."

I caught his hand and held it. "I never meant it, you know. I was nineteen, just beginning to study the Craft. I loved you so much. I wanted to marry you. I wanted . . . I wanted children with you."

He barely nodded. "And I wasn't ready. It wasn't you. It was me, Beth. I was so crazy about you, but I had to know if it was you or the religion that spoke to me. I needed a little time to make sure."

I closed my eyes against the memory. "And I took it personally. I didn't want to wait." Three lousy months was all it took for him to work out his spiritual path and show up at my door with an engagement ring and a proposal. By then, I'd been married to Bobby for two months. "So I married someone else to teach you a lesson." I shook my head. I'd been miserable. Bobby had married me partly to convert me and for the next eight years, we clashed on a daily basis until he finally gave up and filed for divorce from his least favorite Witch. By then, Sam had vanished from my life.

"We were all taught a lesson. You see, we're all part of this architecture of situations that move us toward wholeness. Everyone who participates in the lesson gets to learn something, even if it's brutal. We both learned things that made us better people in the long run." He held his breath, swallowed

the pain, and exhaled. "If you hadn't left me and married someone else, we would never have had this past year together."

"No, we would have had ten more years. I wasted them because of my immaturity."

"They weren't wasted, my love. They weren't. Think back to
the two people we were when you were nineteen and I was
twenty-three. We were novices, in more ways than one. We
didn't value each other then. You partied too much. I spent a little too much time getting high or drunk. We weren't mature
enough to realize how much we could hurt each other or anyone else."

"I know. You're right." We also had no idea how much either
of us would hurt inside because of a split-second decision. We
were wiser now, yes. Bitterly so.

"Imagine if I had married you then," Sam whispered. His
breaths came harder. "As immature as we were, we would have
ruined everything. I would have been drunk all the time or
high. You would have felt neglected and probably cheated on
me all the time."

I didn't move. I wouldn't acknowledge it, but I knew Sam was
right. His neglect was how I had ended up with Bobby.

"Beth, it took your leaving to make me straighten up my life.
I gave up my vices and completely turned my life around. I
don't think that would have happened if your leaving hadn't
shaken my world to the core."

He was right. And I never really appreciated Sam until after
I'd thrown him away. I had learned the value of our relationship
the hard way.

"So you see, my love?" Sam's fingers tightened around
mine. "If we'd had those ten years together that you think we
wasted, we might never have had the love of our lives this past
year. We would have been two other people, probably long since
divorced and hating each other."

I kissed the back of his hand, between the tubes and tape, and then held it to my cheek. I didn't care anymore if he felt my hot tears on his skin. They were honest tears. "How can I let you go? How, when I've finally found you?"

"Because given a choice of ten years of who cares or the past year of the greatest love I could imagine, I will enter the Summerlands rejoicing because I had more joy with you than any man deserves in a single lifetime. And when you're an old woman and you've watched our child grow to manhood and his children after him, then my love, I'll be waiting for you in the Summerlands."

"I love you, Sam. So much."

"And I will always love you." He squeezed my hand with all his strength. "But you've got to let go of the past. Beth, you've got to let *me* go."

He closed his eyes then. I didn't realize it, but his nurse had been standing behind me, just outside the curtain. The man in scrubs padded silently into the room, withdrew a syringe from a canister of medical equipment, and emptied the syringe into the IV in Sam's arm.

I watched, though I couldn't tell where the liquid had mixed with the other fluids, and followed it in my imagination to his skin, to his bloodstream, to his heart. The frowns and ridges of pained muscles seemed to smooth in Sam's face, and I knew he didn't hurt as much now.

"He'll sleep," the nurse said softly in my ear. "But he can still hear you and sense that you're here, if you'd like to talk to him, say your good-byes. It won't be any better than it is now."

I nodded and flattened Sam's palm against our baby. Then I sang. Song after soft song. Every folk song he loved. From "Bonny Portmore" to "The Trees They Do Grow High." I wanted my voice to be the last thing he heard.

Yet he held on still. Even when I was hoarse. I knew then that he would never leave as long as I was in the room with him. Not after the last time, when I'd fallen to my knees, begging Dr. Minter to bring him back. Sam wouldn't do that to me again. He wouldn't make me watch him die. As tired as he was, he would hang on for as long as I stayed by his side.

I knew then what I had to do. I arranged his hands on his chest, both over the heart chakra, the acorns tucked safely in one palm. With a little effort, I wheeled the bed toward the west so the setting sun would linger on his face. I bent and kissed his forehead, then his dry lips. Holding my breath, I lifted the oak staff from his bed.

The nurses in ICU moved aside as I walked down the corridor, the long stick clutched in my hands and tears streaming down my cheeks. Employees in the hallways, dressed in silly costumes and handing out candy to people in the waiting rooms, backed up against the walls. No one tried to stop me. No one spoke to me. Not even Dr. Minter, who stood in a doorway, watching with tears in his eyes.

I took the stairs down to the courtyard. Somewhere along the way, I kicked off my shoes. I stepped barefoot into the cool grass in the late afternoon. Out to the fallen leaves. Out to the stone fence with the engraving I never could read.

> *Not heaven itself upon the past has power;*
> *But what has been, has been, and I have had my hour.*
> —JOHN DRYDEN

I stopped in front of the stone and, with two hands, gripped the raised staff above my head. I felt its energy course through me from head to bare toes. I felt my baby move. I closed my eyes.

Then with all the strength I had, I brought the staff down hard, splintering it into two, on the stone. A great whoosh of energy knocked me to the ground. I felt the gates of the Summerlands open and close.

I will always love you, Beth. The wind caught the words and sang them through the courtyard.

I opened my eyes. Everything had quieted. I dropped the remnant of the staff and wrapped my arms around my belly.

Sam's spells always worked. Always.

Lorna's Calm and Sleep Inducer

LORNA TEDDER

Nerves jangled? Can't sleep?

Before you pop a tranquilizer, try this calming position.

Lie in a comfortable position with one hand on your forehead (sixth chakra) and one on your stomach (third chakra). One will probably feel cold and the other, a different temperature. Close your eyes and concentrate on the energy beneath each hand. The energy will shift and the flow of energy will become even. Let your mind drift.

You'll find yourself calmer if you've been anxious, and if you're suffering insomnia, you'll find yourself getting sleepy.

Also, if a family member is anxious, you can "lay hands" on him/her in this way and calm down your loved one. Try it on a child after a nightmare and the little one is likely to tell you it feels like floating!

Psyche's Tears

CHARLOTTE BRISBON

Meg stepped back to take a look at the Lughnassadh decorations that she and Snowflower had hung in the foyer of Fort Worth Unitarian Universalist Church. "I think that'll do it. Thanks for the help, Snow."

"*De nada, mija.* You're quite welcome." Snowflower, a lovely Hispanic woman with white in her black hair, grinned at Meg as she straightened her robes. "Thanks for inviting us to lead your ritual. We don't get to do many public circles."

Meg grinned back, imagining how the staid, upper-middle-class residents of suburban Colleyville might react to a coven of Witches celebrating in a public park. Then she stifled the grin. The initial shock might be amusing, but the public backlash would not be. The Dallas–Fort Worth metroplex was a bit more liberal than most areas of Texas, which wasn't too hard, but, aside from a well-known, public pagan center in Dallas, the UU churches were the safest havens for pagans and Witches to practice openly.

A voice behind Meg made her turn. "Looks great, ladies."

Kieffer, a stocky, red-haired, thirty-something man who ran the counter at the Mystic Woods Gift and Metaphysical Shoppe on weekends, held up a plate piled high with cornbread cakes. "Where can I put these?"

Meg waved in the general direction of the kitchen. "You know where the kitchen is, Kief. Go make yourself useful."

He laughed, but headed that direction.

Snowflower looked over the decorations, nodding. "They do look good. You guys must've put in a lot of work on those." She indicated the sun wheels they had placed at various places around the foyer.

Meg shrugged.

Snowflower looked toward the door that led to the back grounds of the church. "Did anyone manage to come up with a cauldron? Can we have a fire?"

"Jason found one. And we can have a fire. The county's not under a burn ban, anyway."

"Good." She gathered the skirts of her robe in one hand and picked up a large sports bag in the other. "I'm going to purify the ritual area. Would you send Thorn in?"

"Sure."

Meg found Thorn, Snowflower's high priest, in the kitchen, trying to snag a quick snack, and she sent him off to his high priestess. Caryn, who was overseeing the feast preparations, wiped her hands on a dish towel. "Well, I think that does it." She checked her watch. "And none too soon. Decorations up?"

"Yep. Jason and Martin are out getting wood for the bale-fire."

"Great. Anything else?"

Meg shook her head. "Just wait for people to show up, I guess."

People began to show up about fifteen minutes later. After another thirty minutes, she could tell that there would not be a large group—Samhain and Beltane, respectively, were Evergreen Circle's biggest groups—but they would have more than enough for a decent-sized circle. Wanda and CoCo, owners of the Mystic Woods, were some of the first ones to arrive; they went off to talk to Kief. Meg greeted a young couple who entered a few minutes later, carrying a baby, and started chatting with them.

She felt Caryn give her a nudge a bit later. "Look who's back."

Meg craned her head around and looked. Striding through the front doors, resplendent in a long, slinky black dress and about twenty pounds of silver jewelry, came Desdemona Ankara and her dozen or so attendants. A self-styled Witch Queen, she carried herself with an admittedly fluid grace and more than a slight air of self-satisfaction. She wore her copper hair swept up into an intricate mass of curls atop her head, and the silver circlet of a high priestess, with a crescent moon made of rainbow moonstone, on her brow. She looked like a wealthy, red-haired cross between Morticia Addams and Elvira, Mistress of the Dark. Meg gritted her teeth. "The Bitch Queen," she muttered to Caryn. She hadn't shown her face since Beltane of the previous year. "Who invited her?"

Caryn patted Meg's arm. "Now, now. She *is* a pagan and a sister Witch, after all." Her voice indicated at least as little liking for the woman as Meg had.

"Yeah, well." Meg didn't consider Desdemona her sister. Anyone could call herself a Witch, but making it so was a different story.

Desdemona swept over to her. "*Megan,*" she purred, offering a ring-bedecked hand, as if she expected it to be kissed. Her voice dripped with sarcasm. "I do *so* love your little gatherings."

"I'm *so* glad." Meg ignored the hand. "How's the punk scene, Desdemona?" Desdemona's band, Psyche's Tears, had to be the only all-electric Goddess-praising techno-punk Witch band in existence. Or at least in Texas.

A smile broke across Desdemona's face, a supermodel smile with white teeth in a little too much of an overbite to be perfect. "Just fabulous. We're up to our tails in gigs.

"We thought you might like some music during the feast," she went on, "so we brought instruments."

Meg sighed. Snowflower and Thorn might have something to say about that, but she knew better than to say no to Desdemona. The one time she'd tried, Desdemona had flown into a spitting rage, and Caryn had to threaten to call the police. "Fine. You can set up in the fellowship hall." As much as she hated to admit it, though, Meg did kind of like the group's music. A teensy, tiny bit.

"Lovely. Boys"—Desdemona snapped her fingers in the air, and the male members of her entourage pricked up their ears— "bring the instruments. Girls, see if you can help out here." The group dispersed, with Desdemona sweeping along behind the "boys" to oversee their work.

When they had scattered, Meg noticed a young woman standing by herself, who had evidently come in at the same time as Desdemona's group. She wore her long blond hair pulled back in a ponytail, and she was dressed in a loose white gauze blouse, faded jeans, and glittery blue plastic sandals of the type schoolgirls used to call "jellies." A small, plain silver pentacle on a thin silver chain hung around her neck, and she carried a small drum under one arm. Meg walked over to her and extended a hand. "Hello. I'm Meg Bradley."

The blond grasped Meg's hand briefly. "I'm Feather."

"Welcome, Feather. Have you been to one of our open circles before?" Meg gestured toward a wooden bench near the glass windows that looked out over the shady garden at the back of the church.

"No." Feather sat down, and she nodded in the direction Desdemona had taken. "Des thought I might enjoy coming."

Meg bit her lip and tried to be diplomatic as she sat. "So, you know Desdemona Ankara?"

"We're housemates."

"Ah." Meg wondered what that entailed. Feather seemed like a gentle flower child, not one of the punk-goth set that followed Psyche's Tears around. "You, uh, don't seem like one of her crowd."

Feather laughed, a melodious, almost fey, sound. "Oh, I'm not into that. I'm her cousin. I just came down from Oklahoma to help her out a little."

Meg nodded. "I see. Is 'Feather' a Craft name?"

She looked a bit sheepish and shrugged. "My folks were hippies."

"Mine, too. But they stuck me with 'Megan.' " Meg made a face. Feather laughed again. Meg decided that she liked hearing Feather laugh. She seemed refreshingly *normal.*

They sat and talked while waiting for the last stragglers to arrive. Meg learned that Feather had moved to Texas last winter, from Norman, Oklahoma. She'd been practicing the Craft for four years, and hadn't seen Desdemona in three when she'd come down to Texas.

"So what did you come down to help Desdemona with?" Meg asked.

Feather bit her lip. "Well, I—I really can't say. I mean, I don't know how well you know Des, so I wouldn't want to . . ."

Meg held up her hand, cutting Feather off. "No, that's okay. It's probably none of my business. I don't know your cousin very well." *Or like her, either,* Meg added silently.

Feather relaxed and smiled.

Shortly thereafter, everyone was called into the sanctuary of the church. After Jason welcomed everyone to the Evergreen Circle chapter of the Covenant of Unitarian Universalist Pagans'

(CUUPs for short) Summer Solstice ritual, the ritual itself began. Normally this would be held outside, but the early August heat was intolerable. Snowflower and Thorn led a beautiful harvest ritual, including a circle dance honoring the Corn Mother and incorporating a special service honoring the full moon. It culminated in a group procession out to the area where Jason and Martin had set up the cauldron, with everyone chanting "Horned One, Brother, Son, Leaper in the Corn" and carrying the representations of the Corn Mother (a corn dolly) and the Horned God (a two-foot-tall "wicker man" woven from wheat stalks) in places of honor. Then the balefire was lit in the cauldron, and the wicker man was placed in the flames with great reverence, to burn while everyone meditated on the God's yearly sacrifice of Himself for the sustenance of His children. When it had burned down, Thorn pulled an aluminum foil–wrapped parcel from the flames, and opened it to reveal a loaf of homemade bread. This was broken into pieces and consumed by everyone in the circle, and the ritual was ended. Then everyone went inside to feast and celebrate.

Contrary to Meg's expectations, Snowflower did not seem the least bit upset by Desdemona's band providing music during the feast. She and Thorn went out onto the floor, away from the area where people were eating, and started dancing as the first mad riffs from the electric guitar filled the air and the synthesizer rose and fell in eerie counterpoint at half-tempo. Then Desdemona's rich contralto joined in, a melodious wail better suited to a torch singer than a punker.

Meg headed for the buffet. Being a potluck, there were a large variety of foods to choose from. She soon snagged a large glass of iced tea and filled a plate to overflowing with cheese enchiladas, red beans and rice, salad, fruit, and other goodies. Including the last two of Kief's corn cakes.

She found Feather sitting by herself at a table, picking at a barely touched plate of salad. "Mind if I join you?" Meg had to raise her voice to make herself heard.

Feather looked up, and her face brightened a bit. "Hi, Meg. Go ahead."

Meg sat. "Did you enjoy the ritual?"

"Yeah." She stabbed a bit of romaine lettuce with her fork and fiddled with it. She did not have the aura of someone who was enjoying herself.

"So what's bothering you?" Meg broke a corn cake in two and dunked it into her beans.

Feather sighed. "Nothing more than usual, I guess."

"Want to talk about it?"

She shook her head.

They ate without speaking. Outside, the dusk was rapidly turning into night. The band stopped playing and headed for the food, and a handful of people pulled chairs into a small circle. Soon, drums and percussion instruments filled the air with their steady beat, a peaceful, calming rhythm that grounded the energy raised by Psyche's Tears and rendered speech pointless.

Meg shut her eyes and let herself drift. As people finished eating and joined the drum circle, the rhythm slowly evolved, until it sounded like twice as many were drumming as there really were. Right at the edge of perception, she thought she could hear faint chanting. A good omen, she decided. Drum-speak. The spirits had decided to join in the fun.

Then something changed. It began gradually, so she barely noticed it, a faint chill underlying the summer heat in the poorly air-conditioned hall. As it grew more noticeable, it took on a threatening edge, a growing negativity. Apprehension knotted her stomach, and Meg opened her eyes.

She couldn't see anything amiss. No one new had come into the hall, although a few people were saying their good-byes and calling it an evening. Feather sat motionless across from her, eyes closed, her drum on the floor beside her. Meditating, maybe. The drum circle went on, undiminished, although she could no longer hear the drumspeak.

She got up and went over to a window. Nothing outside had changed.

A hand on Meg's shoulder made her jump. As she turned, Desdemona Ankara smiled sweetly at her. She leaned over so that Meg could hear her. "Megan, *dearest,* the boys and I have a gig tonight. Would you be a sweetheart and tell Feather for me?"

Gagging on the honey that dripped from her voice, Meg opened her mouth to reply, but Desdemona swept off before the words could get out. She sighed.

Feather didn't respond immediately when Meg passed Desdemona's message on to her. She swept her blond hair back out of her face. "Need help with the cleanup?"

"Sure."

The negativity Meg had noticed before dissipated while they were engaged in the cleanup. By the time they finished, it was eleven o'clock at night. Jason told Meg that he'd lock up the church, so she bid her friends good-night and bright blessings, then went out to the parking lot. Feather went with her.

Meg walked Feather to her car, an old Datsun. "It was good meeting you, Feather. Glad you could make it."

"Me, too."

Meg took Feather's hand and squeezed it. "Give me a call if you want to talk. My number's in the phone book."

"Okay." Feather hesitated. Then she gave Meg a hug. "It was a lovely ritual."

"Thanks. I'll pass that on to Snowflower. Safe journey," Meg added as Feather got into her car. She watched her drive off, then turned and went to her own car.

*   *   *

IT was still dark when the phone rang. Meg glanced over at the clock. Three o'clock, it read. Mother Goddess, only three hours of sleep. She bit back the impulse to hurl curses at the phone and pulled the pillow over her head, waiting for the ringing to stop.

The answering machine picked up on the fourth ring. "Hi, it's me!" her voice chirped, annoyingly perky. "Here comes the tone—you know what to do." *Beep*, went the machine. Meg relaxed slightly, hoping whoever it was would hang up.

No such luck. "Megan? Megan Bradley?" came a familiar voice, one her mind was too fuzzy at the moment to identify. "Megan, pick up! This is important."

She couldn't ignore that. Pushing the pillow aside, she sat up and fumbled for the phone. "What?"

The answering machine clicked off as the caller spoke. Her voice sounded distressed, an emotion which, Meg's subconscious noted, was definitely not one she would associate with this person. "Megan, is Feather there with you?"

She sat up. "No." Something clicked. Desdemona. This was Desdemona Ankara. "No, Desdemona, she left the church just before I did. She hasn't been home?"

"Her car's here, but she didn't bring her drum in. I don't think she's been inside."

"Have you called the police?"

"Are you crazy?" Her voice rose to a shrill pitch. "The *cops*? Honey, don't you know the cops think we're all Satanists?"

Meg groaned silently. "Desdemona, I happen to know of several Wiccan police officers. They know the difference, trust me." Well, some of them did.

"Could you call one of them, then?" The desperation in Desdemona's voice seemed pathetic, completely unlike the over-confident Bitch Queen everyone knew and . . . well, whom everyone knew, anyway.

"I don't *know* them personally." A yawn threatened to work

its way out of Meg's mouth. She did her best to quash it. "Anyway, we don't know that anything's happened to her. Does she have a boyfriend?"

"No, she's a lesbian, you idiot!" Desdemona was all but crying by now.

"All right, all right." She tried to think. "Can you get any of your covenmates to come over?"

"I—I can't let them see me like this!"

Meg groaned to herself again. "Okay, listen. Give me directions to your place. I'll come over, and I'll call the police from there. In the meantime, you try to pull yourself together. I'm going to need your help."

"Okay," she sniffled and reeled off the directions. A house in Bedford.

Meg thought quickly. She lived in Arlington. "I can be there in half an hour."

"Hurry."

Meg hung up the phone, got out of bed, and pulled her jeans on. She tucked her oversized sleep shirt into it, then slipped on her flip-flops. After that, she went into the bathroom and splashed cold water on her face.

Meg tried to think. If Feather really was in trouble, they'd have to find her. Didn't the police have a rule that said they had to wait a certain amount of time before they could start searching for an adult? She grabbed her backpack from under her desk, dumped its contents on the bed, and pulled out the plastic tote that she kept under the bed. It held her magickal tools and supplies. She packed her athame, her pendulum, a packet of ground sea salt, a white candle, self-lighting charcoal, a lighter, some purification incense she'd compounded recently, a small metal bowl of sand with a plastic lid to use as a censer, and a jelly jar of rainwater that she'd charged in the last full moon. After a moment's thought, Meg dug out her athame and packed her oak wand instead. To Meg, the athame was a sacred tool of ritual; to the police, it was just an illegally concealed dagger. Best not to take a chance losing it.

After grabbing a bottle of drinking water from the refrigerator, Meg went out, locked the apartment, and hopped into her old Ford. Luckily, at this hour, the freeway was practically empty.

DESDEMONA Ankara lived in an older house with a sandstone façade on a tree-lined boulevard. Two cars sat in the driveway: Feather's Datsun and a dark, not-so-old midsize four-door of indeterminate make and model. Meg would have expected Desdemona to be the sports car type. She pulled up to the curb and parked.

The porch light was on, a cloud of moths, June bugs, and other insects buzzing around it. The doorbell button had black electrical tape over it. She pulled the storm door open and knocked.

Meg barely recognized the woman who opened the door. Desdemona had taken down her hair—it fell in mussed curls just past her shoulders—and washed off her makeup. The dress had been replaced by wrinkled khaki capri pants and a loose black T-shirt that read TAKE BACK THE NIGHT! under a picture of a number of stylized female figures dancing under a crescent moon. Her feet were bare. The jewelry had gone away. Her complexion was blotchy and her blue-hazel eyes were red and puffy. "Megan." She opened the door wider and stepped back. "Come in."

The living room had snowy carpet that looked as if it had never even heard of red wine or grape juice. A nice, overstuffed, if worn, beige sofa nestled against one wall, and the matching loveseat and recliner gathered cozily around it. A cherry coffee table with a beveled glass top glowed in the dim lighting as if it had just been polished. A matching entertainment center with a large television, VCR, and a stereo completed the room's furnishings. "Nice place." Meg took careful steps, afraid of soiling that pristine white carpet.

Desdemona snorted. "Thanks." She shut the door behind Meg.

The two women looked at each other in awkward silence for a moment. Meg shifted her backpack on her shoulder and bit her lip. "I guess I'd better call the police for you now."

"No."

"But—"

"I'd rather you didn't." Desdemona looked uneasy. "They can't do anything 'til she's been gone twenty-four hours, anyway."

"Not even if she's in danger?" Meg felt the back of her neck prickle with outrage.

The redhead turned away. "I don't think she's in danger," she admitted after a moment. "Not right now. She's wandered off before."

"Then why on earth did you call me at three in the effing morning?!" Infuriated, Meg put a hand on Desdemona's shoulder and spun her back around. She had to fight back the urge to strangle the woman. *Mind ye well the Rule of Three,* she reminded herself. *Whate'er ye do comes back to thee. An it harms none, do as ye will.* Meg settled for a scowl instead.

Desdemona shook her off. "Just because she isn't in trouble right now doesn't mean she can't get into trouble!" She glared back. "I should've known I couldn't call you, Miss Goody Good-witch, with your open circles and your college education and your perfect teeth!"

Meg gaped. Perfect teeth? "Look, I didn't come here to be abused. I came here to help Feather. Now, do you want my help or not?"

A thin wail arose from a back room. Desdemona closed her eyes and sighed. "Just a minute." She turned and practically ran to the back room.

She came back a few moments later, carrying a very upset baby about three or four months old. "He's hungry." She waved Meg toward the sofa and seated herself in the recliner. Seeing Meg's hesitance, she added, "Don't worry. Everything's Scotchguarded." Cradling the baby in her left arm, Desdemona cooed and murmured to him while she hiked up the bottom edge of her shirt. He latched onto the proffered breast and nursed hungrily, pulling his arms against his chest. Desdemona leaned back in the chair, eyes on her son and an uncharacteristic look of bliss on her face, a Wiccan Madonna in a T-shirt.

Meg sat down on the edge of the couch and put her backpack on the floor. She hadn't known Desdemona had a baby. That must be why she hadn't been to one of Evergreen Circle's rituals in at least a year. Meg bit her lip, wondering how else she had misjudged the woman. "Um, Desdemona?"

"Denise," she replied absently.

"Huh?"

"It's Denise. Denise Taylor. Desdemona Ankara is my stage name."

"Denise, then." So she had a normal name, too. Meg suppressed a yawn, feeling the urge for a Diet Coke now that the adrenaline was ebbing. "What about Feather?"

"She's, um, not quite right, you know?" Desdemona—Denise, Meg corrected herself—seemed embarrassed to talk about it. "I mean, she's okay most of the time, but she gets these spells where she just goes weird. She gets depressed and starts doing bizarre things, like stealing things, running away, telling lies." She broke off.

Meg didn't know what kind of mental illness might make

Feather act that way, but she was majoring in literature, not psychology. She understood Tolstoy and Dickinson better than Freud and Jung. "Is she getting help?"

"Oh, yeah, the doctor put her on some medication and it helped for a long time. But she's gotten worse since her mother died and she came down here."

Something nagged at Meg. "She told me she came down to help you out."

Denise chuckled, a soft laugh not unlike Feather's. "Well, she *is* a big help. She keeps the place clean and does the cooking. But I wouldn't leave Ian alone with her." She stroked the baby's fine, scant, reddish hair. "No, she and I are all either of us has. When Aunt Marion died, it made sense for us to be together. Feather needs someone to look after her."

Meg chewed on her lip. What Denise said made sense, but, calm as she seemed, nervous energy poured off of her. She was usually so shielded that Meg could never read anything from her. She was avoiding something, Meg decided. Something that might help them find Feather. "You said she steals things?"

"Oh, yeah." Denise laughed again. "Once, when we were kids, she stole the Baby Jesus out of the Christmas crèche at the Baptist church and left a ransom note. I thought her mom was going to ground her for life."

"What about recently?"

Denise fell silent. The nervous energy flowing from her increased to the point that Meg started to get a headache. She reached down for her backpack, then stood. "Fine. If you don't trust me enough to cooperate, then I'll go get some sleep and you can get your covenmates to help you." She started toward the door.

"No!"

Meg looked back. Denise had half-risen from her seat,

clutching her child to her. Her eyes were wide, fearful. "I—I can't. I just can't."

"Why not?" Meg walked back to the couch and sat, this time on the arm. She held on to her backpack.

"She—" Denise covered her face with her hand, although whether it was a consciously dramatic gesture or not Meg couldn't tell. "She took our coven's book. How can I face everyone and tell them that?"

Meg didn't say anything. She'd always been a solitary practitioner—never a member of a coven—but she knew that a Book of Shadows had considerable significance. Meg's own Book of Shadows held rituals, spells, recipes for potions, incense, even witchy desserts, but it was more than a grimoire. She also used it to chronicle her thoughts, her aspirations, her spiritual journey. A coven's Book of Shadows would have all the rituals and spells that the group used, but it would also contain any covenant they made together, their history, their spiritual voyage. Its loss would be a severe blow.

Denise had collapsed in her chair, curled up with her baby, but tears streamed down her face. "I know I come across as a know-it-all high priestess, but that's just part of my stage act. You always have your circles on Saturday nights."

And Saturday night would be the busiest night of the week for bands, Meg realized. They probably had to go straight from the ritual to their first gig, with no time to change in between. Not a surprise, once Meg thought about it, that Denise had to come to the CUUPs circles in her stage persona. Meg put her backpack on the table and started unpacking. "So you're not a high priestess?"

"We rotate. We don't use a degree system or a hierarchy—it's too patriarchal. I just got passed the wand at Samhain." Denise pronounced it *SAHvain* instead of *SOWwen*, an alternate pronunciation. She gently broke the suction between the baby's lips and her nipple with her pinky, then moved him to the other breast. He sucked away happily.

Meg felt a contented lethargy creep over her, and she yawned. Then she looked over at Denise, who had leaned her recliner back and closed her eyes. "Stop that."

"What?" She didn't open her eyes.

"Making me sleepy. You've been broadcasting energy like crazy ever since I got here." Meg laid her pendulum on the coffee table as another yawn threatened to take the top of her head off.

"Sorry." The lethargy lifted from Meg as Denise put her psychic shields back in place. Then Denise yawned. "Ooh. Baby hypnosis strikes again."

Meg pondered her supplies and tools for a moment, then selected her wand, the pendulum, the candle, and lighter and put the other items back in her backpack. "Do you have a Tarrant County street guide?"

Denise waved a hand toward the couch. "Rand McNally. Under the center cushion."

Meg reached under the cushion and pulled out the thick, spiral-bound book of street maps. She opened it to the index, found Denise's street, and turned to the page with the appropriate map. She laid it flat on the coffee table, then picked up her wand. "I'm going to cast a quick circle and do some divining."

"I'm just not going to get anything definite out of this thing tonight." Meg frowned at her pendulum, which circled mindlessly over the map. She'd tried every map within possible walking distance of Denise's house, with the same results. Yet the pendulum had ruled out the possibility that Feather had been taken somewhere more distant. So she had to be in walking distance of the house. "I wonder if Mercury's gone retro-grade." The candle flickered in her breath as she spoke.

"No, but the moon's full." Denise, returning from tucking her son in, cut a doorway in the circle with her hand, stepped through, and closed the doorway behind her, sealing it with a pentagram drawn in the air. She sat down beside Meg.

"That should make divining easier, not harder."

"Maybe it has. We do know she is in walking distance of the house."

Meg looked at Denise. She did have a point.

"And you're tired," Denise went on. "That would keep any-one from divining well."

Score two for Denise. "If we raised some energy, that might help us narrow things down a little," Meg mused.

"How about a chant?" Denise suggested. " 'Earth My Body'?"

"Sounds good." Meg stood up and stretched. "Let's move around a bit, though. I'm falling asleep."

They ended up chanting and dancing around the coffee table. Meg felt the energy start to rise, up through her legs, up from the earth, a warm, quiet exuberance that washed her weariness from her. As the energy built, she and Denise in-creased their pace, increased the tempo of their chant, until Meg's head spun and the fine hairs on her arms stood on end. She felt the energy take form around them, a cone with its base on the floor and its point reaching up through the ceil-ing. "Now!"

Meg stopped so abruptly that Denise bumped into her and the two women tumbled to the floor. Buzzing with energy, Meg disentangled herself and crawled over to the table. She picked up her pendulum and dangled it over the open map, holding it still with her other hand. She felt Denise put her hands on her shoulders, felt the extra energy surge through her, a sudden high that made her dizzy. Meg took what energy she needed from the surge, fed it to the pendulum, and shunted the rest into the floor, grounding it back into the Earth. She focused her intent, willing the pendulum to reveal Feather's location, and removed her hand from it.

The pendulum hung still for a moment, then slowly began to swing side-to-side. *No.*

Meg turned the book to the next adjacent map, stilled the pendulum, and focused again. On her third attempt, the pendulum swung back-and-forth—a "yes" response—then made tight circles over the map grid directly beneath it. Meg put down the pendulum and looked at the map. "Bedford Boys' Ranch Park."

"That's about an hour's walk from here. We'll take my car." Denise cut a doorway and let herself out of the circle, closed the doorway, and headed back to the nursery.

BEDFORD Boys' Ranch Park lay about three miles west of Denise's house in east Bedford and about a mile north of Texas Highway 183, give or take a bit to allow for meandering streets. It took about five minutes, once Denise had Ian safely in his infant seat in the back of her car, for them to get to the park entrance. Meg knew that Denise had probably broken a number of traffic laws.

The park had been an actual boys' ranch at some time in its past, but now it had a small lake surrounded by public recreational areas. Denise parked her car at the entrance, which had a low gate across it to keep people from driving into the park after it closed. "We'll have to walk." She opened her door and undid her seat belt.

"Any idea where in the park she might be?" Meg got out and shouldered her backpack, hastily repacked with everything except the candle, which had been full of molten wax.

"There's a circle of sandstone boulders not too far in, over-looking the lake." Denise put on an infant sling that snuggled against her like a backpack worn the wrong way around, then took her son from his car seat and put him in the sling. He fussed a little, but soon settled back into sleep with his head on his mother's chest. "I took her there a couple of weeks ago, and she loved it. She got high on the energy—I had to ground her so she could sit still." She reached into the rear floorboards and took out a large flashlight, the type used by police officers. Then she sketched a sigil in the air over the car, whispered a few quiet words that Meg didn't catch, and turned toward the park entrance. "Let's go."

The air had lost its summer heat and turned cool from the proximity of the lake. Meg pushed the backlight button on her watch and checked the time as they hiked into the park. Four twenty-three. Dawn was not far away. Assuming Feather had gotten home about eleven thirty, it would have taken her a little while to go into the house and find the book before coming to the park. Say she got here around midnight—incidentally, a prime time for working magick under the full moon. Then she'd have been out in this chilly air for over four hours. Meg picked up her pace a bit.

They reached the sandstone circle, which sat off the park road at the top of a slight rise. It was smallish as stone circles went, none of the stones standing more than about knee-high, optimal for sitting on. Two larger stones were in the center of the circle. And curled up on one of them, pale in the light of the setting moon, lay a small, slight figure.

Denise broke into a sprint and reached Feather first. As Meg crossed into the stone circle, she felt negativity slam into her. Reeling, she caught herself against a stone and sat, trying to ground the negative energy and sort out her confused chakras, which still hummed with the energy they had raised earlier. Someone, probably Feather, had tried to do a magickal working here, but the spirits Meg could sense seemed confused, chaotic. Most were benign; some were not. She wondered if Feather had even cast a sacred circle to protect herself.

"Got her," Denise called. "She can walk. Let's get her out of here."

"Not yet." Meg got off the stone and went over to them. "We need to cleanse this place before we go."

Feather started weeping. "I'm sorry. I m-messed up everything. I j-just wanted . . ."

Denise put an arm around Feather's shoulders and hugged her. "It's okay, sweetie. It's okay." She looked at Meg. "Can you do the cleansing yourself?"

"Sure."

"Then we'll wait for you in the car."

Meg looked over at the second center stone, where Feather had set up a makeshift altar. A thick binder lay on it, between a pair of black pillar candles. The coven's Book of Shadows, no doubt. She picked it up and gave it to Denise. "I think this is yours. You'll need to cleanse it."

"Thanks."

Meg waited until Denise and Feather had reached the road, then set her backpack on the stone and took out the ritual items she'd packed. She'd have to make do with Feather's candles. Black wasn't the best choice for full moon magick, but it would be perfect for absorbing negativity.

She set up her ritual items on the first stone: salt in the north to represent Earth, censer in the east for Air, jam jar of charged water in the west for Water. One of the black candles went in the south for Fire, and the other in the center for Spirit. Meg used her lighter to ignite a briquette of self-lighting charcoal, then set it, sparkling and popping, in the bowl of sand. She opened the medicine bottle that contained her purification incense and set it beside the bowl. She picked up her wand.

Starting in the east, Meg walked clockwise around the outer perimeter of the stone circle and used her wand to cast the sacred circle. In her other sight, she saw the energy flow from the wand, a brilliant white flame. "Naught but Love enter this place," she chanted as she paced the circle, "naught but Love flow from here." She traced the circle three times, then went to the center of the circle.

She put down the wand and picked up the bottle of incense. Then she turned to face east, her arms uplifted. "Guardians of the East, Spirits of Air, I ask you now to watch over my circle. Join me as I cleanse this place." She felt a slight wind stir her hair. Meg poured the incense onto the glowing charcoal, then picked up the lighter.

She invoked the Guardians of the South, West, and North in that order, just as she had invoked the Guardians of the East, lighting the candle in the south, and presenting the water and the salt to their respective quarters. Then Meg turned to the center candle. "I call on the powers of Spirit, the Akasha, that from which all things come. I ask you now to watch over my circle. Join me as I cleanse this place." She lit the center candle.

Meg picked up the censer and carried it, using her hand to waft smoke from the incense over the altar, the ground, the stones, even the items that Feather had brought to use in her magickal working. "I cleanse this place by Air and Fire." She focused her intent, willing spirits to return to whence they came and for negativity to ground itself and become harmless.

When she had done with the incense, she replaced it on the altar. She took some of the salt and put it into the jar of water, then swirled it to dissolve the salt. Starting in the east, she began sprinkling everything she had cleansed with the incense. "I cleanse this place by Water and Earth."

Finally, she put down the water and picked up the center candle. She took it around the inside of the sacred circle and let its light fall on everything she had sprinkled and wafted. "I cleanse this place by the powers of Spirit." When she returned the candle to the center of the altar, the aura of the place seemed lighter, more at ease.

Meg paused and rested for a moment. The negativity had been banished, but if it was not replaced by something more positive, it would return. Finally, she turned and faced the setting Moon. She lifted her arms into the Goddess position, as if she were cradling the world, and lifted her eyes to the fair, round face of the Lady. "Mother, this place has been cleansed and the adverse energies sent to rest. I ask you now, Bright One, bless this place, and fill it with peace and with Your love, that negativity may not return. By the free will of all, and for the harm of none, so mote it be, my will be done."

Meg closed her eyes, feeling the moonlight, the love of the Lady, wash over her and pour into the circle, filling it with a sense of serene contentment. She felt the arms of the Lady enfold her and a gentle breeze brush her face, and she knew it was done. Opening her eyes, she silently thanked the Lady for Her aid.

She finished the ritual in silence, giving mute thanks first to the powers of Spirit as she snuffed the center candle, then to the guardians of each of the four quarters, for their assistance. She snuffed the second candle and covered the charcoal briquette with sand. Then she picked up her wand and traced the sacred circle in reverse, releasing the energy that formed it. "May this circle be open, but never broken. So mote it be."

Exhausted, Meg packed up her ritual items. She poured the wax from the candles into the sand in the metal bowl. She'd replace it with clean sand later. Meg found a small sports bag that Feather had used to carry her own things in and packed those items—the candles, a small athame, and a large amethyst—into it. Once she'd determined that she'd gotten everything and was leaving no litter behind, Meg checked her watch. Five fifteen. She shouldered her backpack and Feather's sports bag and hiked back to the park gate.

When she got to the gate, Denise's car was gone. Meg groaned and plopped down on the ground. "Boogers." She was too tired to think of a proper cuss word. Just when she was thinking Denise might actually be worth getting to know, the woman had to pull this stunt.

Then headlights fell over her, and a car drove up to the gate. Meg stood, grabbed the bags, and wobbled over to it. Feather slept in the front passenger's seat. Ian slept in his car seat. Meg opened the rear driver's side door, dropped her backpack and the sports bag onto the floorboards, and slid inside. "Sorry about that," Denise told her as she shut the door and put on her seat belt. "A cop came by and we had to move. I got back as soon as I could."

Meg relaxed against the back of the seat. She decided not to make a big deal out of it. "That's all right. Buy me breakfast and we'll call it even."

"After everything you've done for us? You've got it." Denise put the car in gear and headed back to the street.

"Did Feather say anything about why she took your book?"

Denise sighed. "She wants to be a Witch. She was angry because my coven wouldn't take her as a student. She didn't believe me when I told her that we're not a teaching coven. So she tried to perform a self-initiation."

"Ouch. In her mental state, no wonder the spirits were confused." So Feather hadn't been practicing the Craft for four years, after all. Meg tried to stifle a yawn and failed miserably. "You know, she didn't even cast a circle."

"Good Goddess." Denise sounded shaken. "Who knows what she could've stirred up."

"But she didn't. And the area is cleansed and blessed by the Lady. It'll be all right."

"Good."

They rode in silence for a while. Meg noticed that Denise drove more slowly and obeyed all the traffic laws this time. "You know, if Feather wants, I could teach her Wicca," she finally suggested.

"You would?"

"Well, there would be conditions. She'd have to go back to her doctor and get more help for her mental problem, for one thing."

"Oh, she's going to do that, all right," Denise agreed. "I'm going to call her doctor personally. What else?"

"I want her to start getting out more, doing mundane things. No magick. I have a feeling she's trying to use Wicca as an escape, and she needs to be well grounded in reality before she tries to tackle magick." Meg yawned again.

"All right."

"And she's not to come to me to be taught before Samhain, at the very earliest. She needs to decide if she really wants to commit herself to the path of Wicca first."

"I'll make sure she has time to consider it." Denise turned on her right turn signal, and Meg closed her eyes.

MEG saw no sign of Denise or Feather between August and October. As she worked on her preparations for the CUUPs Samhain ritual, she wondered if they would make it to this circle. She'd decided to write and lead the ritual herself, to become a more active participant in Evergreen Circle's activities as the Great Wheel began its new cycle. It would be good to see Denise and Feather, to find out how they were doing. She wondered how much Ian had grown.

A crowd of about sixty gathered for the Samhain ritual, most of them dressed in Halloween costumes or robes. With Jason acting as her high priest, Meg led the group through the ritual. They enacted a drama of the God's passing over to rule the Otherworld during the dark of the year, and they celebrated the Final Harvest with apples and cider. Before the ritual ended, they would honor their loved ones who had already made the Crossing to the Otherworld. But before that, Meg went to the center of the circle and stood with her arms spread in the darkness as the balefire in the cauldron spilled its light over her.

"Samhain marks the ending of the old year and the beginning of the new in the reckoning of the ancients. It is a time of endings and beginnings, time to release old sorrows and to embrace new joy. For though the darkness is growing, we know that the light will one day return."

She nodded at Jason, who, with a couple of assistants, moved around the circle and passed out small pieces of flash paper from a magician's supply shop to those gathered there. Meg fingered her own piece. "You will receive a small piece of flash paper. Imbue it with that which you wish to be rid of, then, as you are willing, approach the cauldron and throw the paper in." Meg stepped closer to the cauldron and tossed in her slip of paper. It burned in a puff of sparks. "I choose to rid myself of my suspicions of those who are different, and to strive for a friendlier, more open heart." She stepped back into the shadows.

One by one, people approached the cauldron and tossed in their papers. Some spoke of what they were ending and beginning, and some chose not to. A red-haired woman in a Xena costume carrying a baby on one hip approached the cauldron, and Meg recognized Denise. Meg smiled, and Denise gave her a silent wink as she tossed in her paper. Then a blond with short, fine hair and dressed as Xena's sidekick, Gabrielle, came up to the cauldron and tossed in her paper. "I choose to be free of my mental illness, and to embrace my friends." She caught Meg's eyes with her own, tears glistening on her face.

It was Feather.

Meg Bradley's Purification Incense (A Little Kitchen Witch Magick)

CHARLOTTE BRISBON

Needed:

- ☾ mortar and pestle
- ☾ 1 part dried parsley
- ☾ 1 part dried rosemary
- ☾ 1 part dried thyme
- ☾ 1 part dried white sage (sagebrush)

Put equal parts of the herbs in the mortar and grind with pestle. As you grind, focus your intent on the purifying qualities of the herbs, and project your intent into the herbs, charging them with magickal energy. If you don't have a mortar and pestle, you can use a food processor, but the physical effort of grinding the herbs by hand is magickally more effective because it helps to focus intent. If you like, you can chant while grinding, perhaps something like, "Parsley, thyme, rosemary, sage / Drive all baneful energies away." (Or you could sing the folk song "Scarborough Faire," which has "Parsley, sage, rosemary, and thyme" in the chorus!). When finished, put the incense in an airtight container and store away from light.

Burn this incense on a charcoal briquette when magickal purification is needed. It has a pungent odor, so be sure you have plenty of ventilation. You may wish to experiment with the proportions of the herbs to adjust the scent according to your own personal tastes.

A note on the herbs used: Parsley, rosemary, and thyme can be found in any grocery store. White sage (sagebrush) is sold at metaphysical stores and other stores that sell supplies for Native American religious practices. If you can't find white sage, you can substitute regular kitchen sage. This herb is not usable for purification, but it does have a quality of magickal protection, so using it would make a purification/protection incense.

Enjoy!

At Midnight in the Garden of the Gods

PAMELA LUZIER

Mournful howls split the night, jolting Kay Price out of her meditative trance. She muttered an imprecation, placing a hand against her chest to still the pounding of her heart.

It sounded like a pack of wolves just outside her bedroom window, but she knew better. There weren't any here in Colorado Springs—it was just the dogs next door, howling at the moon. And it seemed as if every time she tried magick lately, they let loose. She'd been told animals could sense the energies, but this was ridiculous. Her ritual was ruined now. At this rate, she'd never find her spirit guide.

Resigned to the inevitable, Kay concluded the ritual then opened the circle, feeling a little clumsy. She was new at this, but ever since she had taken the local Wicca 101 class, she knew she had found her spiritual path in life. Unlike other belief systems she had tried, Wicca allowed her to tailor her life and environment in creative ways to develop her own personal path for improvement in harmony with nature. Since her job as a CPA in the corporate world left her feeling stressed and very *un*harmonious with nature, the Wiccan principles resonated deep within her, filling a need she hadn't known she had.

Unfortunately, it was proving harder than she'd expected to practice. She gazed out the window at the moon, looking for answers in its pale, serene face. She certainly hadn't gotten any answers through meditation, though, the Goddess knew, she had tried hard enough.

And her question wasn't all that difficult, either. Though it wasn't required of a novice Witch, Kay felt as if she needed a specific deity or animal totem, one of the many aspects of the Goddess, to work with. Her teacher, Shardae, was very patient and helpful, but Kay wanted to progress to the next level, to work with a personal guide of her own on the spiritual plane. And, seeing how Shardae's bear totem gave her strength, purpose, and— most of all—focus, Kay yearned to have the same for herself.

But a study of potential patron deities and spirit guides had left her nothing but confused. It wasn't that she didn't find any of them interesting—the problem was that they were *all* intriguing and she just couldn't decide which was best for her.

Shardae had suggested a number of methods to find her guide, but it was harder than Kay had imagined. Magick wasn't as clear-cut as the numbers and accounting methods she dealt with as a CPA. Magick was fuzzy, nebulous, and at times frustrating. Especially tonight.

She sighed, realizing she still needed assistance. Maybe Shardae could help when they met tomorrow.

*   *   *

AFTER work the next day, Kay drove to Old Colorado City and maneuvered her car around the city's ubiquitous orange traffic cones to reach the Celebration New Age Store, where she had arranged to meet Shardae. As Kay exited the car, her ears were assaulted by the sound of jackhammers and the construction workers' radio blaring out oldies. Kay frowned, wondering if the noise would be this annoying inside.

Shardae drove up then, and as she joined Kay on the sidewalk, the workers let loose with whistles and ululations of approval. Kay wasn't conceited enough to think any of it was directed at her—her tailored suits never inspired such approval. It was all for Shardae.

A petite dynamo with skin the color of sweet milk chocolate, Shardae was dressed in a bright orange and black sleeveless caftan that skimmed her trim figure, the soft fabric clinging in all the right places so that when she moved, it revealed more than it concealed. Matching chunky bracelet, earrings, and necklace completed the look to make her appear not only Wiccan, but sexy at the same time.

And she obviously took the accolades as her due. Casting a mischievous glance over her shoulder at the workers, she led the way to the meeting room with a provocative sway of her hips.

Kay followed her with a shake of her head, wishing she had Shardae's confidence.

Once they were inside and the closed door cut out most of the outside sounds, Shardae planted her hands on her hips, gave Kay the once-over, and shook her head. "Girl, how do you expect to do magick lookin' like that?"

Kay glanced down at herself, nonplussed. She thought the tailored peach dress with its matching duster was pretty, plus it concealed the extra ten pounds on her hips. "What's wrong with it? It's what I wore to work."

Shardae cocked her head. "That's what's wrong with it. You look uptight, all closed in."

"But I'm not uptight—I'm comfortable." She knew many women found suits uncomfortable and stifling, but she wasn't one of them.

Dropping her saucy attitude and becoming all teacher, Shardae said, "But to do Magick before the Goddess, you need free-flowing clothes."

Kay frowned. "I don't know why She should care what I wear."

Shardae rolled her eyes. "I didn't mean She's a fashion critic. But loose clothing with natural fabrics allows the energies to flow freely, not stay bound up within you. And it gets you in the right mood."

"The right mood?"

"Sure. Just as wearing suits to work makes you feel professional, wearing special clothes for ritual will make you feel in tune with the energies."

That made sense. And Kay was willing to try anything if it would work. "Okay, but I don't have anything to change into for today." She glanced down at her dress. "This is natural—it's silk. How about if I take off the jacket?"

Suiting actions to words, she took off the jacket, then, at Shardae's suggestion, removed her belt and shoes as well and let her long blond hair loose from its confining chignon.

Her teacher surveyed her thoughtfully, then said, "The pantyhose have got to go." At Kay's doubtful look, Shardae added, "Hey, just be glad I'm not asking you to work skyclad."

Shivering at the thought of working nude at any time of the year in Colorado, Kay sighed in resignation and shimmied out of her pantyhose. "Okay, but that's all I'm taking off."

Shardae laughed. "That's enough. Now, come sit down and tell me about the problems you've been having."

Feeling a little odd without her shoes and pantyhose, Kay nevertheless sat, squirming a little before she explained. "I've been trying to find my spirit guide using the methods you suggested, but nothing works. Every time I try, something goes wrong."

"When you asked for guidance, did you say that it was for the greatest good of all concerned?"

"Yes, of course." Kay paused, frowning. "Does my failure mean that it *isn't* for the greatest good?"

"Not necessarily. You might just have problems hearing the answer. Did you ask for it to come in your dreams?"

"Yes, I tried that last night." After the meditation had failed.

"And what did you dream about?"

Kay smiled ruefully. "Doing the tango with Kevin Costner." And answering an entirely different kind of wish.

She expected Shardae to laugh, but she just cocked her head and regarded Kay thoughtfully. "Are you sure you're not getting anything? It doesn't work like a telephone, you know. You can't just call up the gods and tell 'em you want to hang out. And you won't find a big neon sign with arrows pointing to it, saying 'This is the answer.' "

"I know." Obviously, or she wouldn't have so many problems getting this. "But how *does* it work?"

Shardae shrugged. "It's different for each person. Some see visions, some hear words in their head, some just get a feeling. Different deities and guides choose different ways to make themselves known." She paused, then added, "Maybe you're getting a response, but you're just not hearing it."

"It's possible, but I doubt it. I've been trying for weeks now with nary a glimmer." She gave Shardae a pleading look. "Could you help me?"

Shardae sighed. "All right, but we shouldn't need a ritual for this. We'll do an exercise that should help. Come, sit on the floor."

Just like in class, Shardae led Kay through grounding and centering herself. Once Kay was completely relaxed, Shardae spoke softly, leading Kay through a guided imagery process, asking her to go to a beautiful place in her mind.

Kay found herself in a peaceful garden with many paths. She chose one of those paths at Shardae's suggestion, and followed it to its termination in a peaceful, sunlit clearing.

"Now," Shardae whispered, "as you turn your head, your guide will reveal itself to you. What do you see?"

The light brightened with Kay's anticipation, but just as she was about to catch a glimpse of her guide, the radio volume outside suddenly increased, blaring out the chorus to "The Leader of the Pack," complete with the workers' off-key accompaniment and a revving of the jackhammers.

Jolted out of her trance, Kay felt like cursing. Instead, she said, "See? Every time I try this, something happens to mess it up." And she had been so close. . . .

Shardae seemed disappointed in her somehow, but it wasn't anything Kay could control. As the volume reduced to a bearable level, Kay asked, "What can I do?"

"Maybe the tarot will help you understand," Shardae suggested. "You seem to have an affinity for the cards." She pulled a deck out of her purse and instructed Kay to shuffle them and pull one card.

Kay shuffled, concentrating on her desire to learn who her guide was, then cut the deck and turned over the top card. "The moon," she murmured.

"You've been studying the tarot," Shardae said. "What does this card mean to you?"

Kay frowned. "Secrets, hidden things, psychic feelings."

Heck, she already knew that the answer was hidden from her. She suppressed a sigh. It didn't appear that this was going to help any more than the other methods had.

"Never mind the book answer. Study the card and tell me what you see, what the symbolism means to you."

This was a standard Rider-Waite deck so Kay was familiar with it, but she studied it anew. "The moon has a woman's face in it. . . ." Sudden realization struck her. "Could it mean the Goddess?"

"Maybe. What else do you see?"

Kay studied the card, trying to make sense of it. "There are two stone pillars flanking the moon, and a golden path between them to the Goddess." Excitement rose within her. Maybe the answer *was* here. "And two dogs looking up at it—one tame, one wild."

"And what do these things suggest to you?" Shardae asked.

Kay couldn't remember what else she had read about this card and was afraid to guess, afraid she would give the wrong answer—she was much better with numbers than esoteric concepts. "I'm not sure."

"The pillars, or towers, represent the conscious and unconscious mind. The dogs represent the two aspects of your nature—wild and tame."

That was kind of what she had figured, but Kay didn't think she would have been able to phrase it that neatly. "What about the lobster coming out of the sea below them?" At Shardae's raised eyebrow and expectant look, Kay decided she'd better try to guess it for herself. "Uh, moving from one element to another?"

"That's good. So put it all together—what is its message for you?"

Perhaps she did understand it after all. "Maybe . . . in order to evolve and find my path to the Goddess, I need to find a balance between the tame and the wild, my conscious and unconscious sides?"

Shardae nodded. "Sounds like a good reading to me. What do you think?"

"I think I still don't understand it."

Her teacher sighed, making Kay feel particularly dense.

Patting her hand, Shardae said, "I think what it's trying to tell you is that the psychic level of your unconscious mind needs to be reconciled with the conscious. In other words, your subconscious is sending you messages, but you're not getting them."

It was the same old theme—Kay couldn't understand because she tried too hard. But if she didn't try, how would it ever make sense? Even this interpretation didn't help. "It still doesn't tell me what I need to know. What should I do?"

Shardae frowned as she looked at the card. "Well, the imagery here of the moon and the two pillars also suggests something else to me, something more concrete that might help you."

"What's that?"

"A ritual in the Garden of the Gods."

Kay was familiar with the thirteen-hundred-acre park near the base of Pikes Peak, and while she acknowledged that the towering red sandstone formations gave the place a magickal feel, she couldn't imagine how it would help. "But people are there all the time," she complained. "Lots of tourists, especially now that the weather has warmed up. I don't see how I could perform a ritual without being interrupted."

"Not at midnight."

"Midnight? Isn't the park closed then?" And she wasn't sure she wanted to wander around out there alone at night, either.

Shardae shrugged. "It's not barricaded, so it's easy enough to get in." Obviously noting Kay's reluctance, she added, "The Garden of the Gods is a magickal place, and there's no more powerful time to work this kind of magick than at midnight on the full moon."

"But . . . isn't it dangerous? Bears and mountain lions have been seen there." And every time she'd tried this sort of thing, something had interrupted her. Up to now, the interruptions had been rather benign . . . but what if it turned out to be a wild beast next time?

"They're usually not in the main area, especially not this time of year. There's plenty of water up in the mountains now, so they won't need to come down."

"I don't know. . . ."

"And I'll be there, to keep you safe from harm."

Kay sighed. Though she wasn't entirely comfortable with the idea, she had to do *something*. "Okay, if you think it will work." Nothing else had, that's for sure.

Shardae gave her an exasperated look. "If this doesn't help you find your spirit guide, nothing will." She paused and lifted an expressive eyebrow. "Did you ever think that maybe you are getting the answer, but you're rejecting it? Are you sure you want to learn what it is?"

"Of course I want to know." Then, suddenly apprehensive, Kay said, "Why do you ask? Do you think my guide might be something weird, like a lizard or a toad?" She couldn't bear the thought of a reptilian guide. *Ick.*

Shardae laughed. "No, it's not. Trust me on that."

"How do you know?" Sudden realization struck her. "You know what it is, don't you?"

Her teacher hesitated, then said, "Yes, I saw it in your aura very clearly during the guided imagery session."

Elated, Kay exclaimed, "Great! What is it?"

Shaking her head, Shardae said, "I'm sorry, this is something you must learn for yourself."

When Kay slanted her an exasperated look, Shardae added, "I'm not being difficult. If I told you, your link with your spirit guide would be nowhere near as powerful, or as intimate, as you hope. You don't want that, do you?"

"I guess not." Kay felt a little disappointed, but not too much so. At least she knew she *had* a guide now. "Will you help me do what it takes to find out for myself, then?"

"I can give you guidance and stay nearby, but you'll have to do the ritual yourself."

Then she didn't have much time to prepare—the full moon was only a week away. "Okay, I'll do it."

But she was tired of constantly being frustrated, tired of searching for elusive answers. If it didn't work this time, if Kay didn't learn who her spirit guide was, she might have to take it as a clear sign that it just wasn't meant to be, that she should give up Wicca forever.

WITH Shardae's help, Kay spent her free time over the next week designing a ritual and gathering the necessary ingredients. The night of the full moon, Kay arrived at the Garden of the Gods parking lot near the rock formations known as Kissing Camels and North Gateway Rock at half past eleven. She found Shardae already there, sitting on a boulder and drinking in the moonlit beauty of the huge red monoliths that thrust up from the earth.

Kay felt a little foolish in the white Roman-style toga she had made especially for this ritual, but maybe Shardae was right about clothing making a difference—it made her feel different, more open, more . . . spiritual.

Shardae rose and gave her an approving glance. "Very nice. Did you make that yourself?"

"Yes—you said it was better if I did and I didn't want to do anything to mess this up."

Her teacher peered at the wide gold band she had trimmed it with. "And what's this?"

"Isn't it beautiful? The clerk said it's supposed to represent Romulus and Remus. Since Romulus founded Rome, I thought it apt to trim the Roman toga."

"Very appropriate—more than you know."

So Shardae was going to continue to be mysterious, was she? Well, no matter. With her mentor's approval, Kay was sure to be successful tonight. Buoyant with the promise of achieving her goal, Kay asked, "So is this how you found *your* spirit guide?" She still found it amusing that the petite Shardae worked with a huge bear.

"No, for me, it was totally obvious. For weeks, everywhere I turned, I saw images of bears—black bears, brown bears, polar bears. You name it, I saw it."

Ruefully, Kay said, "I wish it had been that easy for me."

Shardae just laughed, saying, "Well, maybe it will be tonight."

"I hope so." She couldn't help fearing that her whole future as a Witch was riding on this.

"Are you still worried about the beasties?"

"A little," Kay admitted.

"Well, this should help." Shardae pulled a necklace over her head and gestured for Kay to bend over so she could drape it around Kay's neck.

The necklace consisted of a heavy metal circular pendant suspended from a cord and inscribed with a pentacle. As Kay grasped the disc, it felt warm and alive in her hand, pulsating with energy. "What is it?"

"I made you a talisman. It should shield you, keep you from harm."

Kay tried to thank her, but Shardae waved her thanks away. "Enough, already. Go now. You have only twenty minutes until midnight. The night is clear, the moon is bright, and the time is perfect."

Feeling safer now, Kay grabbed her pack with all her paraphernalia in it and headed down the path toward the spot she had chosen near the Three Graces and the Cathedral Spires. It seemed very appropriate to conduct her ritual before the elegant fingerlike formations that reached beseechingly toward the sky.

When Kay reached the intersection of two paths, she faced east so she could see both sets of spires framed between South Gateway Rock and Cathedral Rock. Yes, this felt right—this was the place to hold her ritual.

Using a nearby flat boulder, she laid out her black velvet altar cloth then placed the items she needed in the appropriate spots.

Filling a silver goblet with water, she set it in the west position, then lit incense to represent the element of Air in the east, filled a ceramic bowl with rice to represent the Earth in the north, and lit a candle in her small brass burner to represent Fire in the south.

There—the four elements were represented. Now for the other magickal tools. To open the spiritual realm and aid in the incantation, she placed hellebore and vervain in a small bowl, then laid an opal and a moonstone on the cloth. Finally, she situated her most prized possession on the altar—a wand made from a clear glass rod wound with silver and tipped with amethyst. She hadn't found an athame yet that felt right, but she didn't need the ceremonial dagger for this ritual.

Kay sighed. Everything looked just right, and the full moon made the opal and moonstone shimmer with radiance. Now she was ready.

She hoped.

She glanced up and took a deep breath. As the scent of pine and juniper filled her nostrils, she really noticed her surroundings for the first time. During the day, the verdant spring vegetation contrasted with the red sandstone rock to create a scene of spectacular loveliness. But it was no less dramatic at midnight. The full moon lent an otherworldly beauty to the scene, the towering rock formations casting fey shadows to produce scattered pockets of mystery.

Anything could be lurking in those shadows. . . .

As a chill passed over her, Kay grasped the talisman and quelled her misgivings. Tonight would be a night for joyous exploration, to celebrate what she could see in the light, not fear what was hidden in the dark.

The talisman helped her banish her apprehensions, and her surroundings took on a mystical, dreamlike quality, one far more suitable for her purpose. Peace stole over her.

I'm ready.

Taking a deep breath, she picked up her wand and used it to cast a circle around herself and the altar to ensure the power she raised would stay where she wanted it. Once the shimmering circle was cast, she concentrated on invoking each element in turn, thanking them for being there. Then, taking a pinch of the mixed herbs, she ground them between her thumb and forefinger and let her offering fly away in the wind, asking the Air element to open the veil to the spirit world.

So far, so good. Satisfied she had done everything right, Kay turned to the next step—raising power. Luckily, that was one aspect she had never had problems with. In fact, her success in that area had given her the confidence she had needed to go on despite her failure in others.

By now, she no longer needed to work at it. Instead, she knelt and concentrated, simply holding her palms together. When she pulled them apart, the energy appeared, cupped between her palms, ready to do her bidding.

As always, the feel of the magick vibrating against the sensitive skin of her palms filled her with awe. But it wasn't yet strong enough for her purpose. She sang the names of the Goddesses as she was taught, over and over again, to build the magick until the power was at its peak. At that point, she formed the question in her mind, focused the energy, and let it go.

As it flew off into the night, she took the cool, smooth stones from the altar and held them to her breast, then closed her eyes and opened her mind with rising excitement and expectation.

Her inner consciousness unfurled, opening and expanding to reveal . . . what? Yes, there was a Being there, though Kay could only make out a shadowy figure. She sensed it was trying to tell her something, but she couldn't understand.

"Who are you?" she cried. "Will you tell me your name?"

A female voice, rich and powerful with wisdom, answered her, resonating with something deep inside Kay. "I have told you many times, but you do not heed. Return to me when your understanding is full."

With that, the vision in her mind's eye vanished and Kay opened her eyes with an exclamation, begging the Goddess to come back.

Only silence answered her.

No, it's not enough. I don't understand. What did the deity mean when She said She had told Kay many times?

Impatient, Kay wanted to search for answers right away, but she had to complete the ritual first. Pulling snacks out of her pack, she had refreshments to ground herself back in the physical plane, then thanked and released the Gods, devoked the elements, and opened the circle. The ritual was complete.

Kay gathered all her implements together and stowed them back in the pack, frowning as she pondered what had happened. She now knew she had a spirit guide, but who—or what—was it? As she hurried back up the path, she realized that, once more, she would have to rely on Shardae to interpret the meanings of these events.

All Kay knew was that though she had finally contacted her patron Goddess, the Goddess had seemed to chastise Kay for not paying attention. Attention to what, though? Kay was still as clueless as when she had gone in. And frustrated. She was no closer to understanding who and what her guide was than she was before. Obviously, she was just too magick-deaf to understand.

Her pace slowed as defeat overwhelmed her. She still hadn't found out what she had come here to learn. True, she had gotten further than she had before . . . only to be scolded by the being she had hoped would help her. She had failed.

Was this an omen that she should give up trying to be a Witch? She might have thought that earlier, but now Kay quickly rejected that idea. The thought of abandoning her study of Wicca just didn't feel right. Besides, her innate stubbornness wouldn't let her give up and the ways of the Witches were just too compelling, too . . . too . . . right. Achieving full understanding might prove more difficult than she had expected, but so was doing anything worthwhile.

Maybe the problem was with her—with her approach. Everything seemed to point to the fact that she was trying too hard. Maybe that was it. Maybe she should stop searching so hard and concentrate on learning other things.

Now *that* felt right. Pausing for a moment on the path, Kay closed her eyes to better feel the magick in this mystical place and spoke directly to the listening spirits. "I trust you to let me know when the time is right." So saying, Kay let go of her obsessive search with a shrug of her shoulders and felt the burden fall away. In its place, there was only vast relief and a sense of rightness.

I have to tell Shardae. Hurrying back once more, Kay rounded a corner and jerked to an abrupt halt as she came face to face with a huge, menacing beast. She felt more than heard a challenging roar and her heart rate tripled as the brute loomed over her, blocking out the moon.

Dear Goddess, it's a bear!

Frozen in her tracks, Kay instinctively grasped the protective talisman Shardae had given her and prayed for deliverance.

She got it. Power surged through the talisman into Kay, sweeping away the fear. A protective spirit filled her with courage and her hackles rose, her ears laid back, and she bared her teeth in an answering, challenging snarl. Her guardian wolf had arrived!

For one tense moment, the bear stared at her, then it dropped its powerful forelegs and backed off. As Kay watched, breathless, its form dissipated and shredded into nothingness, revealing it as nothing more than a phantom of her imagination and leaving Shardae standing where the bear had been.

Her teacher held her hands out in an appeasing motion. "It's only me, Kay."

With the threat gone, Kay felt the spirit of the wolf leave her, content that it had finally made its presence known. Shaking with excitement and unspent adrenaline, Kay asked, "Was that me?"

"It sure was. Whooo-ee, girl," Shardae exclaimed. "Your spirit guide sure showed with a vengeance, didn't it?"

Yes! "A wolf. It's a wolf." Much better than a lizard or a toad.

"I know," her teacher said smugly. "So, how do you feel?"

"Elated." But now that she thought about it . . . "And stupid." She felt like smacking herself upside the head. "The signs were there all along, just like you said. I just didn't recognize them." The wolflike howling of the dogs, the wolf whistles of the construction workers, "Leader of the Pack" blaring at her at the appropriate moment, the wild "dog" on the tarot card, and her own choice of Romulus and Remus—the twins raised by Lupa, the wolf Goddess—to border her gown.

Even the dream made sense now. She hadn't been doing the tango with Kevin Costner. Lupa had been trying to tell her she was dancing with wolves. . . .

"Now that I think about it, I've been seeing and hearing wolves in everything lately." Kay groaned. "I'm so dumb—I don't know why you continue as my mentor."

Shardae grinned. "You're not dumb. You're just not used to thinking sideways yet—you're still too linear. But from now on, it'll be easier, now that you know what to look for."

Shardae was absolutely right. True magick wasn't showy like the false illusions made by stage magicians. It didn't happen with a blinding flash and a boom—it pervaded everything in subtle ways.

Kay hadn't been able to understand that message until she had stopped trying to force it. That was the lesson of the tarot card, the lesson Lupa had been trying to teach her.

And now that she had such a powerful and protective spirit guide, Kay was confident that her training would proceed much faster. Just as Shardae had promised, the answers were all around her. All she had to do was pay attention, let go . . . and learn to howl at the moon.

I Am

CHARLOTTE BRISBON

I am Earth
Green, blue, brown
In all Her Majesty
Ocean eyes, snowy cloak,
and flowers in Her hair

I am Moon
Pale white, black, grey
Aged and ageless
Changing and changeless

I am Virgin, Woman
complete unto Herself
Huntress in the shadowy wood
And Maiden in the meadows

I am Mother, Creatrix,
cradling my child in my arms
I birth all Life into existence
in the rush of the waves

And

I am Crone, wise, ancient
Barren trees on the moonlit moor
Grandmother waiting by the cooking fire

I am the wind in the trees, laughing, singing,
And I am the trees, with leaves in my hair
I am the rain
and the earth that receives it
I am the pale light at dusk that casts shadows,
and I am the shadow,
Dark, mystery

I am Life

I am Goddess

I AM

The Spelling Error

JEN SOKOLOSKI

Flick.

Flick. Flick.

"Damn!" Lucy Dane dropped the lighter and sucked on her thumb. She still couldn't believe she was doing this, willfully disobeying her father. And worse, it was the rule she'd promised she'd never break. But there were some things that didn't belong in the realm of dads. Best friendship was one of them. Her best friend, Brianna James, had come to her last week and asked for her help, really nervous and formal-like. It made Lucy nervous herself, since Bri knew that she could count on her for anything.

Even a love spell.

Normally, she would have said, "No way"—Bri knew how her dad would flip if he found her casting spells.

But Bri had bought a book on love spells and threatened to do it herself. That couldn't happen. For starters, Lucy's dad had drilled into her head that spells and magick changed the world around you. And that could mean killer consequences. A simple spell for rain could cause a flood. Or get the rain, but have the entire Midwest suffer a drought because you worded things wrong. She also knew from listening to Morgana, her dad's waitress, that love spells were notoriously easy to screw up.

Flick.

"Don't curse, it's not nice and if my mom hears you, she'll have a fit." Bri pushed on the old beach towel she'd stuffed under the crack of her bedroom door to hide the light from the hallway outside.

Flick.

"Sorry." Lucy picked up the lighter again and ran her sore thumb down the rough-edged wheel.

Fizzzzzz.

This time a tiny flame lit up the darkness. "Aha! See? I told you we could get it to light."

Lucy touched the flame first to the wick of a pink candle, then a red one, then a white one. "And it only took ten whole minutes."

"Shh. I think I hear my mom."

"Oh, for Pete's sake, Bri, your mom cannot hear through walls!" She set the lighter down.

Bri's stuffed animals loomed, vaguely threatening in the soft candle glow. Rows of glassy eyes peered down at her from the nets on the wall. Lucy couldn't help but think that they could see what she was doing and tattle to her dad.

"You don't know my mom."

"Yes, I do, and if you think she'll have a fit over fire in your bedroom, it's nothing compared to what my dad will do if he finds out I snitched this." She rummaged in her black velvet backpack and pulled out a plastic bag. "I was so afraid I'd get caught with this in school."

Bri took the baggie and squished the dried leaves inside it. "Why? They can't bust you for thyme, can they?"

"Wanna bet? Candy Patasky got busted last week for having ibuprofen—three days detention. Do you really think they'd believe me if I told them it was thyme? My dad would kill me twice—once for snitching from his herb cabinet and once more for getting detention. And this—?" She waved her arms at their ceremonial circle. "I don't even want to think about it."

Guilt made her belly twist. Her dad was pretty cool and this would hurt him if he knew. Most of the time, he treated her like a real person instead of a kid, and if somebody twisted her arm, she'd tell them that she even liked hanging out with him. And he wasn't a lump on the couch like Bri's, or a drill sergeant like Candy Patasky's dad, who wouldn't let her wear makeup or even go to the mixer dances in the gym. In fact, Lucy's dad was pretty reasonable about dances, makeup, and overnighters. But there were a few things that he was just unreasonable about. Like magick.

Most of the time, she didn't even miss not having a mom.

"I don't understand this whole thing your dad has about not letting you cast spells until you're thirteen. When he explained it to my mom, he said that your religion wasn't harmful or dangerous."

That puzzled Lucy, sometimes, too. "It's not supposed to be. I guess you could do spells to wish ill on somebody, but it seems a lot easier to just put an old banana in the bottom of their gym bag or something."

Bri snorted. "Scott Dunphy stunk up the entire class with that thing."

Lucy giggled. "He started it when he filled my locker with packing peanuts." The Styrofoam flew from her locker between classes, sticking to her and everyone who passed by.

She'd had to stay after school and clean up every one, including the ones that had somehow found their way down into the basement wood shop, into the nurse's office, and even into the old classroom with the leaky roof where everybody stacked their broken chairs and old desks. She'd been filthy and exhausted when her dad picked her up hours later. And he had the nerve to laugh.

Stacking the four big boxes next to his truck, he'd said, "Laugh!" pointing at the still open containers.

"What?" All she wanted to do was go home and take a bath. The last thing she wanted to do was laugh.

"Laugh into the boxes, Lucy. Let's make some magick." To demonstrate, he leaned over an open box and laughed, loud and obnoxious. "Now you try."

Making magick was the only thing that would get her to do something so silly. She leaned over a box. "Ha ha ha."

"That was a sad laugh. I know you've got more giggles in you." He started tickling her and pretty soon, she was stuck in a giggle fit.

They ran around the boxes and filled them with laughter. Every time she laughed, it felt like she'd accidentally snorted ginger ale, like the bubbles got inside her, fizzy and sweet.

When they finally plopped down on the sidewalk, she said. "That was fun. Only I hope nobody saw me doing that."

"Whatsa matter, kid? Your street rep taking a beating?" he teased her.

"Why did we do that? Was that real magick?"

"That was laugh magick. When we take those peanuts to the recycling center, everyone who gets a package with some of those peanuts in it gets a little of our laughter."

That was her dad, always making ordinary stuff special by throwing in a little magick. But when it came to letting her do magick on her own . . .

"Geez, these things are putting out heat." Bri brought her back to the present.

The candle flames burned straight and high, smelling of apple-cinnamon and vanilla. Lucy thought of the pastries her dad baked at the coffee shop.

She inhaled once, deeply, and held out her hands above her head, not at all certain of what she was supposed to do.

Bri just looked at her. "Now what?" she whispered.

Lucy frowned. "Did you write down what you wanted to say?"

Bri pulled a folded piece of pink notebook paper from the back pocket of her jeans and held it out for Lucy to read. "I tried not to be too specific."

Seeing what she wrote, Lucy hissed, "You said 'like Tommy Robinson.' I already told you we can't manipulate any one person!"

"Okay, I won't read that part then. Sheesh."

"It matters, Bri. If my dad taught me anything it was that spells are not to manipulate people. It's *Isfet*." She used the term he always used when he spoke about bad things.

"That's another Egyptian word, isn't it? Your dad really believes that old junk, doesn't he?"

Lucy felt a flash of annoyance at her best friend. "Bri, that 'old junk' is no different from your Ten Commandments, like don't kill people and don't steal your neighbor's stuff."

"Sor-*ry*," Bri mumbled, "it's just hard to think it's not weird when your dad dresses up in a skirt every Halloween, pretending to be King Tut."

"Not *every* Halloween—and it's a kilt. But let's not even go there. Look, the candles are going to burn out. Do you want to do this or not?"

Bri nodded solemnly.

Lucy glanced down at Brianna's paper. "Umm . . . you say you want a boy to like you. Better to just ask for some*one* to like you, otherwise a boy your kid brother's age could like you."

"Eww. The last thing I need is another eight-year-old. Are you going to wish for something, too?"

Lucy thought about that. "Yeah. For someone who can love me for who I am."

"That's pretty general."

She shrugged, suddenly serious, raising her hands again. "Beloved Netjer, awake in peace. We come to you to ask a boon."

The air took on a quiet hush and she had the sudden sense that yes, the Gods really *were* listening.

MILES from his darling and disobedient daughter, Paul Dane knelt before a cedar box—his merchant's shrine to Ptah—in the storeroom of his deserted coffee shop. A box he'd painstakingly hand-painted with hieroglyphs, using India ink and a reed pen he'd cut himself from the banks of the creek across town.

Inside the box, a brass incense burner carried the charred coals of frankincense tears and sandalwood powder, carefully measured to provide just enough sweet-smelling smoke to fill the room, but just under enough to trigger the sprinkler system. A hand-blown glass oil lamp provided the only light, glinting off a gilt and lapis replica statue of the blue-skinned bald god of craftsmen and, depending on who interpreted, great architect of mankind.

Right at this moment, he really needed a great architect if he had any hope of keeping house and home together.

"My water is the water of Ptah, the water of Ptah is my water. It is pure, it is pure." The words rolled out of him effortlessly, he was so attuned to them. He slipped into that beneath-consciousness state that purified his mind while he went through the motions of purifying his body. A sense of expectancy hovered around him. The Netjeru provided, but on their own terms, which was why he rarely asked Them for much. Now desperate enough to ask, he was willing to accept whatever they served up.

He focused on what was best for Lucy. If only the coffee shop would turn a little profit, he could afford to keep the house, the business, and, most importantly, his daughter.

MIRA Taggert finished packing Jeremy's things into the last box, the final evidence that she'd shared her life with someone for the past two years. Cradling the phone in the crook of her shoulder, she dragged the box into the yard to join eight others. "He dumped me, Mom. Just like that. In the middle of Hawaii."

"Oh, sweetie, I'm sorry. Do you want me to turn him into a toad?"

"It'd be redundant." She almost laughed until she remembered that the whole occult thing was what was responsible for their breakup. Faced with the truth on a sunny beach, they'd had it out.

"You're telling me that my religion—my *faith*—is childish nonsense?"

He sighed. "That's not what I meant. Look, I'm about to make partner in my firm. I can't have a flaky wife who talks to ghosts and believes in Witchcraft. I need a wife my partners will respect. Someone who won't make waves." He flicked her tiny crescent moon earrings. "Why can't you just wear some simple pearls?"

If he thought her tiny pentagrams and tasteful earrings were flaky, he had no clue. She'd left most of the trappings of her religion behind when she was old enough to realize that faith came from the soul and not the jewelry around one's neck.

She turned from him and laughed, feeling the power of the ocean, the sand beneath her feet, the clear air, and the volcanic energy that pulsed through the islands like a great heartbeat. She longed to call on those waves and that power and lash out at him with a nice big typhoon.

Not that she really could—that kind of great, mystical power only existed where very skilled special-effects people got paid lots of money to do it. Nevertheless, as she stalked away, dignity shredded but somewhat intact, she liked to imagine that the sky had grown flatter, and the waves wilder.

Her mother's voice drew her back to the present. "Honey, you sound drained. Join me for a while at the center. Besides, there's a favor I needed to ask you anyway."

Her mother's favors always made Mira nervous and she began to pace back and forth between the living room and the kitchen. "I've told you, Mom. I can't help your friends' stores. My business consulting wouldn't get them anywhere they'd want to go." The Psychic Mall was more like a haphazard hybrid between flea market and charity than a group of businesses. Palm readers, aura readers, mediums, and crystal sellers came and went as they pleased, no advertising, and gave their services away if the mood struck them.

"Not the mall. A man, new in town, just opened a coffee shop, and he needs your help to make it work."

"A coffee shop, huh?"

"Yes. He has the most charming twelve-year-old daughter, Lucy. She visits me quite a bit and she's worried about things. Her father's raising her alone, you know." Kendra tsked. "And Paul—Lucy's father—is Atlantean royalty and not used to working for a living."

Mira stopped in her pacing tracks. "Mom, you know I don't believe in that Atlantis junk. Besides, it doesn't matter what people were in their past lives. It's this one that counts."

"Yes, dear. And in this one, he's Atlantean royalty who needs your help."

THE coffee shop was empty, but Paul was optimistic. He could feel it as he whacked the cappuccino maker's basket on the edge of the counter. His prayers had worked.

In the middle of the last round of thumping spent grounds into the trash bin, he noticed a woman had entered the shop and the sight of her sent his internal alarm bells into spastic mode.

Gods above and below, he thought. *Please don't let it be* her.

Her back was to him but he thought he recognized the caramel-colored fall of her hair and the peculiar way that a tie-dyed kaftan hung on her shoulders. *Anyone but her. Anyone but my ex-wife, please.*

The woman turned and smiled at him. "I've been sent here."

His knees went watery with relief. Not his ex-wife. Not come to take away his child.

"You were sent here?"

She nodded and leaned on the counter. The closer he looked, he realized she didn't look like Heather at all. Maybe the hair color . . . and the same hippie clothes designer.

"By Fate?" he asked skeptically.

She smiled, a dreamy smile touched with sadness. It made him want to pull her into his arms and comfort her. He put his hands firmly on the stainless steel counter between them, thankful for the barrier. Definitely no hugging. His eyes fell to the gape of her loose neckline, and there was something so sensual about glimpsing a sliver of curved breast that his eyes nearly rolled back into his head.

Gods, I need a social life, he thought, realizing he hadn't been with a woman in so long he was hallucinating about a long-gone ex.

"Actually, by my mother. But she's been known to assume the guise of Fate when she wants things to go her way."

Mira had had plenty of time to take in the décor of the place, and she already knew what she would suggest to her client—a total makeover.

Insane-asylum green paint covered everything, brick walls, floor, even the tin ceiling that at one time might have been elegant. The place looked like a vintage prison, sans barred windows. Elvis singing in striped overalls wouldn't be out of place.

What spaced her out though was the prison warden—or rather, the owner, and he was just stunning enough that her mother's Atlantean-prince description didn't do him justice.

"Well, since your mother, Fate, or both sent you here, I'll have to assume they sent you for coffee." Paul Dane—or His Atlantean Highness—stood six foot five if he was an inch, and the industrial glare of the bulbs in the caged prison-lamps hanging from the ceiling gleamed off his chrome-dome bald head. A wry grin lurked behind his way-too-long goatee.

She blinked. The force of that smile sent warmth rushing through her. Impossible. She was still nursing a broken heart, wasn't she? And besides, she got hot over smooth jaws, not smooth heads.

"Well?" His voice even sounded like it had been sent through a grinder, scooped carefully into an unbleached filter, and percolated with only the purest mountain spring water from someplace in the Himalayas. And served up to her in a fine china cup with just the right amount of real cream and sugar.

Voices like chocolate were easy to come by, but a voice like coffee was enough to do a girl in. *Earth to Space Station Mira.* She shook her head to clear it.

"No, you don't want coffee?"

Her own voice finally remembered what it was designed for.

"Um. Yes. No. I mean, yes, I want coffee, but no, my mother and Fate are fine, thanks."

"Okay. Now can you tell me what kind of coffee you want?" The java-voiced query was slow and patient.

"Business consultant."

One sandy eyebrow went up. "Oh, we don't grind up people with the coffee here. It interferes with the integrity of the bean."

"No! I mean, *I'm* a business consultant." Good gods, but she was making a mess of things! She sounded like a simpleton even to her own ears. Her eyes fastened on a word on the blackboard behind him. "Mochaccino?"

"Now we're getting somewhere. I'll get you a mochaccino."

Had she really said that? "No! Not a mochaccino." That much sugar on an empty stomach would knock her right out. "Just a Kona blend. Decaf."

"Right."

He turned away from her and her brain came back from its sabbatical. She knew staying at the center with her mother was a bad idea. She'd stayed up way too late in a women's drumming circle last night and the iron shorted out on her this morning, leaving her business suit too wrinkled to wear and a tie-dyed kaftan her only other option for today's session of Embracing Her Inner Moron.

"Kona blend decaf." He slid the mug over the counter to her.

She held out her hand. "Mira Taggert."

Both of his eyebrows shot up. "You're Kendra's daughter?"

She nodded, smiling. At last, they'd made a connection! "I'm here to help you save your business."

HE was in trouble. Her smile was blinding even if the woman could barely put two sentences together! Kendra Taggert's daughter was supposed to be a hotshot corporate suit—a real savvy businesswoman. Kendra was a bit of an eccentric, even in the pagan community, but he never expected her flights of fancy to include complete denial about her daughter. Beautiful, admittedly, but dumb.

He went to the end of the counter and circled it. "Let's sit down over there and talk." Somehow, he'd find a way to thank her for her offer and get rid of her. Sure, he admired alternative ways as much as the next pagan, but he needed good business sense, not crystals and fairy dust.

She threw her head back to drink, bringing the cup to her lips with both hands wrapped around it. Her eyes closed halfway and she pursed her lips around the cup rim. He found himself momentarily mesmerized by the delicate curve of her throat and his eyes wandered lower for another peek at the barely hidden curves that encouraged thoughts he didn't need to be thinking.

He forced himself back to the look of pure abandonment crossing her face. He knew it was good coffee—he made it himself, and he knew good coffee beans. She might be a flake, but the woman drank coffee like an urban hedonist.

"Gods, that's good. And that was the decaf?"

"Uh-huh. Now you see why we don't grind up people in it."

THE coffee, thank heavens, hit her brain almost instantly, restoring most of her faculties. She followed him over to one of the small tables in the corner. He held out a chair for her and her eyebrows went up. Chivalry? Why not? Maybe princes from Atlantis learned this stuff in their underwater star kingdoms. He even pushed the chair in for her without knocking her knees as she lowered herself onto the battered cushion. The warmth from his body seeped into hers, almost as if they were touching auras.

She looked up to find him looking back down at her. His eyes were the most liquid dark hazel she'd ever seen. A girl could drown in those eyes.

Focus, she told herself sternly. This is a client, not a romantic daydream. She fished in her bag for the folder she'd spent part of yesterday working on. He looked slightly stunned when she slid it across the table.

Her mental meltdown must have been contagious. "I, uh, um, well," he said, as if that covered it all.

She helped him out by opening the folder and tapping the outlined business plan, relief flooding her as her confidence seeped back in. "First thing, of course, is an overhaul of the décor. I can have decorators' quotes for you within twenty-four hours—"

"No," he murmured as he turned a page.

"I can be very persuasive with local decorators," she said.

"I'm not redecorating."

There was an audible screech as her train of thought came to a halt. "Why not?"

"I like the place the way it is."

She glanced around. "Empty, you mean?"

"No, retro."

Meet the eccentric business owner, she thought. The worst of the lot. "We can do retro. Retro *and* full of customers if we do it right."

"And you have a plan for that?"

She nodded. "Oh yes." She turned to her portfolio and pulled out her business plan, neatly bulleted and formatted on bright white paper. The paper seemed shrunken in perspective to his large, long-fingered hand.

He seemed to barely glance at it before passing it back. "No."

"No?" Unease slithered into her stomach, making her wish for the antacids in her purse. If she could just discreetly reach for them . . . "Why not?"

"You're missing two major details. One, the selling strength of the product itself, and two, the vision of the owner."

Heat bloomed in her face. "Owners usually rely on me to clarify their vision," she said, a tad defensively.

"Well, this owner might have blurred vision, but he knows exactly what he *doesn't* want." He pointed to the outline. "I will not be a clone of you-know-who. If I wanted that, I would have shelled out the cash for a franchise license at the get-go and saved myself some headaches."

Hurt welled up in her big whiskey-colored eyes. Paul felt like a jerk, but the bottom line was still Lucy and he didn't have time to pander to dreamers. He'd expected more from Kendra Taggert's daughter, not that hers was the worst business plan he'd seen, but it was generic enough to have been pulled from a college textbook. And turning his place into a cheap knockoff of that West Coast chain was something he'd expect from a mundane, not someone whose mother claimed she understood the subculture.

"I'll revise the plan," she said tightly. "This was only a starting point."

He wasn't sure he wanted to spend more time on a hopeless cause, but his sense of *Ma'at*—justice—wouldn't let him turn her away without a fair shake.

Looking around with sad eyes, she pleaded. "I *can* help you."

He pictured her sitting down with crystal sellers and occult dealers. Her job would be pretty simple—teaching them some basic bookkeeping. "Convince me."

She licked her upper lip, unknowingly reminding him that he was a full-grown male complete with all the requisite hormonal functions, then let him have it with both guns blazing.

Too stunned to speak, he revised his earlier opinion—she might dress like a hippie, but the similarity ended there. Put her in a business suit and even Ralph Reed wouldn't be able to find

fault with her. She was starting to scare him. *Think of Lucy.*
Mira Taggert was starting to make some sense, and if she kept
going the same way, he just might find a way of keeping his cof-
feehouse and his daughter.

"I'd like to meet again to fully revise the plan as soon as possible, if that's okay."

While Lucy was at the center of this, she was far from his
thoughts as he answered, "Dinner. Tonight."

In the back of his mind, it occurred to him that he was actually asking a woman out on a date.

She nodded. Small wonder, since he seemed to be using the
Caveman School of Romantic Seduction to communicate. *Just
don't let me start beating my chest*, he prayed to whomever
might be listening.

LUCY knew she was in trouble as soon as she walked into the
coffee shop. Morgana's response to her "Where's Dad?" question was to grab her arm and drag her to one of the couches.

"Listen, kiddo. When you asked me about love spells, I never
thought you'd go out and cast one!"

"I didn't cast a *love* spell." Not *technically* a love spell, anyway.

Morgana frowned at her. "Don't lie. It's bad karma. Do you
know where your dad is right now?"

"Duh, that's why I asked you."

"He's out—on a date."

Lucy's world tilted. "A date?" she stuttered. "With who?
Who'd date my dad?"

"Some businesswoman he hired."

Her jaw dropped. "A businesswoman? And my dad? You've
got to be kidding. Dad wouldn't date a businesswoman at gunpoint!"

"He might at *spell*point," Morgana said.

Lucy bit a fingernail. Her dad and a woman? Did her spell backfire? On some level, she knew that he was his own person, but the thought of him doing non-dad things creeped her out. Worse, it made her feel lost. When he wasn't being her dad, where did that leave her? Would she end up with a wicked step-mother who turned her dad's brain to mush? Would he stop loving her best?

WHILE his daughter worried about her fate, Paul worried about his own in the restaurant two blocks away. He hadn't been on a date in too many years to count and he had no idea if the rules had changed since the Stone Age. He was pretty sure there was a moratorium on dragging the little woman back to the cave by the hair, but he didn't know much else, and the more time he spent with her, the more he did want to drag her back to his cave by the hair—or maybe just walk her the four blocks south to his house, send Lucy to spend the night at her friend's, and have a grown-up slumber party of his own.

Funny, Kendra had never mentioned Mira's incredible beauty, but she hadn't exaggerated her daughter's business sense.

It took Mira all of ten minutes to come up with a sound, viable business plan that he could live with. By the time their food arrived, she was already on more personal ground.

"I have to say it," she said. "My mother told me you have a thirteen-year-old daughter but you barely look old enough."

"She's still twelve for the next few days."

She shook her head. "You look way too young."

He shrugged. "I'm thirty-four. Plenty old enough. I was twenty-one when she was born. Old enough to understand responsibility."

"Most men that age aren't," she said.

"I had to be. Heather—Lucy's mother—and I, we married young. She didn't understand responsibility. I'm not sure she does yet."

"Is Heather still around?"

He found himself willing to talk about his ex-wife. Surprising since her image usually invoked anxiety and heartburn and more than a little worry. "Nah, she lives in a commune in California. She left me when Lucy was still a baby, but her parents live nearby. They're waiting for any chance to take Lucy away from me, which is why I have to keep the coffee shop solvent."

Mira's doe eyes softened. "I'll do everything in my power to make sure the coffee shop turns a profit. I swear," she said earnestly.

He blinked. Her eyes were totally honest, and she meant every word. It was shocking to him to realize he wouldn't be the only one thinking of Lucy behind every decision. And humbling.

He turned the conversation before she could say more. "What about you? Ever married?"

Her mouth turned down. "My ex just dumped me for being what he called 'childish,' meaning that because I'm a pagan, I wouldn't make a good trophy wife."

"Ouch," he murmured in sympathy, while thinking something along the lines of *more for me.*

"Yeah, we were on vacation in Hawaii. I came home and showed him childish—I stuck all of his things in boxes in my front yard and cast a rain spell that actually worked."

He bit his cheek. "My assistant, Morgana, would really like you."

"We already talked a little, while you were behind the counter."

"Gods help me. And the male population of West Monroe High School."

"Let 'em fend for themselves. Next question—my mother says that Lucy visits her all the time. . . ."

Time to be diplomatic, he thought. "Yes, Lucy spends a lot of time at the center. Much as I try, I can't be all things to her."

She nodded in understanding. "There are some things only a mom can do."

He nodded. "That bothers me. Not that I can do anything about it."

"Well, if it's any consolation, there are some things only a dad can do. I grew up without one, and I felt the loss. But I can't picture you happy about Lucy spending so much time with my mother. She just doesn't seem like the type you'd encourage."

Her accuracy was uncanny. And left him no room to maneuver. "Umm, well, I think she picks up some ideas better left unpicked-up."

Even though she held some of those thoughts herself, Mira couldn't help but be offended on her mother's behalf. "Ideas like feminine empowerment, perhaps?" she asked coolly.

He shook his head. "Ideas like prehistoric feminist utopias. Revisionist history. Sloppy scholarship."

She rolled her eyes. "You think a thirteen-year-old is interested in footnotes and source citations?"

"My thirteen-year-old is. Besides, letting people believe that a mix of Victorian folk magick, Celtic poetry, and Star Trek philosophy is ancient tradition is downright irresponsible."

"My mother does not do that. She makes it no secret that her tradition is thoroughly modern." Intolerance among mundanes, she expected. But from a fellow Pagan? Whatever happened to the idea that "we recognize all paths as having validity"?

"And then she tells people she's descended from an unbroken line of Witches in existence since the Bronze Age."

"She does *not!* Not anymore." Not since Mira had traced the family history and proven without a doubt that the

women of the Taggert family had been everything from Pres-
byterians to prostitutes, yet none had practiced any sort of
Witchcraft while doing it. "And besides, you'd better step
down off that soapbox until you stop telling people you're
from Atlantis."

First he gaped. Then he groaned. "Oh, Lord, I knew that
would come back to haunt me."

"Instant karma," she shot back.

He laughed. "Maybe so. I told that one to Lucy when she was
little. To make her feel special about our differences."

She raised an eyebrow. "And you didn't think that was at all
revisionist?"

He had the grace to blush. "Well, it does have a basis in fact."

"Really? Do tell," she drawled.

"My maternal grandmother is from the island of San-
torini. One of the prevailing theories about Atlantis is that it
was the kingdom located in the center of the island of San-
torini, or Thera, as the Greeks call it. Said center of island was
blown to smithereens courtesy of a volcano in the classical
era. If that theory is right, then we are Atlanteans. At least
partly."

She had to laugh at that. "You are one sick puppy, Paul
Dane."

"A sick, well-researched puppy," he replied.

Against her will, her lips curved upward. Of its own accord,
a laugh bubbled out of her throat. "Okay, I give up."

"You know, you should do that more often."

"What, give up?"

"No. Laugh."

THE twilight breeze was just a touch humid, bringing with it
that sense that the night was alive. It accompanied the feel-

ing crawling through her that said this was a powerful
night—a night where destiny rode the wind, even though
her mind shied away from even thinking in terms so poetic.
"Where to now?"

"My house."

"Your house?" Mira arched an eyebrow at him. If he thought
that dinner would get him a piece of her— He put one hand
lightly on her back in a courteous gesture and she shivered at
his touch. Hell, he might be right.

"The place is a little messy, but Lucy is there. I want you to
meet her."

Was it so wrong to admire the way his voice softened with
affection when he talked about his daughter?

"And I'd like you to see my reference library."

She stopped beneath one of the old sycamores that lined the
street. "I'm sorry I was a bitch back there. I hate it when people
automatically write us off because of a lack of history. It forces
other people to invent history so we'll be taken seriously. In the
end, everybody loses. You hit a hot button."

He turned to face her, his face hidden in shadow except for
the faint gleam of his eyes. "I wouldn't mind hitting a few more
of your hot buttons," he said quietly.

Her breath caught in her chest, kick-starting her heart into
high gear. A moment caught her up in the age-old female
dilemma—flight or flirt, and she decided to flirt. "Is that a line,
Mr. Dane?" she asked coyly.

"More of an opportunity crime, I think. Did I just lose cool
points for it?"

It seemed like the most natural thing in the world when his
hand lifted to brush a stray lock of hair away from her forehead.
His fingers were large—one hand could easily grab her whole
face—but his touch was gentle. "No. It was a good line. Very
clever," she said.

He lowered his head a little. "I'm not as good with actions, but this feels right," he said softly.

He was going to kiss her. She was going to let him. It felt right. "Go with that," she murmured, turning her head up to meet him.

His lips touched hers. She felt the rush and sizzle of attraction simmering in her soul boil over and flood her. She wrapped her arms around his neck and he deepened the kiss.

He left her breathless and wired. The leaves of the sycamore fluttered in a sudden breeze. Right there, under that tree with him, she felt an absolute sense that she was exactly in the right place at the right time, and focused on the right thing. Nothing else mattered.

The sound of a pickup truck gunning its engine around the street corner broke the spell. She looked away first and he let her go—there were no other words for it. She felt sure he could have kept her under the sycamore forever if he truly wanted to.

"LUCY?" Paul called out as he opened the door of the little brick Cape Cod.

"In the dining room, Dad," came the muffled reply.

Mira followed as he led the way.

"Meet my daughter, Lucy. Lucy, this is Mira. She's Lady Kendra's daughter and she's going to help me with some business in the coffee shop."

Mira looked down at Lucy, perched on a dining room chair. The girl was lovely, yet very little betrayed her as her father's daughter. Her skin was a beautiful dusky olive, and her hair was midnight black. The only clue was in the stunning deepness of her eyes, the same as Paul's. Mira held out her hand. "Hi, Lucy."

Lucy's manners were excellent. "Hello, Mira."

After standing to shake her hand, Lucy continued to hold it. "Come on, I'll show you around."

The library made her green. Paul and Lucy, and a handful of others, practiced Kemetic Reconstructionism. While Mira's faith was a mix of modern philosophy and traditional folk practices whose origins didn't really matter, Reconstructionism demanded a more scholarly approach. Lucy summed it up best. "We try to do things the way the ancient Egyptians did them, and when we change things, we need a good reason."

Paul opened a book with Egyptian hieroglyphs and read a few passages to her, then translated them into English. She was doubly impressed when Lucy showed her the framed pieces of papyrus around the den. "They're the Maxims of Ptahhotep. Like proverbs, only ancient Egyptian. I drew them out, then put the translations below them. Dad helped, but I did all the artwork. Did you have fun on your date with my dad?"

Mira blinked at the sudden change in subject. "Er . . ." Wasn't she a little young to be asking that? "I had fun, thanks."

"Cool. He can be a dork sometimes, but he's mostly fun to hang around with."

Paul put a hand to his chest. "Wow. The biggest praise for your old man that you can come up with is that I can be mostly fun to hang around with? How am I supposed to score with chicks when that's the best you can do?"

Lucy rolled her eyes. "Dad, you really freak me out when you talk about scoring with chicks. Besides, I can only teach you so much on how to be cool. The rest you have to figure out for yourself, Grasshopper."

"If anybody can teach me to be cool, it's you, kiddo. Now get off to bed so you can recharge your cool-o-meter for tomorrow."

Mira watched their exchange with fascination.

When Lucy had gotten herself off to her room, Paul looked at her.

"She's a great kid," Mira said. "She's really crazy about you."

"I think she's crazy about you too. She's never shown any other woman this room, not that there have been many women, but I was surprised that she brought you in here."

Mira chewed her lip. "Did she do something wrong?"

"Not at all, she just let me know that she approves of you—" Paul lowered his head, nibbling her bottom lip as he pulled her into his arms—"of us."

MIRA had lots of opportunities to talk with Lucy during the next few days and found an ally—Lucy hated the look of her father's coffee shop as much as she did. She was the one who came up with the perfect idea to get Paul's buy-in on redecorating. "Feng shui," she said, and handed a book to Mira.

It made sense.

All Mira could express was that the place's aura felt wrong. Paul didn't want to hear metaphysical reasons. As he put it, "I'm only spending real money on real reasons."

Lucy had found a reason real enough to present to her father. After studying books from the library and visiting together one of the local decorators who incorporated feng shui into his work, they had enough ammo to go as a team to present their idea to Paul. Outnumbered, outgunned, and outclassed, he reluctantly agreed to a few changes to the décor.

To celebrate, Mira took Lucy out shopping for "girl stuff"—a double celebration since it was also Lucy's birthday. Lucy wanted, rather, needed, a bra, and like Mira had said to Paul earlier, there were some things dads just couldn't do. Paul wouldn't know to take his daughter to be measured properly for a well-fitting bra, nor would he hold with taking her into Victoria's Secret for something pretty and grown-up looking.

Afterward, they went to the makeup counter in the big department store and got free makeovers, just to be silly.

"Your dad isn't going to be mad at me for putting makeup on you, is he?" Mira asked when the makeup girl removed cooling cream from her eyelids.

"Naah. For our big temple celebrations, he wears thick black eyeliner, and I have to do it for him because he can't get the lines straight. It's a little hard to tell your kid she can't wear makeup when she's just done yours."

At the end of the shopping trip, Lucy cocked her head to the side and said, "You know, you're not half bad to be around."

"Umm . . . thanks, I guess. You're pretty fun to hang out with, too." Mira knew better than to get all emotional, but inside, her heart swelled. This young girl accepted her, and her father maybe did, too.

Lucy's friend Brianna and her mother came over for dinner, cake, and ice cream, and afterward, Brianna's mother took both girls home with her for a sleepover. Mira picked up her purse as the girls were leaving, even though she didn't want to go. "I'd better get going, too."

"Stay," he said simply, quietly, right in front of his daughter. Mira's jaw dropped open.

"Come on, girls," Brianna's mother said crisply. "If we leave now, we can stop at the video store before it closes."

Lucy kissed Paul's cheek. "G'night, Dad. I'll be back early tomorrow to help with redecorating." She then stepped up to Mira and hugged her.

Surprised, Mira hugged back. "Happy birthday, sweetie."

"My dad likes you, you know."

Mira nodded, unsure of what to say or do.

"It's okay. You can like him back."

"Oh, I do."

The girls left with Brianna's mother and they went from being a happy crowd to just herself and Paul, facing each other across the open doorway. She still had her bag over her shoulder, ready to go at a moment's notice.

He stepped toward her and cupped her face with his hands. She never could get over how big his hands were, and how gentle they could be. "Stay," he said again.

Her heart pounded in her chest. No going back if she said yes. Forward held only question marks. She couldn't stay here forever. But she very much wanted to stay here now. She nodded, and he lowered his head to hers.

MIRA woke up slowly, going from unconsciousness to a long, lazy stretch. The unfamiliar walls gradually intruded on her until she realized she hadn't slept at the center last night.

A glance at the alarm clock told her it was after ten. Geez! Her lazy stretch turned into outright panic. Gods help her if she didn't get moving and out of bed before Lucy came in and found out exactly why her dad had been so gung-ho about her staying overnight at her friend's.

She pulled on Paul's bathrobe and opened the door. Lucy's startled face was right on the other side.

Mira's jaw dropped to the floor. She struggled for words and discarded every trite thing that came to her mind.

To her credit, Lucy's face returned to its usual shape. " 'Morning," she said. "Dad said to tell you that he's got fresh Danish down at the shop."

"Fresh Danish," Mira echoed stupidly. A thirteen-year-old girl was handling this better than she was! "Umm. Great?"

Lucy snorted. "You're more incoherent than Dad in the mornings. I'll be in my room. Let me know when you're ready to leave for the shop, okay?"

"Sure," Mira mumbled. Her face must be sixteen shades of purple.

"Have a shower," Lucy prompted.

"Right. A shower."

The teenager shook her head. "You *are* worse than Dad. At least he goes in the direction I point him." She gave Mira a light push toward the bathroom.

ONE long hot shower later and Mira was feeling more herself. Embarrassed to hell and back, but herself. If Lucy didn't want to make a big deal out of what obviously happened last night, well, then, neither would she. Stepping from the bathroom dressed in her work clothes, Mira smelled something unmistakably familiar, even comforting, almost. The scent led to Lucy's cracked-open bedroom door.

"Reverse this spell I spake in haste, let my magick go to waste. Release us all from love's fine curse, reverse my spell, reverse, reverse. Set all free that have been bound, turn my wishes back around. Release the glamour I have wrought, release, release the lovers' knot."

No comfort there. Mira froze. The unmistakable tingle she felt at the words was something she'd spent years around. Now, she couldn't ignore it, and it scared her.

"Lucy?" She blinked rapidly at a sudden blur in her vision.

"Mira?" Lucy came out of the room. "Are you ready to— what's the matter?"

"Lucy?" Her own voice came from far away, in a tunnel somewhere. "Lucy, what did you do to me?"

"Omigod. Mira! Oh, shit, what have I done?" Lucy pressed her knuckles to her teeth as Mira slid down the wall, unconscious.

*   *   *

SHE woke up with a pounding headache and several concerned faces hovering around her. "Mom? Paul?"

"You haven't been taking care of yourself," her mother chided gently. "The spirits are displeased. Dr. Bowden agrees with them."

Chelsea Bowden, one of her mother's friends, introduced herself. "Your blood sugar was pretty low. Your mother tells me you're supposed to eat something first thing in the morning. Lucy said you hadn't eaten anything and you slept late."

She wanted to cover her face with the pillow and have somebody press on it until she stopped struggling. Did the world need to know what she'd been doing last night, and with whom?

She thought again of Lucy and the undoing spell she'd heard. Then she looked at Paul. What if their irrational attraction was indeed the result of some spell? A few days ago, she'd have scoffed. Now, she floated in a sea of unsurety. She bit her lip.

Last night was wonderful. Incredible. *Magickal.* Maybe too magickal. What if that beauty and truth—that *Ma'at*, as Paul would call it—what if that was all the influence of some misdirected teenage energy? The notion was ridiculous, of course. But it wasn't. If she'd made it rain on Jeremy's clothes, then Lucy could have created something artificial between her and Paul.

There was only one way to find out for sure.

"YOU'RE leaving," Lucy stated.

Mira nodded, fastening her suitcase. "My work here is done. You got your wish, kid. I'm unbound and set free." The words hurt deeply, even though she managed to mask them in a carefree tone.

To her surprise, Lucy started to cry. "I messed up bad, and I don't even know how, and now you're leaving because of me."

Mira shook her head and took the girl into her arms. "Hey, it's okay. Why don't you tell me the whole story and then we'll figure out if it's all your fault or not." Her heart went out to the girl. After all, she was just as confused as Lucy was.

Lucy sniffed. "I cast a spell. Before you came. I wanted to find someone to love me. I know I wasn't supposed to, but I just wanted somebody so bad, you know?"

"And you wished for a boyfriend?"

Lucy shook her head. "You're not supposed to do that. I kept things vague because I didn't want a boyfriend that would turn out psycho or anything. I was thinking something more like a dog."

Things clicked into place then. "And you got me. Woof, woof."

Lucy sniffed and laughed at the same time. "I didn't want my dad to find a girlfriend. Then you showed up and when you spent the night with him at first I thought it was great."

It was, she thought, biting her tongue. "Why did you think it was great, and what happened then?"

"I thought it was great because my dad really does need somebody. I can't take care of him forever, you know."

"Maybe you ought to have mentioned this to your dad first."

Lucy rolled her eyes. "He's a *guy*, Mira."

She snorted. "Can't argue with that. Anyway, what happened then? Why did you cast the undoing spell?"

"I got scared. There you were, making Dad happy and making me happy, too, and it was all because of my spell. I manipulated you into coming here and sleeping with my dad."

"That's a new one. First time a teenager takes credit for two consenting adults."

"You're not taking me seriously!" Lucy protested.

Mira sighed. "Yes, I am. You're taking yourself *too* seriously." It came to her then, the whole why of it. "Sometimes," she said slowly, "um, you know about *Ma'at*, right?"

Lucy nodded.

"*Ma'at* isn't necessarily what's good, is it? It's what's right. And that has nothing to do with good. I'm coming to understand something myself here. I'm thinking maybe you got what's right for you, rather than what's good for you. It's not what you think you want, it's what *Ma'at* says you need. And maybe that was me, for a time."

"But you're leaving," Lucy wailed, fresh tears starting.

"I have to." It hurt too much to stay around. "It isn't what I want, either. It's what *Ma'at* says I should do."

PAUL polished the same spot on the new counter for the umpteenth time as the door opened. He didn't need to look up to know it was her. "You're leaving," he said. It wasn't a question.

It was right that she should. Her work was done, they were too incompatible to stay together long, and he wouldn't subject Lucy to a short and fiery affair that would leave them all hurting in the end.

The counter reflected the new lamps' glare coldly. *Ma'at gives you what it thinks you need.*

"Yeah," she said hollowly. "Um, maybe one last coffee before I go?"

"Sure." He turned away and poured from the carafe. *I need this,* he told himself.

He put the cup on the counter and finally looked at her. Her golden tiger-eyes shimmered and he couldn't stop his hands from reaching out to brush his thumbs against her cheekbones in the lightest of touches. She'd come into his life and kick-started both his business and his heart from surviving into living. Now she was leaving and it was back to surviving again.

She turned her head into his hand, like a cat seeking.

Hell, he thought. *I need this like I need a hole in the head.* This was not *Ma'at*. This wasn't right in that bone-deep sense he expected from something truly *Ma'at*. This hurt and it was wrong. "No," he said.

"No what?"

"No I'm not letting you leave."

She looked up at him. "If this is about—"

"It isn't about anything but me and you and how we feel about each other."

"But Lucy—"

"I know Lucy cast a spell, and I know she undid it. She told me everything, and I know it had nothing to do with us."

"How can you be sure? I can't build a relationship on the vagaries of misdirected energy."

"This isn't vague, and I'm pretty sure it isn't misdirected," he said and kissed her. The sense of rightness rushed through his veins. When he was done—and he took his time—he looked down at her flushed face and asked, "Does that feel any different than before she undid her spell?"

Mira blinked rapidly. "I—this—but—"

"But nothing. I'm talking about how I feel about you. I love you, Mira. Lucy loves you. It isn't *Ma'at* to have you anywhere but by my side."

Mira felt something unlatch in her chest. What did she think she wanted? Hell, she didn't know. But she did know that this—Paul, and Lucy, and the coffee shop—seemed to be part and parcel of something *Ma'at* knew she needed. Her heart swelled and she knew what *right* felt like. "I love you, Paul. And if that Lady with the feather weighed my heart right now, She'd find it floating."

"So you'll stay?"

"I'll stay."

He hauled her over the counter into his arms, knocking the coffee cup onto the floor, where it shattered amidst the applause of everybody in the coffee shop who'd just witnessed one of the better moments in the history of the universe.

Pagan Family Values

JEN SOKOLOSKI

There is a recurrent theme throughout ancient Egyptian history of the love shared by fathers and daughters. It resides in tales of the Netjeru (gods) all the way down to the average Joe working classes. The sun god Re is inspired to cross the heavens each day just to see his daughter Hathor. There is an abundance of Amarna period art depicting King Akhenaten showing open affection to his six young daughters. The following song was dedicated by a pharaoh in praise of his daughter, Mutirdis, and inscribed on a stela, now in the Louvre. It is not hard to see that paternal acts of greatness didn't start with anybody's million-man march, and that "Daddy's little girl" isn't just a concept of modern times.

> Sweet, sweet of attraction,
> the Hathor priestess, Mutirdis,
> Sweet, sweet of attraction,
> says King Menkheperre,
> Sweet, sweet of attraction,
> say the men,
> Lady of attraction,
> say the women.
> She is the royal daughter,

sweet of attraction,
The most beautiful of women,
A virgin never seen before.
Black is her hair like the blackness of night,
Like grapes and figs . . .
Her breasts are firm on her body.

Tambourine Moon

ZELENA WINTERS

Ki shan I Romani,
Adoi san' I chov'hani

Where Gypsies go,
There the Witches are, we know.
—Old Romani poem

Like a beacon in a North Atlantic fog, the ghost light stood at the end of the stage, casting a burst of white throughout the otherwise darkened Jernigan Theatre, flooding the empty orchestra pit with shadows.

Izabella Banning felt every one of her sixty-four years as she stooped to retrieve another discarded program from the floor. She slipped the booklet into the green plastic bag she dragged behind her. The bag grew heavier as she lumbered through another row, another row, and yet another row of empty seats. Last night's show, whatever it was, had been a success.

Her legs ached. It must be close to six A.M. She had been here nearly two hours and still had three to go. Her first three months on the job had been fraught with challenges. She had never ridden a bus before—much less flown in a plane—never paid taxes, never used a vacuum cleaner. But she had mastered them all. The greatest challenge, however, still remained.

For now, all she needed was a few minutes' rest. She sat in the aisle seat and sighed, slowly bent forward, and rubbed her ankles.

Some said the ceiling of the Jernigan arched like that of a cathedral. Some said the long, narrow torchère sconces lining the walls were reminiscent of votive candles. Tour guides would point with pride to the award-winning art deco style: wide floor-to-ceiling panels of ivory-colored Greek keys; brushed gold medallions with silver suns, moons, and stars; and the cloud-filled mural that graced the massive ceiling, the largest of its kind in the country.

To Izabella's eyes, the bow of the ceiling recalled the inside of her wooden *vardo*. The lacey wrought-iron sconces were the torches to light the horse's way for night travel. With so many stars scattered on the carpet, it took little to imagine the sky over the open roads she left behind. It took nothing to remember the sound of friends laughing, of old men singing ballads about princesses and bandits, of the winter wind answering her summons.

She reached down and retrieved another program, paused, and studied the cover. Ah, the violins. So they played them in this country too. Good. But those poor men! All of them in black, trussed up like fowls and forced to sit cheek by jowl, ramrod straight on the spindly metal chairs that still crowded the stage. What manner of music could birth from such confinement? Prisoners, the whole lot of them. Not a Rom in the pack—she'd wager her last gold coin on that.

In her clan, a man wore a full-sleeved white shirt, a vest embroidered in red and gold, a bright silk *diklo* tied round the neck, and pants of heavy cloth, cut to the knees for ease in riding horses. His music would have the sweetness of a meadow in spring and the power to tame the wildest storm. When he drew the bow across the strings, the trees would dance. The land itself would sing.

Izabella glanced at the cover photograph again. No, there'd be no Rom among all these stiff-backed *gaujo*s.

She reached into the *poachy* of her housedress for her handkerchief and felt the keys to the apartment she shared with her daughters. She had named her first-born Katarina, not Kate, and the little one Piroska, not Priscilla. Their dear father, He Who Has Crossed Over, chose the names himself. Kate and Priscilla—those were *gaujo* names! She spat into the green plastic bag. She had been so sure of success when she crossed the ocean to be with them. She was, after all, *chovihani* to the Banning clan, her magick unrivaled. When the time was right, she would use it.

Izabella looked up and gazed into the white-gold glitter of the ghost light, a naked bulb on an ornate metal floor lamp. When the stage was alive with performers there was no need for the light. But with none of the living to claim the stage, it was fair game for the spirits. Only the light kept them away. Her new friend Delia Jones had warned her that theater people were superstitious. Izabella had taken great comfort in the notion.

"HERE we are. Finally." Priscilla stood at the top of the second-floor landing. She fumbled with the key while jostling the bulky bag in her arm.

Izabella took the bag from her. "Look at you with your shackle of keys. If you keep yourself cooped like a chicken you will never taste freedom."

Turning the doorknob, Priscilla mumbled, "Better than sleeping in a field."

Izabella followed her daughter into the apartment the three of them shared on the second floor of one of Hartford's grand old Victorians and placed the bag she carried on the kitchen table. Seven o'clock and the late-April sun had given way to evening shadows that slipped in through the window screens, tumbled across the walls, and stretched across the hardwood floors, everything the lifeless color of sand. To Izabella's eyes, the only redeeming feature was the assortment of polished brass planters overgrown with green-and-white ivy, herbs, and deep purple violets in full bloom. To her way of thinking, the bookshelf groaning with leather-bound volumes crowded the space. The first time she saw the collection of pearl-pink seashells she spit on the floor.

"Ah, what is this?" Izabella frowned as she bent down and picked up a battered saucepan from the wastebasket. She examined its handle. "You will fix it, yes?"

"I will throw it away."

"A good copper pot like this? Your uncle Gardner, he could fix this in no time. Make it strong. Make it shine."

Priscilla grabbed the pot from her mother's hands and jammed it back into the wastebasket. "We can afford a new pot. Besides, we aren't tinkers."

"I am still your mother and you would fare well to hold your tongue!" Izabella wagged her finger. "Uncle Gardner is a good man. His hands are gnarled now like old rope, but when we pull into town people still flock to his *vardo*." She retrieved the saucepan and held it against her chest. "He would see the life clinging in this pot."

"You're in *this* country now. The days of fixing pots, weaving baskets, telling fortunes, and roaming the countryside in those horse-drawn, gaudy, painted *vardo*s are gone. And I say— good riddance."

Izabella opened her mouth to speak, but two things kept her

silent—the sound of Katarina's voice from the front door, and the unmistakable glitter of tears in Piroska's eyes.

"Hello. I'm home." Kate walked into the kitchen, placed a white plastic bag on the table, and spoke to her sister. "I couldn't remember if you put salt on the grocery list so I picked it up myself."

"You shouldn't have. We don't need it."

"We don't have any. I checked the pantry this morning."

"We don't have any because we don't *need* any."

Izabella stepped between her two daughters and picked up the box. Should a family run out of salt, the man would lose his potency. She poured a generous pyramid in the palm of her hand.

"What on earth are you doing?" Priscilla said. "Be careful. You'll spill that on the floor."

"What am I doing?" Izabella paused and studied her daughters. There was Piroska, twenty-nine years old, thin as a reed, buttoned up in a gray suit and white blouse, her dark curly hair shorn like stubble. She had yet to take a man to her bed. Some things a mother could tell. At thirty-four, Katarina fared little better. Five years since she and her husband had come to the crossroad and walked their separate ways. More meat on her bones than her younger sister had, Katarina always dressed in the colors of mushrooms. She carried her sorrow in her dark eyes, and kept her chin-length hair tucked obediently behind her ears. At least the girls had kept their ears pierced, holes for the mischievous spirits to easily flee when chased away.

From Izabella's ears dangled hoops of gold coins. Her dear husband had given them to her on their wedding day, promising to add more coins with each child she gave him. But despite the joy in their efforts, there had been only the two girls before the sudden storm, with its deadly lightning, claimed him. Katarina had been twelve, Piroska seven.

Looking at little Piroska now, Izabella's heart remembered the sadness, the way a bruise remembers the injury. She gazed at the pyramid of salt still weighting her palm. Piroska didn't know it, but she *did* need the salt. So did Katarina.

In one swift motion, Izabella tossed it into the air.

Both daughters gasped.

Trained as a *chovihani*, Izabella had learned to stop time. While Kate mumbled about the waste and Priscilla grumbled about the mess, Izabella watched the thousands upon thousands of white crystals float through the air like the slow streaming tails on fireworks, settling like fairy dust on each daughter's hair, eyelashes, nose, lips, shoulders, breasts, belly, hips, legs, leaving puddles at their feet. She held out her arms, palms up, and in Romani called, "As the salt lays the trail, may the lusty hand of a good man follow."

Kate blushed crimson. "Momma!"

"Ah," Izabella said with a wide smile. "You remember more of our language than you admit."

Priscilla brushed the salt from her shoulders. "Let me guess. She wants to see us married." With added determination, she brushed the salt from her sleeves. "Well, as they say, 'From the movie *Fat Chance* . . .' "

"And why is that?" Izabella asked. She longed to hold and comfort her child, but Priscilla stormed to the closet, where she retrieved a dustpan and broom.

"Because," Priscilla answered as she gripped the broom handle and jammed the straw against the floor, "because Gypsies are filthy. Horse thieves. Beggars. Baby snatchers." She glared at her mother. "And I don't want to be one of them."

"Don't talk to Momma like that!"

Izabella held up her hand to stay Kate's protective embrace. "No, no, no. Let her speak." She had heard it all before, the accusations, the taunts; but never had the words cut so deeply.

"So, my filthy little Piroska, show me the horses you stole, the babies you snatched." There was no answer. "Well? Where are they?"

"My name is Priscilla."

Izabella spit on the floor. "That is not the name your papa, He Who Has Crossed Over, gave you."

"Zoltan—"

Izabella covered her ears and quickly turned her back, but there was no stemming her daughter's anger.

"His name was Zoltan"—Priscilla's voice caught—"and he has been dead for more than twenty years!"

"And now you have called his spirit." Izabella staggered against the sink. "Now he will never know peace."

Kate rushed over. "Here, Momma, sit down." She dragged a chair from the table. "And you"—she wagged her finger at her sister—"you be quiet! You know what the doctor said." She pressed two fingers against the side of her mother's wrist. "Do you feel all right? Do you need your pills?"

"A sip of water."

Priscilla grabbed a glass from the cabinet and filled it from the faucet. "Here," she said as she knelt down next to the chair. "I'm sorry, Momma. I didn't mean it . . . all those things I said . . . I didn't mean to upset you."

"I know, I know." Izabella drank slowly, then closed her eyes and whispered, "Forgive them." Louder, she said, "Have no fear, girls. I have no plans to die today."

"You didn't plan that heart attack either," Kate said, stroking the long snowy braid that hung down her mother's back.

Izabella nodded, remembering Uncle Gardner's frantic phone call to the United States. "And now I am healed, good as new—better even—and as eager for home as dry land for a rain cloud."

"But we're your family," Kate said.

"Does that mean you will return to the clan with me?" Izabella looked at Kate, then Priscilla. Neither answered. "You girls are of my blood. Anyone can see the fire we share."

"But we aren't part of your world." Kate clasped her hands and drew them to her lips. "We left that world behind."

"So you did."

Priscilla walked to the window. She fussed with the café curtains, red and white gingham with starched white ruffles. "You could make this your world," she said.

"Become a house-dweller? *Dordi, dordi,*" Izabella said, shaking her head slowly. "No, you see, I'm—"

"Don't tell me you're too old to make such a change."

Izabella stood, braced both hands on the back of the chair, and smiled. "I will never be too old." She filled her mind with the images of a world and a crumbling way of life she had left behind. "But, you forget. I am needed there. I am *chovihani.*"

Priscilla locked her arms across her heart. "You're needed here, too."

"Yes. I could teach you to read the cards. How to use those pots of herbs on your sill. Tell you stories of the *Biti Foki.*"

"No, not for those things," Priscilla said, "for . . . for . . . I don't know."

"You don't know because you have yet to glimpse your *tacho paramoosh,* your own shamanic path."

"I'm not going to be a *chovi*—a Witch! And neither is Kate." Priscilla turned to her sister. "Are you?"

Kate shook her head. All the while, she had been silent, examining the copper pot Izabella had retrieved from the wastebasket. "We chose to leave, remember?" She gazed at the metal. "To escape the crowded *vardo,* the constant dust, the persecution." She lowered her eyes and her voice. "To stay in one place, become house-dwellers."

An uncomfortable silence settled about them like a fog, until Priscilla asked her mother, "Do you hate us for leaving?"

"For leaving the clan? No, I don't hate you. But mark my words. The day will come when you will ache to live as the Romani you were born . . . and it will be too late."

In a voice barely above a whisper, Kate asked, "What about leaving you? Do you hate us for that?"

Izabella clutched the small drawstring *putsi* that hung from the leather cord around her neck. Inside was a locket of her husband's ebony hair, a piece of charred wood, and snips of the two cords that had once tethered each babe to her belly. "I missed you." She looked away, remembering their eagerness to pack the faded carpet satchel she had reluctantly bought for them. "But you are of my flesh. How could I ever feel anything but love for you?"

Resting her hands on the back of the chair, Izabella closed her eyes to see the past. Her younger sister Mara had married a *gaujo*, knowing she would be banished from the clan for such a betrayal. To lose Mara had been bad enough, but the worst had come five years later when she returned, dressed in worldly clothes, her hair shorn scandalously, her pockets filled with paper gold. With photographs of a seaside cottage, picket fences, and flower gardens, Mara had lured Izabella's girls away. At sixteen and twenty, they were old enough to go. In all the years that followed, they had returned several times, though never to sleep in the camp. Their letters, delivered by friends who knew the annual routes, spoke only of their happiness, not the ache in their hearts. But some things a mother knows.

Katarina had always been the one to seek the peace. Izabella was not surprised to feel the comfort of her daughter's embrace. Nor was she surprised to hear the sound of Piroska's retreating footsteps as the one with the fiery and fragile heart ran from the room.

IN the weeks that followed, Izabella learned more of her daughters' lives, the memories they treasured, the sorrows they hid. In turn, she reminded them how the future was revealed in dominoes, tea leaves, and beans. They paid no attention. When Piroska had a sore throat, Izabella made a syrup from the fruit of the blackthorn shrub and said it would balance the energy line that connects the throat to the womb. Piroska scoffed and sought a prescription from a *mullomengro,* a dead-man maker. When Katarina encountered a problem at work, Izabella made an amulet of protection, from mugwort and blue feathers. Izabella found it on the living room floor next to a pile of *Science Digest* magazines. On May Eve, she gathered greenery and spread it about the house. She baked small honey cakes and burned sandalwood incense. At midnight, she went to the backyard, wrapped the clothesline pole in ribbons of red and white for the blood and milk mysteries of the Great Goddess, and lit a bonfire. Neither her daughters nor the men from the fire department were interested in hearing about Beltane and the need for creative flames on the night that called all nature to mate.

Izabella shared her frustrations with Delia Jones as they rode the bus home from work.

Delia lived on the ground floor of the house next to Izabella. It was Delia who had gotten Izabella the job at the Jernigan Theatre. She was a large-boned woman with skin the color of cocoa and a voice that always rose and fell like gentle ocean waves. Where Izabella always wore something of red and gold, Delia always wore white. Sitting on the near empty bus, she rummaged through the large straw satchel braced across her thighs and retrieved a plastic container of cut fruit.

"Glory, all that commotion last night! Three fire trucks? What mischief got into you, girl?" She opened the container and offered it to Izabella.

"*Parika tut.* Thank you." Izabella took a chunk of pineapple.

"I sought only to bring love and fertility to my daughters." She clutched the *putsi* hanging from her neck.

"What you hiding in that little pouch? Coins? Candy?"

Izabella looked long and hard at the woman who had become her friend, then whispered, "Magick."

Delia cast a knowing glance. "Ah, yes," she said and held up her wrist to reveal a bracelet of pink and yellow beads. "To honor Obba, guardian of the tombs."

Izabella loosened the strings of the bag, inserted her thumb and forefinger, and, with appropriate reverence, withdrew a piece of wood. "Once, this held the life of an ancient oak, struck by the fire bolt of Zeus. I was witness to the death."

Izabella gazed at the piece of char, seeing the green of its tender time as a sapling, the moist and glorious golds of its bounty years, and the seven shades of black that mourned its death. She took in a draught of air, long and deep, then closed her eyes and willed her breath to slow. Slow enough to blur the confines of the bus. Slower still to conjure the aromas of a cook fire on a chilly autumn morn . . . the bite of frost on her bare feet . . . the sweet of her husband's mouth on hers just before he ran after Piroska's pony . . . the open meadow . . . the crackle of dry leaves . . . the gray leaden sky . . . the distant rumble of thunder, the oak tree that was to tether the animal for only a moment, and the sudden strike of lightning that changed her life forever.

"Girl, you all right? Wake up now, you hear me? Wake up."

Izabella felt like a rag doll, her arm being shaken gently by one who knows the nearness of other paths.

"I am back," she said simply, then turned her face to the window.

*   *   *

WHEN the Jernigan was full there were nearly three thousand people. Now Izabella was the only one sitting in the seats. With her chores behind her, she had come for a few minutes of solace in the theater's shadows. Loneliness could wound without drawing blood or leaving scars.

The heavy doors behind her opened and Delia came rushing in, waving a program in her hand. "Don't be sleepin' now, girl! Look what just come in!"

Izabella pointed to the trash bag full of discarded programs. "I don't need another."

"Glory, no!" Delia stood before her. "Just heard about the new show loading in next week. Gonna play Thursday and Friday night. Here," she said, shoving the program toward her. "These just came in. Look at that picture. Isn't that one of those painted wagons you used to live in?"

Izabella cried out loud. There on the cover was a mammoth full moon and a horse-drawn wooden *vardo* intricately carved and colored with flowers. Next to the wagon stood a beautiful black-haired woman with bare shoulders and bare feet, in a white peasant blouse, dark ruffled skirt, red and gold ribbons streaming from her waist. She held one hand defiantly against her hip. In the other hand, she held a tambourine.

"I'LL have three tickets," Izabella said to the woman at the box office window. "Thursday night. The best seats you have." She turned to Delia and grinned.

While the clerk pulled up the computerized seating chart, Delia said, "You are certain you want to spend all this money? I can show you a secret place where you can stand and watch for free."

"No, no, no!" Izabella clutched a fistful of bills then carefully slid them into the silver trough. She watched the woman on the other side of the glass partition scoop them up and count. She turned to Delia, "My girls must see what they have forgotten. They must."

The clerk slid a small envelope back into the trough and smiled. "Here are your tickets and your change. You're in the center orchestra, row E. Please note, the tickets are nonrefundable. Enjoy the show."

KATE ran down the sidewalk after her sister. "Calm down, Prissy. It's not that bad."

"Not that bad? Our mother is up there in our kitchen *dukker*ing for old Mrs. Watson—the neighborhood big mouth! That doesn't bother you?"

"Come on, we can't expect her to give up the only way of life she's ever known."

Priscilla pressed her lips together as though to stem her anger. "She's got that ratty old 'sky' cloth on the kitchen table, tarot cards spread all over it, and candles burning everywhere. I'm surprised she hasn't hung up bead curtains."

Kate stifled a grin. "She's a Gypsy, not a hippie."

"Don't laugh at me!

"I'm sorry. I know you're worried about—"

"I've worked for this for years." Priscilla glanced up at the second floor. "All I have to do now is pass the character reference test. I've been finger-printed, had my finances examined, my handwriting analyzed, been interviewed by a panel of shrinks. The agency is sending another one over next Thursday. You're damn right I'm worried!"

"It'll be all right." Kate reached out and grabbed her sister's trembling hands. "You're not even thirty. There's still plenty of time to have a baby the old-fashioned way."

"Having a husband doesn't guarantee anything." Priscilla

pulled away. "Look at you. You had a husband but I don't see any baby."

"*Have.* Hank and I are separated, not divorced."

"I wouldn't brag about it. You haven't seen the man in five years. Where do you suppose he is now? Tahiti? The Klondike? Cairo? Anywhere the wind blows, right?"

"Shh! Here comes Mrs. Watson."

A plump woman in purple sandals and a flowered mumu fluttered down the sidewalk toward them, grinning. "Why, if it isn't . . . oh, what are those cute names? Piroska and Katarina. That's it. I didn't know you girls were Gypsies!"

The sisters froze.

"You have to stop all this." Priscilla waved her hand across the large colorful cards strewn on the kitchen table. "Lighting bonfires. Reading cards. Telling fortunes."

"It's called *dukker*ing."

"I know what it's called!"

Slowly, Izabella spread the fingers of her left hand and let her palm hover over the cards, all the while looking into her daughter's eyes, listening to the vibrations of her voice. Such fear. Such loneliness. Her palm came to rest above the image of a *vardo* carved with hearts and flowers, the card some called the Ace of Cups. "Love is not to be seized, little one, only accepted."

Priscilla turned to Kate. Tears filled her eyes and her voice quivered as she pleaded, "Make her stop."

Kate sat down across from Izabella. "Momma, I know this is hard for you to understand, but Prissy and I . . . well, we don't share your ways."

"You used to. You could again if only—"

"No." With her left hand, Kate picked up several cards from

the table. "We aren't demanding that you give up your ways. Only that you keep them to yourself. This isn't Europe." She gathered the rest of the cards and eased them into a pile. "People here aren't interested in Gypsies and *vardo*s and *dukker*ing and all the rest."

Izabella reached into the *poachy* of her flowered housedress and withdrew the brochure and the three theater tickets. "Oh, but they are," she said as she spread the items on the table. "Look."

Priscilla came closer and stood beside her sister. "What is all that?"

"See for yourselves," Izabella said, easing the tickets toward them.

Kate picked up the brochure and read aloud. "Gypsy Caravan—An Authentic Passport to Music and Magic. Eight o'clock, Thursday and Friday, June—"

"That's next week." Priscilla read from one of the tickets. "Center orchestra seats. You paid for these?"

"No, I stole them." Izabella laughed. "Of course I paid for them. They're for us . . . you girls and me. If you like it, we can go again Friday. Oh, how good it will be for you girls to hear the music of your destiny, to see—"

"We're not going." Priscilla slapped the tickets on the table. "I'm sorry. You'll have to return our tickets. We can't go. Impossible. We have plans." She gave her sister a meaningful look.

"The theater allows no refunds," Izabella said, unable to hide her disappointment. "Can you not change your plans? Just this once?"

"No!" Priscilla snapped.

"Prissy doesn't mean to be so harsh, Momma. But she's right. We do have plans that night. In fact, we were hoping you and Delia might get together that evening. Maybe she will go to the show with you."

"Delia is going to her son's home in Brooklyn."

"I'm sorry. If only you had asked us first."

Izabella gathered the tickets and the program and tucked them back into her *poachy*. "I see. At last."

CENTER orchestra, row E. Izabella sat in the center of the row, an empty seat on each side of her. As a peace offering to her daughters, she had worn the outfit they had given her: conservative navy blue suit, white blouse, sensible shoes. She had refused, however, to abandon her gold earrings, the coin-filled hoops her late husband had given her those many years ago.

Far more importantly, she had a plan.

Earlier that night, just before Izabella left the house, Piroska had pressed a small, red leather purse into her hands. "Take it," she had insisted. "It has everything you need. Money, tickets, tissues, and a comb." When Izabella opened the bag to retrieve her ticket for the usher, she saw what else the purse contained. Now, as she watched the show, she clutched the bag close to her heart, trying to soothe the sadness within.

At her feet was her large leather satchel, the one in which she kept the tools for making magick. In it was the red and gold wedding scarf she normally wore on her head, her blue altar cloth, a pouch of fresh thyme, a willow branch, a candle, and a small cauldron.

Tonight she would call the ancestors.

HER palms still tingled from applauding the *lautari*—men who played the accordion, violins, double bass, and cymbals carried around the neck. She had shown equal pleasure for the women who danced with passion, snapping their skirts as they twirled in bare feet around the campfire. But the theater was empty now. Almost.

Izabella had hidden in a supply closet backstage and waited for the performers, patrons, ushers, and staff from the box office, marketing, and facilities to leave. She waited while the sound engineer stored the microphones, the prop man arranged the small items used in the show, and the wardrobe mistress readied the costumes.

The last onstage was always the head electrician. She waited while he performed the ritual of carrying the ghost light to the edge of the stage. He plugged it in, turned off all the other lights, and walked out, the security guard close behind.

At last, she was alone.

The heels of her sensible shoes echoed as she walked across the stage.

Her chest felt heavy as she stood still and faced the empty seats. She knelt down. That her bones creaked didn't bother her; she had lived to be a crone. Not everyone was as lucky. The hinges on her old leather satchel scratched the air as she opened the bag. The contents were minimal but sufficient.

While at work that morning she had cut a six-foot length of willow from the tree outside the theater, wound the supple branch in a circle, and tucked it in her bag. Now she removed the willow, held it by the cut end, and let the slender whip fall gracefully from her fingers.

The air vibrated with the memory of music and the mingling scents of perfumes. She raised the willow over her head and circled it slowly round her body three times, till the tendril brushed against her face, her breasts, her hips. The energy gathered.

She stretched out her arm, letting the willow drag along the floor. Standing straight, her chin lifted, she raised her voice. "I call the East, and the Spirit of Air. With your powerful wind, cleanse this space. With your gentle breeze, ease the way for those I call to this night's circle."

She made a quarter turn, and as she did, drew the tip of the willow along the floor. "I call the South and the Spirit of Fire. Fill this night's circle with passion, that those who enter will walk without fear on destiny's path."

Again, she turned a quarter, drew the willow along the circular path, and stopped. "I call the West and the Spirit of Water. Soothe the hearts of all who enter this night's circle."

One last turn. "I call the North and the Spirit of Earth. Bring the bounty of all your seasons to nurture all who enter this night's circle."

The circle cast, she laid the willow at her feet. Palms down, she moved the air around her feet in waves. She drew it up like rising water. It lapped at her knees, rose past her hips, swirled about her throat. She lifted her arms above her head, drawing the air along the path made by her palms till all around, above, and below her pulsed with a readiness for magick.

She knelt again. In the center of the halo created by the ghost light, she spread the Persian blue cloth her grandmother's grandmother had embroidered in symbols ancient and long-forgotten by most. She groomed the silky fringe with her fingers until all four edges lay flat and smooth against the hardwood floor.

From her satchel she retrieved a small, three-legged iron cauldron and centered it on the cloth. Into it, she placed a white candle. She had given up her pipe long ago, but still carried matches. She struck one and reverently brought the flame to the wick, saying as she did, "With fire, I pledge devotion to the hearth and hearts of the Wise Ones who now walk the path on the Other Side. I call you now. Guide me."

She had taken a snip of thyme from the pots growing so orderly on the sill of the kitchen window. She pulled the herb from her satchel and pinched off several of the tiny dark green leaves. She bruised them between her fingers then dropped them on the flame.

Like chords of music, the scents of musk and evergreen, damp earth, curry, and warm horse flesh played around her. She dropped more thyme on the flame.

From all directions, a glittering fog rolled in and shrouded the plywood props.

As though being summoned, Izabella stood. She gazed across the stage as light and mist gathered in a column.

"My Zoltan!" Her voice caught as she stared at the man she had married so long ago, the man she had loved every day since. With his raven black hair and eyes, he looked as young and handsome as the day he had been struck down. "My Zoltan," she murmured. He stood with his legs apart, his feet in thigh-high leather boots, his dark pants cut wide above the knees, his white full-sleeved shirt open at the neck, a red and gold *diklo* knotted at his throat. A small gold hoop—the one she had given him—pierced his left ear.

She walked toward him. As the fog enveloped her feet, her shoes disappeared. The skirt of her navy suit loosened and became a circle of red and green ruffles. Ribbons of gold and white streamed from her waist. A breeze fluttered her hair. Long, lustrous, and black, it billowed about her shoulders, left bare now by the white lace blouse that skimmed across her breasts. "My Zoltan."

In the silence she heard his heartbeat.

He smiled and took her hand. "Bella."

At his touch, she heard the plaintive cry of violins and felt the heat of the campfire. Her *vardo,* the one she and Zoltan had shared, stood in place of the pressboard wagon. The moon, once a painted prop, grew luminous, big, and round, pale gold like the tambourine now in Izabella's hand.

He traced her cheek with his fingers. "Dance for me, Bella."

Like it was yesterday, she slapped the tambourine against her hip and the heel of her hand. She twirled around him, her steps sure and graceful. In his eyes, she saw the fire of the passion that marked their wedding night. In his smile, she saw the love that filled their marriage.

Breathless, she stopped in front of him and held out her hand. "Dance with me, Zoltan."

Smiling, he slid one hand around her waist, and with the other, drew her close.

Izabella pressed her lips to his chest. From the violins that had been so spirited now came a hungry sound, slow and undulating, hot as fever, sultry as the sheen on his skin. They danced.

"Like apple wine," he whispered just before he kissed her.

It could have been yesterday, so familiar was the ritual of his touch. "Come," Izabella said as she led him to their vardo.

"Ah," he said with a grin while his hand slid below her waist, "you aim to bewitch me?"

"I already have."

Hours later, they sat on a log in front of the glowing embers, all that remained of the fire.

Zoltan kicked the coals with his boot, sending a column of flickering red sparks into the air. "I long to see our girls again."

Izabella hung her head. "They are house-dwellers now."

"Both of them?"

"Hooked by the lure of a seaside cottage with picket fence, that was Katarina. And our little Piroska, well . . ." Izabella looked across the stage where the red clutch lay on the floor. "Her heart is heavy."

They sat a while in silence, his arm around her waist, her head on his shoulder.

"Come with me," Zoltan said, his voice ragged.

"In time."

"Now." He took her hands and drew her to her feet.

"But, Zoltan—"

"I don't want to lose you again."

She had waited so long to be with him. But the time was not right. She had told no one the secrets of healing, of seeing time past and yet to be.

"You hesitate? Think with care, Bella, for I cannot come to you again."

She stepped back. Others in the clan knew how to cast a circle, to draw down the moon. But she had given her magick to no one. If she died now, it would die with her.

With confidence in his stride, Zoltan walked to the altar on the floor. "Why would you summon me if not to join me?" He picked up the willow wand, rolled and tied it like a rope, and packed it in the satchel.

"But it was not you I summoned." Izabella joined him. "I called the ancestors."

"What was it you sought from them?"

"Guidance."

Zoltan picked up the red clutch. A piece of paper, tightly folded, crisply creased, fell from it. "What's this?"

"The weight on Piroska's heart."

Zoltan read aloud.

My Mother,

I seem unable to speak without hurting you. I don't wish it so, but so it is.

I write this letter to ask your forgiveness. For my harsh words, yes. But most of all for my actions that morning so long ago . . . for disobeying and leaving my pony untethered, for making Poppa run after it into the meadow, beneath such an angry sky.

Please find it in your heart to forgive me. If I could make amends

by following your path, I would; but that is impossible. The Gypsy
blood in me runs cold.
Priscilla

Zoltan looked up with anguish in his eyes. "The child blames herself?"

Izabella nodded, her throat too tight to speak.

"But the fault was my own!" Zoltan said, rising. "When I felt the air stir with menace, felt the sting on my skin, I knew to drop to the ground. But no, I stood tall, daring the gods to challenge me."

A sound from the lobby startled them.

"No!" Izabella cried. "Not yet!"

The frantic voices of their daughters grew louder. Izabella reached for her husband.

"Bella!" he called as his image faded before her eyes.

The music stopped. The stars vanished. The fog disappeared. The *vardo* returned to a pressboard prop.

The girls shoved open the door to the theater, a security guard close behind.

"Momma!" Kate called as she ran down the aisle toward the stage. "It's all right! We're here!" She hurried through the door that led backstage and in seconds stood at her mother's side.

Izabella stumbled for words as she saw the confusion on Katarina's face and then Piroska's as they both stared at her. Her navy skirt, unzipped, had twisted to an odd angle. Her half-buttoned blouse hung outside the skirt like a disheveled rag. She stood in stockinged feet, only one of her sensible shoes nearby, the other tossed across the stage.

"Momma, what happened?" Katarina looked in her mother's eyes.

"You know good and well what happened," Piroska said.

The guard joined them on the stage. "What's going on here?"

Katarina gently finger-combed Izabella's white hair into a braid.

"I think that's obvious," Piroska said as she retrieved the shoe from across the stage. "Our mother is ill." She set the shoes in front of Izabella and nudged her to put them on. "She had a heart attack not long ago." She guided Izabella's arms into the jacket of her suit. "And right now, all we need is to get her home where she can rest." She took Izabella's arm by the elbow. "Come on, Mother. We have to go."

They took several steps toward the door before Piroska turned back, a look of panic on her face.

"Don't worry," Katarina said as she knelt by the satchel. "I'll take care of this." To the guard, she said, "Please help my sister get our mother to the car. I'll be out in a few moments."

The guard looked concerned. "For heaven's sake," Piroska said, "my mother works here. She's not going to steal anything."

"I wasn't implying—"

"No," Piroska snapped. "Of course you weren't."

"I just thought maybe your mother needed an ambulance."

"No! Just help us get out of here."

The guard stepped in front of Izabella. "Ma'am, I got the ambulance number on speed dial and I know all the EMTs. You want me to call?"

Slowly, Izabella shook her head. "My daughter is right. What I need is to go home."

Guided by her daughter and the guard, Izabella left the stage. Halfway up the aisle toward the lobby, she paused and looked back, just long enough to see Katarina kneel down next to the satchel and pick up the cauldron. The tambourine moon still glowed with the iridescence of magick.

"WELL, I don't know about you two, but I can't sit here forever." Priscilla eased her chair back and stood.

Early morning light caught the crystals hanging in the kitchen window, spilling prisms onto the table where Kate and Izabella still sat.

Kate reached across the table to pat her mother's hand. "She's right. You should go to bed now."

"We should all go to bed now," Priscilla said, "or skip sleep altogether." She yawned and stepped away from the table. "I'm too tired to think."

"A moment, please," Izabella said, "I have something to say." She smiled at Priscilla, sad to see such apprehension on her face. "Sit down," she said and tapped her hand gently on the table.

When both girls were again seated, Izabella reached across the table and took Priscilla's hand. "The burden you carry is heavy and not rightly yours."

"Oh, no. Please, I don't want to discuss this. Now now—"

"Listen to me. You did not cause your poppa's death."

Priscilla pulled her hand away and covered her face. With shoulders hunched as though to hug herself, she sobbed softly.

"It was his time." Izabella looked from one daughter to the other. "Just as it is time for me to return to the clan. My destiny lies unfulfilled, so I must go, with or without your help."

"No, Momma! Not now!" Katarina jumped up from the table and rushed into the other room.

She returned with the leather satchel, placed it on her chair, and reached inside. As she pulled out the branch she looked in her mother's eyes and said, "A wand to cast the circle. Made of willow to call the dead. Yes?"

Izabella nodded. Shimmering in the air between them, she saw Katarina standing on the Jernigan stage, a glittering fog swirling about her feet.

"And this"—Katarina held up the candle—"to welcome the spirits."

"Yes," Isabella said. The word turned to vapor as it floated to the vision and became a flame in Katarina's outstretched palm.

"And this"—Katarina held the small cauldron—"for casting spells."

"So," Izabella said, "You have not become a *gaujo* after all. Good."

The kitchen became a meadow, with a circle of dazzling *vardo*s hitched to horses with silver bridles. Children ran freely, squealing at the puppies nipping their heels. The older children crowded around a group of men playing violins.

"But what of this?" Katarina held a pinch of green leaves.

"Thyme. To thin the veil between the worlds." Izabella gestured toward the window. "Snipped from your sister's herb garden."

Priscilla grabbed a napkin and wiped her eyes. "They're for cooking."

"They are for many things."

Katarina bruised the leaves in her fingers, brought them to her nose, and inhaled.

Zoltan appeared in the sun-drenched meadow. The twinkle in his eyes matched his booming voice as he called to the musicians. "Play a lively tune! I wish to dance with my daughters." Only one figure joined him.

Katarina stared at the herbs in her hand. "Momma, please stay . . . show me how."

Izabella arched a brow in mock confusion. "To cook?"

"No," Katarina said softly, her breath suspended. "To conjure."

"Kate!" Priscilla gave her sister a look that was, at first, puzzled, then resigned.

Izabella leaned back in her chair and nodded slowly. "*Parika tut,*" she whispered. "Thank you." Eyes closed, she envisioned the clan moving on without her, but so mote it be, for she had at last found the vessel for her secrets.

It would take years to teach Katarina. Eyes still closed, Izabella saw her first-born comfortable under the mantle of *chovihani*. She saw little Piroska with a babe of her own, conceived on a blanket under the stars, in an open field.

"About last night," Katarina said, then paused. "We need to talk."

"Ah, yes, about last night." Izabella felt her husband's arm about her waist, then tucked the memory in her heart. "Girls," she said with conspiratorial delight, "I danced with your poppa last night."

Priscilla bit her lip as though to bar her thoughts from spilling, then said simply, "I'm glad."

Katarina picked up the cauldron and grinned. "So did I."

A Spell for Seeing Your Path of Destiny

ZELENA WINTERS

Destiny is a wide road. Many of us travel with unsure feet, and eyes blind to the signs along the way. To illuminate your own path, cast this spell.

Materials:

- A white candle to signify your pure intention
- A black candle to absorb your fears
- 13 stones to symbolize your path

Preparation begins at the first quarter moon, when the tension of separation is strong.

During the week between the first quarter moon and the full moon, spend time walking and thinking about your life over the last twelve years. Remember journeys taken, classes studied, influential movies and books, jobs (both those you took and those you left), relationships (those that brought joy and those that scarred your heart), moves, accidents and discoveries, joys and disappointments, friends and family who entered and left your life. Pick thirteen stones to represent thirteen such steps along your path. The stones don't have to be uniform in size, shape, or color; they don't have to be pretty.

Cast the spell at the full moon:

(Arrange the stones in a circle. As you place each one, notice its physical characteristics. Is the stone rough? Smooth? Plain? Colored? Veined? Chipped? Shiny?

(Place the white candle in the center of the circle. As you light the candle, say the following, or similar words of your own choosing: *With faith in the Divine, I accept my path. I trust that each step leads to the fulfillment of my Spirit.*

(One at a time, pick up each stone and meditate on why you selected that particular stone to represent a particular person or passage in your life. As you return each stone to the circle, say *Thank you for your lesson.*

(Place the black candle in the center of the circle, next to the white candle. As you light it, say the following, or similar words of your own choosing: *With faith in the Divine, I release my fear. I accept the courage to walk my path.*

(As you blow out the candles, say: *So mote it be.*

(Place the stones where you can see them daily as a reminder of both your path and your progress.

I recommend keeping a journal devoted to the wisdom gained from casting this spell.

The Letter

CELIA MOON

The letter came on a Thursday morning. It was in a pale gray envelope of very good quality and carried no return address. Fern's name and address were written in clear, utilitarian hand-writing on the front.

She did not receive much personal mail, at least not in the mailbox. What she did get came via e-mail, on the computer, so the letter intrigued her enough that she spent an enjoyable few moments running through the possibilities—a long-lost high school friend, maybe, or a note from a student, or a kind letter from a faraway aunt or cousin. It was a quiet morning, sunlight gilding down to the porch in melted-butter waves, and the only sounds were the chirping of finches in the pear tree and, high above, the drone of an airplane. A perfection of summer, which created a perfect expectation of good.

It was true it might only be a solicitation from a real estate salesperson, or some other thing of that nature. She checked the postmark, however, and she couldn't quite read the town, but the bottom of the circle showed MONTANA in little capitals. Hmm. She didn't know anyone in Montana that she could think of, but that didn't mean anything.

With a small smile of anticipation, she tucked the rest of the mail under her arm—her husband's *Sports Illustrated,* the water bill, the school newsletter, and a note from her mother— and flipped the pale gray envelope over. She slid a fingernail beneath the flap and suddenly felt a wave of fierce warning.

She paused. Should she simply throw it away, then? This emotion—fear and warning mingled in a rich stew—had protected her many times during a very terrible time in her life. She was loath to ignore it.

But as she stood there, sunlight gilding her bare feet, the warning passed. Taking a breath, she extracted a single neat sheet of paper. In standard Times New Roman, twelve-point face, was a letter that began:

Dear Fern,

I have no right to come into your life this way after so long, but I have been so haunted the past few weeks that I will have no peace until I write this letter. Forgive me if it causes pain. I think in the end, it will give more peace than sorrow.

Fern took a breath against the sharp sense of body memory that clutched her lungs, and the mail that had been tucked under her arm fell out suddenly, scattering over the wide oak boards of the porch. The words on the page blurred in a sudden rush of dark memory, and she took a hiccuping breath.

She folded the letter and tried to fit it back into the envelope, but found she could not do it because her hands were shaking. Instead, she fitted them together, envelope and letter, back to back, then bent down and picked up the dropped magazines and newsletters, her mind on stun.

Would she never be allowed to forget all of it?

Going inside to the kitchen, she left all of the mail in the usual spot next to a blue glass vase that just now held a spray of exuberantly sexual poppies with their trembling, shivery stamens. The petals were pink with black spots, and scatterings of black pollen fell to the table. Fern took a glass from the cupboard above them and turned on the water at the sink until it was cold, filled the glass, and drank it down as fast as she could.

It helped and she did it again, drinking the second glass more slowly. On the windowsill was a second vase, this one made of crystal that caught the evening sunlight and threw dancing rainbows into the room as she cooked supper. It held two dried white roses and a sprig of dried rue. The aromatic seed pods of the rue released some of the very last of its tiny scrap of scent as she rubbed her fingers on them.

"Oh, Mother!" Fern whispered. "How much longer? Lend me wisdom and strength. Protect me from myself and others."

She turned. The letter lay in the open, where Fern's daughters might see it, and she picked it up and leaned one hip on the counter, holding the paper loosely in her fingers. The sun moved, reflecting from the window next door, and a fingering of light danced inside the cut crystal vase. Memories crowded in, sad ones and joyous ones, good ones and bad ones. Resistance built in her chest and she almost wanted to cry. Hadn't she paid long enough for her abuse of the Rede?

A soft voice in her heart said, *What we resist will persist,* and, with a sigh of release, she let the memories come.

Three Years Before

"I shouldn't be giving you this." The words were spoken by Gina Walters, Fern's only connection to the larger pagan community in her town. Fern was a solitary, a hedge Witch with an

eclectic tradition gathered in equal measures from the earth religions of her youth, and her time in Haiti, and her studies of
Wicca. Her training was not formal, but she was devoted to the
Rede, the single, simple directive given to practitioners of
magic: Harm none.

It sounded obvious. Whatever you did came back to you times
three, so the guiding principle of life was to put out only good in
the world. In theory, it was so simple that even the smallest of
children could grasp it. In reality, it was quite difficult at times.
Witches were, after all, only human, given to the same longings
and hungers as the rest of the population. Knowing that there
were spells out in the world to summon a particular lover or
bring bad luck to an enemy was sometimes a hard thing.

It was quite human to want to manipulate events to bring
about a heart's desire. Once an old Witch had told Fern that re-
sisting rationalizations for working magic against the Rede was
as difficult as staying on a diet and it was better to just keep the
tempting stuff out of the house—or her head.

So that was what Fern had done. She knew manipulative
spells existed, but she chose not to read them, think about them,
give them any room in her life.

Until now.

And there was worry in her as she held the paper in her
hand, close to her palm. "I know," she said, dashing away the
tears that threatened to fall—by the heavens, she was sick of
weeping!—and took a breath. "You know I wouldn't ask it if I
had any other options, but I really feel that I'm battling something big here, something huge, and so monstrously misguided
that if I don't act, many lives are going to be damaged, including hers." Joyce, the other woman, who had deliberately set out
to take another woman's lover. Very bad, that.

Fern let go of an exhausted sigh. Was it just a rationalization?
"I am so lost. But it feels all wrong, Gina. It really does."

Gina put her hands around Fern's wrists. Her own blue eyes filled with tears. "I know, sweetie. Just be careful, all right? Guard against negativity. Search your heart."

Fern nodded. "I've thought very seriously about this, I promise you. I will only protect myself and my family and only halt any evil influence she has. And I'll only bind her for a little while, until I'm sure it's safe to let her go." She bit her lip, fighting more tears. "I won't interfere with his free will, either."

"I know," Gina whispered, and flung her plump arms around Fern's neck, pulling her close and rocking her back and forth for a long, deep moment. "I wish you didn't have to do this, that it had never happened. And if it helps at all, I'd probably do the same thing."

"Thank you," Fern whispered.

BACK at home, Fern waited for the girls to go to bed—at fourteen, eleven, and nine, that was a lot later than it had been. Even then, she waited another hour to be sure they were asleep before she slid her movable altar (which doubled as the breakfast bar) quietly away from the wall to the middle of the kitchen. She'd mopped the floor and cleansed the area earlier; now she scrubbed the table and covered it with the altar cloth she kept tucked in a special drawer. The smell of incense drifted out of it as it fluttered into place. She smoothed it flat and set up the candles for Lord and Lady, a bowl for incense, a chalice for holy water, and a small crystal dish of consecrated salt. When it was ready, she cast a protective spell over it, to keep the area clean until she came back to it. The usual order was to cleanse oneself, then set up the altar, but Fern was prompted to do it differently tonight.

It was herself who needed the most powerful cleansing tonight if she were going to work good magic. She was fearful.

She was exhausted. She was sorrowful. To make sure she didn't release harm into the world, into her life or the lives of the others she was involving tonight, she had to remove as many of those influences as she could.

At first what she mainly did was stand beneath the shower spray, wishing that she was just getting ready for bed as always. That she was going to get out of the shower and go climb into bed next to Jake, her big warm bear of a husband. Jake with his thick black beard and laughing blue eyes and solid round of tummy that she liked to rub. They had been together since junior high, since she had walked into biology and saw him sitting there in his red shirt.

There had never really been anyone else, though they'd taken a year off once, when Jake was twenty-two and Fern was twenty-one. She went to the Dominican Republic to teach with the Peace Corps. Jake wandered, taking odd jobs, sleeping with bartenders, and briefly involving himself with a nurse in Austin, who tended a leg he broke on a construction site. Fern had believed for a time that she might be in love with another man, a fierce crusader of a doctor who offered her a vision of the future—and herself—that was not at all what she saw with Jake. Tenderly, she had imagined a life spent in service to others, nurturing lost children and poverty-stricken mothers, spreading love and joy through the world. It had seemed so very noble.

But then her doctor had asked her to marry him, and Fern cried all night. Somehow, across the miles and the hours, Jake had sensed her distress, and called her from a pay phone in a Seattle bus station. They talked for two hours, and by the end of the conversation, they knew the inevitable. They were homesick apart from each other. Three months later, the day Fern returned to the United States, they were married in a simple ceremony in an adobe church, surrounded by sweet-smelling pines.

And all these years, it had been good. Not just acceptable. Not just okay. Good. Peaceful, full of laughter and sex, struggle and honor, tenderness and ferocity. Any fighting was punctuated by a recommitted sense of union.

Standing in the shower, tears running down her face, Fern tried to hold to that vision of her union with her husband. It was powerful and real.

This breach was the illusion. She did not know why things had suddenly gone foul between them. She didn't know why he had strayed into another woman's arms—a woman who was so agonizingly lonely that Fern found it difficult to even hate her for her deliberate and successful attempt to seduce Jake into her bed.

In truth, Fern didn't blame anyone. Things like this just happened sometimes to mundanes. The woman was lonely. Jake was lost.

The past couple of years had been undeniably difficult in Fern and Jake's lives. Little things—a fender bender with the car, extra dental work on one of the girls, a seemingly endless list of plumbing problems in their old house. All the little things added up, and it seemed they never had quite enough money for anything extra, like fun. A mistake, she realized now, though she'd just been trying to be a good steward.

Then there were some very big things—Jake's old, beloved dog simply died one night in his sleep; there was a major reorganization in his company and half the crew was let go before the dust settled; one of their friends was diagnosed with leukemia, and Fern spent a lot time to help care for her and her children.

Through it all, Fern struggled to hang on to a sense of perspective—life had its ups and downs, and they were just going through a down cycle, a dark phase. Sooner or later, the sun would come out again.

Jake was moody and sorrowful and sometimes distant, but she gave him his space, cuddling up to him at night as she'd always done. And as he'd always done, he lifted his arm to give her room to tuck herself next to him. At night, holding each other, things settled. They were home.

Which was what made his announcement, three weeks before, so unbelievably shocking. He had met another woman. Fallen in love. Was moving out. Now.

Fern was blindsided. She kept blinking, looking at this man she knew like her own body, wondering what demon was speaking out of his mouth. She just couldn't seem to get past her shock, even when he packed his things and actually moved. It was unreal, absurd.

A classic response, her friends said to her. Men can do that, be duplicitous, change horses in the middle of the stream. Go ahead and grieve, they said, then let it go.

And she might have. Except that Jake did not seem particularly happy about it. He called her every day, just as he'd always done, to remind her to see to the light on the porch or get a tool for the car. He brought her plants from a patio job where they'd had to dig up the backyard. He cried over his girls, who were trying to be loving and were very angry.

That was the really weird thing—the girls. Jake might love another person. That part wasn't so hard—he was a generous, giving kind of man. He liked taking care of people and giving them a good vision of themselves, and the woman—whom Fern had decided to meet on her own—was a very lost, hungry kind of person. But Fern did not see that Jake would leave his children. It went against all that he was, all that he believed. Divination had shown her, over and over, that there was a malevolent, misguided force at work.

Not, she didn't think, the other woman. Something preying on that other woman.

And yet, what to do? What was there ever to do when people fell away from themselves? In the depths of her sorrow and loss, Fern had cried out, "Mother, help me!"

And as if the Goddess came and sat with her right then, Fern felt a great sense of calm move in her. A directive came to her mind—she often heard the Lady in a musical voice like this: *Do not despair, daughter. Do not give up. You must fight for your family. For him.*

So Fern fought, using methods both mundane and magical. She called a therapist. She did magic nearly every night, rituals, communication rituals, loving rituals. She asked for blessings for all involved. She sought the advice of all the elders she could ask, and went to the library to flip through books on the grief process and on midlife crises. She wrote letters to the other woman, asking her to consider what the cost to Jake might be.

Nothing. The situation, only four weeks old as she stepped out of the shower that November night, only worsened. Jake looked more haggard each time she saw him, as if he were being devoured by some internal evil. He was sleeping in a fleabag hotel, stuck between two choices, and their daughters were beginning to look for ways to exploit the situation.

The sense of impending doom continued to grow until Fern could barely eat. Somehow, Jake was in trouble in this if she didn't do something. She had no idea what or how or when, only that she was the only one who could act.

Whatever it cost her, she had to free him.

She called her friend Gina for help. Major magical help.

Which she would work tonight. Wiping the mirror, she saw that her own face was haggard. There were circles under her eyes. She'd lost weight. "Not much of a warrior," she said to her refection. Her mouth went grim. Hard.

She was the only warrior she had.

Adorned in her robes, she went back downstairs and gathered her tools. Two black candles and one white; rosemary, rue, and dragon's blood to scatter on the floor and altar, one red string and one black one. A piece of paper with the woman's name on it, and the paper that Gina had given her with the spell on it.

She lit candles on the counter and turned off the light, then cast her circle by walking the perimeter three times, scattering salt and rue seeds as she went. Salt to cleanse and rue to protect. And as she walked, she chanted a purifying spell—to purify herself of ill-intentions, anything she knew and anything she didn't. The chant eased her. Sorrow and worry slid away—here was the truth of all things, in the sphere of Spirit, where woman and Goddess connected.

Returning to her starting place, she lit the candles and called the forces of the Goddess to help her. Power shimmered in her egg-shaped bubble, taking a silvery hue as she began to speak. Tonight she would call Hecate to her aid, a Goddess who understood the need for dark action.

When the opening rituals were finished, she lit the black candles and picked up the rolled-up piece of paper and the black string.

And a jolt of something hot went through her chest. A flash of anger.

For a moment, she hesitated, wondering if she needed to cleanse herself further. She nudged it. A spark only. Not enough to ruin the ritual, surely, even one as delicate as this.

Taking the black string in her right hand, she said, "I bind thee, thief, from acting in harm." She wrapped the string around the scroll, over and over, chanting, "I now bind thee, I now bind thee."

In that instant, Fern saw a flash of the woman's face and heard her name loudly in her mind: *Joyce.*

She froze, the black string wrapped tightly, ready to be tied, and waited for what was to be revealed. Breathing in, she closed her eyes. "I accept what must be shown," she said, and she saw a vision of her own hands upon Joyce's head, drawing out a black mist.

Fern cried out in protest, "I can't! Don't ask it!" She had been called to put her hands on people only a few times—on a boy who was dying of his alcoholism, on an old woman standing next to her at the grocery store, and a few others. The experience was not easy, but the call was so compelling she'd never been able to resist it.

Not this time. No. Fiercely, defiantly, she chanted, "I bind thee!" and tied the black string.

There was more. The red string had to be tied in a long ritual using a chant, one meant to discourage thieves, and Fern managed to get it done, her voice becoming a thin whisper as she worked through to the end, tying a total of nine knots in the red string. When she finished, closing out the circle and thanking the Goddess, it was all she could do to clean up and put things away before falling, exhausted, into her bed.

In the morning, she awakened feeling very calm for the first time in weeks. She wandered out to the garden with a cup of coffee. Wrapped in a sweater, she listened to birds chirping and whistling in the trees. A soft gray sky covered the world with a gentleness, and Fern felt that she could breathe again.

"Thank you," she whispered to the heavens, and she felt a sense of the Mother with her once more, long fingers smoothing her hair from her face. And with a jolt, she saw again the lowered eyes and high brow of the other woman—*JOYCE!* said a voice in her head—and Fern's own hands on Joyce's head.

No.

Fern took a breath, feeling her resistance thicken. It might well be wrong, a sin, something that would haunt her, but not even at the urging of the Goddess could she imagine putting her hands on her enemy in a spirit of healing. The very thought made her tremble in fury.

This once she could not do it.

Besides, how in the world would she manage it? Just walk up to her husband's mistress and say, "Uh, excuse me. Mind if I put my hands on you?"

Shaking her head, she turned to go back inside, and started when a figure emerged from the house. "Oh!" she said, putting a hand to her chest even as she recognized Jake. "You scared me to death." Moving toward him, she tried to be calm and without rancor. "What's up?"

He stood on the porch step, the silver threads in his beard catching the light just so, and his blue eyes were solemn. "I want to come home."

She halted, a soft surety in her heart, and waited.

"I've been so lost and I've made huge mistakes and I don't know what I was thinking, but I miss you and the girls and nothing seems real without you." He spread his hands open, palms out. "I don't deserve it, and I don't know how to make it up to you, but I'd really like it if you'd let me try."

Fern moved across the grass, put her coffee cup down on the table, and put her arms around her husband's neck. "Oh, I have missed you," she whispered. "Like a limb."

And there would be dark days ahead, sorrows to overcome, trust to rebuild, but when Jake pulled her to him, burying his face into her neck in a gesture of relief, all she felt was purest joy. *Thank you*, she silently whispered. *Thank you.*

AND that, Fern thought, was that. Jake came home and worked to make things right. Fern worked to let it all go, take joy in the fact that she'd seen the truth of the situation and acted to correct it, even if it had meant manipulative magic. The evil was broken.

But within two months, Fern discovered a fly in the ointment: wherever she went, she saw the other woman, Joyce. She saw her buying milk at the grocery store, discovered she was in the car next to her at the car wash, they were in the same department store, in the same aisle, reaching for the same coat.

They did not speak. One or the other would turn away, jaw set, and they would go in opposite directions, hearts pounding. Or at least, Fern's heart pounded—in murderous rage, rage so wild she sometimes got a headache from it and had to go home and lie down.

And the graphic, physical nature of her rage was terrifying. When she saw Joyce, her unhappiness like a drab gray cloak around her shoulders, Fern did not feel sympathy. She didn't wish to reach out and take away the suffering, as she'd been prompted to do.

No, she wanted to use her hands as weapons—she wanted to peel the flesh from the woman's cheekbones, grind her bones to dust, hear her scream as she pierced her nails into her skin.

One dark May day, Fern turned a corner in a rose garden and there stood Joyce. She hunched her shoulders and started to walk away, making Fern think of nothing so much as a street dog that had been kicked too often. Her shoulder blades poked out of her back like ears.

But it didn't kindle sympathy. Instead, the wild black-and-red rage swirled out like mad insects. "Why did you do that to my family?" Fern cried after her. "Don't you understand how much pain you caused me?"

The other woman turned. "I didn't mean to hurt you. He just made me feel so good. I needed him more than you did."

The rage trebled, blinding and choking her. Fern stumbled, as if she'd been pushed, and she turned away, her blood pounding, screaming, her hands burning hot. In her imagination, she saw her hands on Joyce, but the power was so destructive that her hands left blackened, burned marks where they had landed.

Walk, said the Mother. *Breathe and walk and keep moving.*

It made Fern ill, the ferocity of her rage. And it gained in power as the months passed, even as Joyce began to wither right in front of her eyes, growing thinner and thinner until she looked as if she might disappear.

At last Fern went to see Gina, the Witch who'd given her the binding spell. "What do I do?"

Gina flung her long bushy hair away from her face. "You've bound her to you," she said with a serious expression. "I'm not sure where the rage is coming from, but maybe if you stop seeing her so often you'll be able to let it go and the rage will just disappear."

"I'm afraid to unbind her," Fern confessed. "What if she decides to take him away again?"

Gina raised her eyebrows. "Then maybe she was supposed to."

Fern bowed her head. Nodded. She couldn't live with the anger that was eating her alive. In the end it would destroy her. That evening, she went to the secret drawer and took out the scroll with Joyce's name on it, cut the black string around it, and tore the piece of paper to bits, blowing them into the wind in the backyard. "I release you," she said.

She'd also taken out the red string with its nine knots, and this she tucked into her pocket, then she went to find Jake. "Honey, do you feel like taking a walk with me?"

"Sure," he said, putting aside the newspaper and rubbing his nose where his glasses had made a mark. He'd been working off his little paunch, and they often took a walk after supper these days.

"Which way?" He said as they stepped onto the sidewalk.

"East," Fern said. The direction of new beginnings.

Overhead, the evening sky was softly purple, the horizons going pinker as the sun lowered at the end of a day. From her pocket, Fern took the red string with its nine knots and intoned silently, *I unbind thee,* as she worked on the first knot. It was very tight, and it took a lot of prying to get it free, which for some reason made her chuckle.

"What?" Jake asked.

"A joke one of the girls told me," she said lightly. "Tell me about your day. How did the architect like your suggestions?"

Jake took his cue, launched into a tale of his day, a simple, happy thing she would never take for granted again. As he spoke, she untied the knots in the opposite order from the way she'd tied them, struggling once in a while to get one free. A lot of anger went into those knots, she realized.

Anger she'd only barely acknowledged to herself.

As she worked on the very last one, she said, "Do you ever run into Joyce?"

He started, a frown on his face. "I don't want to fight, okay? Let's just let bygones be bygones."

"I won't fight," she said. They'd topped a hill with a view of the town tucked into the river valley like a string of diamonds. "I was just curious."

"No," he said. "It's kind of funny, really, because I used to see her all the time." He lifted a shoulder, cleared his throat. "She saved jokes to give me."

Fern held the last knot between her fingers. "But you don't see her now."

He shook his head, then gave her a very serious look. "It wouldn't matter, though, Fern. You're my love. My wife. The only one." A slight shimmer of tears showed in his eyes and he blinked hard. "I don't know what happened to me. Maybe I never will, but I swear on all that's holy that you never have to worry about it again."

A wind swirled over them, and Fern lifted the untied string into it, letting it go before she leaned in and gently kissed her husband. "I love you," she said. "Thank you for coming home."

AND that should have been that, Fern thought, holding the letter from her nemesis in her hand, wondering if she had the courage to read it. Once she'd undone the binding, Fern stopped seeing Joyce all over the place, stopped seeing her anywhere at all, in fact. Fern wondered if Joyce had left town.

But of course, that wasn't that at all. Turning the letter over, then over again, Fern took a breath and let the last memories come to her.

ONE bright August day, Jake took the girls to the mountains for fishing—which Fern the vegetarian could not bear—and Fern went to see Gina in her bakery. It was midmorning, a lull time, and they carried bear claws and large mugs of café latte to a table by the big picture window. "So?"

Gina said. "Feeling any better?"

Fern gave her a wry smile. "I've learned a lot," she said ruefully. "About why manipulative magic is so dangerous and why we shouldn't use it."

"Ever?"

"I don't know," she said slowly, considering the question carefully as she stirred her coffee. "There was something wrong there—and the spell seemed to shatter the bad influence."

"Is it possible she cast a love spell over him?"

Fern straightened. "I never considered that. I suppose it's possible. It would explain a lot."

"Yeah," Gina said. She took a breath as if to add more, then hesitated.

"What?"

"I don't know. It was just such a weird response from Jake. Of all the guys. I just never thought he'd ever stray."

Tears sprung to Fern's eyes. "He wanted to take care of her. There I was, charging through the world with my herbs and cures, running the children around, taking care of everybody, and I didn't even see him. Everybody made me feel so needed and I just took it for granted that he'd say something if he needed me." She took a breath, squared her shoulders. "And there was this wounded bird in his path who needed him. That's his way, you know?"

"You're a lot more understanding than I would be, sister."

Fern shook her head. "No. We're just so connected. I had to admit to myself recently that I wouldn't have been able to keep a distance between us even if our marriage split up. I mean, it would be like divorcing a sister or a parent or an uncle. He's just a part of me, my life." She smiled softly. "I'm really glad things turned out this way, though. I like having him as my lover best of all."

Gina reached over and took her hand. "It was a bad season," she said, and they both thought of their friend Lida, who'd finally succumbed to her leukemia two months ago. "We all have to go through them, don't we?"

"Yeah, we do."

"So, the anger is gone. Anything else going on with it?"

Fern narrowed her eyes. "How did you know?"

"It's not finished."

"Why do you say that?"

"Two things: I've had seven dreams about the two of you— you and her, not you and Jake—and then I saw something in the paper that I want to share, but only in a minute."

"Dreams?" Fern's heart gave a guilty thump. She, too, had been having dreams. Almost every night, in fact, and all of them were variations on a theme: Joyce was in terrible trouble. A small flash of annoyance pushed the guilt away. "I don't think I should have to deal with her anymore. I think I've been pretty bloody magnanimous. I even wrote a letter of forgiveness—and did she send me a letter of apology in return? No." She huffed, flinging her body against the chair. "I mean, enough is enough, don't you think?"

Gina smiled softy, her motherly face with its rosy cheeks making Fern feel even guiltier. "I thought so. You're supposed to do something else, aren't you?"

Fern stared out the window at a cat washing its face in a puddle of lemon-colored sunlight. She wiggled her foot and didn't speak.

"Look," Gina said, more firmly. She pushed a newspaper clipping over the table.

Reluctantly, Fern picked it up. The small, bold headline read: SUICIDE THWARTED BY GOOD SAMARITAN.

Fern's heart dropped and she lifted alarmed eyes to Gina, who nodded soberly.

The article read:

A teen on his way home from work spied a forty-one-year-old woman in a car parked on the street and, worried that she seemed sick, opened the door to discover she was unconscious. He called 911 to get an ambulance. When attendants arrived, they discovered the woman in a coma, and she was rushed to a local hospital, where it was discovered she had taken a dose of barbiturates that would almost certainly have proved fatal without intervention. She was in serious but stable condition Monday morning.

Fern buried her face in her hands. "Oh, I have been so evil!"
"Take care of it."

*   *   *

So it was that Fern found herself on the way to the hospital after a ritual cleansing that took more than an hour. First she ran a hot bath, filled with Dead Sea salts, and bathed in it to cleanse her aura, her skin, her attitudes. Then she showered away the negativity that had been clinging to her, and waited as she filled the tub one more time, this only to a sitz bath level. Into it she poured a special combination of herbs—lavender for peace, rosemary for healing, cedar for purification. Into a tiny, embroidered bag she kept in a Tupperware bowl of salt between uses, she poured a combination of the same herbs. Then she lit three candles—white for the Goddess, pink for honor and love, and pale blue for health and healing.

Lowering her naked body into the bath, she rinsed herself head to toe with the herb-infused water, and then closed her eyes.

"Dearest Mother," she breathed, "in my pain and confusion, I have ignored your edict. I rededicate myself now to you and your purposes, knowing that you see what I cannot, that you lend truth and power and beauty to even the darkest of moments. I ask your forgiveness, and hope that you will grant another opportunity to put this sad situation to rest at last."

And there, in her tiny bathroom, Fern felt the all-loving, all-giving beauty of the Great Mother fill her up, pet her head, touch her face. *You are both my daughters*, She said. *I need your hands.*

In release and peace, Fern wept. And there, in her heart, she saw what the Goddess illuminated: a tight, hard ball of darkness in her heart, a ball made of sorrow and distrust and fear, a ball of negativity that would poison her eventually.

Harm none. Not others, not yourself. It was the way of the Rede, as simple and clear as anything that had ever been written.

Harm none.

*   *   *

FERN had to lie to the nurses, say she was family, to get into the room. She figured it wasn't much of a lie, anyway, since the Goddess Herself had said they were both Her daughters. Which made them sisters.

It was dim and quiet, the silence disturbed only by the soft electronic beeps of an IV pumping saline into the painfully thin arm of the woman lying so still beneath her sheets. For a moment, Fern was wracked with terror—what if Joyce awakened and freaked, and called for Fern to be kicked out? Then they'd never be free of this whole mess.

But although Joyce's eyelids fluttered a little, it was clear she was unconscious. Fern took a breath and really looked at her enemy. Really looked.

She could not weigh more than a hundred pounds, a sore point for a long time, since Fern was not exactly fashion-model slim. Okay, she wasn't even mother slim. She was an old hippie in a soft body, with breasts that had gone too many years without a bra and hips that showed some dimpling after three babies, and a tummy that wouldn't see daylight again in this lifetime.

Seeing Joyce the first time had cut right into all the motherly things Fern once liked about her body and made her feel diminished.

But what she saw now was that Joyce was starving. Starving for love, for peace, for something to believe in. She had thought she'd found it in Jake, and who could blame her for trying to claim that?

The tight ugly knot in her chest spun like a yo-yo, gathering power. *I can blame her!* it said.

No, Fern said to herself.

She closed her eyes and cast a circle around the bed and herself, then drew down the power to her hands—the healing power. The first time it had happened, she'd been unsure of herself, not wanting to use manipulative tactics on an old man lying in a doorway. But the Lady had insisted—*Put your hands on him*—so Fern had done it.

She'd only been called five other times in her life, but the feeling was unmistakable. It was as if all the light in the world gathered in her palms, a light both blindingly bright and infinitely good. And as if it were liquid, she only had to pour it out. She could see it going, a golden flow from her hands, through the air, into Joyce's feet. For a moment, Fern wondered if she should switch positions, go to the head of the bed, but a quiet kind of nudging kept her right in place.

Pouring love, light, hope, dreams, joy, excitement, satisfaction, love, love, love into those long bony feet with their too-long nails.

Seeing it flow up those long legs, into Joyce's belly, through her breasts, neck, head, out the top.

It lasted a long, long time. Or so it seemed. Fern stood with her hands outstretched over the prone body of a woman who had been her enemy, and let sunshine flow through her.

And as it flowed, the dark knot of sorrow and fear that lived in her own heart began to dissolve. She saw it as clearly as if it were sitting in front of her—it simply began to melt, bits of it dripping away into the light, absorbed and rendered harmless by the vast flow.

At last, it ended. The light faded. The circle erased itself. Fern opened her eyes, half expecting to see Joyce glowing like a picture of a saint. Instead, there was no visible change. Except, perhaps, the eased sound of breath moving in her lungs, through her mouth. Maybe a little color, high on those gaunt cheeks. "Peace be with you," Fern said and headed for the door, her task done.

And also with you.

As she walked down the hallway, back to her own life, Fern knew the situation was not entirely whole, not yet. What the

Mother had done for them today was offer them the start of healing. Fern would struggle with anger and suspicion. Joyce might fall sometimes to despair. But at least it was a beginning. The rest was up to them.

IN her kitchen, Fern remembered the light and, feeling stronger, opened the letter once again.

Dear Fern,

I have no right to come into your life this way after so long, but I have been so haunted the past few weeks that I will have no peace until I write this letter. Forgive me if it causes pain. I think in the end, it will give more peace than sorrow.

I write only to offer a most earnest apology. I will tender no excuses, for there are none. I pursued your husband, knowing he was your husband, and I believed it was my right to do so. I saw that he was a little lost, that he was getting to that place men sometimes get to, where they don't know what things mean, and I preyed on it, for months and months.

Forgive me for that. Forgive me the days and weeks and months of sorrow I gave you. In a strange way, knowing you both—the love you bear for each other—healed a heart that had been broken too often. And I am now to be married myself, for the first time. May it be as rich, may I be free enough to love as you do. May he be as devoted as your Jake.

Thank you, Fern. Peace be with you.

Joyce

In her kitchen, in the heart of the home she'd fought to save, Fern opened a drawer and looked at the candles within, trying to decide a color to use. In the end, she chose a yellow taper, to symbolize sunlight and healing, and she put it on the breakfast bar. "Thank you, Mother," she said, and lit the candle, then lit the letter on fire, not in anger, but in letting go, holding it over the sink until the end. As the last bit of it burned, sending up smoke to the heavens, Fern heard the soft, warm chuckle of the Goddess.

Thank you, daughter.

Magickal Housecleaning

MAGGIE SHAYNE

Here are some tips to make your mundane housecleaning into something supercharged with magick, to rid the house not only of physical dirt and grime, but negative energies, astral nasties, bad vibes, and all the spiritual gunk that collects in the corners. Methods such as these have been recommended by spiritual teachers from Dion Fortune to Scott Cunningham. Opportunities for further study abound.

- ☾ Add a few specially charged herbs to your mop and other cleaning water: Rosemary. Citrus rind. Angelica. Spearmint. You "charge" the herbs by pushing energy into them mentally, holding them while envisioning them glowing with the light of God, or Goddess, or angels, or positive forces of any kind.
- ☾ Once the herbs are charged, mix your cleaning water as you normally would, but add a pinch of each herb and a dash of salt, which is known to purify. As you add the herbs, chant a little rhyme. Use this one or make up one of your own:

> *Golden glowing light of love,*
> *From below and from above,*
> *Cleanse my home of all that's dark,*
> *Purify my home and hearth!*

❨ As you clean your house, always move in a counterclockwise direction, cleaning the rooms in the north end first, then west, then south, then east, and working back to north again. Mop and scrub in counterclockwise circles. This motion banishes the astral echoes of the dirt you're cleaning away. (Be sure to complete your circles. Work all the way back to where you began.)

❨ Finish by adding some of the charged herbs and salt to a spray bottle of water, and walk once more around the house counterclockwise, spraying a bit as you go. Then walk around again, this time with some sage or other purifying herb smoldering, waving the smoke into all the corners, counterclockwise through the house. You have just purified your space by the powers of earth and water (the water and the salt with herbs in it) and by air and fire (the burning sage and its smoke).

❨ When the cleaning is finished, you must complete the magick by filling the house with positive energy. Otherwise, there's a vacuum left behind. Something has to fill the space left by the energy you have banished. You want to make sure it's something positive. So now you are going to move through your house in a clockwise motion, the motion of creating.

Charge some white candles you've chosen specially for this purpose. Choose candles with scents that please you. Again, you charge them by holding them in your hands, and envisioning the results you want them to bring, see them glowing with the light of positive energy. You can rub them with oils or engrave symbols of love and happiness in their faces. When they are ready, take one to every room in your house, beginning in the north, then east, then south, then west, moving clockwise this time. As you light each candle, say this rhyme or make up one of your own:

Light of love, I call you forth,
Fill this space with happy warmth,
Grow and glow within my place,
Shine your light on every face.
All who enter here will feel
The energy I know is real.
And no one who intends us ill
Shall pass across our threshold sill.

As you let these candles burn, take a specially chosen oil, and draw a symbol you view as protective on every window, door, and every other opening, such as heating ducts, vents, electrical outlets, etc. Suggested symbols include the equal armed cross, the pentacle, or a protective rune such as Algiz. This will seal your work, keeping negativity out.

Continue to fill the space with positive energy by playing happy, joyful music, playing with children or pets, watching a funny film, anything that brings laughter and love into the house.

Never leave candles unattended. Put them out when you finish your work, and know their flames and energy continue burning in the astral. Light them whenever you feel the room you are in needs a boost of positive energy.

The Reluctant Psychic

Valerie Taylor

"She pushed me."

The voice spoke straight into her left ear in the silence of the library, and Hilary Chance almost fell off her stool in surprise. She caught herself and turned in extreme annoyance, ready to show that annoyance to whomever had startled her so badly.

No one was there.

The room was empty, except for the microfiche librarian on the other side of his desk twenty feet away. He couldn't possibly have spoken in her ear. Besides, it had been a woman's voice. A young woman.

The microfiche reading room was full of carrels. If someone wanted to play a joke, she could certainly hide herself. But that fast? And Hilary hadn't recognized the voice.

Well, she was too busy to play games. Her editor's latest Fantastic New Project actually was a pretty good idea: a series of columns investigating older, unresolved murder cases to see whether they could be solved by modern forensic methods. Perfect project for a science writer. But her editor wanted the first column yesterday, and that meant a lot of research fast.

She turned back to the microfiche reader, squinted at the old newspaper story on the microfiche screen, and found her place again.

. . . tension ran high in the courtroom as the jury foreman unfolded the scrap of paper and read, "In the charge of murder in the first degree, we find the defendant, Edward Howsum, not guilty." Howsum sagged and put his face in his hands, and his attorney pounded him on the back. A buzz of outraged conversation went up from the crowd, and Eleanora Claymore's mother fainted into her husband's arms. Judge Morris pounded his gavel and demanded silence. He removed his glasses and frowned at the defendant. "Edward Howsum, I can't say the jury gave the wrong verdict, but I don't believe justice was served. This was a shocking crime. To kill a young woman because she wouldn't marry you."

At this point, Howsum tried to interrupt, but his lawyer silenced him, whispering urgently into his ear. Howsum shook his head but remained silent.

The judge frowned and spoke again. "Edward Howsum, you are free to go. And may God have mercy on your soul." Once again outraged conversation erupted in the courtroom, and the judge did not bother to silence it. Edward Howsum left the courtroom with his attorney beside him and an angry crowd behind him.

"He didn't do it. She did."

This time Hilary whipped around on the stool, determined to catch the jokester before she could hide again. But again no one was there.

She realized the librarian was watching her, his gaze one of wary curiosity. She gave him a weak smile. "I think there's a fly in here or something." She flicked a hand around her head.

Shoo, fly. He gave one quick upward nod, mouthing "Ah!" and went back to his work.

Hilary turned away, her heart thumping. She would absolutely have sworn there was someone standing just behind her shoulder speaking directly into her ear.

Obviously she needed a break. She'd been sitting there squinting at microfiched newspaper stories for nearly ten hours. No wonder she was starting to hear things.

She could finish up at home. With Mrs. Northcutt around, it might not be any quieter, but at least Hilary'd never hallucinated there. She printed off the final story and stuffed the pages into her laptop case.

When Hilary pulled up at home, she saw her landlady sitting on the shady front porch sipping from a stemmed glass. ·

It was a welcome sight. She could use the sustenance of a glass of Mrs. Northcutt's favorite tawny port. Just the break she needed to get a fresh start. Plus, Mrs. Northcutt would probably get a huge kick out of Hilary's hearing things. That kind of thing was probably right up her alley. Hilary smiled tolerantly.

SILVERBLADE, née Joanna Horry Northcutt, sat on her veranda watching her boarder march up the walk, her black nylon case slung over her shoulder. Not a hair out of place, while Silverblade's own hair was an exuberant graying mass, frizzy from the humidity. No nonsense, that was Hilary. Silverblade smiled tolerantly.

Hilary plopped her laptop on the floor and herself into the little wicker chair across the chintz-covered table from Silverblade. "Got a glass for me? Today, I need it. I'm officially going nuts."

"Really, dear? What happened today?" Silverblade reached for the second tulip-shaped glass on the small cart beside the door, poured an inch of the deep golden wine into it, and handed the glass to Hilary.

Hilary took a sip. "It was the strangest thing. I've worked too many hours in a row before, but this is something new." She laughed in apparent disbelief. "I was at the library today reading old newspaper stories of a murder trial that happened fifty years ago. The murderer wasn't convicted because the evidence was at the time circumstantial. I'm trying to find out if there was any evidence that might have convicted him today. Anyway, I thought someone spoke to me." She tapped her left ear. "Directly into my ear, it sounded that close. Like someone was leaning over my shoulder talking. But when I turned around, no one was there. Honestly, it happened *twice*. Finally I realized my brain was so tired of sitting in the same place for hours on end staring at a screen that I was hallucinating."

Silverblade wondered. She took a small sip of her port. "Perhaps you weren't hallucinating?"

Hilary shook her head, sharp and definite. "No, no one was there. Either time. I'm sure of it. The room was empty, except for the librarian, and he was across the room. Besides, the voice was a woman's."

Silverblade set down her port. She picked up the decanter and splashed a tiny bit more of the golden liquid into her glass. "What did she say?"

"Pardon me?"

"The voice, what did she say?"

"It said . . . uh, something about he didn't do it, she did it."

"And you were reading about a murderer? One who wasn't convicted due to lack of evidence?"

Hilary stiffened slightly, but Silverblade wasn't giving up just yet. "Perhaps she was there but you couldn't see her. Perhaps you could only hear her."

"You mean, like a ghost?" Hilary started to laugh but covered it with a cough. "Mrs. Northcutt, I'm sorry, but I don't believe in ghosts. Believe me, I've done plenty of work on so-called supernatural phenomena. My 'Ask a Stupid Question' column gets reader questions about such things nearly every week. I investigate some of them—it's part of my job—and 95 percent of the claims can be explained very easily."

Silverblade could hear how carefully Hilary spoke, obviously fighting to keep the amusement out of her voice, bless her heart. As if Silverblade hadn't encountered closed minds before. "And the other five percent?" Silverblade shrugged and sipped her port, but she watched Hilary carefully over the top of her glass.

Hilary took the last sip of her port and stood. "Well, I really better try to grab a nap and then get some work done. Thanks for the drink! I'm so busy with this project, I probably won't have much time in the near future for friendly little chats."

Silverblade just smiled.

Hilary escaped into the cool of the house. *Yegods and little fishes, save me from the true believers.* She and Mrs. Northcutt had got along fine until now with no deep discussions of spirituality, and Hilary saw no reason to leap that particular gap at this point. Those who believed just ached to evangelize, as if convincing others could somehow validate their own superstitions. Strange how easily people could convince themselves of what they wanted to believe.

She grabbed a soda from the refrigerator on her way to the kitchen stairs and climbed the two flights to her rooms under the eaves—really the maids' quarters, back when Mrs. Northcutt's great-grandparents built the old mausoleum—and set her laptop case down with a feeling of relief at having dodged a bullet. Hilary'd known the old lady considered herself some sort of pagan—the pentacle earrings made that much clear—but she hadn't seemed all that *woo-woo* about it. Hilary figured she was the earth-mother type, sort of revering nature and respecting the universe. Maybe a few forays into tarot and runes, the occasional spell. Who knew it went beyond that and into a belief in actual magic and ghosties and such?

It was almost funny, if it hadn't been slightly sad.

Hilary knew about Witches—her column got occasional questions about them—and she knew they were harmless people and simply deluded the same way believers of any other faith were deluded. Some folks believed prayer worked, Witches believed spells did. Just as no good Christian ever prayed for something evil, no good Witch would ever cast a spell to cause evil.

And Hilary believed in the power of both prayer and spells, for purely practical, logical reasons. Either one was a perfect example of self-fulfilling prophecy. Pray—or cast a spell—for the strength to get through something difficult. Add a firm belief that help will arrive in response, *et voilà!* You find the strength. Pretty damn divine, that.

But ghosts? Honest-to-goodness ghosts? Or "resident spirits," she guessed Mrs. Northcutt would probably term it. Or maybe "spirit guides."

Good grief.

Oh, well, she could just avoid any conversation with her landlady that threatened to turn to spirituality or the supernatural. Certainly the old lady had never once tried to bring up the subject before this, so it shouldn't be difficult.

Well, she didn't have time to waste on possible future difficulties. She pulled the final newspaper account of Edward Howsum's trial from her laptop case, opened the soda, and curled up in front of the window overlooking the rooftop and front yard.

HOWSUM LYNCHED!

WITNESSES MAKE WILD CLAIMS!

Edward Howsum was abducted at gunpoint from his home last night by a group of about seven armed and masked men. Deputies found his body hanging from a tree in the woods behind Joseph

Claymore's farm early this morning. Sheriff John Moody said there were no suspects.

Two men who claimed to have watched the hanging reported that Howsum had no final words but that when the horse ran out from under him, Howsum appeared to hover for a moment before he dropped suddenly. He kicked for several minutes before he died.

The two men, who appeared to be drunk and would not give their names, claimed to see an apparition of a weeping woman in a nightdress standing in the dust beside the hanging tree, shaking her head, her arm extended upwards toward the dangling body.

"He didn't do it. Please, you must see that."

Hilary gasped aloud and spilled her drink down her shirt. She stumbled from the chair, scattering papers.

This wasn't happening. Auditory hallucinations were a pretty good sign of mental illness. Severe mental illness. Schizophrenia. Or maybe a brain tumor.

No. It was just the job. Overwork. She was tired, exhausted really. It was getting to her, all these silly questions about the supernatural, and now a case that seemed to have a connection to supernatural beliefs. Plus her landlady hadn't helped. Hilary knew how strong the power of suggestion could be. She just hadn't realized she was personally so susceptible. She was a science writer, for God's sake. She knew better.

At least she was done reading. She had enough research in the bag to come up with a first draft detailing the methods a modern forensic scientist might use to give the jury clearer evidence with which to convict Edward Howsum.

First, the girl's nightgown. Only a few small spots of blood had spattered onto it, and there hadn't been a pool of blood around her. At the time, the explanation had been that the knife in her neck had severed her spine and her heart had stopped beating immediately so that she hadn't bled much. But . . .

"Please help him. She pushed me."

Hilary stood, abrupt and awkward. She paced the room, and her eyes lit on her headphones. She grabbed them, slotted in a tape of white noise she sometimes used to screen out sounds when she worked in the newspaper office, shoved it on her head, and turned the sound all the way up.

She sat back down and cautiously turned to her laptop again. She worked. Worked some more. No voice. Nothing.

The relief was almost overwhelming. She worked in blessed peace for another half hour, then sat back for a moment to eye her work . . .

And noticed movement beyond the laptop screen. Beyond the window.

Three floors up.

Headphones still blasting in her ears, she stepped toward the window. Another step. One more, and she stood before it. She reached toward the gauzy curtains, the fingers of her right hand sliding between the two panels, grasping the rough lace edge, pulling it back.

A young woman in an old-fashioned nightdress, long brown hair mussed as from sleep, stood on the rooftop staring in at her. White noise still filling her ears, unable to move, Hilary watched as the young woman mouthed something at her, a hand coming up, reaching toward Hilary as if in supplication.

Hilary screamed and couldn't hear her own scream. She snatched off the headphones, stumbling back from the window.

She raced out of the room, not knowing where she was going, just away.

SILVERBLADE was just contemplating doing a tarot spread with Hilary in mind when she heard the scream. She jumped up and ran into the house, entering the kitchen just as Hilary burst through the yellow door at the bottom of the kitchen stairway. Hilary stopped, staring at her, panting, her eyes wide.

"Hilary! Was that you screaming? Whatever happened?"

Hilary babbled out an explanation, barely making sense. "I saw a woman, a woman, on the roof. Outside my sitting room window. On the roof, just standing on the roof. She was trying to talk to me." Silverblade saw tears start in Hilary's eyes.

Silverblade put her arm around her boarder and led her to one of the bright red chairs at the kitchen table. "Here, sit here." She poured her a glass of ice water and sat down beside her. "Now, tell me about it. Perhaps we can figure out what this means for you."

Stupid of her; it was completely the wrong thing to say at the moment. She saw Hilary's jaw tighten. "Mrs. Northcutt, I'd like to believe this was only a ghost. Clearly that would be a better option than that I'm hallucinating. But this is obviously a medical problem, and I'm not going to waste time pretending it's anything else. Please, if you want to help, call my doctor."

Well, the poor girl was frightened. If she needed to prove to herself there was nothing medically wrong with her, that was probably smart. "I'll see if I can get you an appointment, and I'll drive you over." There would be no more discussion of other possibilities, at least for now. Silverblade turned to pick up the phone.

HILARY sat in the grim little office, surrounded by diplomas testifying to Joe Bodiman's ability to solve her problem. Finally the door opened and Joe came in. He smiled. "Well, the news is good. The MRI shows everything is normal, the scan was fine. All your levels are fine. You seem to be in perfect health."

She waited, but that seemed to be all he was going to say. "But there has to be *something*. The voice, the woman on the roof." If anything, things had been getting worse; over the past week she'd been seeing doctor after doctor. "Isn't there anything else you can check?"

"I'm afraid we've pretty much been through it all. You don't seem to be depressed; you haven't used any drugs." He shrugged. "My advice would be to ignore it."

"I can't ignore it!" Hilary heard the shrill emotion in her own voice. With an effort, she sat back in her chair, relaxing her hands where they'd clenched the arms. "Look, I don't think I can ignore the voice. I want it to go away. And the woman in the nightgown. Isn't there something you can give me? A drug? Electroshock therapy? A lobotomy?" She laughed, only slightly hysterically. "I just don't want to see or hear anything that isn't there."

He nodded slowly. "We can try Risperdal, if you like. It's an antipsychotic. Very safe, especially at low doses." He pulled out his pad and started to scribble. "You may not see any change for a while, but give it some time."

She grabbed the slip as if it were a lifeline and nodded. Anything, if it would help.

He was right. It took a while. She tried to ignore the woman's voice, and one morning Hilary realized she hadn't heard from her in several hours. It was an odd feeling, this new, old aloneness.

Finally, maybe she could get some work done. Her editor had been patient with all the medical issues, but enough was enough. Hilary was ready to take her life back.

She worked into the early evening, making a list of all the things the cops could have investigated if Edward Howsum had committed his crime today instead of fifty years ago. Hair and fiber evidence. DNA on the bloodstained nightgown. Fingernail scrapings from the victim.

From time to time she looked around her. Nothing! She heard nothing; she saw nothing out of the ordinary.

The vague sense of aloneness was still with her, so after she finished for the evening and closed up her laptop, she went in search of Mrs. Northcutt to suggest a cup of tea. No more port for Hilary, unfortunately.

SILVERBLADE sat with her boarder on the veranda, sipping tea. The girl seemed a lot calmer now that she was no longer receiving unwelcome visits from her spirit guide. Maybe Hilary just wasn't a good candidate for such help. It pained Silverblade to think that anyone would reject such a gift.

Hilary sighed. "Well, I guess I'm officially psychotic, since antipsychotics seem to work so well for me."

It almost seemed an opening, so Silverblade decided to go with it. "But Hilary, don't you want to know why it was happening?"

"That's the same thing the psychiatrist said." Hilary shook her head. "I don't know. Stress? Overwork? I'm not depressed and I don't think I'm particularly anxious, but I guess that can creep up on you. I just never thought I was vulnerable to stress before. I know that's ridiculous, but it always seemed so . . ."

"Intangible? After all, if you can't see it, it isn't really there." Silverblade grinned.

Hilary gave an answering grin, and Silverblade was glad to see her able to poke a little fun at herself. It was a good sign the girl's mind wasn't totally closed, even if she herself thought it was. Maybe there was hope for Hilary yet.

IT was late evening when Hilary finally said good-night and returned to her rooms. In the dusk, she could see the screen of her laptop glowing gently. Strange, she was sure she'd turned it off and closed it. Maybe forgetfulness was a side effect of the

Risperdal. Well, if so, she could live with that. She closed the laptop before brushing her teeth and dropping into bed.

The next morning as she got out of bed, Hilary tripped over the open bottom drawer of her nightstand. "Ouch!" She stood looking at the open drawer stupidly as she rubbed her foot.

She knew she hadn't left it open. For one thing, she'd have had a hard time getting into bed with it standing open. Besides, it was empty. She hadn't gotten around to storing anything there yet. So there was no reason for her to open it.

Could she have opened it in her sleep? She'd have to ask Joe if Risperdal could cause somnambulation or other sleep activity. Great, a second possible side effect.

Well, it was still better than the alternative.

After she dressed, she walked downstairs. In the empty kitchen, the refrigerator door stood wide open. Hilary took out a container of cottage cheese and one of raspberries and made her breakfast. She smiled at herself as she made sure to close the refrigerator before taking her breakfast into the dining room. Mrs. Northcutt was sitting at the lace-covered table with the morning newspaper, drinking coffee and eating a dish of fresh peaches.

"Morning, dear! How was your night?"

"Great, except I think I'm discovering some side effects of this drug." She told Mrs. Northcutt about the laptop and the open drawer. "But I guess forgetfulness isn't only for Risperdal users. I found the refrigerator door standing wide open this morning. How long were you refrigerating the kitchen?"

Mrs. Northcutt frowned slightly and set down her spoon. "I don't think I even had the refrigerator open this morning."

When Hilary went back up to her room to grab her laptop, she found all the drawers in her dresser standing open. She had to laugh. It looked as if the Risperdal was turning her from a neat freak into a slob.

When she got home from work that evening, she found Mrs.

Northcutt sitting on the porch with an empty glass and an empty decanter. "Hilary, please go inside, then come back out here and tell me what you see."

Hilary frowned, but she set down her laptop and walked inside. The hair on her neck stood on end, and she stifled a small scream.

Every drawer, every door, every window was open. Draperies were open, and behind them blinds were open.

Hilary walked into the kitchen. The oven was open. The microwave. The refrigerator. The kitchen faucet was turned on full, the water running down the drain.

Inside the refrigerator, the milk stood open, its cap on the shelf beside it.

The door to the kitchen stairs stood open, but Hilary didn't go up. Couldn't go up.

She retraced her steps to the front porch and barely made it into the chair beside Mrs. Northcutt.

Her landlady fluttered a hand at the empty decanter. "I found the decanter open and couldn't get it to remain stoppered. I'd put the stopper in, go back in the house, and when I walked past again, there it was. Just sitting there on the table beside the decanter. I even tried to put a spell on it." She blinked. "I had to finish what was in it. I'm rather afraid to open another one."

Hilary nodded and stared into the front yard blindly. "I don't understand. What is happening?"

Mrs. Northcutt gave her a considering glance. "Do you really want to know what I think?"

Hilary turned her head to look at her landlady. *She means do I want to hear she thinks this is something supernatural.*

Hilary almost laughed. What else could it be? Some enemy of Hilary's who was sneaking into the house to open things in an attempt to make her think she was crazy? That was even crazier than . . .

Even crazier than believing in ghosts. She nodded. "Yes, I want to know what you think."

Mrs. Northcutt took a breath. "I think the spirit that is trying to contact you has a lot of flexibility and doesn't bear frustration very well. When you tried to shut her out with white noise on your headphones, she made an appearance. When you changed the chemistry of your brain to make it impossible to pick her up that way, she started this poltergeist stuff." She shrugged at Hilary's appalled look. "You asked me what I thought. I think you should try to accept this, whatever it is. But it means you're going to need to pry open your mind a smidge."

Hilary bristled. She was an extremely open-minded person. Just not credulous or gullible. Belief in the supernatural was for the gullible. Like Mrs. Northcutt.

Except . . . Mrs. Northcutt didn't seem the gullible type, either. Not at all. Other than the fact that she believed some things Hilary didn't believe. But maybe, Hilary thought for the first time, just maybe she had reason to.

Hilary shook her head, impatient with herself. Even if the voice *were* real, which wasn't possible, it would still be a problem. "How can I accept it? It won't leave me alone."

"Did you try asking her to be quiet?" Mrs. Northcutt hesitated for a moment, as if trying to make a decision, and said, "I may have some ideas that can help."

"What, spells? You think a spell is going to work?" Hilary laughed, but it felt hollow.

"Unless you try, you can't know." Mrs. Northcutt gave a sigh. "All I know is, we can't live like this. If it were me, I'd go off this medication, at least see if that stops the poltergeist business. If it does, maybe you can learn to live with the voice, even if you can't accept that it's real."

"Mrs. Northcutt, the medication is not doing this. I don't know what is, earthquakes maybe, tiny ones we can't feel."

Mrs. Northcutt gave her an amused look, and Hilary suppressed a slightly hysterical urge to laugh at the switch in their roles: Mrs. Northcutt skeptical, and Hilary suggesting something preposterous.

Hilary took a breath. "Okay, it's not a very good theory. But there must be an explanation for this."

"Look, try not taking the Risperdal. Just long enough to see if the poltergeist stops. If it doesn't, fine, go back on it. But if it does, we'll know there's a good chance that's what's causing it. At the worst, you'll get the voice back. How can it hurt?"

It could hurt a lot, if Hilary couldn't get any work done. If the voice really did come back.

"And if that happens, try asking her to be quiet, if she's interrupting you. Maybe say, 'Not now, please, I'm busy.' Maybe you could even try listening once in a while."

The very idea made Hilary anxious.

Mrs. Northcutt reached over and patted her arm. "Besides, now that you know how you can stop the voice, what's to prevent you from going back on the Risperdal again if you need to? After you move out, of course." Mrs. Northcutt smiled, but Hilary suspected she wasn't being completely facetious.

Well, Mrs. Northcutt was right about one thing—Hilary couldn't live like this. It was worse than the voice. She'd actually been starting to get used to the voice by the time it shut up. No way could she get used to this.

So Hilary stopped taking the Risperdal. And soon all the drawers stayed shut.

And then one morning a voice spoke in her ear.

A new voice. This was a man's.

"I don't care anymore, but she's right. I didn't do it. She says it was her stepma."

And then the familiar voice of the woman. "I asked him to

come. I told him you needed to hear it from someone else. Now do you believe me?"

Hilary stood up. She paced to the window and looked out. There was no one on the roof. There was nothing in the room. At least it was back to being just a voice. Well, voices. She guessed that was the consequence of fighting the first voice: Now she had two.

At least nothing was open. Or running.

Her heart beat faster. She felt as if a chasm yawned before her, a merciless dark void over which she was considering jumping. A one-way trip, she knew. If she made the jump, there was no way ever to return to the other side. The safe side, where everything made sense and where science writers knew what was real and what wasn't.

But the safe side no longer seemed safe either.

She turned and perched on the windowsill. "All right," she said to the empty room. "What is it that you want from me?"

And as if that were all it took, that one tiny, immense crack in the very fabric of her self-image, suddenly she heard dozens of voices, all talking directly to her, all trying to get her attention. Not loudly, not shouting, just *there*. Right there, right in her ear. She tried walking away, tried putting her hands over her ears. Finally she screamed, "Shut up!"

It wasn't exactly the polite request Mrs. Northcutt had suggested, but it worked. The voices stopped. Blessed silence. But the silence felt pregnant. They were waiting, but they wouldn't wait long. She could tell.

She needed a plan. And she needed help, and she knew where to start. Mrs. Northcutt would know. Spells, or meditation, or whatever people used to control this stuff, God only knew. Or the Goddess, she guessed she should say. Hilary almost laughed.

Maybe, just maybe, this was going to be an exciting journey.

*   *   *

SILVERBLADE sat on the veranda, a cup of coffee before her, enjoying the coolness of the summer morning. The screen door opened behind her and Hilary stepped out onto the porch.

Hilary hesitated a moment, and Silverblade could tell there was something rather large behind the hesitation. "Mrs. Northcutt?" she finally started. "Can I ask you a few questions? About . . . well, spirit guides, and how I can . . ." She hesitated a moment. "How I can find out what this means for me?"

Silverblade turned to her, a broad smile on her face. "Of course, dear. My path was a difficult one to find, too. I'd love to help you find yours. And, please, call me Silverblade."

Mom's Charm and Ritual

VALERIE TAYLOR

As a pagan mom of young children, I want to show my kids paganism is useful. I also want to make rituals interesting and fun enough that they want to participate next time I suggest one.

Kids, even more than adults, find it easier to visualize when they have something tangible to focus on. So empowering objects, like charms, is a perfect way to introduce a child to magick. (Note: Charms containing small items are only appropriate for children over the age of three, as younger children may be tempted to put the charmed items in their mouths.)

Children also have short attention spans. So our ritual, while complete, is very simple. For a longer child-friendly ritual, I like the ideas in *Circle Round* by StarHawk, Diane Baker, and Anne Hill.

Dreams Charm

When my five-year-old was having nightmares, we made a Dreams Charm to help him have only the kind of dreams he wanted to have. (We were careful to phrase it just that way, to avoid preventing dreams that might be scary but were still important or helpful dreams.)

Help your child choose a piece of cloth that appeals to him. Something with smiling stars and/or moons would be ideal for a child's literal visualization. A piece cut from a favorite pair of outgrown pajamas would also be great, but make sure it's the child's choice and not yours—his associations with the material are what count, not your fond memories of how cute he looked in those jammies! You'll also need a piece of yarn or ribbon about eight inches long.

Cut (or have your child cut) the cloth into a rectangle ten by four inches. Fold, right sides together, into a five-by-four-inch rectangle. Stitch up the two long sides and turn inside out so the right side of the fabric (the side with the pretty print) faces out. Attach the very center of the ribbon to the bag about an inch down from the opening. The more of the bag your child can make himself, the better—for instance, instead of you sewing the bag, perhaps your child can staple the sides together. Perhaps the ribbon can be tied to a safety pin and the safety pin attached to the bag.

If you have a pagan or magickal supplies shop which carries stones or a gem shop nearby, allowing your child to choose his own stone(s) from the bins is best. If you don't have such a store nearby, you can also order the stone(s) from the internet or from a catalog.

Have your child select one or more of the following stones, all of which have traditionally been considered to have antinightmare properties. Again, allow your child to make the selection, which he will probably do based on size, shape, color, shininess, and texture of the stones.

- Amethyst (peaceful sleep)
- Carbuncle (wards off nightmares)
- Citrine (wards off nightmares)
- Coral (wards off nightmares)
- Garnet (wards off nightmares)
- Iron (protects against negative energies while sleeping)
- Malachite (protects young children from evil spirits while sleeping)
- Peridot (dispels night terrors)
- Rhodonite (soothes nightmares)

For the spell empowering the charm, you'll need:

* A black candle
* A white candle
* A small bowl of salt
* A small bowl of water
* Some sprigs of dried thyme or white sage
* The stones your child has chosen
* The bag the two of you made
* A muffin or other offering your child will enjoy sharing, on a special plate

Magickal timing: The most auspicious time for a child's spell is today or tomorrow, and at a time of day when your child will be alert but not too wound up.

Arrange your space: Have your child spread your altar cloth and place the items on it.

Purify: Have your child sprinkle some of the salt into the water, stir gently with his fingers, then sprinkle you and himself lightly. Say, "So we cleanse ourselves."

Ground: Stand together before the workspace. Say, "We are trees, our branches reach up to the skies, our roots reach into the earth." Stretch your arms up, close your eyes, and imagine your fingers are brushing the clouds, your toes are digging deep. Close your eyes and breathe in slowly, breathe out slowly. End by saying, "So we ground our energy."

Cast the circle: Have your child carry the bowl of salted water around the area you've designated for the circle, sprinkling the water as he goes. Say, "So we cast the circle."

Call the quarters: Stand with your child facing east and fan your hands to move the air, saying "So we call the Air." Turn to the south and hold up your hands and flutter your fingers to simulate flickering flames, saying, "We call the Fire." Turn to the west and move your hands in a scalloping pattern before you to simulate the movement of waves, saying, "We call the Water." Turn to the north and hold your two fists together to suggest the shape of the earth and pull them into your chest, saying, "We call the Earth."

Invite the Goddess: Say, "Demeter, we invite you to join us and welcome you into our circle." We choose to ask Demeter to bless this charm because she loves small children.

State your purpose: Say, "Demeter, protectress of children, we have come here to ask you to bless these stones and help Michael have only the dreams he wants to have."

If you use a chant to start your rituals, you can use it here.

Light the candles and run the dried herbs through the flame, just enough to perfume the air. Say, "We ask a blessing on these stones to guide Michael's dreams in the ways he wants them to go, and to turn away the dreams he doesn't want to have."

Have your child pick up the stones, one by one, dipping them into the salted water one at a time and placing them into the bag, as you say:

Every dream,
Every night,
Will be helpful, good, or bright.
As we will, so mote it be!

Have your child tie the bag shut, or tie it for him.

Thank the Goddess: Say, "We thank you, Demeter, for joining us." Break the muffin into three pieces and share it with your child, holding the third piece over the flame for a moment and then leaving it on the special plate for the Goddess. Say, "As we eat, we share. Blessed be."

Open the circle: "Earth, Air, Fire, Water, the circle is open but unbroken. May peace go with you. Merry meet, merry part, merry meet again."

Your child can place the charm under his pillow each night, repeating the spell's rhyme when he does so.

A Solitary Path

EVELYN VAUGHN

"I am *so* sorry it didn't work out with you and Joe," said Judy. Which might have been sweet if this weren't the fifth time she'd said so.

Today.

Tobi looked up from half-heartedly tracing a maze on a fast-food placemat. "Ya know, Jude, I think you're sorrier than I am."

Judy, blond and solemn, nodded. "You're probably right."

Tobi groaned.

"Really! It's just . . . I hate to see you so alone."

Now Tobi groaned *loudly*. They were in a mall food court; she couldn't spread her arms out for fear of hitting another person.

Judy just raised her voice. "You know what I mean. I'm so happy with Bill—what's wrong with wanting the same thing for you? Couldn't you do a love spell or something? You're a *Witch*, for heaven's sake!"

Then she said, "Oops," because an elderly couple to their

right started clearing their trays. Of course, they might have simply finished eating.

"One," clarified Tobi, pointing her ballpoint like a tiny wand, "some Witches might disagree with you there—rumor has it I don't take the Craft seriously enough. Two, if I were still in the broom closet, I wouldn't be wearing my pent. And three, the best part about dating Joe was it *did* make you happy. And Mom. And some folks from work, several of whom apparently thought I was a lesbian."

They added in unison, "Not that there's anything wrong with that."

"Which, by the way, doesn't make sense," added Tobi, snitching one of Judy's fries. "If I were a lesbian I wouldn't be dating *nobody*—I'd be dating *women*. Still, though I love you all, I need a better reason than that. Making you happy, I mean. Not dating women."

Judy shook her head. "Better reason? How long were you dateless before you went out with Joe?"

"Six years," Tobi admitted easily; it wasn't like she hadn't had offers. A gaggle of teenage girls, one table back, blatantly stared. They hadn't been surprised by a Witch at the mall, but they were shocked by celibacy? And yet from the leftover buns on their trays—and the look of their bony arms—Tobi could see they were all on that no-carbs diet. To each her own. "And I was perfectly *happy*," Tobi added. "I'm *still* happy—more than when I was dating the wrong guy."

"Maybe it just takes practice," insisted Judy. As if dating, like sushi, were an acquired taste.

"Or maybe we both deserve something more clearly special."

"But how will you find special if you aren't even trying?"

Simply shaking her head wasn't enough—Tobi buried her beringed fingers and her pen in her curly brown hair to keep her head from exploding. "What I meant was, *if* I end up with *anybody*, it should feel special. Special enough that we'll find each other without stressing about it. I'd rather not bother with anything less in the meantime. It's not like there's a hurry. If we don't catch each other this time around, there'll be other lifetimes."

Judy stared. "That kind of reasoning may be why the Church ditched the idea of reincarnation in the sixth century." Judy said *Church* with a capital *C* because she was Catholic. But a liberal Catholic. Clearly.

"I'm not wasting this life! I have my work, and my writing. I have Habitat for Humanity once a month—and my religion."

"Which you practice alone."

"I attend some open circles." But she'd observed Beltane, aka May Day, alone. And Spring Equinox. And Imbolc. She'd had fun, too. Punxatawny Phil had featured significantly in her February celebrations.

She'd attended an open circle for Yule, anyway.

Unable to comment on open rituals, Judy took another bite of her burger. Tobi returned to the placemat puzzle. Mazes were always most difficult when you played along, working from the outside in. "The right guy has plenty of opportunities to come along," she insisted. "And he will. Until then, why dwell on his absence—why *empower* it—by giving up what I do enjoy?"

"Like television?" Judy knew her too well.

"My favorite magic," agreed Tobi, trying a different entrance on the paper maze. "Why do that, just to seek something that may be premature anyway?"

"TV's not real."

"Tell that to Ted Turner."

Judy widened her eyes in pseudopatience. "What if this perfect guy isn't real, either?"

"What if he is?" Some things she just knew—the same way she knew that words and stories had power and that worlds existed beyond their own. But Tobi knew she could never wholly explain it to Judy.

She wasn't sure she could even convince another Witch!

Tobi's brand of Wicca was eclectic, urban, and so firmly anchored to pop culture that some of the more traditional pagans she knew, locally and online, dismissed her as a fair-weather Witch . . . even after eight years. Personally, though she understood the pagans' concern about image, Tobi didn't get how a magic user could laud the power of the moment—the now—and yet scoff at fads. How could someone worship at the altar of ancient myths—literally, even!—while dismissing a mass media that wove new mythology every day?

Very few people, pagan *or* mundane, could hear Tobi's theories about TV and Dreamtime without questioning her sanity. Lacking substantiality, the astral world was too often mistaken as lacking substance as well. Most magic didn't just work by natural means—sometimes it hid behind them, easily dismissed against more obvious "realities."

Busy with everyday life, Tobi rarely thought about *him*—whoever he was—Mr. Special. But when she focused into herself, she felt their connection as powerfully as she felt the pull of Mother Earth right here in the splashing fountains and ficus trees of the food court. She knew him as surely as she knew the presence of Father Sky through the airy skylights, tinted against the worst of the midwestern sun. Her someone might not exist in this world, but worlds overlapped. She didn't need to find a wooded grove to commune with nature, and she didn't need a Friday-night date to feel loved.

By whoever he was.

"I *sense* him," she said finally. "What if I settled for someone else, and wasn't available if he shows up?"

"And if you end up alone?" There Judy went with her one-path-to-happiness paradigm.

"One, there are worse fates than staying single. Two, I'm not alone. I have friends, family . . . my cat. I'm not cutting into my life for anything less than magic. And yes"—Tobi raised a flat hand to fend off more concerned protests—"I realize that a relationship isn't all magic. But doesn't the magic have to be there at some point, at least early on? Just a *little* toe curling, just a *little* 'Yay, I'm going to see him tonight' shivers?" *Just a little swelling background music as their eyes met?* "If not, why bother?"

Now it was Judy who groaned. "I reserve the right to worry. Especially with you coming and going at night all the time, and that mugger running around loose."

"Two attacks in four weeks hardly constitutes a crime wave."

"If you were still dating Joe, you could call him if you heard someone breaking in."

Tobi doubted anybody would break into her home, as many wards as she'd placed around it. She also had good, solid, mundane locks. "Or here's a thought. If I hear someone breaking in at night, I could call the police."

"I just worry, is all," insisted Judy. Again. "Promise me you'll be extra careful until this guy is caught, okay?"

Tobi felt so relieved that the issue had moved off her love life, she was happy to comply. "I promise."

And as their conversation turned to Judy's new position at work, Tobi smoothly completed the paper maze—by starting at the center and tracing her way out.

Not *every* path had to be fumbled down by trial and error, did it?

SHE should have had better sense than to watch the news the next night. But it came on after her favorite show. Tobi hadn't wanted to disturb the almost sensual satisfaction of a good story—or the purring cat in her lap—by getting right up. Next thing she knew, she was watching a report on a third mugging in the area.

Her area. The TV station's map graphic showed that all three had taken place within a four-mile radius of her.

Peachy.

A rune-pull didn't prophesize full-out danger, but it recommended action be taken. So did her Magic 8-Ball. So Tobi did what any smart Witch would do—she called her boss to ask about a shift change. Yes, it was a little late, but they were friends.

"Don't tell me you're worried about the mugger," teased Steve. "Our little Witchipoo?"

Some Witches kept a low profile to avoid very real bigotry and persecution. With Steve, Tobi instead endured a weird kind of enthusiastic teasing. She guessed it was better than him tricking her into attending a Christian revival, like the head of finances had done.

"*Natural means,* Steve," she reminded him patiently. "You've got to act in accord. Any Witch who does magic and then ignores it to wander around at midnight wearing a T-shirt that says MUG ME isn't grasping that particular concept."

Actually, midnight—the big Between-Time—might prove safe. But not three-thirty in the morning, which was when she generally got home from her part-time job assisting auto-club distress calls for a White Knight service.

"Oh yeah," said Steve, remembering. "Like the big-screen TV." Though no Witch, he'd once played with a spell to afford a big-screen TV, and ended up getting three straight weeks of overtime. Well, it *had* paid for the television . . . but it also explained why a TV addict like Tobi got by with a twenty-five-incher, magic or not.

He said, "Look, I can ask around, but it'll be tricky. Not

everyone loves the graveyard shift the way you do." He'd made plenty of jokes about that, too.

"Just see what you can do on your end," said Tobi. "I'll see what I can do on mine." She'd promised Judy . . . and to break her promise would be to weaken the power of her word.

"You got it. Hey, Tobi?"

She waited.

"You do be careful, okay? I know Stanley doesn't like the idea of work-at-home, but this is the twenty-first century; we can rig something. You don't need to be driving in every night if you don't feel safe."

And Judy thought Tobi needed a boyfriend to feel loved? "You got it, Steve-o. Thanks."

Now she'd promised her safety twice. After hanging up, the idea of working protective magic lingered. She felt safe in her third-floor apartment. She'd warded the place with a bubble of protective blue light—blue on the astral plane, anyway—powered by a centrally located crystal. She had hidden black onyx near each doorway. She'd charged a household guardian with the protection of her home—her childhood teddy bear, whom she felt certain had a big bear spirit. Nobody had ever broken in. She doubted anybody would. But what about when she was walking in from her car—the time when, according to the news, women were most vulnerable? The Magic 8-Ball had warned her: OUTLOOK NOT SO GOOD.

Tobi had no reason to believe that the Powers That Be couldn't use kitchy plastic to communicate.

Always glad for a reason to explore her collection of magic books (most of them paperback), Tobi settled on the carpeted floor of her dining alcove between her bookshelves, her altar, and her microwave, and she started skimming. A protective talisman? Couldn't hurt. Perhaps a binding spell on the mugger?

She considered that one before rejecting it. The temptation

was to go Warrior Witch and try protecting the whole damn city, but she knew better. One, she didn't have enough information; too many variables existed for proper control. Two, she doubted she could handle it; even a Warrior Witch couldn't protect the whole city single-wandedly. And three, nobody had asked her. Unlike the sisters on *Charmed*, Tobi had never been given the responsibility of protecting humankind in general . . . and a lucky thing for humankind that probably was. Nope, pretending that magic made her omnipotent would be condescending and dangerous.

Better to do something she could fully control. As if to confirm her decision, her book fell open to the perfect spell. "A thought form," she told Sophie, her cat. "Of course!"

Like personal archetypes, thought-forms were creations who took on a level of reality through the focused belief of humans. For magical purposes, they were generally envisioned, charged with a specific job, then dismissed with thanks once that task had been accomplished. It was the closest Tobi could come to the faithful, imaginary friends of her childhood. The more she studied Wicca, the more she came to believe that "imaginary" was just another way of saying "from other realms" . . .

. . . and that magic was a way of accessing them.

"THOUGHT-form, huh?" asked Oz, as in the Great and Powerful. It wasn't his real name. He ran the Shop-a-Spell store in a local strip mall. Tobi wasn't sure what magic shops were like in New York or California, but here in the urban Midwest, the Shop-a-Spell had two full walls of windows and enough stained glass and prism-refracted sunlight to satisfy Ra and Apollo put together—not to mention Iris, Goddess of rainbows. "I like it. Very *you*. Have you decided on specifics yet?"

The more clearly one envisioned a thought-form, after all, the more likely it was to succeed in its task.

"At first I thought I'd hitchhike my spell onto an existing character," admitted Tobi. "The more people who believe in him, after all, the stronger he'll be. . . . And you've got to admit, the idea of having, say, Ares, the god of war, from the old *Xena* shows patrolling my parking lot is pretty cool."

Oz widened his eyes.

"I know," she said with a laugh. "The god of war might not be the best poster child for 'Harm none.' Besides, a thought-form empowered by hundreds of thousands of people should probably be used for magic meant to help more than one Witch, so I've decided to work from scratch."

"I think that's wise," agreed Oz. "So you want something to time out about a month's worth of rent-a-guardian, huh? I've got just the thing." And he led her toward the back of the store.

Oz looked more like a grizzled old biker than a Witch— complete with a long gray braid and tattoos. A biker wearing two pentagrams, a triskel, *and* a Thor's hammer pendant. But he kept good stock, and he knew magic.

As Tobi passed a cluster of twenty-somethings by the "Ceremonial Magic" shelves, one of them sniggered, "Nice shirt." Two more laughed and hushed him.

She was wearing her *Bewitched* shirt, showing a curvy, blond cartoon Witch on a broomstick.

"I was gonna say the same thing," agreed Oz, raising his voice. But *he* meant it. "Where'd you find it?"

"Off the internet," she admitted. "I also downloaded a desktop theme for my computer. It plays the *Bewitched* song when I boot up, and whenever I execute a file, it makes that tinkling, nose-wiggle noise."

"Does it call for Dr. Bombay when you get an error message?"

She laughed. "No, but I like that idea."

"Some of my coveners and I noticed something you can maybe explain." He kneeled beside some shelves and started opening the drawers underneath, where he kept some of his overstock. "The men in those shows never want the women—like Samantha or Jeannie—to use their magic. What's with that?"

"Oh, there's a *definite* patriarchal subtext there! But have you noticed they aren't doing it anymore?" When he glanced up at her, quirking a shaggy eyebrow, she added, "Well, yes, Darren Stevens and Major Nelson are; they're stuck in the celluloid past. But like on *Charmed*, none of the men seem to be asking the Witches to give up their powers. Sometimes they're even the cheering section. It makes me proud to be a couch potato."

"The times, they are a-changing." He'd gone back to digging, and whooped in triumph, handing her a large, colorful square of silk. She lifted it up by two corners, admiring a stylized picture of a medieval knight, painted over an odd design that looked both geometric and ancient.

"Niiice," she admitted, though unsure what he meant her to do with it. "The dragon on his coat of arms is a cool touch." In old stories, dragons often symbolized paganism. Thus when St. George slew England's dragon . . . well.

"That whole batch had the cheapest dye job I've ever seen," admitted Oz, standing with creaking knees. "If you tie it outside, like a knight's standard, by the time the month's through it'll be sun-bleached to obscurity. That's when you'll know to release your guardian."

"Perfect!" Odd . . . she'd been using that word a lot in regards to this project. When the bell rang from the counter, Oz headed toward the front to wait on his other customers and she admired the scarf a little more. A knight—that certainly fit the role she was asking her thought-form to play. Silk was a natural fabric, and woven! The idea of magic as spell-weaving had always appealed to her. Her instincts said, *Go for it.*

Up front, Oz was ringing up the purchases for the twenty-somethings. One of them was critiquing a flyer for an open Midsummer Ritual, out by the lake. "They didn't know what they were doing," he said. "At Beltane, the guy who dismissed the South blew out the quarter candle."

"No!" exclaimed the girl beside him.

He nodded and rolled his eyes. Tobi noticed another customer, a young businesswoman, watching from near the selection of tarot cards. Once the paganier-than-thou group had left, the younger woman asked, "What's wrong with blowing out candles?"

"Some traditions consider it an insult to the element of Fire," Oz explained easily, taking the scarf from Tobi and tapping the cost onto his adding machine, then calculating tax. "Or the element of Air. I forget which. Maybe both."

"Elements can get *insulted?*"

"Some practitioners think so," said Tobi. "Maybe they're right. But those guys are probably newbies, still looking for rules to define that One True Path. When you're just starting, you take everything so seriously."

"Luckily for me, Fire isn't all that picky," Oz said with a grin, accepting the money she handed him. "Now, Water . . ."

"Talk about your moody elements!" Tobi and Oz nodded wisely together.

The girl looked from one of them to the other. "You're goofing me."

"Yeah," admitted Oz. "We are. But *I* think it's a sign from the universe that Tobi should celebrate Midsummer by the lake." He even tucked a yellow flyer into her package before handing it over. "At least she knows those guys won't be there. And there'll be labyrinths."

That caught Tobi's attention. "Like in the David Bowie movie?"

"Actually, that one was more of a maze . . . most labyrinths are simply drawn on the ground and walked for meditative purposes, not solved. But they're really something."

"I'll think about it," she hedged, accepting her change.

She'd decided to be a lot more careful with her promises.

Tobi's thought-form would be a man, envisioned and then asked to patrol the parking lot from one full moon to the next. She tried considering a woman instead—she knew plenty of warrior Goddesses, by reputation anyway, who set a good example—but for some reason, her imagination kept latching onto a man.

Maybe Judy's concerns about her not having enough male energy in her life were having an effect.

He wouldn't actually materialize in front of her, of course. That was *not* how magic worked. But if she envisioned him clearly enough, and charged him powerfully enough, his very existence—even in a separate if interpenetrating realm—might dissuade predators.

She took several nights to plan him, jotting thoughts into her Palm Pilot between calls at work, deleting as many qualities as she kept. The last time she'd tried listing the traits of the perfect man, even before she'd become a magic user, she'd nevertheless drawn to herself a guy who possessed every ingredient. He'd been handsome, charming, attentive, creative. . . .

Unfortunately, since she'd been doing it blind, she hadn't remembered to add such qualities as "responsible," "loyal," or even "honest." *Be careful what you wish for. . . .*

"Responsible," she decided firmly, copying the list off her PDA and into her leather-bound Journal of Shadows. She sat on the floor again, Sophie the cat stretched comfortably beside her,

Enya music surrounding her. *Sometimes* she remembered to turn off the TV. "Honest. Alert."

Wouldn't do to have a guardian who didn't actually notice the mugger.

"Even-tempered." She didn't want the police scraping the remains of the mugger off the asphalt, either. Just in case.

Oh, and—duh. She added something fairly important, pleased with how the milk-colored gel ink looked against the black pages of the journal. "Protective."

The next step was to decide what he looked like. The more clearly she pictured him, the more surely he would exist on the astral plane. She knew he would have dark hair, clichéd or not. He would be tall, with wide shoulders and a broad chest and . . .

She laughed. Unless he was patrolling the parking lot topless, not to mention corporeal, it wouldn't matter what his abs looked like. Although if she put him in a tight shirt and well-worn jeans, it couldn't hurt, either.

White T-shirt, she decided. *So that the mugger's subconscious can better see him.*

Strangely, despite how certain she felt about his hair color and size, she couldn't envision the thought-form's face. And normally she had such a *good* imagination! She knew he would be handsome, at least to her own eyes . . . one of the many advantages of an imaginary man. Still, she felt as if she were squinting her third eye to get a good look at someone, and he was ducking his face away from her. Frustrated, she went through clippings from her "cute guy" file—where she kept favorite pictures from magazines and catalogs—and found an image that was, well . . .

Perfect.

The picture fit so well that she wondered if she'd been subconsciously remembering it all the time . . . a possibility that in no way invalidated the effort she'd put into him so far.

The magazine picture, an ad for some kind of dot-com company, showed a dark-haired man from behind, standing in heavy mist. He wore tight jeans and a tighter shirt, just a little of his hard jaw visible over one broad shoulder, a lock of dark hair hiding the rest of his face. The tag line read, WHAT DO *YOU* THINK IS OUT THERE?

He had a cute butt, and she hadn't even ordered that.

"It's you," she whispered, holding the page, and her breath fell shallow even as CD music swelled. She felt as if she knew this man, wholly and instinctively . . . and as if everything she knew about him pleased her.

Maybe it was a sign that this working was meant to be.

One of the many benefits to having her own place—along with keeping her own hours and watching whatever she chose on the tube—was that Tobi didn't have to hide her tools from roommates or parents or even disapproving spouses. She did, however, keep her most sacred items in a carved oak cabinet, away from dust and sunlight. On her night off, which she'd made sure was the full moon, she opened the cabinet's doors to release a delicious cloud of scent, from incense and herbs and candles and oils, and retrieved four well-used jar candles. They were in the standard quartet colors—green, yellow, red, and blue—and she set them to four sides of her living room to mark the directions of north, east, south, and west, respectively.

Her coffee table became her working altar. She laid a blue cloth with a pattern of gold and silver stars over it, then set out her athame, her bell, and her spirit candle. Two artistically faceless figurines in white ceramic, male and female, represented the divine forces of God and Goddess. It had taken her well over the standard year-and-a-day after she'd discovered Wicca to move past the "collecting cool props" phase of her individual study . . . by then, she'd collected quite a few. She made sure now that the photograph model for her thought-form lay on the altar, as well as the new scarf, washed in saltwater to cleanse any clinging energies.

She turned off the telephone ringer, set her VCR for the shows she would miss, turned her answering machine's volume all the way down, and lowered her halogen lamp to the barest of glows. Pressing "repeat" and then "play" on her stereo released the familiar instrumental soundtrack to *Conan the Barbarian*, one of her favorite working CDs. She'd already showered and now wore a sleeveless silk robe, which had come off a peignoir set but which she reserved for magic. Usually a kitchen-witch, Tobi did not always go through all this ritual to do magic, but tonight's working felt far bigger than her usual day-to-day charms.

Tonight felt momentous.

Standing straight in front of her altar, she stretched her arms out wide, her athame—a distressed replica of an antique dagger—in one hand, reaching up and up until it pointed to the ceiling. "It's showtime, folks," she murmured softly, to whoever and whatever might be listening.

The athame seemed to quiver in her hand as she walked the perimeter of her circle. Even as she set it back on the altar, before she'd lit quarter candles, Tobi felt the air inside her sacred place—*between* and *of* all space and time—falling heavy and still. It wasn't just because she'd cut off the air-conditioner so it wouldn't startle her or blow out the candles.

"Element of Earth, power from the north, I call on you," she stated clearly into the shadowed room. "Be with me in my sacred circle." Then she lit the green candle, near the one houseplant that had ever survived her care, and envisioned the fertile energies of earth power gathering around her to that side of the room. When it felt proper, she stepped to her right, under the wind chimes that hung from her living room ceiling, by the yellow candle.

"Element of Air, power from the east, I call on you. . . ."

And so on. After the calling of the quarters, she requested her Lord and Lady attend her circle as well. From the feel of the energies that began to thrum around her and the delicious shiver up her spine, she could not doubt they'd assented.

Tobi had done group rituals before. When they went well, the power was incredible . . . but one fidgety or cynical group member could easily destroy the night's magic. A benefit to being a solitary practitioner was not having to worry about anybody's missteps but her own. This private circle in her living room felt safe as few places could. The candlelight, the scent of copal, the gurgle of her table fountain on the west side of the room, the music—all combined with her breathing exercises to ease her into a gentle alpha state . . . or, as she better liked to envision it, to move into the world beyond worlds. It was a place she *went*, after all . . . the same way somebody *got* on the phone or *went* on the internet.

Kneeling on the carpet before the altar, she let the world outside her circle fade as she focused on the picture, then on the empty space beyond it. If her guardian were just over six feet, that would put him . . . yes. Tobi could see exactly where he would come to, standing against the opposite wall.

First she envisioned his shape, slightly warping the reality around him like a particularly good invisible-man effect in the movies. *We can rebuild him. Stronger. Faster. . . .*

She repeated her breathing exercises, to better concentrate.

Visualization was Tobi's forte. After tweaking the shape of her creation—widening his shoulders, remembering that men tended to taper down into their hips instead of flaring out again—she needed only a few more breaths to lend him color and substance. Dark hair. White shirt. Tanned arms. Tight jeans. . . .

She could picture the tight jeans very nicely. If only he were real. . . .

"But he's not," she reminded herself sternly, as if Judy were watching over her shoulder—and knew her stupidity even as her image of him vanished to reveal only her wall, framed photographs, doorjamb.

Catching herself before she sent out any more negativity by cursing, she calmly and firmly started over. One, steady breathing. Two, alpha state. Three, hulking male form in her living room. Despite the negation—out loud, yet!—she recalled him with surprising ease. Kneeling, she would have to look up to take him all in—so she did. That made him seem even taller and more protective in her mind's eye.

It also gave her an intriguing vantage on those imaginary jeans.

He is real, she kept telling herself to the beat of barbarian drums, slowly perceiving the highlights of his hair, the plane of his cheeks, five-o'clock shadow, eyelashes. *He is real. He may not be of my world, but here and now he is real. . . .*

Soon, his shade stood before her as surely as if she were watching him on TV. Oh, she could also see the doorway beyond him, the display of photographs through him. He hadn't materialized anywhere but in the astral realm and in her own perception of it. But by focusing on his presence, not his absence, she could "see" him clearly indeed. The way his dark eyes stared silently back at her, she even felt his presence with her, in this sacred circle. She imagined the scent of him, a faint mix of soap and musky aftershave. For a moment, it seemed almost as if she could reach out across the altar and . . .

But no, she had a spell to cast.

Claiming the scarf, she laid it on the opposite side of the altar from herself, at his feet—and saw that her thought-form wore brown cowboy boots. Who would have thought? Then, sitting back, Tobi spoke what she'd written:

I ask thee, guardian, for a boon—
from now until the next full moon.
Protection, against anyone
Who means me harm. Yet harming none,
I bid thee, guardian, if you will
Patrol these grounds against all ill
As long as these, thy colors, fly—
Or if thou won't, bid me good-bye.

Then she waited. As her creation, he would probably do as she asked . . . but as soon as something became real, it got free will. He seemed so *very* real, she found herself holding her breath—then releasing it, relieved, when he shrugged one shoulder and took an easy step forward onto the scarf. He had accepted.

"Then I bid thee," she said, "to fulfill thy duty with the following virtues: Responsibility. Honor. Protection. . . ."

At one point during this recitation, angling her gaze upward and imagining his face, she thought she saw a hint of a smile. She liked it, liked the lips she'd envisioned for him. If this weren't the middle of a fairly hefty spell, she might even smile back. . . .

Tobi suddenly felt glad that she'd limited his existence to a twenty-eight-day cycle . . . and anxious to bind the spell!

"If this working be correct," she cautioned, "and allows others to be free, so I will it, so I shape it, and so mote it be."

And in the blink of an eye—*poof?*—she was alone again. Well, alone except for the masculine and feminine faces of God and the elements of Earth, Air, Fire, Water, and Spirit. But no tall, broad-shouldered, fictitious hunk stood before her.

She couldn't shake the idea that, just before vanishing into the standard, he'd winked at her.

Wow!

She took extra time to ground herself before thanking and

bidding farewell to the Lord and Lady, as well as the elements—"Go if you must, stay if you will." As she walked the circle again, envisioning the bubble of protective light receding back into her athame, the air seemed to move again, to drop several degrees. It had been warm in-circle. She'd been there awhile.

"My circle is open yet ever it remains, within me and without." Putting down the athame, she allowed herself to stretch a bit, then gathered the scarf from where she'd imagined her guardian stepping onto it. Into it.

It was such soft silk. The stylized knight painted on it was dashing, and the faint, geometric design behind him . . . was it a labyrinth? She almost hated to set it out where it could fade. But that, too, was part of the spell, and a small cost indeed. She'd asked the guardian to be with her one moon's cycle, and that was that.

So she went out onto her apartment terrace, into the quiet summer night, and tied the scarf to the wrought-iron railing, where it moved slightly in the warm breeze, in the cloud-shrouded moonlight. It was a romantic night, soft and heavy. "As long as this standard flies," she whispered, trailing her fingers across it, "so may you walk."

Good spell, she thought, then shivered—her magic shiver.

A motion from below her caught her attention.

For a moment, Tobi felt self-conscious . . . maybe nobody could have heard her, but they might wonder what she was doing on her balcony, well after midnight, in a peignoir! But then she looked closer, and felt a different self-consciousness—

—at the glimpse of white T-shirt as a tall, dark-haired man rounded the corner of the apartments beyond hers!

"Ho-ly crap," she whispered—and immediately regretted having said that out loud, in case she empowered it!

*   *   *

MAGIC *isn't supposed to work this way,* she typed on her PC to Cybele, one of an e-mail listing of Wiccan friends across the country who liked to call themselves a cybercircle. Cybele was the only one online to receive instant messages when Tobi, desperate to unburden to another magic user, logged on. That's probably because Cybele lived in Hawaii. It was much earlier in the day, in Hawaii.

The few moments Tobi had to wait after typing a quick overview of her spell, before her friend's response scrolled across her monitor's screen, felt like torture. Then, accompanied by a harplike strum of magical sound-effects from *Bewitched*:

CYBELE63: *What way, exactly?*

Tobi quickly typed, *Creating real people! One thing to form/summon being from pure energy. Other thing when it leaves footprints!!!*

As soon as the initial shock had allowed her to move—and she'd changed into something less likely to get her arrested or jumped—she'd hurried outside to check. Not with candles but with a really big flashlight. Nobody stopped by to see if she was the mugger, which seemed a mixed blessing.

So had the footprints.

Frankensteiny, she added. Then she hit "enter" and waited.

CYBELE63: *Just because man you saw was real doesn't mean he's man you created. Maybe was mugger.*

Also not a lot of comfort . . . but, surprisingly, it was a little.

Tobi typed the word that was so intricately linked with magic—a word that almost defined "natural means." *Coincidence?*

CYBELE63: *Maybe connected, but not your doing.*

Tobi considered that—and realized what was happening. One way to cope with magic was fearful self-doubt. With power came responsibility. Gods knew, enough B-grade movies had pushed that little lesson—what if she had "meddled in powers beyond her understanding?"

Frankensteiny indeed, she thought.

A second knee-jerk reaction was to dismiss magic as coincidence. She of all people should remember the message of Between-Times—that when magic was involved, things could be coincidence *and* more.

Her computer let out another harplike chord.

CYBELE63: *You cast a circle?*

Tobi typed, *Yes. Enter.*

CYBELE63: *You clarified good of all & free will & harm none.*

Cybele didn't even add a question mark, which soothed Tobi considerably. She wasn't some teenager practicing out of her first book-o-spells. She knew her magic couldn't create human beings, not unless other powers in the universe were involved— and she knew her own actions had been careful and correct. So she answered, *Yes.*

CYBELE63: *Don't give away power. Wait & see.*

Tobi took a deep breath, and whispered thanks for friends and fellow practitioners . . . and for the technology that allowed her to contact one in real time, even if Cybele was far away and they'd never actually met.

Thank you, she typed. *Merry meet.*

CYBELE63: *Merry meet. Tell me what happens.*

And they signed off. When Tobi heard thunder in the distance—so much for her full moon—she shut down her computer. As it closed Windows to the tune of *Bewitched,* her outlook shifted from dismay to careful excitement.

What if magic sometimes *did* work like that?

TOBI felt tangibly aware of her thought-form when she woke the next day . . . though maybe she should blame that on the

dream she woke from. She couldn't remember anything concrete from it . . . uncaptured dreams faded even faster against
"reality" than unrecorded instances of successful magic. But the
feeling of it lingered like a full-body memory, a delicious sense
of being safe, held . . . loved.

She stretched in bed, luxuriating in that feeling, and then she
sat up and thought, *He's out there.* And she smiled. She didn't
have to wonder. She just knew.

He was out there, doing what she'd asked of him, and it
felt . . . nice. It added something pleasant to her day.

Later, when she left for work, she cheerfully said, "Hello,"
into the evening—and she would not have been wholly surprised had somebody answered. She stopped by the twenty-
four-hour supermarket on her way home, and when she lifted
her packages out of the car, she half-expected her thought-form
to step out of the shadows and help carry the bags. *Welcome
home*, the energy at the edge of the parking lot seemed to say.

"Thank you," Tobi said softly, fully aware of how crazy she
would look if anybody were in the parking lot at four A.M. to
hear her. She would look as crazy as people seemed when talking on a mobile phone hands-free, she supposed, before you noticed the earpiece. As crazy as someone dancing and singing to
music on a Walkman. People who heard things others didn't always seemed crazy, even when they weren't.

"I'm glad to be home." And she blew a kiss toward the shadows, where he might be standing, as she passed.

Oh, she knew he wasn't rea—*NO!* She knew that he was *not
of this realm.* That was as much disservice as she would do her
creation. But it didn't hurt to enjoy the dream of him, did it?

It might even empower his protective abilities!

After changing into shorts and a tank top, Tobi sat out on the
terrace, reading by candlelight, sometimes fingering the soft
scarf that occasionally moved or shifted against the railing

where she'd tied it. It was a beautiful, gentle night, the moon only one day past full. That had to explain how incredibly . . . *fulfilled* she felt.

Two nights later, she saw him again—just for a moment as she rounded the corner of her car, and from the back. She still hadn't seen his face except in her dreams—and then she couldn't remember it. But she felt pleased, all the same. She felt safe.

She typed regular reports to her Witch list, who tuned in for daily updates as if Tobi's life had become *Passions* or *The Guiding Light*. She printed copies for her own journal, and at one point drove by Kinko's to make a color copy of the picture of the man, from behind, in the mist. The tag line made her laugh.

WHAT DO *YOU* THINK IS OUT THERE?

"HAVE you got a new neighbor?" asked Judy when she came by a week later, and Tobi took a deep, intrigued breath as she slipped her feet into sandals.

"Why do you ask?" she said, gathering her purse and a plastic sack of snacks. Judy's husband was out of town, and the two friends planned to catch an early movie before Tobi left for work.

Inside, she was thinking: *Did you see him? Huh? Did you?* But asking that would probably color Judy's objectivity.

"I thought I saw a guy standing near your car. Then when I looked again, he wasn't there."

Yes yes yes! He wasn't even waiting until full dark anymore; it was only sunset! Then again, Between Times like dusk and dawn, midnight and noon, allowed the best magic because of the overlapping of worlds. Tobi asked, "What did he look like?"

But Judy knew her too well for that. She stopped in front of the door before Tobi could open it. "What's going on?"

"I'll tell you in the car," promised Tobi—the movie would be starting with or without them, and she did have her priorities. "But you may not believe me."

"Hasn't stopped you before." Suspicious, Judy nevertheless stepped aside so that Tobi, after a last kiss for her cat, could head out.

Every step down from her third-story apartment felt imbued with an extra awareness. The path out to the parking lot, past neatly cut grass and an empty beer bottle, seemed even more so. Tobi savored it as she'd been savoring it for two weeks. It felt like expectation—like opening the mailbox on her birthday, or heading out on a vacation, or picking up the phone when her Caller I.D. showed it was someone she'd been hoping would call.

Someone like a man?

Not just any man.

Judy unlocked her car by remote—it made a chirping sound and flashed its lights, as if happy to see them—and Tobi climbed into the passenger seat, trying not to search the surroundings for her guardian. She'd been seeing him on and off all week, but never by looking directly at him. Always with her peripheral vision.

"You would not believe the problems Bill had catching his plane," Judy said as she started the car, and went on with something about paper tickets and credit cards, none of which Tobi wholly heard until, "You aren't listening, are you?"

"Sort of," assured Tobi, her gaze just over the mirror out her window . . . so that, *in* the mirror, she could almost see a dark-haired figure standing at the edge of the parking lot, where they'd just come from. *Bye,* she mouthed fondly. *See you later.*

Gods, but he was gorgeous. His white T-shirt looked orange in the sunset.

"This is starting to creep me out, Tobe," said Judy. "What's going on?"

Tobi told her. Enthusiastically. All the way to the theater.

"So he's like a ghost?" demanded Judy, circling the cineplex lot in search of a parking space.

In the Patrick Swayze sense? "Only in that he's overlapping from another realm. But he's not the soul of a dead person, if that's what you mean. I have a feeling he's more than just my creation—that I tapped into something bigger. Better, even. But I'm not sure what that is, what *he* is." *Except mine.* "I'm so excited you saw him too."

"*Maybe* saw him," Judy corrected. "I didn't get a very good look."

"My Witch list will freak, all the same. Not many of them have ever had magic turn out so . . . definitively. Well, except for Merlinna, but some of us have doubts about her; her stories tend to sound like scenes from *The Craft*. You know how the Internet is."

"So you've been e-mailing about this guy a lot?"

"And dreaming about him—and I cast circles around my bed, to make sure nothing dangerous gets in." Though if an incubus looked like this guy, or like she *felt* he did despite not remembering the dreams, would she mind? "I write down what I can remember, as soon as I wake up, and it's pretty interesting reading. For me, anyway." Things like *he gets home tired but then we make out on the couch* and *laughing with him, hiking by the river, he gives me his extra water.* "I wake up happy."

"You sound happy." Judy's voice had tightened and not, Tobi thought, because they were still looking for a parking spot.

"You don't," she noted warily.

"Should I be? You're more excited about this guy than you ever were about Joe."

"All the more reason to be glad Joe and I broke up. Jude, we're going to miss the coming attractions. Would you like me to . . . ?" And Tobi rolled her fingers. Her Parking-Space Song didn't always work, but sometimes it helped. And it always made them laugh.

"*No.* Last time we tried that here, the power went out in the entire theater."

Which had *really* made them laugh. "I told you that wasn't related. Probably."

Giving up, Judy pulled into a space some distance from the building and cut the engine. "Still."

Tobi felt frustrated. She wanted to gush about her hunky thought-form, and Judy was practically radiating negativity. "You know I'm a careful magic user. It's never worried you before."

"You've never fallen in love with a figment of your imagination before."

Tobi considered that as they unbuckled, made sure their cola bottles and candy bars were hidden deeply enough in her purse to smuggle in, got out of the car, and started the long hike toward the theater. The day's heat hovered over the asphalt, despite that the sun had set. "One, the only people I've *ever* fallen in love with have been imaginary. Think about it." Even once when she'd thought she was in real, corporeal love, it had been with someone she'd imagined the man to be. If she added her favorite movie and TV heroes into the mix . . . well, some of her sexiest moments had been wide-screen.

Judy didn't argue it.

"Two," Tobi said, "I am not falling in love with my thought-form."

"You're not the only one with instincts." Judy shook her head. "I think I'd rather you don't date at all than that you date someone make-believe."

"I'm not dating him," insisted Tobi. "I can't even *see* him except from the corner of my eye." *Or asleep.*

"Mmhm." Judy bought the tickets, so that Tobi wouldn't

have to open her purse and risk revealing their contraband. They got to the screen just in time for the coming attractions, which ended the conversation for the moment. But the movie— a love story—helped clarify things, all the same.

Tobi had several theories about the magic of movies. One was that occupying one part of the mind with fiction allowed a deeper part to work things through unimpeded. Another was that a good romance connected viewers to Universal Love Energy. It reminded people who were involved of their loved one, and soothed those who weren't involved, offering quiet assurance that romance really did exist. Usually, Tobi fell into the latter category.

That evening, she found herself in the former.

She wanted to be with him. She felt like calling home and talking to him. Too bad he had no voice. No phone number, even. No *face!* That she could see.

But she would know it if she saw it.

When she saw it.

Oh, my.

"I think you're half-right," she admitted to Judy afterward, still wrapping the softness of the movie's happy ending gently around herself. "I'm not *falling* in love with my thought-form."

"Good," said Judy. "But . . . ?"

Tobi tested the idea with words. "I think my thought-form is the one I've been in love with all along."

CYBELE63: *Interesting theory. Why?*

Tobi typed, *Explains why details seemed so set. Also explains familiarity. Even dreams—having his energy nearby opens portals.*

On top of all that, it felt right. All she had to do was say, "It's him," and she got her "magic shiver," a delicious shudder down the spine, ending with a tingle in her hands and feet. It meant potent powers were afoot.

With a chiming noise, a different name scrawled across their chat.

MERLINNAGURL: *Yu didnt do luv spell? I once did & wuz STOCKED!!!*

Tobi assumed she meant "stalked." That happened with badly done love spells—not just in the movies. She decided not to put energy into wondering whether it had ever really happened to Merlinna. So she simply typed, *No love spells. No names.*

In fact, it was standard to give a thought-form a name, but she hadn't felt . . . qualified. As if he already *had* a name, and it just wasn't time for her to know it. Yet.

CYBELE63: *M, that's why love spells are dangerous. T, Maybe he saw chance for a visit.*

Unless I'm going crazy, admitted Tobi, and hit "enter."

CYBELE63: *Why crazy?*

B/C I'm in love with someone, talking, caring, and he's not even . . . No. She wouldn't doubt his reality again. It would be like refusing to clap one's belief in fairies to save Tinkerbell. She deleted that, and settled on: *He's not really here w/me.*

CYBELE63: *Neither am I.*

She had a point. An argument could be made that Cybele didn't even exist at the same time as Tobi; it was still yesterday in Hawaii. But she was real, and Tobi was real to her. Now Merlinna . . .

The computer chimed.

MERLINNAGURL: *Why not use names?*

Luckily, Cybele began to patiently explain the ethics against naming anybody but oneself in any magic for which one did not have explicit permission. Normally, Tobi would have joined her—it was for opportunities like this that they endured Merlinna's usual hubris. But if her thought-form was really, well . . . *him* . . . he only had two weeks left of his visit.

Merry meet, she typed, and signed off before Cybele had to bother responding.

She wanted to go sit on the balcony, in the warmth of his presence, and wrap her hand in the rapidly fading scarf.

Tobi made an extra effort to stay involved with the outside world during the next two weeks. It was partly precaution against dissociative behavior—magic or not, she balked at crossing the line into mental illness—and partly preparation. When the full moon came again, she had to take down and bury the scarf and release the thought-form. She'd promised.

Better not to have isolated herself when it happened.

So she built houses with other Habitat for Humanity volunteers one weekend . . . but amused herself with the image of the man she loved in a work-belt, shingling the roof beside her.

She resisted the temptation to take extra time off work, and was surprised when a colleague asked if she was dating. "You're wearing makeup," he explained. "And those are new clothes, right?"

She was, and they were. She'd also bought herself flowers.

She went to dinner with her family and enjoyed reminiscing about her late grandparents. Not long before leaving, she turned down her big sister's invitation to a party on the twenty-first. "That's Summer Solstice," Tobi explained, thinking quickly. "There's a big festival going on at the lake."

"Oh, well," said Teresa, and shrugged. "Maybe some other time. It'd be nice for you to get out and meet people."

Other than the people from work, from Habitat for Humanity, and all her friends? Not to mention . . . "It's a big festival because people will be there."

"I meant normal people," said Teresa, which led to their semiannual no-such-thing-as-normalcy fight. Driving home, Tobi found herself justifying her side of the argument to the empty passenger seat. She could almost hear a man say, *She worries because she loves you.* Then, *Who can blame her?*

But the parking lot was empty when she got home.

Her phone was ringing when she reached her apartment—Judy. "Turn on channel five. Fast!"

The reporter was interviewing a young woman who'd had a close call with the mugger, only half a mile from where Tobi lived. "But then he looked at the parking lot, nervous, like someone was coming," she gushed into the anchor's microphone. "And he ran off!"

They now had a police artist's drawing of the man's face which, Tobi felt relieved, was nothing like her guardian's face at all. She might not be able to picture it outside of dreams, but she knew she would recognize it.

Wow.

She went out onto the balcony and fingered the scarf. It had faded to a pale blur of pastel-faint color, and its edges had started to unravel. Not even a week left. "You're supposed to stay in this apartment complex," she chided softly into the night air. "We weren't going to save the whole city."

No answer, of course. But she thought about the girl on the news, with her college T-shirt and glasses, and she understood him all the same. She suspected that she usually did.

"Good job," she added. She'd always known he was a hero.

When esbat—the night of the full moon—arrived, she received at least four e-mails and a telephone call reminding her that she was loved, that her friends cared. All because the visit of someone she may yet have imagined was ending. She knew she was supposed to be depressed, but she felt . . . lucky.

She untied the bleached remnant of the scarf from her railing, having to do deep breaths and envision the knot sliding loose in order to manage it. Then, inside, she readied for her ritual. She turned off the telephone ringers and turned down the answering machine. She chose the same CD as before, lit incense, and set out her quarter candles. She cast her circle, bid the presence of the four elements and her gods, and finally kneeled before her altar, alone in her circle and yet touched by so many people of her world and beyond. She felt a strange *lack* of depression about this . . . but she could think of only one person qualified to discuss it, and it was neither Judy nor Cybele.

"Perfect," she whispered, yet again.

Lying back on her carpet, still in the safety of her circle, Tobi sank into guided relaxation, feet first, then calves, knees, thighs . . . until she'd reached a deep and meditative state. She imagined herself surrounded by a brilliant silvery light, protective and powerful. Then she envisioned a well beside her, into which she tossed all the negativity of her week like a handful of dirty pennies. She felt her astral form turning away, even as her concerns plunked into the cleansing waters of this dream-world. Leaving her body was *not* Tobi's forte. . . .

But when she opened her eyes—her astral eyes—she found that the silvery light had become a thick, gentle mist surrounding her.

And then she saw him.

The man's back became visible to her first, through the fog— his T-shirt, his jeans. She knew that back, those shoulders. She knew that hair, as if her fingers had buried themselves in it for countless lifetimes.

"It's you," she whispered.

He turned to face her, dark eyes lighting with recognition, and Tobi felt full force his joy, acceptance—love. Probably because it was hers, too.

It was him, all right.

"You were expecting someone else?" he challenged, and she heard in his voice countless endearments, nighttimes, lifetimes together. No wonder she hadn't given up on him.

"Never," she promised, going to him. She raised her hands to his chest, her fingers curled slightly, afraid to really touch. Touch didn't work the same way in the astral realms. Surely it would disappoint. "But you're taking your time, this time around."

"We agreed to it before we started," he reminded her gently, brushing a callused hand over her hair. Clearly he didn't follow the same no-touching-in-the-astral-realm rules. "You probably don't remember. My physical self doesn't, either. The point of incarnating is to forget and then relearn, right? It's part of the fun."

"But I remembered you," she insisted. "Part of me has always remembered you."

"Some things are impossible to let go." He drew his hand down her cheek now. "But it's time to pretend to, isn't it? I can feel the moon."

It took a long moment, through the satisfaction of being with him again, to remember her spell. "I've got to dismiss you from the task. I promised."

"And you keep your promises," he agreed quietly. "Always. So spell away."

Somehow, Tobi remembered her closing spell.

> *"Upon this moon, upon this time,*
> *I release thee with this, my rhyme,*
> *And with my thanks, and with my heart—*
> *So merry we meet, and merry we part."*

He nodded. "You always were handy with the couplets. Now, one more thing. . . ."

And he kissed her.

It was not a physical kiss because they were not, at the moment, physical beings. It was more. Deeper. It was a melding of their auras, their energies, their souls. She felt surrounded by him, imbued with him . . . and as sure of him as she was of her own heart. No wonder she wasn't interested in looking elsewhere! This was worth waiting lifetimes for.

Soon, she heard—or felt—him promise. *Now close it.*

"If this be correct, and allows others to be free: So I will it, so I shape it, and so mote it be."

She opened her eyes to see the ceiling fan above her, shadowy in candlelight. Alone again . . . but never completely.

Her body wasn't relaxed anymore.

Her toes were curling.

BY the time Tobi made it to the big Solstice Festival, she'd buried the scarf with the original picture, been to another movie with Judy, and seen on the news that the mugger had turned himself in. He'd said he felt he was being stalked. Though he didn't mention a dark-haired man in jeans and a white T-shirt, Tobi had her suspicions.

At the festival, she enjoyed spending the long, hot afternoon with other pagans—the heat wouldn't last forever, after all. A live band played Celtic music, with anyone who'd brought a drum—and many had—joining in. Others clasped hands and danced in circles, like a magical ring-around-the-rosie, the brave ones weaving in and out under the arms of their companions. Almost everyone brought potluck for the feast, from store-packaged cookies to homemade vegetarian dishes.

Oz was there, flirting with a white-haired earth mother and wearing a tank top which read THINGS HAVEN'T BEEN THE SAME

SINCE THAT HOUSE FELL ON MY SISTER. He waved when he saw Tobi.

One woman, who Tobi thought was HP—high priestess—of a local coven, did a spontaneous recitation of the Charge of the Goddess. It gave Tobi magic shivers, especially the part which went: "For if that which you seek, you find not within yourself, you will never find it without."

Best of all were the labyrinths. As Oz had predicted, the event organizers had created a whole selection of them—a replica of the Chartres labyrinth, a Cretan "seven-circuit" maze, and a Medicine Wheel Walk for those pagans on Native American paths. The designs had been chalked into the grass like multifaceted baseball diamonds.

Tobi chose the replica of the labyrinth from Crete. It struck her as Greek . . . *Pygmalion*-y. Though resembling a maze, it only had one way in and one way out. She liked that the point wasn't to struggle through dead ends and false turns. The point was simply to choose one's path and then trust it, to walk it deliberately . . . and at one's own speed.

As she took steady steps between the chalk guidelines, she focused on letting go—of societal expectations, of fears, of self-doubt. She realized, as she reached the center, that she felt truly happy. Hot, but happy. Bug-bit, but happy. Alone . . .

But she wasn't alone. As she'd told her sister, it was a big festival. Besides . . .

A breeze stirred the hair stuck to her neck, and she smiled as she sensed his presence. *If that which you seek, you find not within yourself . . .*

"Merry meet," she greeted softly into the coming dusk. The standard pagan greeting was short for "Merry meet, merry part, and merry meet again." Why waste energy mourning separations, when reunions would so surely follow?

Soon, he'd said. She remembered that much.

"I'll be here," she said. "I promise."

Pygmalion's story ended happily, didn't it? Why couldn't hers?

Tobi turned around and as she paced her way slowly across the grass, tracing the labyrinth back out, she drew to herself: one, confidence; two, happiness; three, hope. He was out there. She felt him, as surely as she felt the Goddess in the nearby lake, the God in the late-sinking sun.

In the meantime, she would enjoy the company, the sunshine, the day—then have her own, solitary ritual later tonight.

She decided to use Beach Boys music, and laughed. Whoever he was, he liked Beach Boys music, too.

She said, "Perfect."

Star Trek Time-Travel Survival Spells

EVELYN VAUGHN

Question: Are these spells, or survival techniques?
Answer: Yes.

Like Tobi in "A Solitary Path," I'm a great believer that much of the power of "Betweens" (crossroads, midnight, etc.) comes from releasing the need to cling to "either/or" thinking. Also like Tobi, I take a great deal of inspiration from television. One particularly powerful world that TV has given us is Gene Roddenberry's *Star Trek* universe—if you don't believe some of those characters have become powerful thought-forms in their own right, be sure to read Janet and Stewart Farrar's *Spells and How They Work*! Admit it. Isn't it fun to consider that all those Trekkers who've had to put up with uninspired "get a life" jokes (only Shatner's was inspired—the rest are derivative) might actually be more sensitive to other dimensions than the mundanes?

The first version of the following spell is from a facet of *Star Trek* that many have forgotten. Not any of the prime-time TV series. Not the books. Not even the movies. No, this is inspired from the animated, Saturday morning cartoon of *Star Trek* and an episode called "Yesteryear" (written by D. C. Fontana). In it, Mr. Spock goes through a time portal back to Vulcan and his own past. There are now two of him—the adult Spock he is, and the child Spock he was, and he ends up saving his own life. Yes, that could be seen as a time paradox; if he hadn't saved himself, he could not have become the adult who saved himself. But paradoxes only confuse those of us who can't do Betweens.

This episode, and possibly another D. C. Fontana offering from *Land of the Lost,* got me thinking even as a child: Wouldn't it be cool if our future selves could time travel back to our own present and give us help and encouragement when needed?

Eventually I began to think: Why can't they?

Thus is born the first of my Star Trek Time-Travel Survival Spells.

When to Use Them

For the first two: use them whenever you're in a time of great stress and would really appreciate some reassurance that things are going to get better, from someone who understands you and should clearly know whereof s/he speaks. For the last one: use it when you're feeling on top of the world and want to save the feeling.

Supplies and Ingredients

None, except your imagination. At least, no supplies are *needed* beyond that.

However, if you find that your ability to visualize is greatly enhanced by props, then by all means, feel free to find some that work for you. Props that set the mood for magic include special music, candlelight, and incense—of particular use would be a scent that you associate with yourself or your own magic. If you're a fan, you could use *Star Trek*–type props (a fake phaser, a flip-phone used as a communicator, a uniform, even a button that says TO HELL WITH THE PRIME DIRECTIVE; I'M GOING TO KILL SOMEONE). Or, on a more serious note, you might try the kind of prop that you can imagine a future-you would bring back to the present-you, in order to prove that she's you (something you can't imagine ever parting with).

Preparation

Sometimes I do this spell in the midst of a crisis, and so do no preparation. If you have time to prepare, however, consider casting a circle. The standard method is to trace the boundary of a circle around yourself, envisioning the blue light spreading into a bubble around you. A down-and-dirty way for impatient, fire-sign types is to simply concentrate (maybe holding your breath) and then imagine that—*pop!*—a blue eggshell of protective energy has appeared around you. Either way, believe that the protection is real. Validate that by saying something like: "This is my circle, I am safe" or "Around me, above me, below me, may nothing harmful enter or leave this place." If you wish to invite the elements or your God(ess/esses), by all means do so.

It is also of course useful, if you have time and ability, to make yourself comfortable sitting or lying down.

Spell #1: A Visit from Future-You

❅ Envision yourself from the future—five years, ten years, etc. I recommend you don't overdo it and try to contact yourself at age 103. Not because you won't live to 103 (why wouldn't you?) but because really, at 103 won't you have better things to do than travel back in time to reassure your younger self? Besides, there's less chance you'll give away too much information, the less time that exists between Present-You and Future-You.

❅ Imagine Future-You saying something like, "Hi! What's the problem?" If s/he'd hug you, then allow that. If you need proof, let her/him convince you. Then tell Future-You why you're upset.

❅ Now imagine/listen to what Future-You will say to that. Generally, s/he'll be pretty good at putting things into perspective for you.

Have you lost your job? S/he'll remind you that you've lost other jobs, but continue to find new and often better ones. Have you lost a loved one? S/he might comfort you as nobody outside yourself can, and tell you there will be, while not replacements for the friend you've lost, people in your future still worth living for. Since Future-You won't be zinging through the cosmos unless s/he is in a strong place, the story should always be a good one.

Note: *The wise future-you will avoid specifics.* Why? So as to avoid those time paradoxes. Why not play it safe?

- ℭ Feel yourself relaxing to the realization that things will work out, that although we sometimes have to redefine what "work out" means, things always do.
- ℭ Thank Future-You for coming, and wish her/him safe journeys on the trip home.
- ℭ Know that things will get better. If you can't trust yourself, whom can you trust?

Spell #2: A Glimpse Forward

- ℭ Find a place where you can sit and be comfortable for at least a minute or two.
- ℭ Breathe deeply in order to relax your body, even if you fear you can't relax your soul.
- ℭ Imagine a good moment in the near future, where whatever is bothering you has passed. It particularly helps to envision something you are very likely to do, and enjoy doing. If you are afraid your cat is getting ill, then envision sitting with it, healthy again. If your car has broken down, envision driving it without problem. Another option is to imagine doing something you've always longed to do: a special trip or activity.
- ℭ Say something like, "So mote it be" or "I have this to look forward to."

❰ Relax, encouraged by the goal set by that glimpse of the future.

❰ Make sure you then do what you envisioned yourself doing. If you encouraged yourself by visiting Paris, then visit Paris. Keeping your word is important in magic.

Spell #3: The Giving End

You know those moments that seem golden? Everything's going wonderfully and you feel like you're breathing straight nitrous oxide, you're so happy? You may not be able to bottle those moments, but you can send them out to yourself.

❰ Breathe deeply.

❰ Say something like, "I send this to myself" or "May I always remember this."

❰ Imagine that the happy you is now heading out to visit your younger self, at some time when s/he was anxious or depressed and needed encouragement. It is important to keep your word, after all. We certainly want to avoid those pesky paradoxes, just in case!

If all else fails, call on your favorite character for help. But realize they're more likely to appear in a dream (night *or* day) than on your doorstep. And remember to thank them!

The Iron Bride
(A Bast Mystery)

ROSEMARY EDGHILL

"Truth is an iron bride."
—Traditional

Dedication: This one's for Jim Macdonald, who should be able to guess why.

Sociologists and cultural anthropologists would tell you that new religions commonly spring up when the old ones can no longer address common psychological needs. Feminists would tell you that the reemergence of the universal feminine to challenge the patriarchy is long overdue. Ceremonial Magicians would say that the Aeon of Horus has begun, and New Agers would talk about harmonic convergence and the Age of Aquarius.

None of these explanations completely covers my territory. My name is Bast, and I'm a Witch—or, if you prefer, a member of the nonpastoral, nonproselytizing, adult-conversion polytheism known as Wicca, sometimes called the Craft of the Wise.

Wiccans, or Witches if you prefer, practice in small groups

known as covens, and the conviction among my friends for quite some time had been that I was long overdue in starting one. I wasn't out of delaying tactics yet, though. It is a truth universally acknowledged, as Jane Austen almost says, that every working coven needs a coven sword, which was my current excuse for not starting an Outer Court, or preinitiate coven: good ceremonial swords aren't all that easy to come by. Of course, there are the blades prominently displayed in the windows of esoteric boutiques like the Serpent's Truth (aka the Snake) and the Sorcery Shoppe, but at 300 percent markup they—along with the dried bats and wizard hats with which they share the window—are mainly for the tourist trade.

Normally I would have just hit up Ironshadow for the work, but when I'd gone looking, Pat seemed to have dropped out of sight. This explained why I was moping around the Snake—the oldest and proudly tackiest occult shop in lower Manhattan—late on a Thursday night in June, staring wistfully, or so I told myself, at the case containing the Genuine Grimoire of Armandel Ritual Sword and Matching Dagger (rhodium-plated) and wondering if either my conscience or my Visa would ever forgive me for buying a blade—any blade—at the Snake's prices.

"Shopping?" Lark asked, after watching me stare at the tourist sword for about ten minutes.

Lark was here because Trismegistus, the Snake's owner, had hired Lark last spring as the Snake's new manager. And to my vague surprise, Lark made a pretty good manager, or at least as good as the Snake was ever likely to either deserve or attract.

I explained my problems to him, which is to say, I complained for about ten minutes about the unavailability of a good custom swordsmith.

"I know a guy who makes blades," Lark said. "Wayland Smith. He's up in Poughkeepsie."

"Poughkeepsie? It sounds like a disease," I said. It also

sounded like it was outside the city, and the last time I ventured upstate, it hadn't ended well.

Lark smirked, something he does irritatingly well. He reached down and pulled out a wrapped bundle. "He did this," he said, placing it in my hands. It was heavy. I turned back the cloth and looked.

The blade was plain iron, heavily oiled and inlaid halfway down the blade with fillwork symbols in fine (i.e., *pure*) silver. I couldn't interpret the characters, but I could admire the workmanship: sharp and even. The furnishings were highly polished jeweler's bronze, and there were more runes running in a circle on the face of the disc-shaped pommel. The hilt itself was carved amber.

"Nice," I said, handing it back reluctantly. Good blades are my weakness, and with my paycheck, I can't afford many. "Poughkeepsie?" It was starting to sound more attractive.

"Why don't we drive up and see him?" my cheerful coenabler said. "I've got my spare helmet with me."

POUGHKEEPSIE, besides being a joke, is a midsized city situated along the Hudson River halfway between Manhattan and Albany—or Entropy and Death—with nothing much to recommend it including location. Its main pastimes are real estate fraud and murder, with more drug trafficking than you'd think possible in a city with a population of under a hundred thousand. Despite several area colleges, the local tone is somewhere between Urban Slum and God's Mistake. Of course, I might not have been seeing the Queen City of the Hudson at her best, since it was after one o'clock in the morning when Lark's Harley crossed the city line. They'd rolled up the sidewalks hours ago.

"Do you think he's going to still be up?" I asked Lark when we stopped at a light.

Lark nodded and said something muffled by his helmet. The streets we rode through were blessed with a surplus of decaying and badly modernized Victorians, souvenirs of the days when a river location meant a thriving metropolis. A few minutes later, we pulled into the driveway of one that was in better shape than most of its neighbors. I could see lights on at the back of the house, but the front rooms were dark.

Lark balanced the Harley on its kickstand and swung off. I pulled off my helmet and tried to work circulation back into numb extremities while he skipped up the steps.

"The front door's open," Lark said, with an air of positive discovery.

"Don't go in there," I said quickly, but men are different from real people. Disregarding the obvious common-sense explanation that the reason the door was open was because the house was already filled with brain-eating alien Terminators from the future, Lark disappeared inside. I followed more cautiously, heartened by the lack of screaming. Since I still didn't hear anything when I reached the door, I reluctantly followed him inside.

Wayland Smith's living room was decorated in Early Testosterone Oblivious: state-of-the-art electronics, ratty secondhand furniture, and heart-stoppingly gorgeous swords. The man was obviously a bachelor without a steady girlfriend.

"Hey, honey?" Lark called in a strange voice.

There are very few people I will permit to call me "honey"—or "baby" or "sweetie" or "dear"—and Lark is no longer on that list. But there was something in his tone that made me swallow my automatic protest and follow his voice into the back of the house.

"Oh," I said inadequately, when I saw what Lark had seen.

Wayland Smith was sprawled in a chair behind a desk in what was obviously his office. He would not be taking orders for swords tonight, or any night in the future. Wayland Smith was dead and, like Marley, there was very little doubt about it. His throat had been cut and there was blood everywhere, great sloppy horror-movie amounts of it. Around his neck Smith wore a large formerly shiny silver pentacle—the star-in-cicle that's the badge of our stretch of the Aquarian Frontier. Whatever else he'd been, Smith had been one of us, or at least a fellow traveler, and his death disturbed me on the level where self-interest lives.

"Fuck," Lark said reverently.

I stared at the body, entranced in the way one can only be by very real things. It takes about ninety seconds to bleed out from a severed carotid; long enough for the victim to think about what's happening to him. It feels like drowning, so I'm told.

"I can't be here," Lark said, empirical evidence to the contrary.

"Yes, you can," I said firmly, grabbing his arm. I didn't know our friends the police all that well, at least the Poughkeepsie flavor, but I knew they really frowned on people who fled crime scenes. "You didn't kill him and you've got an airtight alibi. You were in the store when it happened."

"Like you know when he was killed," Lark snarled.

"Well, it was less than three hours ago. The blood's still red," I reasoned, out of too much experience. The blood stood out in pools on Wayland's black shirt, and the air was full of a smell halfway between fresh copper and bad hamburger. It occurred to me belatedly that if the body was that fresh the murderer might still be hiding somewhere in the house holding a nice sharp sword, and a sword has always been a killing weapon, whatever its magical uses.

"C'mon, Batman." I headed outside, dragging Lark with me.

*   *   *

THE police were, of course, overjoyed to be called to the scene of a flashy murder by a couple of dubious civilians. We got a nice assortment of Law: two City, one Town, a Sheriff, a displaced Statie, and an unmarked car full of grumpy detectives. Lark and I gave our statements several times and would probably be asked to give them several more. Nobody was really happy about Wayland Smith's profession, or Lark's, or about the fact that two New Yorkers had come up here after midnight to discuss buying a sword from the deceased.

Everybody (including us witnesses) stood around on the street drinking coffee from the Zippy Mart around the corner while the good guys waited for Crime Scene to finish up inside. Lark had gone to hunch over his Harley like a morose, denim-clad biker Jesus, but I was standing close enough to eavesdrop, more or less by accident, on a conversation two detectives were having. Either they hadn't noticed I was there, or (more likely) didn't care.

"They can't find the hand," one of the plainclothesmen said.

"Well, did they look?" the other answered.

"Geez, Benj, I don't know. D'you suppose the guy took it with him?"

"What would a drug dealer want with some guy's hand?" Benj asked reasonably. "C'mon, Row. It's probably in the river by now."

About then the EMTs brought out the body, strapped to a gurney and wrapped in a sheet. (Was Poughkeepsie too poor to afford body bags? Did it have so many murders they'd run out of them?) There were faint wet splotches around the chest where the blood had pooled, and also further down, on the body's right side.

They can't find the hand.

The penny dropped, and I realized what the two LEOs had been talking about. Whoever murdered Wayland Smith had also cut off his right hand, the way Romans used to do to sui-cides. And considering Smith's profession and clientele, I could think of only one reason someone'd do that.

"You're looking for a Christian ritual magician," I blurted out.

Both Benj and Row turned to face me.

"THAT was one of your brighter moments," Lark said to me around noon that same day. We'd spent the whole morning making formal statements at the cop shop, which turned out to be about six blocks from the murder site. I had been encouraged to explain my peculiar announcement, but life is not an episode of either *Buffy* or *The X-Files*, and nobody was going to drop everything to go off in search of masked Templars and other mythical beasts on my say-so. As witnesses after the fact with alibis and addresses, we were eventually allowed to go home. We'd gone to the nearest diner first, having missed dinner, breakfast, and a night's sleep.

"Look, I said I was sorry, okay? I shouldn't have said any-thing," I admitted placatingly. Lark has a tendency to belabor the obvious and require large amounts of appeasement, but if I liked him better than I do we'd still be lovers.

"Yeah, right," Lark said, rubbing his eyes. "There go my spe-cial orders. I sent Way half a dozen. Even if they're done, they're probably impounded or something."

"I'm sure it wasn't Smith's idea to get whacked," I said, but that begged the question to which nobody was going to give me the answer: whose idea was it? The New Aquarian Frontier is not a place noted for flashy murders and bloody internecine re-ligious warfare, no matter what stories we like to tell ourselves. "Do you know any of his other clients?" I asked before I could stop myself.

"Are you going to start this detective shit again?" Lark grumbled.

I shrugged. Apparently I was. Because there was something I believed that the police didn't, and so I didn't believe, as Detective Rowland P. Morrisey and his brethren did, that Smith had been killed in a burglary, or even as part of a drug deal gone wrong. I thought he'd been deliberately *executed*.

Anybody might cut a guy's throat—but damned few of them would take the trouble to cut off his right hand before, during, or after the whack. That took a killer who believed in magic—and who didn't like Smith's brand of the same—a Christian magician.

"Christian magician" might seem to be an oxymoron, but for about as long as there have been Christians, there have been Christian magicians—ranging from necromancers, who explicitly conjure demons in the name of Christ, to those esoteric souls who publish long lists of formulae for the evocation of angels.

"Forget about it," Lark advised, and shoved the check at me so I could split it.

THOUGH I didn't have a lot of choice about staying out of the investigation, I couldn't forget about it. It wasn't that I felt some spiritual appointment to solve the case, or even that I had any desire to avenge Wayland Smith, a man I'd never met. My interest was more in the nature of a purely intellectual exercise, because Smith's killer and I shared certain assumptions about the nature of reality that it would take the City of Poughkeepsie a good deal of time to catch up with.

Fact: Someone had killed Wayland Smith, cutting his throat and then removing his right hand to keep Smith's ghost from striking back out of the afterlife. If someone was taking those particular precautions against postdeath payback, the odds were it was a Christian Ceremonial, and that led me down a trail of other assumptions.

That I could find him, for one.

A Christian Ceremonial Magician had to be getting his ritual supplies from somewhere a little more advanced than the gift shop at St. John the Unfinished, and while your basic occult stores—Chanter's Revel, the Snake, the Sorcery Shop, Mirror Mirror—are fine on herbs, oils, candles, and even church incense and saint's statues, when it comes to holy relics, consecrated Hosts, and a few other items, you'll probably have to look elsewhere.

Where?

Unfortunately for my peace of mind, there were ways I could find out.

I offered to babysit the cashbox at the Snake one evening later that week when Lark had an errand to run, and in the best amateur sleuth tradition, I took the opportunity to burgle the files. The little cubbyhole office next to the temple in the back was crammed with copies of *The New Age Retailer*, *Gnosis*, and *Green Egg*, as well as various bills and receipts from suppliers. At the back of one of the battered file cabinets I found Lark's record of vendors for specialty supplies and custom work.

Most of it was mundane and a lot of it was familiar. Some of it was exotic special-order stuff, like suppliers of real lambskin parchment (sheets or bound books), or alchemic glassware, or athanors. There were things specific to Santeria, to Asatru, to Mithraism . . . to Christianity.

I leafed through the folder. Icons, rosaries, handmade prayerbooks, saints' relics, scapulars, consecrated church incense, holy oil, official liturgical vestments . . . items most of my fellow travelers would see no need for. The list of addresses was short: a shop in Canada, a monastery in California, what looked like a private address in France (with a note in Lark's left-handed scrawl that they were Cathars), another one in Maine, and a shop in Westchester County called the Kingdom. The contact was listed only as Brother Samael. Lark had noted that the Kingdom supplied both holy water and consecrated Hosts to "qualified buyers."

That alone was enough to blip my radar: you don't go selling the body of your god on the open market unless you're pretty spiritually adventurous. So the question was: Was Brother Samael adventurous enough to think he had a mandate to execute pagans and heretics?

IT took me two days more to talk myself into going up there to find out, and what I saw when I arrived wasn't at all what I expected. Despite Lark's notes, the Kingdom apparently catered to the sincere but lightweight Protestant flavors of the faith. The whole place had a light airy open look that almost blinded me, and the keynote colors were mauve, peach, and Pepto-Bismol pink. Wearing Basic New York Black in the middle of all this made me feel like a spider on a birthday cake, and I checked to make sure my pentagram was tucked securely into my T-shirt.

It was midafternoon, and I was the only person in the Kingdom besides the clerk. I wandered around the aisles and displays for a while, a bit daunted by all the spaniel-Jesuses and Precious Moments Bibles. There were a lot of angels and affirmations scattered about, but despite its harrowing attempts at perkiness, the Kingdom had the faintly discouraged air of a business that isn't doing well.

Now that I was here, I wasn't sure why I'd come. Lark's files had listed this place as a supplier of heavy-duty Christian ritual supplies, but I didn't see a thing that would qualify, other than some silver boxes of frankincense and myrrh and a display of censer charcoal. Lark's note had to be somebody's idea of a goof, or his own perverse aide-mémoire.

I went outside, feeling flatter than a close brush with mundainity could account for. I'd been sure there'd be some answers here, someone I could question just like a paperback detective to get a lead on Smith's killer. And despite the harrowing ordinariness of it all, I had the unsettled feeling I was missing something.

When you get that feeling, the thing to do is stop long enough for your unconscious mind to establish communications with the conscious one. I looked around the street, scrupulously cataloguing my surroundings just for something to do while my mind entered that state that is not so much trance as *stillness*.

I was in one of the less-affluent Westchester commercial zones. The Kingdom shared retail space with a nail boutique and a karate studio on a street full of two- and three-story buildings: deli, antique shop, photographer, music store. In common with its neighboring structures, there was an alleyway between the building and its neighbor, which had a florist on the ground floor and an accountant above.

In New York, trash goes to the curb in cans or bags. In the burbs, the preferred offering to Cloaca the Trash Goddess is made via the Dumpster in the alley. Since I was here anyway, I thought I might as well have a look at what was in there, just so I could tell myself I'd been really thorough. As far as I knew, looking through somebody's trash wouldn't be breaking any really important laws. If somebody questioned me, I'd say I was an ethnographer.

I ankled up the alley, eased up one of the two halves of the heavy green lid, propped it back, and looked inside. The Dumpster was nearly full, implying a Monday or Tuesday pickup, and the garbage inside looked hauntingly normal, just as everything else had. Boxes that didn't qualify as recyclable cardboard.

Styrofoam peanuts, shredded newspaper, spoiled bags, shrink-wrap, unidentifiable pieces of plastic. Nice dry unmessy stuff, though I put my gloves on before I stuck my hand in to rummage further.

What was I looking for? A clue? Was I killing time, or was my subconscious finally making itself heard? What I know for sure is that after a few minutes of digging, something gleamed gold near the bottom. I dug down until I reached it, with an unhappy premonition of what I'd find.

It was a sword.

I felt my stomach tighten into a melancholy fist. Brother Samael wasn't just supplying the killer. Brother Samael *was* the killer—or else there were two loose-cannon Christian Ceremonials in the Mid-Hudson Valley.

Nobody would have thrown out a sword like this in any normal universe. I was looking at a minimum of forty-five hundred dollars' worth of custom work, and that only if the blade had been a stock blank. I reached in to pull it out, hesitated, and decided not to. A charged and dedicated blade will bite, and I wasn't interested in a week of nightmares. And whether you believed in magic or not, the whole thing screamed intention and purpose.

I believe in magic. My skin crawled with the force of what I saw. I had no trouble believing that this was the blade that had killed Smith. I settled for clearing the detritus away until I could see all of it.

The blade was oddly too-clean, without even a smudge or random fingerprint. There were Greek letters down the side of the blade I could see, and I was betting it had Hebrew on the other side. The crosspiece held a row of ten semiprecious stones, and the hilt was wrapped in a mix of red, white, and purple yarn and gold wire. There were two reliquaries built into the sword; one just above the crosspiece, the other at the pommel. They held brownish, dried-up-looking objects.

"Okay," I said to nobody, stepping back from the Dumpster and taking a deep breath. The blade in the Dumpster was the last piece of the puzzle. "How" had never been a mystery, and from the moment I realized the hand was missing I'd been pretty sure of "why." Now I knew "who," and knew that I knew it.

The story I postulated goes like this:

Once upon a time, a murderer with exclusionary religious principles commissioned a ritual sword. There aren't that many bladesmiths in the occult community, and most of them are booked solid for years to come. By propinquity, serendipity, or plain bad luck, our murderer settled on Wayland Smith.

In one sense, the murder was as much of an accident as a traffic fatality would have been. The killer hadn't been out hunting occult bladesmiths—why stop at one, in that case? Why throw away your weapon if you're on a crusade? The fact that the sword had been abandoned here argued persuasively that the murder had been a disastrous crime of passion, to which Smith had contributed, if only by not stepping out of the way. Had he been too complacent, or just not paranoid enough? And how much paranoia *is* enough?

But I knew that there had been warning, if not fair warning, because Brother Samael, when he placed his order, would have made very clear what he wanted the sword to be, which meant being very clear about his principles. Whether Smith misled him to get the commission or whether Brother Samael really hadn't managed to figure out what sort of person he was dealing with was something I couldn't even guess at, but I was pretty sure that when Brother Samael went up to collect his merchandise on Wednesday night, he discovered that Smith wasn't all that Saved—that he was, in fact, what Samael would have to consider one of Satan's handmaids: a black magician.

When one's interior life is dragged out into the light of day, when one is confronted in the flesh with one's assumptions, strange things happen. I'm not sure Samael was ready for the strength of his own beliefs and what they would demand he do. Or perhaps he was looking for a pretext to bring fantasies of violence into the real world. In any event, discovering what Smith was shocked him enough that he executed Smith with the closest available weapon, the commission he'd come to pick up. Panicking, he made sure Smith couldn't work any more mischief from the next life, and took the sword with him when he left.

But then he got it home, and it occurred to him that a sword made by a black magician might not work real well for a soldier in the armies of Christ. Or else he was horrified by what he had done and blamed the sword. So he ditched it . . . here.

It wasn't as odd a thing to do as you might think. I've had some experience of those who kill without understanding the irrevocability of the act. We have more conscience and humanity than television would persuade us of; the accidental killer— in fact, as opposed to fiction—nearly always does everything but turn himself in. Throwing out the murder weapon in the back of his own store fit right in. Given time he might even confess, or maybe convince himself he'd never killed at all. But no matter what he did, he would have to do something. Murder is the great betrayal, and treason must be recompensed.

The emotion I felt wasn't precisely guilt, though it was just as painful. After a moment, I identified it. Shame. I hadn't been needed: the police would have found/would find him eventually, because though Wayland Smith might not have feared god or devil, he would certainly have feared the IRS. Detailed business records would list his customers, and Brother Samael would be one of them. Even if the trash collectors didn't notice the sword on Monday, even if there wasn't the equivalent of an APB for inanimate objects out on the blade, it was only a matter of time before the police got here.

I'd pushed myself into this for sport, but such meddling carries its own automatic retribution. One of the first teachings of the Craft is that knowledge carries responsibility, and now I had knowledge I didn't want. Knowing gave me the responsibility of acting, and it was a responsibility I did not want. I knew now exactly how Lark had felt back in Wayland's house when he'd wanted to bolt. Being here was bad. No good could come of this.

This was why I didn't want a coven, why I'd been dragging my heels for so many years. I would never feel wise enough to meddle in others' lives, nor happily irresponsible enough to do it anyway.

But now I had to. I'd destroyed my own choices. To live is to act, to act is to judge. The consequences were inescapable, both for Brother Samael and for me. And so, eventually, I found myself back inside the store.

The man behind the counter looked at me suspiciously as I came in again. The smart money was on its being the owner himself, Brother Samael, and when I met his eyes they were the eyes of a pilgrim lost in a universe without design. I know that look too well by now. My guesses outside had been right in every way that mattered.

I had to justify my presence, and I still did not know what to do. I grabbed a couple of useful items at random—frankincense and a roll of charcoal—and approached the counter.

"Are you Saved, sister?" Samael asked as he rung up my charcoal and incense.

I'm a Witch. As a tribe, we are an unruly people, not given to absolutes. But I believe, as many of us do, that the only one who can save you is yourself, though you have to know how. Brother Samael's path had taken all the tools of self-knowledge away from him, and when he had tried to take them back he found them sharper than he'd expected.

There was only one right course of action for me to follow.

"You know," I said conversationally, handing over my money, "even if you didn't make an appointment with Wayland to pick up your blade in Poughkeepsie that night, the police are going to get around to questioning you sooner or later. You're in his records."

His hand went up to the cross around his neck as if it were a weapon. It was the kind made to look like two old-fashioned hand-forged iron nails, which in turn is meant to suggest the nails used by the ancient Romans to crucify a man, though those were bronze and considerably longer.

" 'And the woman said unto him, Behold, thou knowest what Saul hath done, how he hath cut off those that have familiar spirits, and the wizards, out of the land: wherefore then layest thou a snare for my life, to cause me to die?' "

Samuel I, 28:9. A verse for every occasion. I picked up my bag. "You need to know that they know. They are going to find you. You have to know."

More knowledge. And what he'd do with it, I didn't know. But I knew that what I had to do wasn't finished.

THERE was a pay phone on the Metro-North platform. I dialed Detective Rowland P. Morrisey's number off the card in my wallet. I got a bored clerk, who became less bored as I talked and passed me over to Morrisey's partner. Detective Benjamin Adriance also didn't sound happy with my news. He told me to wait where I was and he'd send a cruiser for me.

A train heading for New York stopped and I got on it. I wouldn't be here when Adriance—or Morrisey—showed up, but I figured that the police were probably used to that. And Samael would confess. He'd been trained to it by his path, as I had been trained by mine to judge. And now we had both acted according to our natures.

But as I thought of that, I realized that wasn't completely the truth. My path gave me the tools to know myself, and the responsibility to give those tools to all who asked. That was where my responsibility stopped. Not with their lives, but with the tools I helped them forge. Judgment was also a tool, sharper than most.

I'd started by seeking a sword, and that had also been why I'd come here today. It's the symbol of a coven, but it's the symbol of something else as well, and always has been—of the knowledge that cuts both ways, and cuts deep enough to kill. I'd found the sword I was looking for, and it was foolish to be surprised that the sword had been sharp enough to cut me when I took it up. The pain would all have been for nothing if I set it aside now. It was a high price, but knowledge never comes cheap.

What I'd given to both Brother Samael and Detective Morrisey today was nothing more or less than knowledge.

A sword is a tool, and tools are for use.

PERMISSIONS AND COPYRIGHTS

ABOUT THE CONTRIBUTORS

MAGGIE SHAYNE's Witch trilogy—*Eternity, Infinity,* and *Destiny*—has broken new ground in the paranormal romance genre. Extremely well known as a writer of "the weird stuff," Maggie has published more than thirty novels and several novellas for five publishers since 1993. She is a *New York Times* and *USA Today* bestselling author, and five-time RITA Award nominee. She is currently writing for Silhouette and MIRA.

Maggie has also written for television, including several long-term story lines for the CBS soaps *Guiding Light* and *As the World Turns.*

As a Third-Degree High Priestess and cofounder of the RavenMist Circle, Maggie is recognized as Wiccan clergy, and is a licensed minister of the Wiccan religion.

CAROL LYNN STEWART, also known as Allae, is author of *Door in the Sky,* a novel of magic and mayhem in the Middle Ages, published by Hard Shell Word Factory. *Twilight Visions,* an anthology of short science fiction/fantasy stories published by Dark Star Publications, has another of Allae's stories: "Healing Song," the tale of the centaur Chiron and the water nymph Chariclo. A Witch since 1979 and member of two covens— Serpent's Egg and Moonweavers—Allae toils for her daily bread at a major university, cooking data and mumbling incantations over the bright young heads of freshmen. She also reviews strange and magical books for *ForeWord Monthly News and Reviews: The Magazine of Independent Publishing.* The real boss of her house, Demonspawn the tuxedo cat, rules both Allae and her thirteen-year-old son, forcing both to supply copious amounts of noxious, pasty cat dinners.

LORNA TEDDER followed an eclectic path of Wicca and Druidry for four years before becoming a dedicant of the Black Forest Clan, a tradition of Euro-American Wicca. She holds a Ph.D. in metaphysics, wins fencing tournaments, and manages the PagansDonate.com site. She has published over a dozen novels for Silhouette Books, Kensington Books, and Spilled Candy Books.

CHARLOTTE BRISBON has been published in *Marion Zimmer Bradley's Fantasy Magazine*. She lives in Texas with her husband and son.

A former industrial engineer turned writer, PAMELA LUZIER has much in common with the heroine of "At Midnight in the Garden of the Gods." Like Kay, Pamela took a Wicca 101 course in Colorado Springs and became fascinated by its possibilities, resolving to learn as much about it as possible. Unlike Kay, Pamela has explored the world of Witches through her writing, penning short stories like this one about those who practice the Craft, and including as much magic as her editors will allow in the romance novels she writes under the name Pam McCutcheon.

JEN SOKOLOSKI's humorous short contemporary romances have made the finals in multiple Romance Writers of America contests. Her nonfiction articles (on subjects ranging from the writer's voice to the logistics of urban yuppie-ism in the pagan subculture) have been published on the AncientVines network, the eCauldron, and in several RWA chapter newsletters. Jen has also authored training materials for a wide variety of clients ranging from Fortune 500 companies to her local romance writers' group. Jen practices "Kitchin Witchin' " and is studying Kemetic (ancient Egyptian) Reconstructionism.

ZELENA WINTERS is the pseudonym of Zita Christian, author of three historical romances published by Harper. Descended from a lineage of storytellers, healers, spiritual leaders, and what some might call wizards, Zita draws on her heritage to spin tales of Magick in the lives of ordinary people.

Since 1996, she has taught a six-part course on the basics of writing commercial fiction at the annual conference of the International Women's Writing Guild. She has taught the same course, as well as an advanced course, at the Hartford College for Women.

In addition to writing and teaching, Zita hosts a weekly hour-long television show on Cox Cable's public access channel in central Connecticut. The show, *Full Bloom*, counters the negative implications of aging by acknowledging the contributions of men and women who, despite their age, have not retired from life. Zita is a member of the Circle of the Cosmic Muse, a coven associated with the Covenant of the Goddess.

Under several names, CELIA MOON has written more than two dozen novels and has collected a plethora of awards, including three RITAs and the Colorado Book Award—the first one ever awarded to a romance.

VALERIE TAYLOR has published two contemporary romances with Harlequin. She was named Notable New Author of 1997, and her first novel won the Holt Medallion. She currently is working on a domestic suspense, a supernatural mystery, and a cookbook, and regularly casts spells asking for help focusing. She follows an eclectic path.

YVONNE JOCKS—aka Von Jocks and Evelyn Vaughn—believes in many magics, particularly the magic of stories. She has written since she was five and, at twelve, received payment of a transistor radio for a short story published by a local paper. Soon after that, she decided writing wasn't lucrative enough to pursue professionally (transistor radios aside). Luckily, this decision did not last like the magic of writing did.

As Evelyn Vaughn, she has written four romantic suspense stories for Silhouette Shadows and now DreamScapes, and an upcoming paranormal romance for Silhouette Intimate Moments. She uses the nickname Von Jocks for most of her work in fantasy anthologies such as *A Dangerous Magic, Constellation of Cats,* and *Creature Fantastic.* And as Yvonne Jocks, she writes historical romance novels, mainly the Rancher's Daughters series for Leisure Books, as well as her academic work like editing the reprint anthology *A Witches' Brew.*

A long-time resident of Texas, Yvonne still loves the magic of stories, movies, books, and dreams. An unapologetic TV addict, she lives happily with her cats and her imaginary friends and teaches junior-college English to support her writing habit . . . or vice versa. She is a member of the Covenant of Unitarian Universalist Pagans.

ROSEMARY EDGHILL is the author of more than two dozen books since her first short story publication in 1984, and says she's "never met a genre she didn't like." She started in Regencies and, like so many Regency authors, turned to murder: her Wiccan amateur detective, Bast, has previously appeared in three books from Forge: *Speak Daggers to Her*, *The Book of Moons*, and *The Bowl of Night*, recently collected into the anthology *Bell, Book, and Murder*.

Rosemary lives in the Mid-Hudson Valley with theatrical cats, laughing Cavaliers, and far too many books. Her latest releases are *Summoned to Tourney*, an urban fantasy with Mercedes Lackey, and *Leopard in Exile*, second in a series of contrahistorical magical Regencies written with SF Grand Master Andre Norton.

Rosemary has been an initiated Witch of a British Traditional line for over twenty years.